Courage
of the
Railway Girls

Maisie Thomas was born and brought up in Manchester, which provides the location for her Railway Girls novels. She loves writing stories with strong female characters, set in times when women needed determination and vision to make their mark. The Railway Girls series is inspired by her great-aunt Jessie, who worked as a railway clerk during the First World War.

Maisie now lives on the beautiful North Wales coast with her railway enthusiast husband, Kevin, and their two rescue cats. They often enjoy holidays chugging up and down the UK's heritage steam railways.

Also by Maisie Thomas

Courage
of the
Railway Girls

MAISIE THOMAS

PENGUIN BOOKS

PENGUIN BOOKS

UK | USA | Canada | Ireland | Australia
India | New Zealand | South Africa

Penguin Books is part of the Penguin Random House group of
companies whose addresses can be found at global.
penguinrandomhouse.com

Penguin
Random House
UK

Published in Penguin Books 2023
001

Typeset in 10.75/13.5 pt Palatino LT Std
by Integra Software Services Pvt. Ltd, Pondicherry

Printed and bound in Great Britain by Clays Ltd, Elcograf S.p.A.

The authorised representative in the EEA is Penguin Random House
Ireland, Morrison Chambers, 32 Nassau Street, Dublin D02 YH68

A CIP catalogue record for this book is available from
the British Library

ISBN: 978–1–804–94219–2

www.greenpenguin.co.uk

Penguin Random House is committed to a
sustainable future for our business, our readers
and our planet. This book is made from Forest
Stewardship Council® certified paper.

CHAPTER ONE

Saturday, 2 January 1943

Standing in front of the dressing-table mirror in her pretty bedroom, Emily drew a deep breath and tried to make her shoulders relax, but it wasn't easy. She felt so miserable and tense these days that her shoulders were practically at the same level as her ears. Just a few short weeks ago, she had been the happiest she had ever been in her whole life, and now . . .

Now, *right* now, this afternoon, she was going to hold her chin up and put on a brave face for the sake of her friends. Yes, *her* friends, she reminded herself, not just Mummy's friends; they were hers as well, and you didn't let your friends down. The thought gave her a feeling of determination and she looked squarely at her reflection. Lord, but she'd changed. She had lost weight and her forget-me-not-blue jumper and navy A-line skirt were looser than they ought to be. Her face was thinner too and her dark hair had lost the shine she used to be so proud of. She looked a fright – but what did it matter? It didn't. She didn't care. Gone were the days when she had loved looking at herself, when she had gloried in gazing at her reflection. Being in love had made her cheeks glow and her blue eyes sparkle – yes, they really had sparkled. She wouldn't have believed it if she hadn't seen it for herself, because it sounded like the sort of daft though rather appealing description you found in books.

1

Well, there was no point standing here gawping at herself. 'That won't butter any parsnips,' she murmured. It was something she'd heard Mrs Green say. She loved Mrs Green. She'd loathed her to start with, but that had been back when she'd still been a silly little snob who didn't know any better.

Emily lifted a hand to straighten the Peter Pan collar of her white blouse before turning away to sit on the bed and remove the slippers she'd been given for Christmas so she could put on her shoes. She'd had to carry on wearing her old school shoes for some time after she'd come home from boarding school until Mummy had taken her to the market to look for a suitable second-hand pair. Mummy had said this was more sensible than splurging precious clothes coupons on new shoes. Emily had longed for a pair of stylish slingbacks, but she'd been more than happy with a pair that had almond-shaped toes and, oh bliss, heels. They were proper grown-up shoes, not silly schoolgirlish flatties. Grown-up shoes for a grown-up young woman. That was what she'd thought at the time; she remembered thinking it. But now she knew that being an adult wasn't all it was cracked up to be.

She went downstairs into the sitting room, where Daddy was reading the newspaper while he waited. Thanks to the fuel shortages, the furniture hugged the fireplace, though Mummy might restore the old arrangement in the summer.

Daddy lowered the paper as she walked in. 'You look pretty, darling.'

Emily smiled. Daddy was always good for a compliment. But she felt a stab of sadness too. She didn't feel pretty; she felt washed-out and wretched and the thought of never seeing Raymond again filled her with despair.

'You're a really nice girl,' Raymond had said when he finished with her.

A really nice girl! He was her whole world and she was nothing more than a really nice girl.

But she was *not* going to dwell on that today. This afternoon, they were going to Mrs Cooper's house in Wilton Close to celebrate Mabel's engagement.

As if he could read her thoughts, Daddy stood up and came over to her, looking down into her face. 'You'll be all right this afternoon, won't you?'

'I managed at Lucy's engagement party, didn't I?' Emily answered. 'I'm an old hand at it now.'

Her old chum Lucy had got engaged at Christmas – the same time as Mabel, as it later turned out – and Lucy's parents had thrown a party for the happy couple in between Christmas and New Year. It was supposed to be an impromptu party, but it was obvious it had been planned down to the last detail. Beforehand, Mummy and Daddy had thought there might well be a party and they had wanted to spare Emily from having to attend.

'Mummy can practise saying, "Oh, what a shame. We have other arrangements for that evening" in case Lucy's mother mentions an engagement party,' Daddy had said.

But when the invitation came, much to her own surprise Emily had second thoughts.

'Mummy, could you please say that we have other arrangements that evening, but we'll drop in for a while on our way?'

'Are you sure, darling?' Mummy had looked concerned.

'No,' Emily said bluntly, 'but I think we ought to.'

'Good girl,' said Mummy.

Her parents always liked it when she did the decent thing. They'd brought her up to be polite and it turned out that the need to be so applied even when you were heart-broken.

After that Mummy had come home from work with the news that Mabel had returned from her Christmas visit to Annerby sporting a ruby engagement ring that she was flashing left, right and centre, 'along with the happiest smile you can imagine,' according to Mummy. And this afternoon there was to be the get-together at Mrs Cooper's, where Mabel lived, for her friends to celebrate the wonderful news with one of the railway friends' tea parties that they all loved so much.

Emily felt better about going to this party than she had about attending Lucy's. Was that because she and Lucy had been friends for simply yonks, ever since they were little girls, and these today were new friends? But that made it sound as if her new friends weren't as important and that most certainly wasn't the case. She'd only known them since the summer of '41 and, truth be told, she hadn't been at all keen in the early days. These days, shame could still make her face tingle when she recalled how she'd looked down on Mrs Green and Mrs Cooper for being working class. Back then, she'd felt ashamed of her mother for wanting to be friends with people of that sort. She hadn't liked Mabel, Alison and the rest either, fearing that they were simply out for what help they could get from Mummy, maybe free legal advice from Daddy. Why else would girls in their twenties pal up with someone of Mummy's age?

How wrong she had been, how completely wrong. Emily had learned to value people according to their characters and their actions instead of making harsh and unsubstantiated judgements based purely on age or class. She'd been rather a twerp, actually, and dearly hoped her railway friends had forgotten her old snobby ways. She still experienced the occasional twinge of doubt in case they only accepted her because she was her mother's daughter, but with her sensible hat on, she knew this wasn't the case.

Emily looked round as Mummy walked into the room. She didn't miss the glance that passed between her parents when Mummy saw Daddy standing close to her. They'd been very protective ever since Raymond dumped her, which was perfectly sweet of them, of course, and she adored them for it, but it could feel a bit, well, smothering sometimes. There were moments when she just wanted to say, 'It doesn't matter how kind you are or how much you watch over me. You can't change the way I feel,' but she never did.

Mummy looked swish but not overdressed in dove grey with her trademark pearl earrings. Mummy always looked nice. Elegant. You'd never imagine she spent her working days out on the railway tracks, dismantling, cleaning and reassembling the lamps belonging to signals as well as to engines, coaches and wagons. In her snobby days, Emily had been obscurely ashamed of her mother's job. Essential war work it might be, but it wasn't exactly suitable for a respectable, educated, cultured lady from the upper middle class. Daddy had thought so too, but they had both come round since then.

'All set?' Mummy asked, smiling.

'We'd better do the blackout before we go,' said Daddy. 'It'll be dark when we get home.'

'I'll do it,' said Emily and ran around the house, pulling first the ordinary curtains and then the blackout curtains, twitching them at the edges to ensure they covered the entire windows plus a bit more. Sometimes it was hard to remember what life had been like before the blackout. Just think: small children who had never known any different would think this was normal.

In the hall, her parents were togged up in their outdoor things, complete with warm scarves and leather gloves. Mummy had a rather gorgeous wine-coloured coat with a top-stitched collar and a grey felt hat with an upswept brim. Emily had been obliged to wear her school gabardine for quite some time after she had come home, until dear Mrs Cooper, who helped with the WVS's clothes exchange, had tipped Mummy the wink about a nut-brown coat in good condition and Mummy had quickly exchanged Emily's gabardine for the brown coat as a surprise. It had been an especially kind thing to do because even though Emily was the one to benefit, it had been her mother who had done the swap and that meant she couldn't visit the clothes exchange again for a whole month.

Emily's new-to-her coat was flattering, with its slight flare below the waist and a tie belt that had to be fastened in a knot. And Mummy's pale pink hat with magenta trim looked especially good with the coat – to the point where Mummy hadn't exactly given the hat to Emily, but she raised no objection when Emily wore it so much.

Not that it mattered these days. Emily had cared most awfully what she looked like when she was seeing Raymond, but now – so what? Looking her best hadn't made Raymond stay in love with her even though he was always telling her how pretty she was. Even when he ditched her, he'd said, 'You're so pretty. You'll soon meet someone else' – as if that was all there was to it.

Shrugging on her coat and winding her scarf around her neck and tucking it in, Emily was soon ready to go.

'Have you got everything?' Daddy asked.

They were taking with them a plate of sardine sandwiches and a coconut pudding, as well as a contribution to the afternoon's quantity of tea leaves.

'You can't have a tea party without plenty of tea,' said Mummy. 'And we're taking a quarter of our Christmas cake. Dot's bringing a quarter of hers too.'

'So we don't all scoff Mrs Grayson's,' said Emily.

'I expect hers will be the best,' said Mummy, 'even though we've all had to make eggless cakes this year.'

They walked to Wilton Close, which took about twenty minutes. The afternoon was chilly and damp. Daddy would probably cut along to the telephone box and ring for a taxi to bring them home later when it was dark and cold. That was the sort of thing he did.

When they arrived, Mrs Cooper opened the front door as they were still walking up the path and they hurried inside. Daddy took their coats and Mummy vanished into the kitchen to hand over her dishes to Mrs Grayson. Then they went into the front room into a flurry of greetings and cries of 'Happy New Year!' Those who were sitting down jumped up to hug Mummy and Emily, and Emily could almost – *almost* – feel she was a true part of what was happening. Everyone knew of her unhappiness and wanted to make her welcome and she appreciated that, she really did, even though it could be rather off-putting knowing that everybody knew the private business of her heart. But all the same, the very unhappiness that the others wanted to alleviate was precisely what made her feel distanced from what was going on.

Still, she could play her part. If there was one thing she'd learned about herself recently, it was that she could act the part of Emily Masters to perfection. So she smiled and offered best wishes for the new year and cooed over Joan's baby and tickled his chin and generally behaved as if there was nowhere else she'd rather be. And then she joined her mother, who was with Mabel, admiring her ring.

'May I see?' asked Emily. 'It's gorgeous.'

Mabel immediately took it off. 'Do you want to have a go? Try it. Everyone else has.'

Emily blinked. Not so long ago, she had daydreamed about her own engagement ring. She had thought that would be the first ring to go on her finger. Next thing she knew, Mabel's arms were around her and Mabel was whispering in her ear.

'Sorry, kid. Me and my big mouth. I wasn't thinking. I'm just so excited.'

Part of Emily wanted to dissolve into floods of tears, but she was made of sterner stuff than that, or at least she wished she was. Pretending she was strong was the best she could do. With a small wriggle, she freed herself from Mabel's embrace before the others could realise.

'That's all right. I'd love to try it on.'

She pushed the gold band with its deep red ruby onto her ring finger. There. It turned out that ring fingers weren't so special after all. You could put any ring at all on them. She took it off and handed it back, making sure she was smiling.

'It's beautiful. Congratulations.'

'Thanks. I'm very lucky.' Mabel replaced her ring and looked at it. The rich red stone was perfect for her colouring. She had such glorious dark brown hair, which she wore scooped away from her face and hanging in natural waves down her back. Mabel removed her gaze from her ring, laughing at herself.

Joan appeared, slipping an arm around Mabel. 'Before Christmas, she'd have been gazing adoringly at Max. Now all she cares about is her ring.'

'I don't blame her,' said Emily and slipped away, duty done, but deep inside she howled in anguish, remembering Raymond, remembering how he couldn't quite meet her eyes when he had dumped her. That was what had set alarm bells ringing, because he'd always loved gazing at her. He was an amateur astronomer, a stargazer, and he'd called her his star on earth, which had made her feel like the most beautiful girl in the world. But despite the alarm bells, she'd had no notion of what was coming. The only thing she could think of was that his call-up papers must have arrived, which was stupid of her because he wasn't quite old enough yet, but it was the only reason she could come up with for the subtle change in his behaviour. If she'd had a hundred years to mull it over, she still wouldn't have imagined he was building up to leaving her.

She spent some time in the kitchen, helping Mrs Grayson, then she volunteered to take Joan's dog Brizo for a quick walk before they had tea. She loved Brizo, with his soulful eyes, his soft, floppy ears and gingery, golden-brown shaggy coat. She made the suggestion quietly so no one would offer to accompany her, but even so, Colette joined her. Emily was fascinated by Colette, but then presumably everybody was. Colette was a quiet individual, softly spoken and gentle in her manner. She seemed like a completely ordinary person, yet she had had to put up with being treated appallingly badly by her husband and nobody had had the slightest inkling of what was going on until Tony had beaten her black and blue and put her in hospital. Instead of being sent to prison, he had been allowed to join the army, which seemed grossly unfair, but at least it meant he was a long way away – but for how long? Everyone was saying that the tide of war was turning.

'I hope you don't mind me tagging along,' said Colette, pushing a strand of buttermilk-fair hair behind her ear.

'Of course not.'

'I'm glad to have a chance to have a word, actually,' Colette added and Emily's heart beat harder for a second or two. 'I just wanted to say that I know what it's like when people are watching – kind people, I mean, people who care and who want to make things better, only they can't, because nobody can. Whatever has hurt you, you have to live with it and find your own way out the other end.'

'That's exactly it,' Emily exclaimed. 'Everybody back in the house knows about Raymond and me, and I know they all care deeply, but they can't make it better.'

'It's the same for me,' said Colette. 'I love my friends and I appreciate everything they've done to help me, but when push comes to shove, I still have to live with my feelings. Nobody can take them away, no matter how much they want to.'

'No, they can't.'

'If ever you want to talk to somebody who – and I mean this in the kindest possible way – won't try to make you feel better, but will just let you feel what you feel, then I'm here.'

'Thanks,' said Emily, feeling that a little piece of her burden had lifted. It was flattering, too, to be paid attention to in this way by someone older than herself and to be talked to as an equal. The other girls were in their twenties, but she was only sixteen, with her seventeenth birthday coming up in March.

They walked Brizo as far as the police station on Beech Road and back again. When they returned to Wilton Close, there was chatter going on in the kitchen, which suggested it was nearly time for tea. Emily slipped into the front room. Fussing over Brizo, she took him into a corner and sat on the floor with him. Soon the room was full and Emily wasn't the only one sitting on the carpet. Plates were passed round and tea was poured while everyone chatted. Emily smiled and laughed occasionally as if she was joining in, but she wasn't really. She felt distanced from what was going on, as if her deep sorrow and heartache lifted her out of the occasion.

She looked round at everyone. Mummy was sitting on the sofa between Mrs Green and Mrs Cooper. It was Mummy who had got Mrs Cooper the job of taking care of this house while the owners, Mr and Mrs Morgan, were away in North Wales for the duration. Mrs Cooper didn't just take care of the house, she took great care of the residents as well, helped by Mrs Grayson, who was a wonderful cook and turned out tasty, nutritious meals in spite of all the shortages and rationing. With them lived Mabel, Margaret and Alison, all of whom worked on the railways.

Joan used to work on the railways as a station porter at Victoria Station, and then briefly in Lost Property, before she had Max. Now she was a housewife. Her husband Bob was here too. Emily liked him. He was what she imagined a big brother would be like, kind and good-natured with a lively sense of humour. He wasn't film-star handsome like Mabel's fiancé, Harry, but he was the sort of person you felt comfortable with and that counted for a lot. Harry wasn't here this afternoon because he'd had to go back to Bomber Command straight after Christmas.

Next to Joan, dandling Max on her knee, was Persephone, who was the most beautiful girl Emily had ever seen, with her honey-blonde hair and her violet eyes, but as Mrs Cooper said, she was lovely on the inside as well. Educated at a boarding school herself, Emily recognised in Persephone the confidence that came from living away from home, but in Persephone's case it was more than private education. It was the confidence that had been bred into her through generations of titled ancestors stretching back to when Adam was a lad.

Daddy was talking to Mr Green and Bob while Mrs Green sat with Mummy and Mrs Cooper. Mrs Green was Mummy's great friend even though they were poles apart socially.

She caught Mrs Green's eye without meaning to and quickly buried her face in Brizo's thick coat before Mrs Green could speak to her. She was quite all right tucked away here in her corner. All she wanted was to be left alone. It wasn't difficult, because Mabel was the centre of attention.

'Where's the wedding going to be?' asked Alison.

'At home in Annerby,' said Mabel. 'Mumsy can't wait.'

Alison pulled a face, but then she smiled. 'I suppose it was too much to hope that you could get married here.'

'Of course she can't,' exclaimed Mrs Cooper. 'She has to get married from her parents' house.'

'It's going to be a June wedding,' said Mabel, 'and I'd love it if you could all come, though I know it'll be tricky to get the time off. I want Alison, Margaret, Emily and Persephone as my bridesmaids and Joan and Colette as matron of honours – or should that be matrons of honour? All I know is, I'll be one blissfully happy bride if I can have all my friends as my attendants. And I want you there too,' she added, looking around at Mrs Green, Mrs Cooper, Mrs Grayson and Mummy, 'though you can't be mothers of the bride for me like you were for Joan.' She grinned. 'I don't think Mumsy would stand for that.'

'I'm so sorry, Mabel,' said Mrs Grayson. 'I really don't think I could travel all that way, not even for you.'

'I understand.' Mabel pressed Mrs Grayson's hand. 'I'll let you off, but only if you promise to bake my wedding cake.'

Mrs Grayson pressed a hand to her chest, looking emotional. 'Oh, I should love to. What an honour. I never imagined . . . not with the wedding being so far away.'

'It wouldn't be a proper wedding without one of your cakes,' said Mabel. 'Will you let Mrs Mitchell help you with it? She's family, as well as the person who introduced me to you, so I'd like her to be involved.'

'Of course,' said Mrs Grayson. 'She's been a good friend to me all these years.'

'The rest of us would love to be at your wedding, Mabel,' said Mrs Green, 'but it'll depend on getting time off.'

'You must tell us as soon as the date is confirmed,' said Mummy.

'It's so exciting,' said Margaret.

'There's something else I ought to tell you,' said Mabel. 'I expect you've already worked it out for yourselves, but I ought to say it anyway.' She pressed her lips together, looking emotional. 'When Harry and I tie the knot, obviously I'll go to live down south. Harry has applied for married quarters.'

'Of course you have to live with Harry,' said Mrs Grayson.

'No, you don't,' Joan teased, though her eyes were suspiciously bright. 'You could get wed and come back to us.'

'I think Harry would have something to say about that,' said Alison and the others laughed, so Emily joined in, though she didn't really feel she was part of the conversation. Not because she was being left out, but because . . . oh, just because.

'We'll all miss you, love,' said Mrs Green and there were murmurs of agreement.

Mabel wiped away a tear. 'But we'll keep in touch, won't we?'

'Of course!' everyone cried reassuringly, dashing away a few tears of their own.

'If there's one thing I can guarantee about this lot,' Alison declared, looking round, 'it's that they're superb at keeping in touch. I was snowed under with letters last year when I was packed off to Leeds.'

After everyone had finished eating, Margaret and Joan went to boil the kettle again so that more tea could be squeezed out of the pot.

'Don't start drinking yet,' said Mrs Green, standing up when all the cups had been refreshed. 'We need to have a toast. It's a shame Harry can't be here, but we all want to wish the very best to our lovely Mabel – a wonderful future and a long and happy marriage.'

'Mabel,' everyone said, raising their teacups, and 'Congratulations,' and 'Harry's a lucky man.'

Emily joined in, but it was like she wasn't really there. She was an observer rather than a participant. Lucy and Charlie. Mabel and Harry. Things were meant to happen in threes, weren't they? She wasn't sure she could bear it if Alison and Joel got engaged too.

Except that she would bear it. It wasn't as though she had a choice. She didn't have a choice about anything these days. The one choice she had made, to be with Raymond for ever, had been ripped away from her.

She watched all the smiling faces around her and saw Mabel's happiness. Was it always going to be this way for her from now on? Was she always going to feel she was on the outside looking in?

CHAPTER TWO

It was time to start being sensible. Mabel had had a whale of a time showing off her beautiful engagement ring to all and sundry, wearing it on a chain around her neck when she went to work, but now it was the middle of January and it was high time she stopped. Removing the silver chain, she dropped it onto the dressing table and took the little velvet-lined ring box out of the drawer to put it beside her bed. She held up her hand for the umpteenth time to admire her ring. From now on, she would keep it at home and wear it in the evenings and on her days off.

Home. She looked around the bedroom. The Morgans had slept in single beds, with a bedside cupboard next to each one. There was a chest of drawers, a dressing table with a triple mirror, and a wardrobe with a long mirror inset in one of the doors. One wall housed the chimney breast and fireplace, which must have made the room as warm as toast before the war.

This had been Mabel's bedroom since the spring of 1941. Now it was the start of 1943 and they were still at war. But without the war, she would never have met her darling Harry, her very own cheeky blighter. Just thinking of him made Mabel go wobbly inside. He was as handsome as any star of the silver screen, with his dark eyes, generous mouth, straight nose and broad forehead with its suggestion of a widow's peak at the temples. Better yet, he was a man in uniform and Mabel wanted to stand taller and breathe more deeply when she was by his side. She was massively proud to be able to utter the words 'fiancé' and 'Bomber Command' in the same sentence.

Just think. In just a few short months, they would be man and wife. There was nothing Mabel wanted more in the whole world, but she hated to think of leaving her friends behind. They were inexpressibly dear to her. How would she manage without them? Yes, there would be letters, of course, which were more important than ever in wartime, but could they really make up for the day-to-day company, the chatting and laughter in the station buffet, the kindness and concern and staunch support that came from all of them being together regularly? Something inside Mabel slumped. Letters would be wonderful in their own way, but it would be a huge wrench to leave her chums behind and have to start again.

Harry understood perfectly, bless him. Others often underestimated Harry. They thought he was all charm, and it was true that with his dishy smile and silver tongue, he could entice the birds out of the trees. But he could be sensitive and insightful as well, though this was a side of his character that he saved for Mabel.

'I can't wait for us to live together,' he had told her after they got engaged, and the deep note in his voice had sent a delicious little shiver all over Mabel's skin. 'But I know you'll miss your pals badly. You're so close to one another and I know it's helped you all to cope with the war.'

Mabel had nodded. 'I can't bear to think of leaving them behind.'

Harry grinned. 'If you arrive at Bomber Command with extra suitcases, I won't be surprised if your friends burst out of them.'

Tilting her head to one side, Mabel pretended to consider it. 'That's not a bad idea.' She reached up and touched his cheek. 'As long as you know that as much as I love and need my friends, I love and need you more.'

Harry kissed her tenderly. 'I'll make sure you're happy in your new home, my love, I promise.'

Her new home! Wilton Close had been a real home to Mabel, thanks to the warmth and kindness of Mrs Cooper and Mrs Grayson. Plenty of girls had billets that were just somewhere to lay their heads and stow their belongings, but number 1 Wilton Close in Chorlton-cum-Hardy was a happy and secure home in the very best sense. Mabel knew she would never forget her time living here, sharing this bedroom first with Joan and now with Margaret, while Alison occupied what used to be the box room at the end of the landing.

Girls living together and getting along so well was like having sisters. Mabel's heart dipped for a moment. Althea, the dear friend she'd grown up with and whom she'd always called the sister of her heart, had died in tragic circumstances before the war and for a long time she had haunted Mabel's thoughts. They had always planned to be one another's bridesmaids and now Mabel was going to get married without her. A wave of sadness washed over Mabel and the world seemed to slow down, but then – an important lesson learned in wartime – she acknowledged the scale and importance of her grief before carefully setting it aside and concentrating on the good things.

There was a gentle knock at the door and Mrs Cooper walked in, carrying a neat pile of garments.

'I've done the ironing, dear,' she said, putting some on Margaret's bed and the rest on Mabel's.

'You do spoil us, Mrs C,' said Mabel. 'We should do our own ironing.'

'There's no call for that. I like looking after you. Everyone fettling for themselves wouldn't be very homely, and I like to think I'm providing a home.'

'You certainly do that,' Mabel replied with a smile.

'I'm only doing for you what I used to do for my Lizzie,' said Mrs Cooper. 'I like to think that your mum and Alison's mum are happier knowing you're being properly taken care of.'

'And if Margaret's mum is looking down on her, I bet she's thinking the same.'

'I hope so,' said Mrs Cooper. 'Are you coming down, chuck? Mrs Grayson is ready to put the tea on the table.'

They went downstairs together, Mabel following her landlady. Mrs Cooper was a small bird of a woman who looked as if a puff of wind might blow her over, but she worked hard, not just here caring for the house and her lodgers, but also as a cleaner in other women's homes. Her cleaning service was called Magic Mop, a name Mabel had coined, inspired by jokes about Mrs Grayson and her magic mixing bowl. Magic Mop had suffered some loss of custom last year through no fault of Mrs Cooper's, but now her list of clients was building up again.

With the three girls all working shifts, it wasn't unusual for mealtimes to be spread out, but this evening they were all there. They bowed their heads as Mrs Cooper said grace, giving thanks for the brave men of the Merchant Navy.

'Weren't you supposed to stay in town and go out with Joel this evening?' Mabel asked Alison as they started on their vegetables baked in potato pastry.

'Yes, but he's got to do a double shift because of another doctor being ill,' said Alison.

'That's a shame,' said Margaret.

'Never mind that,' said Alison. 'Let's talk about the wedding. Does it feel strange having the arrangements going on so far away?'

'In a way,' Mabel admitted, 'but Mumsy would be devastated if Harry and I had a quick ceremony down here. She wanted June because the roses will be in bloom and we can have rose petals as confetti.'

'Lovely,' said Mrs Cooper.

'It seems a shame to denude the rose bushes,' said Mabel, 'but with confetti not being allowed, what else is there?'

'Rice,' said Alison.

'Waste of food,' said Mrs Grayson.

'I read in *Vera's Voice* about rice at weddings,' said Mrs Cooper. 'They suggested shaking hands with the happy couple and presenting them with a bag of rice instead.'

'That's not a bad idea,' said Margaret, 'but rose petals will be romantic.'

'I just hope nothing goes wrong in terms of last-minute hitches,' said Alison. 'Like Joel having to do this extra shift this evening. These things happen, especially to servicemen.'

'Well, I personally won't have a last-minute hitch of that sort,' said Mabel, 'because I'll hand in my notice and finish work before the wedding. You hear about brides being given just two or three days off, four if they're lucky. We'll only have Harry to worry about in terms of duty calling.'

'My sister got married with next to no notice, if you recall,' said Alison. 'She got a letter from her boyfriend with a proposal and a possible wedding date all in one. He came home on leave and they dashed up the aisle, had a weekend honeymoon, and then she had to wave him off again. She hasn't seen him since.'

'A lady in the butcher's queue was telling me about her niece,' said Mrs Cooper. 'She was busy organising her wedding when she got an urgent telephone message saying "Come immediately and bring a hat." Her fiancé was about to be posted overseas unexpectedly and she had to rush down to the south coast. Not that anything like that is going to happen to you and Harry, I'm sure, dear,' she added.

'What shall you wear?' asked Margaret. 'At least you've got plenty of time to sort out a dress – or a suit, if you prefer?'

Mabel shook her head. She had given this some thought. Back at the start of the war, there had been a feeling that it was unpatriotic to have a big white wedding, but now things had changed, and the prevailing opinion was that it was good for morale, not to mention one in the eye for Hitler, to have a wedding that looked as pre-war as possible.

'I'd like a proper wedding dress,' she said. Then she couldn't suppress a smile. 'Mumsy would never let me get away with marrying in a suit. She's been dreaming about this for years.'

'Bless her,' Mrs Cooper murmured.

'And then there's the cake,' said Alison. 'With all the restrictions on sugar, some couples are having chocolate cake.'

'Not in June, I hope,' said Mrs Grayson. 'Think of the mess if it melted.'

'One thing Harry and I decided about the cake before Mumsy could take over absolutely everything,' said Mabel with a touch of pride, 'is that on the top, instead of figures of the bride and groom, we want a V for Victory. Pops is going to arrange for a V to be made specially for us in the factory.'

'V for Victory,' said Alison. 'That's perfect.'

'Yes, it is,' said Mabel.

'V for Victory,' said Margaret, 'and V for Very Happy Couple.'

'Talking of victory,' said Mrs Grayson, 'that reminds me. It said in the paper that there's going to be a Wings for Victory Week in March to raise funds for the RAF.'

'I wonder what's being organised locally,' Mabel said at once. 'I'd like to be involved.'

'Of course you would,' said Mrs Cooper, 'with your future husband in the RAF.'

'I'd like to be responsible for organising something,' said Mabel.

'It would be your legacy here,' said Margaret.

Mabel liked the sound of that. Her legacy. She loved her home town of Annerby in the north of Lancashire and she loved Manchester too, had felt a profound connection to the city ever since the devastating Christmas Blitz of 1940 when she, a trained first-aider, had taken part in rescues throughout those two never-ending nights of death and destruction. She would love to feel she was in some small way leaving a legacy behind her. As much as she longed to be Mrs Harry Knatchbull and as dearly as she was looking forward to living with him near Bomber Command, she knew that part of her heart was going to break when she had to leave Manchester and her wonderful friends.

So it was right and fitting to leave a legacy behind her, and not just the memory of a successful Wings for Victory Week event either, but something lasting. Something permanent. Something that would make her friends proud of her.

'Oh, for a proper bath,' groaned Mabel, 'with deep water and scented soap. Never mind fighting for freedom. Today I've been fighting for scented soap.'

'One of the girls in the engine sheds, Sally, was given a cake of scented soap for Christmas,' said Margaret.

'She wasn't,' Alison breathed.

'She was. She says she's put it on the mantelpiece so she can pick it up and smell it from time to time as a treat.'

Mabel rolled her shoulders. It had been a tough day out on the permanent way, levering up heavy railway sleepers so that the ballast that shifted slightly every time a train ran along the track could be shoved back into place and packed down. It was always hard work, no matter how used to it you were, but there had been thick fog today, with large gloops of stinky yellow-grey mush hanging thickly in the air, which made the job more dangerous. All the lengthmen, and indeed anybody working on the permanent way, had to keep their ears pricked the whole time because it was impossible to see the trains coming. Bernice, who was the leader of Mabel's gang of lengthmen, was a stickler for safety and she had given each of them a long piece of string. They had each tied their piece to Bernice's knapsack, which was left a yard or so away from the outermost track, and tied the other end to their belts, so that when a train was heard through the murky air, no one was in any doubt as to which way to go to reach the scrubby wasteland beside the tracks.

'Take care of my string an' all,' Bernice had ordered, 'and don't go piking off with it at the end of the day. I want it all back. I've had these lengths of string since I became a lengthman when the war started. You can't get new string for love nor money these days.'

'You can't get most things for love nor money,' Bette had added wryly.

Now back at home, Mabel said, 'A foggy day out there really takes it out of you. Rain's horrible because you get so cold, but with fog, you can't stop listening and concentrating for even a minute.'

'Go and have your bath,' said Mrs Cooper, 'and then come downstairs and settle beside the fire.'

Mabel grinned. 'It could be heaps worse. Fog's horrid, but at least we aren't having much snow. Do you remember how bitter it was this time last year? And all because it was building up to dumping six feet of snow everywhere.'

'The entire country disappeared under it for weeks on end,' said Margaret. She waggled her shoulders. 'Brrr. It makes me shiver just to remember it.'

Mabel went upstairs to have her bath. Wearing her dressing gown, she went into the bathroom, where a black line around the inside of the tub showed how much water was permitted. Tempting as it was to let the water run until it turned hot, she put in the plug and switched on the hot tap, praying the water would heat up swiftly. As soon as the water level reached the line, she turned off the tap, hung up her dressing gown and stepped into the bath.

Long gone were the days of plunging the soap into the water before creating a delightful foam on the flannel. Now the technique was to wet the flannel and do little more than show it to the soap. Making soap last until the next ration was released was an art in itself.

Downstairs afterwards, Mabel huddled by the fire for a few minutes because dear Mrs Cooper insisted, but it wasn't fair to the others to hog the warmth, so she curled up in a corner of the sofa.

'Do you think we'll automatically carry on being careful with everything after the war?' she asked. 'Or will we all go mad and fritter everything away?'

'Chance would be a fine thing,' said Mrs Grayson, looking up from her knitting pattern. 'You don't imagine that all the shortages will miraculously end, do you?'

Wouldn't they? It was a sobering thought and not one Mabel wanted to contemplate just now. She was grateful when Mrs Cooper changed the subject.

'Are you still going over to Joan's in the morning, chuck? Would you take a plate back to her? It got left behind after the tea party.'

Oh, the tea party! 'That was just *won*derful,' Mabel enthused. 'You're all so kind. I just wish Harry could have been here for it, but I'll tell him all about it next time I telephone. And, yes, of course I'll pop the plate back.'

Tomorrow was her day off and she was looking forward to spending time with Joan. They had developed a closeness during the time they had been room-mates here. Joan was one of only two people who knew about . . . well, never mind what. That was all well and truly behind her and it did no good to think about it. She adored Harry and he adored her and that was all that mattered.

It didn't take Mabel long to walk from Wilton Close to Torbay Road, with its long line of red-brick houses with bay windows in the front and black-tiled roofs above. Mabel rang the bell and Joan answered the door.

'I was watching for you from upstairs,' she said, standing aside to let Mabel in. 'Breathe in,' she added as Mabel slid past Max's splendid old coach-built pram to get to the staircase.

This was Joan's childhood home, where she and her late sister had grown up, looked after by their fierce grandmother, Mrs Foster. Joan and her little family now lived upstairs while Mrs Foster occupied downstairs and everyone shared the kitchen and the bathroom.

The front room upstairs was now Joan and Bob's sitting room. They didn't possess much furniture, just a couple of armchairs, a table with mismatched chairs, and a wooden cupboard with a drawer at the bottom. Brizo was lying on the rug in front of the fire and Mabel sat down to fuss him.

'Where's that other boy of yours?' she asked.

'Having his morning nap. I'll pop down and make us some tea. I won't be a minute.'

When Joan returned, she settled on the rug with Mabel.

'Are you in line for some of the new Utility furniture?' asked Mabel.

'Forget furniture. I'd sell my soul for a pushchair. Max is going to grow out of the pram eventually. I'm lucky there was a pram in the family, but nobody has a pushchair. Anyway, Utility furniture is just for newly-weds, not for old married couples like me and Bob. Besides,' Joan added with a laugh, 'look at us sitting on the rug. We're not a good advertisement for needing Utility, are we?'

'I'd rather be right by the fire on a day like today.'

'So would I. Sometimes I feel guilty for having two fires on the go in one house, but then I tell myself that if Gran was a stranger who'd opened her home to us, we wouldn't be sharing a sitting room with our landlady, would we?'

'No,' Mabel agreed loyally. Things hadn't always run smoothly for Joan and her grandmother and although matters were good enough now for them to share a house, and by all accounts old Mrs Foster was very taken with her great-grandson, Mabel knew that Mrs Foster and the Hubbles didn't live in one another's pockets. Mrs Foster wasn't neglected or left to be lonely, but while multi-generational families usually lived together in the traditional way, it was better for Mrs Foster and the Hubbles to have boundaries.

'I felt quite emotional at the end of December and beginning of January,' said Joan, 'entering a fresh year with Max. He'll be one in May. I can't believe how the time is passing by.' With a twinkle in her eyes, she added, 'Who knows, you might be a mum yourself before his second birthday.'

Mabel shook her head. 'We've waited a long time to get engaged and get married. I've known Harry since 1940, would you believe. That's a long time these days. We want to enjoy being a married couple before we have a family.'

Joan gave her a push. 'I know you, Mabel Bradshaw, Mrs Knatchbull-to-be. You want to be the belle of the ball at all the RAF dances, don't you?'

'What's wrong with that?' Mabel smiled broadly. 'I want to make the most of being on the arm of the handsomest man Bomber Command has to offer.'

'Well, don't wait too long to start your family,' Joan advised. 'Having a baby in wartime isn't the easiest thing, but don't let that put you off. Kindness and ingenuity go a long way. I must show you the felt dog Persephone made out of an old hat for Max's first Christmas. And a lady up the road is married to a soldier who smuggled home a service blanket, which she made into coats for her daughter and her little boy. The boy's outgrown his now, so she's passed it on for Max when he's bigger.'

'I heard Canada is sending over lots of baby things.'

Joan nodded. 'That's right. "Bundles for Britain", they're called. They're for new babies, not whoppers like Max, but a WVS lady gave me a card of safety pins from a bundle that had two cards by mistake. Wasn't that good of her?'

'How things have changed, when safety pins are something to be grateful for.'

'If you don't want children straight away, are you going to work on the railways down south?'

'I'll have to work at something,' said Mabel, adding with a grin, 'not like some people, slobbing around at home.'

'There speaks someone who isn't a mother,' Joan retorted. 'Actually, I'm going to have to start pulling my weight again with war work.'

'You're coming back to the railways?' Mabel asked in surprise.

'No, I mean looking after children. You've seen the posters, haven't you? I can't remember the exact words, but they say something like, "If you can't go out to work, help a woman who can." In other words, look after her children for her. There's a new word for it: childminding.'

'Is that what you're going to do?'

'I think so.'

'You don't sound bowled over by the idea, if you don't mind my saying so.'

Joan immediately brightened. 'I've been spoilt, being here with just Max. It's been wonderful, such a special time for both of us, but I promised myself that once we got to the new year, I'd do my bit to help someone else.'

'It's important war work in its own way.'

'I know, but it's a bit different to being a station porter. I loved that.'

'You'll love this too. Look what a loving mum you are.'

'Mothers need to make sure their children are cared for properly. How else are they to concentrate on their work? You can't have munitions girls worrying about whether little Billy is all right.'

'That's what I mean,' said Mabel. 'It's important work. Essential work.'

'There are plenty of mothers who would give their eye teeth for a loving, reliable person to look after their children. There are never enough nursery places and even if there were, there would still be mums who'd prefer their little ones to be cared for in a home, like a little family. So that's what I'm going to do.'

And there it was, inside Mabel's head: she knew precisely what her lasting legacy was going to be.

CHAPTER THREE

Persephone read through the typewritten sheet in the big sit-up-and-beg typewriter one final time before twisting the knob on the side that made the drum turn round, feeding out the papers. Three pieces: the top copy, which she would submit to *Vera's Voice*, the precious sheet of carbon paper, which had been used so many times it had almost no copying power left, and the bottom copy, so faint that she was sure she could only read it because she already knew what it said. This she would keep for herself and add to her ever-growing file of articles under her pen name, Stephanie Fraser.

What would *Vera's Voice* make of this one? She had written a lively piece about working on the land through the winter. She'd interviewed Miss Brown's land girls, who lived in the old gatekeeper's lodge at the bottom of the drive. They had cheerfully described their work as 'long hours and back-breaking', providing no end of examples, though it was the odd throwaway remark that had given the article its personal tone. Apparently, one of the very few advantages of being a land girl in the depths of winter was that 'the chickens are happy to settle for the night. It's hell in the summer months with double summer time. They're still clucking around at eleven o'clock and simply *won't* go to bed.'

That was the sort of detail that would raise a smile. But what about her reference to Tampax? Had she gone too far? Sanitary protection worn internally was making a big difference to girls who used it, though, so why not say so?

Vera's Voice was nothing if not sensible. They could always cross it out if they didn't like it – or maybe they would simply return the whole article, unwanted.

Writing articles was how Persephone used much of her free time. Not that anyone had that much these days. Persephone's job as a ticket collector at Victoria Station included compulsory overtime, but she had also spent countless nights fire-watching on Darley Court's roof and sometimes she mucked in and helped the land girls. Darley Court was used as a meeting and training centre for local Civil Defence organisations, such as the ARP and WVS, casualty services such as first aid and ambulances, and engineer services, like gas and rescue. Persephone helped keep the diary in order, ensuring that rooms of adequate size were provided and were never double-booked.

As for what remained of her limited free time, she loved seeing her friends, whether for a chatty evening or a trip to the pictures or an evening of dancing. All of which made it sound as if her writing wasn't all that important, but it was, and she set time aside for it regularly and was always on the lookout for ideas for something new and fresh to write about.

Writing was everything to her. She wanted to be a journalist and writing a wide variety of articles throughout the war was her way of proving it. Her parents weren't best pleased, but at this great distance there was nothing they could do about it, and it wasn't as though she used her own name. Meyrick House was at the other end of the country, down in Sussex, and therefore in danger of Jerry offloading unused bombs on the way home, so Ma and Pa had bundled Persephone off to Darley Court instead. In fact, the entire family had seemed to gang up on her, all her ancient rellies, not to mention her beloved brothers before they'd joined up.

That was another thing her parents weren't keen on – the way they had stopped being Mummy and Daddy and become Ma and Pa. To Persephone, it seemed more grown-up to use Ma and Pa. She wasn't a glamorous debutante any longer. She was a young woman with wartime work to do. Even before she had started on the railways, she'd had a job to do here at Darley Court, which had to be put to bed, as it was called, for the duration. Basically, this had meant covering up the beautiful old wooden panelling with protective hardboard – not that Persephone had done this, of course, though she would have loved to. Her job had been to assist in packing away all the ornaments, the best china and so forth, ready to be stored in the vast cellars. Every box had to be carefully labelled, and a book was kept in which the contents of every crate was listed in detail.

Miss Brown had also offered Darley Court's services in storing items from small museums and private collections. This, together with using the place for Civil Defence meetings, was her way of protecting her home from hordes of schoolchildren running amok or recuperating soldiers looking for ways of alleviating their boredom by using the long gallery to play cricket.

Once the house had been securely put to bed, Persephone had joined the railways. She loved the work and also loved the friends she'd met through it, but she had never forgotten her writing and her ambition to be a reporter.

She'd had a job on a newspaper before the war – and didn't that make it sound grand? Like a real reporting job. It hadn't been that at all, not in her eyes. She had told herself it was just something to get her started. Not that she'd been blasé about it. It had, in fact, been rather exciting. It was just that it definitely wasn't what she wanted for the rest of her career.

But nobody had ever taken her seriously.

*

Oh, that desperately disappointing meeting before the war! Persephone had gone to see Mr Bunting, the newspaper's editor, to propose herself as a junior reporter.

He had blinked at her. 'Great Scott, you really mean it, don't you? You actually imagine you can do this. You think you can be a reporter in London when war comes.'

She sat up straighter, not an easy thing to achieve considering her years of training in deportment. She was sick and tired of not being taken seriously. Nevertheless, she smiled. She'd been taught to do that too. ('No one likes a frowny face, Persephone.')

'I've proved I can write, haven't I?' she started to say.

Mr Bunting cut in. 'My dear young lady, a few lines once a week for the society column is a far cry from what you're proposing.'

'A few lines? Since I took over the column, I've produced simply *screeds*.'

'And most entertaining it has been too,' Mr Bunting said soothingly. 'Just what our readers enjoy. But what you're now suggesting – my dear Miss Trehearn-Hobbs, it wouldn't do at all. You're simply not up to it.'

'Give me a chance and I'll prove that I am.'

Mr Bunting bestowed an indulgent smile on her. 'Your patriotism is admirable.'

Persephone waited for the inevitable 'but', then realised there wasn't one, which made it worse. Mr Bunting found her idea so wholly inappropriate that he didn't feel the need to explain his thinking.

On the verge of huffing a sigh, she caught herself just in time. ('Sighing implies boredom, Persephone, and is very rude.') Instead, she took a moment to smooth her pencil-slim skirt. Being tall and slender, she made what her chums called a first-rate clothes horse. Her flesh-coloured silk stockings grazed one another as she daintily crossed one trim ankle over the other, making sure to keep her toes becomingly pointed.

What could she say to change Mr Bunting's mind? Anyone would think she'd volunteered to ship out with the troops and report from the front line, not write about life at home as war took hold.

She had ventured here into Mr Bunting's office only once before, when she was given the job of writing the society column. She had always sent in her pieces – her copy, she had learned to call it, feeling frightfully modern, clever and professional doing so. Had it been a mistake to keep away? Should she have shown her face from time to time? But her identity as the purveyor of high-society gossip was a secret that mustn't be jeopardised. Besides, Mummy would have climbed out of her tree if Persephone had gone on little jollies to Fleet Street.

What a lark it had been to start with, writing her very own column. It had been part of the fun of belonging to the London scene, which in itself had provided such a contrast to Persephone's growing-up years, when Nanny Trehearn-Hobbs wouldn't permit cake and jam on the same day and Roddy and Giles, her adored older brothers, had disappeared off to boarding school, hardly ever to be seen again, or so it had felt.

Much as she loved her sister, Persephone had lived for her brothers' hols, even though those times repeatedly failed to live up to expectations. Roddy and Giles had seemed incapable of coming home without a squad of pals in tow, leaving the young Persephone aching to have them to herself.

But – and this was the biggest 'but' in the whole wide world – if they hadn't been so gregarious, there would have been no Forbes.

Forbes Winterton. Those eyes of smoky-grey. The eyebrows a darker shade than his mid-brown hair. The easy confidence of the athlete, the clever, piano-trained fingers. ('Don't stare, Persephone.')

Forbes strode into her young life, seized her heart with both hands, then promptly hurled it to the ground and stamped on it. Not that he'd had the faintest idea.

'Is your little sister coming with us?' he'd asked, surprised, when she appeared in the stable yard in her riding togs as the boys were getting ready for a paperchase.

'Oh, yes,' Roddy said dismissively. 'Don't worry. She'll keep up.'

'Good as one of the fellows, eh?' Forbes tossed her a smile that liquefied her bones. 'We'll have to call you Percy.'

And they did, every last one of them, from that moment onwards, even the boys who hadn't been at Meyrick House at the time. It wasn't until years later, when Cordelia had pointed out that Percy was a label given to conscientious objectors back in the Great War, that it had stopped. Back when she was a girl, Persephone had spent the remainder of those hols floating about being as feminine as possible to try to undo the curse and make Forbes see her through new eyes, but it hadn't worked.

She had longed to go away to school herself, but like her sister before her, she'd been educated, if one could call it that, by a series of beautiful French noblewomen who had fallen on hard times, followed by a stint at a finishing school in Switzerland, specially selected for her to meet the right sort of girls.

Then it was time for Persephone's debut London Season, organised by Mummy as vigorously as Daddy had ever organised a military campaign.

Being a debutante was the most marvellous fun. Suddenly all those chums of Roddy and Giles's came into their own. Unlike some poor debs who didn't yet know any young chaps, Persephone danced every single dance right from the start. She became even more popular after she was snapped for the society pages.

'Not that one courts publicity, of course,' her mother purred, 'but it's as well always to wear a pretty smile just in case one of those photographers is nearby. Wretched fellows!'

'You look a delight, Percy,' Forbes observed casually, picking up the newspaper she had artlessly left open at the appropriate page to jolt him into realising he must never let her go. Some hope.

She didn't marry from her first Season for the simple reason that Forbes never asked, drat him. Drat her, too, for pining for the one man who was immune to her charms. She didn't want Algy, even though she could have been a viscountess, and she didn't want Monty even though he sent her orchids every single day. Only Forbes would do and she pinned her hopes on her second Season.

Usually the Season started in the warmth of May, but in 1939, because of Their Majesties' state visit to Canada and America that month, it was scheduled for earlier in the year. Beforehand, Persephone felt particularly chipper, having received a charming letter from the Pond's people, asking if she would consent to be photographed for an advertisement for their face cream. This was an honour that was sometimes conferred on the girl popularly destined to be the most beautiful girl of the Season, but Daddy, who could be a real old fogey, refused permission.

'It's a shame, really,' Persephone confided to her grandmother. 'The money would have been nice. Daddy says I can have a tenner a month for my dress allowance, but that won't stretch as far as one might like.' Talking about money was vulgar, of course, but one could say all kinds of things to Grandmama, who had been a Gaiety Girl before she'd knocked Grandpapa's socks off.

Grandmama gave her an assessing look. 'If you fancy earning a spot of pin money, I have an idea.'

And that was how it had come about. Grandmama knew the author of one of the society columns. Persephone was amazed to learn that 'Clarinda' was really a man. Apparently, he was about to emigrate to America, leaving his newspaper in need of a new Clarinda.

The editor, Mr Bunting, was very much in two minds as to whether to take on a slip of a girl but agreed to a trial period, subject to parental consent.

'But nobody else is ever to know,' he impressed upon Persephone. 'No tittle-tattling with your friends.'

'But it's *work*!' Mummy had cried in horror. 'We didn't bring you up so you could . . . work.' She made it sound like the most degrading thing imaginable.

'Besides,' said Daddy, 'there's a million unemployed. It's wrong of you to want a job. Immoral.'

'But not just anyone can do this job,' Persephone protested in her politest voice. 'Only someone in society can be Clarinda. And it's not really what you'd call a job,' she added, despising herself for saying such a thing. 'I wouldn't go into the office or anything.'

'I should hope not,' Mummy murmured.

'And it would be a deadly secret,' Persephone added. 'Not like the Pond's cream would have been.'

So she had become Clarinda, producing complimentary titbits about who enjoyed cocktails with whom at the Ritz and which couturier had dressed them. She also took her pen with her to country weekends, writing flattering comments about who sat particularly well on a horse and who wore which precious stones to dinner. Feeling devilishly clever, she also included snippets about places and events

35

she hadn't been to, but which she'd heard about on the grapevine.

Yes, she loved being Clarinda, but she would have much preferred writing about the preparations for war that were going on all around her. Sandbags appearing by the thousands, air-raid shelters being delivered, gas masks, preparations for the mass evacuation of children. But Mr Bunting simply wouldn't have it.

And then she'd been bundled off to Darley Court to sit out the war there. She'd had some success with getting articles published, though no magazine had ever offered to take her on, even temporarily. No editor had ever said, 'That's a jolly good idea. Can you turn it into a series?' or 'We're looking for someone to produce a monthly column about such-and-such a thing and we thought of you.'

All she could do was keep slogging away.

When Mabel cycled over to Darley Court on Saturday afternoon, Persephone made sure she had the chance to show off her ruby engagement ring to the land girls, who cooed over it longingly, much to Mabel's obvious delight.

'But I expect it's Mrs Mitchell you really want to show it to,' said Persephone.

Mrs Mitchell, the housekeeper, was related to Mabel's father and when Mabel had first come to Manchester, the Bradshaws had consigned her to Cousin Harriet's care. Mabel, however, hadn't stayed long at Darley Court. Instead, Mrs Mitchell had found her a billet with her friend Mrs Grayson, who at that time had still lived in her old matrimonial home, even though her rat of a husband had long since left her for another woman. After Mr Grayson and Floozy had been bombed out, Mr Grayson had ended up demanding his house back – it was his to all intents and purposes, because his name was still on the rent book – which had been a desperately upsetting upheaval for poor Mrs Grayson, but it had all worked out beautifully in the end, because that was the point where the railway friends had arranged for her to move in with Mrs Cooper.

Now Mabel glanced down at her ring and laughed at herself. 'I want to show Miss Brown too. I shan't rest until the whole of Manchester has admired it.'

'Then we'd better make sure the kitchen cat sees it as well,' teased Persephone. She was happy for Mabel; she was happy for Joan and Alison too. Was it time for her to accept that Forbes wasn't and never would be interested in her in that way? Probably. But she knew she could never bring herself to put him behind her. Her heart was an unutterable twit when it came to Forbes Winterton and his smoky-grey eyes. The best she could do was keep her love a secret.

Mabel went below stairs on her own to see Mrs Mitchell, then the two girls went together to find Miss Brown, the elderly owner of Darley Court – elderly, but sharp as a tack. She had inherited the place unexpectedly back at the start of the century after the last male heir died. Instead of appointing an agent to run the estate for her, she'd done it herself, drawing much criticism and derision in the process until the local gentlemen had been obliged to admit that she was making a jolly good fist of it.

For once, Miss Brown wasn't in her office, with her desk that looked outside and a vast table covered with a map of the grounds, marked up according to the vegetables that officialdom had put into groups A, B and C. Instead, they found her in the small sitting room that she preferred to the morning room. It was a favourite room of Persephone's as well. The deep red velvet curtains and pelmet and the marble chimneypiece made the sitting room feel cosy on a winter's day, while the blue hearth tiles and the cream lining and fringing on the curtains, together with the colourful beaded cushions dotted about on the chairs and the sofa, all made the room feel cheerful on a bright day when the sun streamed in.

Miss Brown admired Mabel's ring. 'Thank you for coming to show me.'

'Thank you for admiring it,' Mabel replied with a twinkle. 'Everyone's been so kind. Anyway, I didn't come here just to do the rounds with my ring. There's a Wings for Victory Week in March and I'd like to organise something for it. I'm here to dragoon Persephone into helping.'

'With pleasure,' said Persephone.

'These weeks are so important,' said Miss Brown. 'The people and businesses of Manchester raised a colossal sum for the Warship Week – last February, was it? After that frightful snow.'

'Yes,' said Persephone. 'The aim was to raise enough to be able to adopt HMS *Nelson,* and the total at the end of the week far exceeded the necessary amount, so now we've got our own battleship.'

'People are so generous,' said Mabel, 'and I want to help encourage that generosity.'

'You'll have to speak to someone on the committee in charge,' said Miss Brown. 'I'm sure they'll welcome all ideas.'

'Last year, volunteers made wooden or cardboard models of battleships that were displayed in shop windows,' Persephone remembered. 'I expect they'll do something similar with planes this time. There was a set-up in London last year that supplied blueprints and instructions.'

'I'm sure they'll do that again,' Mabel agreed, 'but I wondered whether we could organise a display of children's model planes. I'm sure the kids would love to join in.'

'That's a good idea,' said Miss Brown.

'The trouble is,' said Mabel, 'I start off with such determination, but I just don't have the flair for this sort of thing. Give me a job to do and I'll do it, but coming up with the ideas in the first place . . . that's not really me, I'm afraid.'

'So you've come to pick our brains,' said Miss Brown.

Persephone gazed towards the windows, but she wasn't looking out at the view. Her eyes were out of focus, as sometimes happened when she thought hard. 'What about . . .?' Her voice trailed off as the idea took shape.

'What about what?' Mabel prompted.

'Women are doing so much work for the war effort. Why not capitalise on it? I bet we could get hold of a bod from the Air Transport Auxiliary – not a man, but one of the girls who deliver the planes to wherever they have to go. If we could bag ourselves an ATA girl to give a talk, that would raise money.'

'Good idea,' Mabel applauded. 'I knew I was doing the right thing by coming here.'

'And we have to hold a dance – but I expect you've already thought of that,' said Persephone.

'Well, I had,' Mabel admitted, 'but it didn't seem very original.'

'It doesn't have to be original, you silly girl,' said Miss Brown. 'It merely has to be something that people will want to do – and most people love to dance. You may hold a dance here at Darley Court if you like, like we did at Christmas.'

'That's a generous offer,' said Mabel.

'It is,' Persephone agreed, 'but would you mind if we think about it, Miss Brown? The Christmas events we held here were a delight and everyone loved them, but if we want to raise a lot of money, then we'll need a bigger venue – like the Claremont Hotel in town.'

'You mean where Cordelia held her War Weapons Week dance?' asked Mabel. 'That was a gorgeous venue – but might it not look as if we're copying?'

'Now you really are being silly,' said Miss Brown. 'It isn't a competition. If the Claremont is the best place for your purposes, then approach the manager.'

Persephone smiled. 'They do say imitation is the sincerest form of flattery. Let's look into it.'

Mabel nodded. 'Yes, let's.'

There was a quiet tap on the door and Mrs Mitchell walked in. 'The afternoon post has come. I thought you'd want it straight away. And shall I bring tea?'

Taking the proffered letters, Persephone glanced through them – and her heart delivered an almighty thud against the wall of her chest. She knew that handwriting as well as she knew her own and it was a lot more important to her than her own. Forbes. She wrote to him regularly, though not as often as she would have liked. Frankly, she would have churned out letters twice a day if she could have got away with it. As it was, she wrote to lots of people – various relatives and friends, as well as several boys in the services who had been her dance partners in London, one of whom, of course, was Forbes. Nobody had any reason to think she had a particular reason for writing to him. Nobody had any reason to suspect that her heart all but leaped out of her chest when she saw his scrawl on an envelope.

'There's a couple for me,' she said, handing over the remaining letter to Miss Brown.

Usually at this point, as had happened on so many occasions before, Persephone would carry on behaving perfectly normally, smiling and joining in, and never mind that half her brain was going wild with excitement. But not this time. This time – oh, crumbs – Forbes hadn't written from overseas. This was an ordinary letter, not forces mail. Persephone caught her breath.

'Would you mind awfully if I open this now? It's from my brothers' friend. I write to him and . . .'

'Of course, dear,' said Miss Brown. 'Do you wish to be on your own?'

But Persephone couldn't even think about that. She opened the letter at once and scanned it.

'Not bad news, I hope,' said Mabel.

Persephone looked at her friend. It was a moment before she could speak.

'He's been injured and he's been brought home – to England, I mean, not home-home, but to hospital. He says he's going to be all right.'

'I'm pleased to hear it,' said Miss Brown. 'My goodness, what a shock for you, but the main thing is he's going to recover.'

Persephone heard the words but they didn't sink in. She didn't have room for anyone else's thoughts just then. Her mind and her heart were stuffed full to bursting with the words Forbes had written – to her! He asked if she could visit him. He asked *her* if she could get a spot of leave and get down to see him in Hertfordshire.

It's a lot to ask, but if you could possibly . . .

A lot to ask? No! Never. She'd do anything to be with him again.

CHAPTER FOUR

Lord, but it was boring being the office junior. When Emily had first arrived home from boarding school the moment her School Cert examinations were finished, taking her parents very much by surprise, there had been a serious question mark over what sort of job she should be put into. Mummy had been keen for her to join the railways, but Daddy deemed office work suitable, because it was ladylike and also it was the sort of work that would last beyond the end of the war. Then there had been a nasty, almost fatal accident in the marshalling yard where Mummy was working and after that Daddy had put his foot down.

And Emily had been here ever since, in the offices of Wardle, Grace and Masters, Daddy's firm of solicitors. She had loved it at first, because it was new and different and it had made her feel grown-up to be able to say she was 'going to the office'. Each of the solicitors had his own secretary, who had her own small office outside his room. Emily worked in the building's main office, which was beside the front door and was presided over by Mrs Beswick, who was even more of a dragon than Matron had been at school. It hadn't taken long for Emily to realise that Mrs Beswick didn't trust anyone other than herself to do anything and the solicitors' personal secretaries kept well out of her way.

Emily had endured months of so-called training for the simple reason that Mrs Beswick couldn't bear to let go of even the tiniest smidgeon of responsibility. Finally, Mrs Beswick had put her in charge of the stationery cupboard, but only because in these days of wartime shortages the shelves were almost bare and doomed to remain so. Apart from making the tea and going to the pillar box, Emily's main duties were collecting letters from the secretaries twice in the morning and twice in the afternoon, and 'doing the boxes'. This was a daily task that Mrs Beswick had eventually handed over to her because, as Emily had explained to Mabel and Margaret, 'It means being out of the office for some time, so she had a straight choice: give the task to me or leave me to greet visitors and answer the telephone. No contest!' She had hurriedly added, 'Please don't say anything to Mummy.'

Doing the boxes meant descending the steep steps into the basement, armed with each solicitor's list of clients for tomorrow. Downstairs there were long shelves of sturdy boxes of documents, letters, even sections of maps in some cases. Emily had to remove what was required for each appointment, replacing all the items she removed with slips of paper that were now worn out and practically see-through, having been used so many times. The documents had to be taken round to the secretaries and at a later date, when all the new notes and copies had been made, Emily replaced everything in the boxes, taking out all the slips as she did so. At the very least, Mrs Beswick would count all the retrieved slips. Often she scurried downstairs to perform a spot check. It was disheartening not to be trusted.

'It isn't you, Emily,' said Margaret. 'She'd obviously treat anyone else the same way.'

'Try not to take it personally,' added Mabel, but it was difficult not to when you were the one on the receiving end.

In any case, Emily was pretty sure that her work at Wardle, Grace and Masters would be hideously dull even if Mrs Beswick was a different sort of person. Being the office junior just wasn't what she wanted, though she had never questioned it before because she knew Daddy wouldn't let her change to something else. Last year, for a handful of precious months, she hadn't cared how ghastly her job was, because falling in love with Raymond had been all that mattered. She could cope with being bored at work while her personal life was glittering with joy.

But now – now she was both bored and heartbroken and her life was barely worth living. Well, there was nothing she could do about the state of her heart. She was doomed for evermore to endure the utter desolation of being unwanted by Raymond. But if she had to live through that, she jolly well wasn't going to put up with being bored at work as well. It was time to put her foot down.

Emily thought seriously about tackling Mummy first. They did fire-watching together two nights a week on the roof of Oswald Road School and Mummy clearly appreciated the opportunity for some mother-and-daughter chats. Emily did too. And Mummy had wanted her to be a railway girl in the first place, so that, plus Mummy's deep concern for her since Raymond had disappeared from her life, could put Emily in a strong position to get her mother on her side.

But that would put Daddy's back up. He wouldn't be amused if he thought he was being manipulated. And even though he had been dead against her relationship with Raymond because of Raymond's family only being grocers, he had been nothing but loving and supportive ever since Raymond had dumped her. Emily had been surprised at first as she'd fully expected him to be jubilant, but then she'd been ashamed of herself. How could she have thought that Daddy, who simply adored her, would find any kind of satisfaction in her unhappiness?

So she would have to speak to both parents together. She waited until the evening meal had been cleared away and they were all settling down for the customary cup of tea while they waited for the next news bulletin on the wireless. She hoped there wouldn't be anything absolutely dire on the news about the war, because she needed to say her piece straight afterwards so that there would be plenty of time for discussion before Daddy headed off for a Civil Defence meeting later on.

'I want to ask you something,' said Emily. 'It's important. I want to try for another job.'

'Another job!' Daddy exclaimed, looking at her in surprise. 'What's wrong with the one you've got? A solid background in office work is very useful.'

'It's deadly boring,' said Emily, 'and I hate it. I've always hated it, but now—' A sudden pain closed her throat, making it impossible to carry on speaking.

'I didn't know you felt that way about it,' said her mother. She looked questioningly at Daddy and he shook his head.

'It's news to me,' he said.

'I never said anything because there was no point,' said Emily. 'I knew I wouldn't be allowed to leave and I didn't want to sound like a cry-baby. I thought I'd just have to put up with it. After all, if a boring job is the worst thing that happens to me in wartime, I'll have got off far more lightly than a lot of other people. But it's different now. I thought . . . When we went to Lucy's engagement party, I kept thinking it should have been Raymond and me. That's what I was hoping for all along. It's what I thought, *believed*, was going to happen. But now that Raymond's gone, I've decided I'd cope a lot better if I could at least enjoy going to work.'

'Oh, darling,' said Mummy.

Emily sniffed away a few tears, reaching up her sleeve to draw out her hanky. 'I don't care how dramatic it sounds. It's the way I feel.'

'We both know how much Raymond hurt you,' said Daddy, 'but you're so young for all this.'

'For all what?' Emily asked. 'Falling in love?'

'Well, that too, but I was thinking of this matter of packing in a perfectly good job. It isn't a grown-up thing to do.'

'I'm nearly seventeen.'

'You're under twenty-one,' Daddy said seriously, 'and that means your mother and I are in charge of the decisions.'

'It's wartime,' said Mummy. 'All the youngsters are having to grow up quickly.'

'That doesn't mean it's a desirable thing to happen to them, Cordelia,' said Daddy, ever the protective father.

'That's true,' said Mummy, 'but we have to face facts. War changes everything, right down to the tiniest details of our lives. Who would ever have imagined as recently as a few years ago that I'd be going out to work, let alone that I'd be doing a manual job?'

Emily held her breath. Was Mummy on her side?

Her father's chest expanded as he drew in a deep breath, which he released on a long sigh. 'That makes it all the more important to keep Emily's life as normal as we can.'

'We don't have to make any decisions immediately,' said Mummy. 'We can at least discuss it. After all, if Emily is so unhappy . . .' She turned to Emily and, before Daddy could speak, asked, 'Is there a particular job you're interested in, darling?'

'I'd like to apply to the railways.'

'No!' said Daddy. 'We've talked about this before. I'm your father and it's my job to keep you safe, or as safe as I can in these uncertain times, and sending you off to the marshalling yard or a signal box or a level crossing doesn't count as keeping you safe.'

'There are plenty of other kinds of work on the railways,' Mummy pointed out. 'She could even be a clerk.'

No! Not more filing. She didn't want to put anything in alphabetical order again as long as she lived. But Emily knew better than to say anything at this crucial moment.

'When I joined LMS,' said Mummy, 'I simply sat the tests and waited to be told what job I was to do. It was the same for my friends. Emily isn't old enough to apply for war work, so we could perhaps ask what openings are available for a young girl, especially if we make enquiries while she's still sixteen. I could have a private word with Miss Emery. That wouldn't put us under any obligation, but it would help us see where we stand.'

Daddy frowned. 'I don't know, Cordelia, and I'm not going to be pushed into making a snap decision. I'll have to think about it.'

CHAPTER FIVE

Persephone only had to wait until the first week of February for the leave she had asked for, but it felt like for ever. And what if the country endured a snowstorm of the same extraordinary proportions as the one that had happened this time last year? The thought of her all-important journey having to be postponed made the beats of her heart so heavy that their thuds echoed through her sleep. Last year's snow had crippled the country for three whole weeks, followed by all the disruptions caused by a thaw on such a massive scale. What if there should be another snowstorm and while it lasted Forbes got better and vanished from her life once more? That would be just too cruel.

But there was no snow – well, there was, but only an ordinary amount. And the beginning of February brought good news of the war.

'Not just good news,' said Dot when the friends met up in the station buffet one evening before they headed for home. 'The very best.'

They all looked at one another and among the smiles Persephone noticed the sheen of tears in a few eyes. The Germans had surrendered at Stalingrad, deep inside Russia.

'My dad says it's the worst defeat the Germans have suffered since the end of the last war,' said Margaret.

'It's certain to be a major turning point,' said Cordelia.

'We said that a few weeks ago after El Alamein,' said Alison. 'Now we've got another one. After all this time at war, it's just so wonderful.'

'There'll still be a long time to go,' said Dot, 'but we can have real hope now.'

Sitting beside Dot, Persephone discreetly pressed her friend's hand. Dear Dot must be thinking of her two beloved boys, who were both fighting for King and country as part of the North Africa campaign. Dot gave Persephone a smile that crinkled her kind hazel eyes. Dot was a good sort, the very best. She had a generous heart and bags of common sense. She liked to refer to the younger members of their group as her daughters for the duration, and Persephone was more than happy to have this special lady as her honorary second mother.

'Talking of hope,' said Alison, turning to Persephone, 'have you had any more news about how your friend in hospital is getting on?'

Persephone shook her head. 'No, but I'll see him soon.'

'I bet he's looking forward to that,' said Mabel. 'There's nothing like a friendly face to cheer you up when you aren't feeling quite the thing.'

'I hope so,' said Persephone. Not wanting anyone to rumble quite how much cheering up she hoped to do, she added quickly, 'I don't think I mentioned it before, but you've all met him.' That caused a bit of a stir. 'He came here and took me out one evening when he had some leave. It was ages ago – a couple of years. We arranged to meet here in the buffet before we went out.'

'I remember,' Alison exclaimed, then laughed. 'It isn't every day a girl swans into the station buffet wearing the most glamorous evening gown imaginable.'

The others laughed and Persephone joined in. How well she remembered that evening when Forbes had taken her out for an early dinner followed by a trip to the theatre. She had put such thought and care into what to wear, settling on an evening dress of silk chiffon in the softest sea-green.

49

High-waisted, it was fitted in the bodice before flaring into a floor-length skirt. Persephone possessed both a dainty handbag and evening shoes in a deeper sea-green to go with it.

'And then the man of the moment arrived,' Mabel added. 'Talk about a good-looking couple.'

Persephone had specially asked Forbes to pick her up from the buffet because she'd wanted the man of her dreams and the friends who meant so much to her to meet one another. The moment had been hugely important to her and her heart had pitter-pattered like crazy, but to everyone else involved it had just been an ordinary introduction – well, she thought now with a smile, ordinary plus the dazed looks on her friends' faces while they drank in how handsome Forbes was.

'I'm sorry if this sounds shallow,' said Alison, 'but I hope that however he's been injured, he still has his looks.'

'I wish I'd been there to see him,' said Margaret.

'Of course,' said Dot. 'It was before we knew you.'

There was the tiniest of silences, then Colette said in a steady voice, 'Since everyone is thinking it but nobody wants to say it, I'll say it for you. I wasn't there either. I was well and truly under Tony's thumb back then and he hardly let me spend any time with you.' Her words were serious, but then she smiled as if to reassure the rest of them. 'I hope I'll get the chance to see this vision of masculine perfection one day.'

'You and me both,' Margaret added and everyone laughed.

Tiny shivers of anticipation passed through Persephone. She couldn't wait for her leave to come round. She had managed to get two days just before a day off, so she had three full days in all, two for travelling and one long blissful day with Forbes, visiting times permitting, of course, though she had taken the precaution of writing to the ward sister at Ashridge to explain how far she was travelling and politely asking if she could spend as much time with Captain Winterton as possible. ('A few good manners go a long way, Persephone.')

When everyone pushed back their chairs and stood up to leave, Persephone checked that the belt buckle of her caramel-coloured wool coat was fastened and drew on her gauntlet-style leather gloves before they all left the buffet, calling goodbye to Mrs Jessop behind the counter. The concourse was packed solid with passengers, clouds of grey tobacco smoke wafting above their heads. High above was the station's overarching canopy of glass and metal, which had survived an aerial attack by Jerry last May, on the night young Master Hubble was born in the first-class restaurant. Persephone was so proud of how her friends had conducted themselves on that occasion. While Joel had attended Joan during her labour, Margaret and Alison had fought their way up onto the canopy and helped to extinguish the deadly high explosives that fell from the skies.

Outside Victoria, Cordelia said her goodbyes and hurried away to meet her husband, as they were going out for the evening. Dot headed off to her own bus stop and the others joined a queue.

'It's lovely that we get to travel together,' said Colette.

'If we can all crowd onto the same bus,' said Alison.

It was standing room only, but they all piled on. Colette got off first at Seymour Grove, then the bell dinged and the vehicle drove away into Chorlton, Margaret, Mabel, Alison and Persephone all staying on until it swung round in a hairpin manoeuvre into the terminus. Persephone could have caught a bus that would have taken her past the terminus and down Hardy Lane, from where it was a hop and a skip to Darley Court, but she much preferred travelling with her chums when the opportunity arose. As she said ta-ta and watched them walk off, she felt a tug of envy. They were lucky to live together. Not that she minded being in Darley Court, and she thought the world of Miss Brown and Mrs Mitchell, but living with other girls must be the bee's knees. Mabel had lived at Darley Court for a short time, but she and Persephone hadn't been chums back then, and although Colette had moved in temporarily after she finally left Tony, when he was sent off to join the army she had moved back into her old house.

Persephone strode briskly through the chilly, darkened streets, aiming her small torch downwards, its tissue-dimmed beam allowing her a tiny bit of a glow to guide her and stop her bumping into lamp posts or pillar boxes. She walked confidently, but not *too* confidently. Pa had walked out of the village hall, a building he'd been in and out of his entire life, and gone straight into the duck pond because he'd been disoriented by the blackout, and if it could happen to Pa, it could happen to anyone.

If everyone was right and the tide of the war had turned, did that mean they could at long last start looking forward to life without the blackout? How strange that would feel – and how very welcome.

Persephone marched up Darley Court's long drive, perceiving the house as a massive shape of deeper darkness. There was a nip in the air that suggested there would be a frost tonight. Often, Persephone walked round the back to the kitchen door, but in the blackout it made sense to use the front door. She walked beneath the porte cochère, the drive-through porch that protruded from the front of the mansion, walked up the shallow stone steps and let herself into the grand entrance hall. Straight ahead of her, the wide staircase led up to a square half-landing with an arched alcove containing a statue of Aphrodite. From either side of the half-landing, stairs led up to the galleried landing. Above the hall was a vaulted ceiling.

Persephone ran upstairs to her bedroom. She had a half-tester bed with white muslin drapes caught up by bows of faded lavender satin. Removing her coat and hat, she peeled off her gloves and unwound the scarf that Mrs Grayson had knitted for her. She had four scarves she wore turn and turn about, made for her by Mrs Grayson, Mrs Cooper, Mrs Mitchell and Nanny. She hung up her uniform and changed into a tweed skirt and Roddy's old cricket jumper.

Persephone glanced in the mirror to straighten the jumper, which swamped her. Then she stopped and looked at her face. Had Forbes remembered her face and realised he loved her? Would the sight of her when she walked into his ward simply take his breath away? That was why he had written, asking her to visit, wasn't it? It had to be. It simply had to be.

The train was full, which didn't come as a surprise. Persephone had arrived early so as to be as certain as she could be of nabbing a seat, though if an older lady was standing, she would give it up. It was a train with compartments and she had a place beside the window. Her small suitcase was in the net luggage rack overhead and on her lap was a capacious handbag lent to her by Mrs Mitchell.

'It's the only way you'll be able to carry what you need for the journey,' the housekeeper had declared.

It was true. These days, station buffets often closed early because of running out of provisions or else they kept their food for servicemen only. Moreover, there was a serious shortage of crockery, so even if tea was available, passengers could have a drink only if they'd brought their own cups with them. In the vast handbag, Persephone had got a packet of sandwiches and an apple, as well as a small flask.

More and more people climbed aboard the train. Outside Persephone's compartment, the corridor was a solid mass of people. She watched through the window as the guard walked along the platform, slamming doors shut, preparing the train for the off. Then he walked back the other way and Persephone knew he was heading towards the guard's van. She heard the shrill sound of the whistle as the guard claimed the driver's attention. Knowing that once he had seen the guard wave his green flag, the driver would blow the train whistle and the train would begin to pull away, she waited . . . and waited. The whistle blew again . . . and again shortly afterwards. After a couple more whistles, the guard came along the platform, opening doors.

'The load's too heavy,' he shouted into the train. 'You lot nearest the door, off you get.'

'He's turfing people off,' said a lady in Persephone's compartment. She had a bag bigger than Mrs Mitchell's on her lap.

'Needs must,' said another passenger with the complacency of one who was nowhere near the carriage door.

At last, the guard blew his whistle again and this time, after the train whistle made its response, there came a hissing sound followed by a rushing noise, and then the familiar *puh . . . puh . . .* began, slowly at first and then building up speed as the train began to move. There were some creaking sounds as the couplings that held the long line of carriages together shifted and took the strain and then they were on their way.

As the train rounded a curve, the passengers swayed and the lady with the enormous bag pulled it closer to her.

'Be careful of my bag,' she said to the people on either side of her. 'It's full of eggs.'

'You've got eggs?' said a gentleman in a pinstriped suit. 'Would you sell me a couple?'

'What? No. I was joking.'

'Are you sure? If that bag is full of eggs, you've definitely got some to spare.'

'I told you. It was a joke.'

From then on, every so often during the long journey someone would lean towards the lady, gazing narrowly first at her bag and then at her, before asking if she would sell some eggs.

'How many more times?' asked the lady, becoming agitated. 'I didn't mean it. I was joking.'

'Who would joke about something like that?' was the reply.

Finally, the lady got off. Persephone watched as she squeezed her way through the tightly packed crowd in the corridor. Persephone didn't think for one moment that the lady actually had any eggs, but if she did, it was difficult to imagine them surviving such a crush.

Later in the journey, the train pulled into sidings and waited there for well over an hour. Passenger trains often had to give way to freight trains or troop trains, which always took precedence, and there was nothing unusual in sitting for ages in a stationary train without ever knowing why the hold-up had occurred. On this occasion, though, sitting in the sidings turned out to be well worth it for the sheer delight and excitement of seeing a massive US Army loco go past, pulling a long line of British wagons. Persephone realised she was smiling all over her face. Just wait until she told Dot, so Dot could tell young Jimmy, her grandson. Youngsters, as well as a lot of grown-ups for that matter, called the American locomotives 'Wild West trains' because of the vast cowcatcher grills they carried at the front.

In peacetime this journey would have lasted a few hours, but this time it took all day and the train's blackout blinds had been lowered long before Persephone got off the train, obliged to trust the local knowledge of a fellow passenger when he assured her that this really was her stop. On the platform, a porter confirmed it was indeed Berkhamsted.

'Is it far to Ashridge?' she asked.

'It's a good few miles, miss, and the first part is uphill. I hope you aren't suggesting walking there.'

'No, I just wondered how far, that's all. Thank you.'

Her heart swelling with excitement, Persephone would have liked nothing more than to go rushing off straight up the hill, but she must hold on until tomorrow. For now, she had a room in a modest but comfortable little hotel, where she would be staying tomorrow night as well . . . after a wonderful day spent in the company of Forbes Winterton, the man of her dreams. Oh, so many dreams! And stretching back such a long way. And tomorrow, when she entered the ward and he saw her and their eyes met . . . that would be when the moment she had longed for finally came to fruition.

Persephone sat in the back of the taxi as, having climbed the hill, it made its way along the gently winding road through the woodland along the top of the ridge. When the vehicle turned into a driveway, an enormous building came into view, its architecture combining grandeur with elegance. In one of his letters, Forbes had told her that the building had started out as a monastery before becoming a royal residence for a time. It certainly looked the part. You could fit three or four Darley Courts into here.

These days, according to Forbes, Ashridge was an off-shoot of Charing Cross Hospital and it wasn't just for soldiers. It was for Joe Public and included a large maternity unit.

Inside, in a long, gracious hallway, Persephone asked for directions to the Wyatt Room, which was one of the rooms that had been turned into a ward for servicemen. It was on the ground floor at the back, with handsome panelled walls and tall windows looking over a terrace and lawns with a variety of trees beyond. Instead of having a row of beds down each side in the traditional way, there was ample space for a third row down the centre. All the men seemed to be lying up in bed, their pillows securely propped up.

A nurse in a bibbed apron, short sleeves with white sleeve protectors and a white cap worn on the back of her head looked expectantly at Persephone as she hovered in the doorway.

'Good morning,' said Persephone. 'I'm here to see Captain Winterton. I know it must be early for visiting, but—'

She got no further.

'Persephone! There you are.'

Forbes! The sound of his beloved voice made Persephone's heart turn a somersault. She homed in immediately on his position in the ward. He was near the middle, as handsome as ever, his tousled hair making him even more attractive. One pyjama shoulder bulged; presumably there were bandages underneath.

Persephone glanced towards the nurse. 'May I?'

The nurse laughed. 'I think he'll come and fetch you if I say no.'

Persephone made her way between the beds, careful not to knock against them. She smiled politely and nodded to the patients as she passed and then – oh, and then she was beside Forbes, and he was reaching for her hand, lifting it to his lips and kissing it. Persephone's thoughts scattered in a thousand directions. This was what she had dreamed of for years. A kiss from Forbes.

'You came,' he said, his gaze warm. 'Bless you for that. You're a sight for the proverbial sore eyes.'

'Of course I came,' she said quietly. Of course she had. She'd have come a lot further and gone to far more trouble. 'How are you?'

Forbes let go of her hand and raised his fingers to touch the opposite shoulder. 'Pretty chipper. Mending. Can't wait to get back into the thick of it.'

That didn't surprise her. It was the way her brothers talked, the way all their friends talked. Forbes might simply have fallen off his horse, snapped a bone and been eager to get back to playing polo.

'Trust you to get a bed right in the centre,' she said lightly.

He understood her at once. 'The life and soul, that's me.' He patted the bed in invitation, then pulled a face while still smiling. 'Better not. There'd be a riot if the other chaps saw you perched beside me.'

'And if they didn't, Sister would,' said the nurse who had spoken to Persephone. She held a wooden chair. 'Here you are. There's not much space, but I'm sure you won't mind.'

Positioning the chair, Persephone sat down. Being so near to Forbes and having his attention trained on her made her feel madly self-conscious and she made a play of turning round to look through the windows.

'A good view,' she remarked, then she laughed. 'Of course, it must be a lot better at other times of the year.'

'Must be glorious in spring and summer,' Forbes agreed. 'Not that I intend to be here to find out.'

Having composed herself, Persephone turned back to him. Oh, those wonderful grey eyes! Her composure wobbled again, but she sat up straight and smiled. She wanted to hold his hand and wished he would reach for hers in invitation, but he didn't.

'Aren't you going to introduce the lovely young lady?' asked the man in the next bed.

'I hope you're not going to hog her all to yourself,' added another with as much of a grin as he could muster with a significant part of his face covered in dressings.

'Leave him alone,' chimed in a third. 'His lady friend has come all this way to see him. At least pretend to give them a bit of privacy.'

'Oops,' said Forbes. 'Sorry, Persephone. They think that every female over the age of fifteen who puts her nose through the door is someone's sweetheart. It's because they're all so desperate for love,' he added loudly, making the fellows in the surrounding beds groan and laugh. 'Seriously,' he added in a quieter voice as the other men left them to it, 'thank you for coming all this way to see me. I can't tell you how much I appreciate it.'

'It's a huge pleasure, truly.'

'Good of you to say so,' said Forbes. 'I say, you didn't mind the others having a bit of a joke, did you? They don't mean anything by it. I hope you weren't embarrassed at being called my lady friend. The last thing I want is for you to be uncomfortable when you've travelled all this way and shown what a terrific chum you are.'

CHAPTER SIX

The atmosphere in the station buffet was cosy on this grey February day, even though there was no cheerful fire crackling away in the fireplace and the shelves lining the wall behind the counter with its wood-panelled front held only a fraction of the numbers of items that used to be available before the war.

'It's changed from how it used to be when we first started meeting here,' said Mabel, looking around and absorbing the differences.

'Everything's changed since back then, love,' Dot said with a chuckle.

'But the glass display case on the counter has scones and carrot cake,' said Alison, 'so all is not lost.'

'And dear old Mrs Jessop is still there presiding over the teapot,' Colette added.

Mabel felt an inner glow of gratitude for the friends the war had brought her, and gratitude, too, towards Miss Emery, the assistant welfare supervisor for women and girls, who had advised them on their very first day that they would do well to set aside all the usual differences in social backgrounds and decide to be friends with one another. This they had done and Mabel, for one, would be glad of it until her dying day.

'Here comes Margaret,' said Cordelia as Margaret left the counter with her tea and wound her way between the tables to join them. 'Mabel and Persephone, you were going to tell us about the plans for Wings for Victory Week.'

Mabel looked at Persephone in case she wanted to start, but Persephone gave a slight shake of her head.

'We're going to organise a dance,' said Mabel, and smiled when her friends cheered softly.

'It wouldn't be us if there wasn't a dance,' said Dot.

'You'll have a lot to live up to if you're going to match Cordelia's dance in War Weapons Week,' said Margaret.

'Oh, we'll outshine that a dozen times over,' Mabel said breezily, making everyone laugh. 'Just you wait and see.'

'I hope you do,' Cordelia said seriously. 'The more money that is raised, the better.'

'Hear, hear,' said Alison.

'Persephone and I have been to the Claremont to talk to the manager and he's happy to host the dance,' said Mabel.

'That's a lovely venue,' said Cordelia, 'and the staff are excellent.'

'We need lots of ideas for raising money at the dance,' said Mabel. 'All ideas welcome. We've got a few to start with.' She glanced Persephone's way again in case she wanted to list them, but she remained silent, so Mabel continued. 'We're shamelessly going to pinch some of the things from Cordelia's dance, like paying to have a particular piece of music played, and Persephone suggested doing a penny on the drum – you know, like in *The Old Town Hall* on the wireless.'

There were murmurs of 'Good idea' and 'That'll be fun' and Mabel felt encouraged.

'Persephone and I will dream up lots of fiendish clues,' she said, 'so be prepared to lose all your pennies. Aside from that, we've come up with a list of ideas that ordinary people can use at home to raise a bit of money, such as lending your own books at a penny a time and making pretty needle cases. You tell them, Persephone,' she added, not wanting to hog the limelight.

'It's easy to make a little needle case. All you need is a piece of card, circular or maybe heart-shaped. It just needs to be lightly padded with wadding and covered with scraps of material. Miss Brown says we can have some of the velvet sashes the children wore at the Christmas party to cut up so the needle cases are as smart as possible.'

'We want to get lots of local ladies making needle cases,' said Mabel, 'and we can sell them at a bob each.'

'If you have local ladies making them,' said Cordelia, 'these are the very people who would have bought them.'

'We thought of that,' said Mabel. 'We wondered if Mrs Jessop would have them on sale in here, and we can ask Lost Property to have some. There are various places we can ask.'

'The library,' suggested Margaret.

'The Worker Bee,' said Alison.

'Lots of places,' said Dot.

'There isn't a queue at the moment,' said Colette. 'You could ask Mrs Jessop now.'

Persephone got up and went over to the counter.

Leaning forward, Dot dropped her voice. 'Is it me or is our Persephone a bit quiet this evening?'

'She was jolly enough earlier when she was telling us about the egg lady and the American loco,' said Margaret.

'Not to mention the descriptions of Ashridge,' said Alison. 'It sounds wonderful.'

'Yes, all right.' Dot held up her hands in surrender. 'My mistake. It was just a fleeting idea, that's all.'

'She's probably still tired,' Margaret suggested. 'She's had two long journeys and then had to get up for an early shift yesterday straight after getting back.'

Mabel felt guilty. Had it been thoughtless of her to suggest meeting up to talk over the Wings for Victory ideas yesterday evening? But they didn't have as much time as she'd like to organise their events, so every day mattered, and in any case Persephone had seemed fine. She looked fine now too, chatting with Mrs Jessop, and Mabel felt reassured.

Persephone returned and even before she arrived at their table it was obvious from her smile that Mrs Jessop had said yes. The others offered to help in any way they could to support Mabel and Persephone's plans.

'Thank you all,' said Mabel, Persephone echoing her words.

Glancing round to make sure no one was going to add to that particular subject, Cordelia said, 'They may not be the only ones asking for help.'

'Oh aye?' said Dot. 'You mean you?'

'I do, though it'll be a completely different type of help, if it comes about,' said Cordelia. 'Emily has asked if we'll let her join the railways. Her ever-protective father was dubious about it to start with. He had visions of all sorts of death-defying jobs, but Miss Emery has assured me that Emily would be given a post suitable for her age.'

'And you want us to keep a friendly eye on her,' said Dot.

'We'll do more than that,' said Alison. 'We'll expect her to join us in the buffet.' She looked around the table. 'Won't we?'

'Of course,' said Mabel.

'Then she can be the new girl instead of me,' Margaret added, making them laugh.

'What's brought this about?' asked Persephone. 'She's an office junior at present, isn't she?'

'And hates it,' said Cordelia. 'Has hated it all along, apparently, and after being let down so badly by Raymond, she's decided that she needs a fresh start.'

'That's understandable,' said Dot. 'And we'll welcome her with open arms. You know we will.'

'Thank you,' said Cordelia. 'Assuming she passes the tests and is accepted, I just hope she'll be given a position here at Victoria. She might end up on one of the local stations. I'd much rather know she was here.'

'Her father isn't the only one who's protective,' said Alison.

'Has she got a date for her tests?' asked Colette.

'Yes,' Cordelia answered. 'It isn't possible to revise for the English or maths, but she's busy brushing up on her geography by poring over our atlas of the British Isles and begging us to test her.'

The conversation moved on, as it did so often these days, to the latest information about food. There was due to be a decent quantity of tins of English plums available in the shops.

'Thanks to the good harvest last year,' said Colette.

'And have you heard about milk bottles yet?' asked Dot. 'From later this month, it's going to be an offence to hang on to them. They have to be washed and returned at once.'

Mabel's mind returned to the Wings for Victory Week and the success she wanted to make of her own small contribution to the national effort. Then she thought of the personal legacy she hoped to leave behind her when she went to live down south. It was tempting to spill all to her friends and ask for their help, which they would be only too pleased to give, but that wasn't how she wanted to do this. She wanted it to be *her* legacy, something that she personally was going to leave.

'Besides,' she'd told Harry in one of their precious telephone calls, 'I'll have plenty of time to organise it – unlike the Wings for Victory Week.'

'From everything you've told me,' said Harry, 'your Wings for Victory Week is going to be splendid. I'm so proud of you for what you're doing for us RAF chaps. I've told everyone down here and they all think you're a brick.'

'I'm glad to do it,' Mabel said simply.

'As for your other project,' Harry added, 'I think it's a good idea for you to tackle it on your own. It'll give you something to focus on.'

Mabel chuckled. 'Brides are supposed to focus on the wedding. Anyway, why do I need something else to focus on?'

'Because it'll distract you from thinking about how you're going to miss your friends when you move away.'

'Oh, Harry,' said Mabel. 'You understand me so well.'

Her heart swelled with love. How lucky she would be to have Harry Knatchbull at her side for the rest of her life.

Letters that arrived during the day were always put on the mantelpiece in the front room. Unless a letter was from Harry, Mabel would as often as not open it right away, but today, recognising her father's handwriting, she put the letter in her pocket to save for later. She had written to him last week to explain her idea and she hoped this would be a favourable reply.

She was due to go out that night on first-aid duty, though it was some time since her training had last been called upon. There had only been around a dozen air raids over Manchester last year and with things now going better for the Allies, maybe there would be even fewer this year. Fingers crossed.

At half past nine, Mabel cycled all the way down Barlow Moor Road to Withington, where she was stationed in St Cuthbert's School. When the first-aid group had first been stationed here, they'd had the place to themselves, but it hadn't been long before other services had been based here as well – ARP, Heavy Rescue and the gas and electricity men. There might now not be much of the action they'd all trained for, but that didn't mean they were idle. A furniture repair shop had been set up and they gathered all manner of bits and pieces to make toys. Also – a great treat compared to the long nights of aerial attacks early in the war – everyone was given the chance for some shut-eye.

When Mabel was sent to kip down on one of the narrow cot beds, she hung back so as to read her letter from Pops. He approved of her idea. She'd been certain he would, because he had always set aside part of his money to improve the lives of those in need, but she felt relieved all the same. Now she knew for definite that her plans could go ahead.

Have you discussed this with Harry? It's his wedding present too, remember.

Mabel smiled warmly. She had confided in Harry at the same time as writing to ask Pops. Harry thought it a simply ripping idea and he was perfectly happy for it to be their wedding present.

After listening to Joan talking about the importance to mothers of having their children properly cared for while they were out at work, often for punishingly long hours, Mabel wanted to set up a nursery. In the great scheme of things, it was a very small thing to do, and she would only be able to help a certain number of mums and children, but she felt strongly that it was the right thing to do. It was the sort of idea Pops would have instigated, which made her aware of the bond that existed between them. And it was for the community – and wasn't that what the war effort was all about, when you came down to it? Yes, it was a massive national effort to win the war, but at the same time there was the need to look after one another on a local level, because that was how everyone was going to pull through, and she, Mabel Bradshaw, intended to be a small part of that.

She had already identified what she hoped would be a suitable building on High Lane. That is, it looked suitable from the outside, meaning it was standing and it appeared to be empty. It was a single-storey building with big double doors at the front and windows set high in the wall – too high to see out of. Even an adult would need to climb onto a chair to look out, which made Mabel think the building might originally have housed a school.

Now that she knew Pops would provide financial backing, she could start things moving.

On her day off, her first task was to find out who was responsible for the building, which she did quite easily by asking an estate agent – though lettings agent was probably a better description these days. The first agent sent her along to a second one, because they had the keys.

Mabel explained her plans to a pair of sunny-faced gentlemen who could have stuck cushions down their fronts and taken a fancy-dress party by storm as Tweedledum and Tweedledee. They were brothers, Mr Anthony Hayter and Mr George Hayter.

'I'm in search of suitable premises to set up a nursery. I'm not saying that money is no object, but I have sufficient funds to have some improvements done to make a place just right – internal improvements, you understand, not external. I haven't got the wherewithal for that.'

When she said which building she was interested in, Mr George said, 'It was a school for a little while, but it started out as a chapel.'

'It doesn't have a name as such,' Mr Anthony told her, 'but it's known as the Extension, because in the time when it was used as school, this was just a temporary arrangement, albeit one that lasted several years while the school's governors found suitable land and raised money to build the "real" school, as it were.'

'Would you care to look round it?' asked Mr George. 'I'd be pleased to show you.'

He escorted her to the Extension and used a huge key to open one of the double doors. It creaked loudly, but Mabel wasn't put off. Nor was she dismayed by the dust and the cobwebs or the old crates and bits and pieces of ancient furniture that had been there for goodness only knew how long. She knew she had to see beyond all that to what the place could look like when it was done up.

There was a large lobby area that extended the whole width of the front of the building. Then they went through a door in a wooden wall into a big if shabby room, roughly square in shape, on the opposite side of which was another wooden wall with a door that led into a similar room, though this room had a sectioned-off lobby containing the building's side door, which simply refused to budge at all. At the far end of the building was a narrow third room, with a range and a vast sink.

Mabel wrinkled her nose. The whole place smelled of age and neglect, but the walls weren't running with damp or black with mould.

'Still interested?' enquired Mr George.

'It has that sad feeling that buildings get when they aren't occupied for ages. Buildings need to be lived in or worked in. When they're just left to stand . . .' Her voice trailed away. Would Mr George think her daft?

But he nodded. 'It would take a bit of elbow grease to bring this place back to life, but I believe it to be structurally sound, though obviously you would wish to have that checked.'

'Of course,' Mabel murmured. She would need no end of advice. She must write back to Pops this very evening to pick his brains. She would have to learn about various Corporation services, not to mention getting to grips with numerous regulations. Standing here in this filthy, stale-smelling building, she ought to feel overwhelmed, but she didn't.

Instead, she imagined clean floors and sunshine pouring in through gleaming windows; toy boxes and happy voices; children sitting at small tables waiting to be offered something to eat. She was going to bring this place back to life.

On a crisp morning at the end of February, Mabel walked to High Lane, where she had arranged to meet Miss Brewer from the Corporation at the Extension, which stood halfway, give or take, between Wilton Close and Torbay Road, where Joan and Bob lived. Mabel had come early, wanting to be the first to arrive so she would be there to greet her visitor, but as she stepped through the gateway in the low wall, a lady in a navy overcoat and grey hat, with a handbag over her arm, was already there. She was probably a few years older than Mumsy and had a competent air about her.

'Mrs Bradshaw?' she asked before Mabel could speak.

'Miss,' said Mabel, smiling, 'and you must be Miss Brewer.'

'Miss Brew*ster*,' the lady corrected her.

'I beg your pardon,' said Mabel. 'I hope I haven't kept you waiting, but we weren't actually due to meet until half past.'

'No matter,' said Miss Brewster. 'Shall we go in? It's a bit chilly to be hanging about outside.'

She smiled as she said this and Mabel, hurrying forward with the key that the brothers Hayter had lent her, warmed to her. By the time she had shut the door behind them, Miss Brewster was already in the first of the two rooms, looking around in an assessing way while holding a piece of paper or possibly card in the palm of one gloved hand and a pencil in the other. She smiled at Mabel.

'Before the war, I'd have been making copious notes, but with paper so scarce now, I make do with a few choice memory-jogging words on any scrap or on the back of the proverbial cigarette packet. You're smiling, Miss Bradshaw. Have I said something amusing?'

'Not at all,' said Mabel. 'I'm just pleased to see you taking a positive interest right away. That's a good sign – or at least, I hope it is.'

'Yes, it is. We have to make the best of everything. Personally, I have always done so, and taken pride in it, but these days more than ever before we have a duty to do so. There is a further room through here, is there? Do you mind if I . . .?'

Mabel followed her into the next room and gave Miss Brewster a chance to jot down a couple more memory-jogging words.

Miss Brewster looked at her, raising one eyebrow. 'Lavatories?'

'Outside,' said Mabel, 'and they're old-fashioned earth closets, I'm afraid, not with running water, so they'd need emptying.'

'I don't see that as a problem,' said Miss Brewster.

'You don't? That's good.'

'Of course not,' Miss Brewster said bracingly. 'Scouts must do that sort of thing all the time when they're at camp.'

'The Scouts? You think I should ask them to empty the closets?'

'Naturally. Who else should do it? They're the ones who are going to benefit from having this building kitted out for them.'

It took Mabel's thoughts a moment to catch up. 'The Scouts? This building isn't going to be for the Scouts, Miss Brewster. There seems to have been a misunderstanding.'

'I don't believe so. I was specifically told—'

'No,' Mabel put in firmly. 'I'm not setting up a Scout hut. I'm setting up a nursery.'

'A what? A nursery?'

'Yes.' Mabel smiled, glad to have got the confusion out of the way. 'Do you need to take another look around now you know you aren't inspecting a prospective Scout hut?'

'No, thank you.' With a click, Miss Brewster opened her handbag and put the pencil and scrap of paper inside, snapping it shut again. 'I don't need to make any notes at all.'

'Oh, good. The accommodation is suitable, then?'

'No, it is not, Miss Bradshaw, for the simple reason that no accommodation, no matter how well kitted out, is suitable for the purpose of bringing up children outside the home. Children need to be at home with their mothers.'

'I agree,' said Mabel, 'but many mothers are out at work now and their work is essential to the war effort.'

'Nevertheless,' replied Miss Brewster, 'small children should still be in the home, and if they can't be in their own homes, then they should be in someone else's. There are plenty of women these days who look after other people's children. It is a form of war work.'

'But there's still a need for nurseries,' Mabel began.

'The need,' said Miss Brewster, 'is for young children to grow up in a home environment and that is what their mothers should arrange for them. What is a nursery compared to the care and attention of a mother or a daily foster mother? The war is no reason to let standards slip. In fact, it is all the more reason to adhere to the old ways, the best ways. If you wish to do something with this building, Miss Bradshaw, do it up for the Scouts – or turn it into a clothing exchange, or a soup kitchen – but do not, I repeat do not attempt to turn it into a nursery. I won't have it. Do you understand me? I simply won't have it.'

CHAPTER SEVEN

Daddy had agreed to permit Emily to work a shorter notice than normal at the office so that she could start her new job with LMS on the first of the month, which happened to be a Monday. The night before, she lay in bed, wanting to feel pleased that her plan had worked, but mostly fighting against sorrow. This fresh start meant taking a step away from Raymond. Although her head knew she needed to do this, her silly heart was playing up. Even so, Emily was determined not to shed any tears over it. She'd wept buckets over Raymond and achieved nothing more than puffy eyes and a pounding head.

Monday began with her first taste of an early start. Her shifts would vary across the whole twenty-four-hour period. One of the questions she'd faced in her interview had been how she would cope with working nights and also continuing with her fire-watching duties. Emily rather liked the thought of working nights. It was all part of her new beginning and leaving office hours behind, part, she hoped, of Mummy and Daddy starting to see her as an adult.

After passing her tests and the medical, she'd been interviewed by Mr Mortimer, a plump gentleman with a neat moustache who wore a bow tie and a watch chain, and Miss Emery, whose appearance was immaculate, not a hair out of place. She wore a smart brown jacket and skirt with a pale green blouse and she had a short string of graduated pearls. Mummy always wore pearl earrings for everyday. She said she wasn't dressed without them.

'You shall be a lad porter,' Mr Mortimer had told Emily. 'That's how porters start and they work their way up over the years.'

'As a lad porter,' continued Miss Emery, 'you'll be under the wing of an experienced colleague who'll show you the ropes and provide an ear when you aren't sure of something.'

'Sometimes you'll be in Victoria Station, assisting passengers with their luggage,' Mr Mortimer told her. 'At other times, you'll be behind the scenes, moving whatever has to be moved.'

'At current rates, your pay will rise to three pounds a week when you're twenty-one,' said Miss Emery, 'but that's a long way off yet. Of course, you won't still be a lad porter then. You'll be fully fledged.'

'Or not,' Mr Mortimer added. 'I devoutly hope the war will be well and truly over long before then and all our men will be home once more.'

Daddy had said the same thing practically word for word when Emily got home and described her interview. He didn't really want her to stop working as his office junior.

'He can't protect me for ever,' Emily had said to her mother afterwards.

'You know that and I know that,' Mummy agreed. 'Just don't say it to Daddy, that's all.'

Now, at long last, here she was on her first day. She was given her uniform of jacket, skirt and peaked cap. Some of the female porters wore trousers. Daddy didn't like women to wear trousers, but she could work on that. In all honesty, it was a tad disappointing to be back in uniform. She and her friends had all sworn a huge oath after they finished their School Cert exams never to wear a uniform again after they left school, but this was different. It was part of belonging to the railways. Emily was aware of how proud her mother was to work for the railways and she wanted to feel the same.

She spent the morning working alongside a porter called Daphne. With a name like that, she ought to sound all plummy and refined, but actually her voice was pure Mancunian. Daphne had a sack trolley, but Emily wasn't given one.

'This way, we can't get separated by two sets of passengers wanting their luggage to be taken to different places,' Daphne explained. 'Just trot along beside me and I'll talk you through everything.'

Emily spent a busy morning on the concourse and various platforms. She knew the concourse well because of having met Mummy here in the buffet sometimes. The ticket office was housed inside a long room with wooden panelling of golden-brown on the outside, where passengers queued at the little windows. High above, hanging from a metal gantry, was an imposing clock with Roman numerals on its face. The boards that showed all the departures were set within a wooden frame and there were noticeboards with further information and advertisements in between the platform entrances. The restaurant with the elegant glass dome in its roof, the buffet and the grill room were all tiled in the same pale yellow, with their names depicted in capitals against deep blue above the doors. The bookstall, which also sold newspapers, had the same yellow tiles, with BOOKSTALL over the top.

The smell was familiar too: smoke, steam, tobacco and the odd whiff of perfume. As she took in the scents and sounds all around her, Emily's senses were alert in a way they hadn't been since she was last with Raymond. It was exciting to have a new job and start her training.

'First things first,' said Daphne. 'The platforms start down there at number one. I know it sounds obvious, but you need to know which way the numbers run. You'll have to learn which platforms are for which destinations. I don't just mean the place at the end of the line. I mean the stops in between an' all.'

'That's a lot to learn,' said Emily, daunted. What if she made a mistake?

'The more you know, the more people you can help, but if ever you don't know, say so. Oh, and be careful of what Annie did until she realised. She learned all the stops along the Southport line so that if someone asked "Which platform for Wigan Wallgate?" she could reel off the stations and tell them which number they had to count up to as they travelled along the line. That was all well and good in daytime when the passengers could see the stations, but in the blackout, when some of the stops happened between stations for some reason, some of the passengers she'd helped ended up stepping off the train into thin air because they'd been counting how many times the train stopped rather than the number of stations.'

'No,' Emily breathed.

Daphne grinned. 'It's funny when you think about it, but not if someone breaks a leg, so think on. I'll show you all the places that passengers will ask for, like Left Luggage and the taxi rank.'

'I know where those are.'

'I'm still going to show you,' said Daphne, 'because I need to make sure. After that, we'll start helping the passengers. Just so you know, when you're on station duty, you don't just float about deciding where you want to be. Everyone has certain platforms and parts of the station to cover and you have to check at the start of your stint where you have to be. Ferrying luggage will take you all over the shop, but you have to end up back where you're meant to be.'

'What if I take someone to the taxi rank and then somebody outside wants me to help them with their things?'

'Then that's what you do, but once you've done it, you need to go back to your own patch. That's how the work is divvied up fairly. Righty-ho, let's get started.'

Apart from when they went for a sit-down and a cup of tea, Daphne and Emily spent the whole morning on the platforms and the concourse, with Emily keeping close to Daphne, helping to put luggage on the trolley and smiling at the passengers, though she took a big step backwards at the end of each job so that if the passenger wished to give a tip, they'd see she didn't expect one.

'There's one hour left before we stop for us dinner,' said Daphne. 'How about going it alone? D'you feel up to it?'

A few minutes later, armed with her own trolley, Emily hovered near Daphne on the platform, waiting for the train to pull in.

'Go further along,' Daphne instructed her. 'Passengers don't like to see staff huddled together. It doesn't give a good impression.'

'And it must be more efficient if porters are spread out along the platform too,' said Emily. After a morning of listening, she wanted to say something sensible.

She made her way further down the platform, past where another porter waited beside a flatbed trolley in the exact place where the guard's van would stop when the train pulled in and all the boxes and parcels had to be unloaded.

Emily couldn't help feeling a little nervous, standing alone, but that was silly, wasn't it? She knew all the places a passenger might wish to go and should she be asked a question to which she didn't know the answer, all she had to do was direct the enquirer to another porter or a ticket collector or to the ticket office. There were plenty of staff who could help.

Shortly, she heard the rhythmic chuffing as the train approached, accompanied by the puffing of white clouds from the funnel. These both ceased as the train coasted alongside the platform, a sharp hiss emerging from the top of the engine. There was the sound of braking and then a deep clunk as the train came to a stop. Already doors were being thrown open up and people were emerging, some in a tearing hurry, others more careful as they stepped down onto the platform.

A pair of middle-aged ladies stood in the centre of a pile of luggage. They looked round and caught Emily's eye. She went straight to them before they could beckon.

'Good morning, ladies. May I help you with your things?'

Excitement spurted through her. This was it. She was working properly now.

Emily Masters – lad porter!

At the end of her dinner hour, Emily was surprised and dismayed to find she wasn't going to spend the rest of the day with Daphne. She had assumed that Daphne was the person from whom she was going to learn the ropes, but she was wrong. It was a shame, because she liked Daphne, but there was no reason why she shouldn't also like the next porter or porteress or porterette, as some people insisted upon calling female porters – just as much.

But instead of being handed over to another female porter, it was to a man – and an elderly one at that. Emily was surprised and dismayed all over again.

Miss Emery had come along to introduce them.

'Mr Buckley will keep a fatherly eye on you,' she explained.

Fatherly? Grandfatherly, more like. It wouldn't be half so much fun as being trained up by Daphne.

But during her first day or two, Emily came to like Mr Buckley. He was a kindly soul who was good at explaining things. He always told her why things were done a certain way and she liked that. It was much better than simply being bombarded with instructions.

Mr Buckley was a short, slightly built man, but Emily soon saw how strong he was as he hefted heavy parcels and boxes around.

'That's what comes of a lifetime of manual work,' he told her.

He showed her the correct way to lift things and provided useful pointers that would make her working life easier – 'Take the trolley to the item, not the item to the trolley' – and impressed upon her that she must always ask for help if she needed it.

'Safety first,' he said, and thinking of the distressing news of the loss of life in the tube station in Bethnal Green where so many people had lost their lives in a crush, Emily nodded vigorously.

Mr Buckley showed her the correct way to stack multiple items onto a sack trolley.

'Biggest and heaviest at the bottom, smallest and lightest at the top,' he said. 'I know it sounds obvious, but it's worth saying. There's nowt worse for a porter than a badly stacked trolley.'

When they were both on the platform as a train came in, Mr Buckley did the same as Daphne had done when Emily was brand new. He kept at a distance, though near enough to keep an eye on her, until they went their separate ways with the passengers they were accompanying. Emily enjoyed feeling that her independence was increasing.

She always took care to stack her trolley properly, but one afternoon an imperious gentleman alighted from the train, summoned her with a click of the fingers and headed straight for the guard's van, not even looking back to check if she was following. How rude! But courtesy was the name of the game at all times, so Emily smoothed her features.

Standing outside the open guard's van, the gentleman called, 'Hathersage, if you please,' in a voice that suggested that no matter what other jobs needed doing, his request should automatically jump to the top of the queue.

A small trunk was lifted down onto the platform. Emily knew how to put a trunk onto a sack trolley – on its end. But then a suitcase followed, plus a Gladstone bag, a long cardboard tube that might have had maps or plans rolled up inside it, and two flat boxes. Crumbs. The trunk would have to lie down, which would be awkward because it would stick out sideways, with all the rest on top.

'Hurry up, girl,' said Mr Hathersage. 'I haven't got all day. Or should I call for a man to do a man's job?'

That settled it. Annoyed, Emily heaved the trunk across the foot of her trolley and then lifted everything else on. Mr Hathersage didn't offer to carry anything. Too late, Emily realised she had done the stacking in the wrong order, but with the disagreeable Mr Hathersage breathing down her neck, she made a split-second decision and took hold of the trolley's handles, placing her weight so that the trolley tilted backwards. Then she set off. She hadn't gone more than a few steps before the luggage toppled off.

'Idiotic girl!' exclaimed Mr Hathersage.

Emily was mortified. She started to scramble about, gathering the fallen items, feeling as if the eyes of the world were upon her, while Mr Hathersage made a great show of tapping his foot impatiently. Crouching over his Gladstone bag and flat boxes, Emily felt like biting his ankle.

Then came Mr Buckley's calm voice. 'Now then, let's get this sorted, shall we?' He began to sort the luggage onto the trolley.

'Oh, good,' snapped Mr Hathersage. 'Someone who knows what he's doing.'

'Miss Masters is very good at her job, sir,' said Mr Buckley. 'Accidents can happen to anyone.'

'Can they indeed?' Mr Hathersage peered around. 'I don't see anyone else's luggage strewn all over the platform.'

Mr Buckley finished stacking the trolley and stood back. 'There you are, Miss Masters. Where to, sir?' he asked Mr Hathersage.

'The taxi rank – if this girl can get me there without casting my belongings left, right and centre.'

'You're in very capable hands, sir,' said Mr Buckley.

As he turned away, he winked at Emily. She took a deep breath and grasped the handles once more, applying her weight to make the trolley tilt backwards towards her. Concentrating furiously, she headed for the taxi rank, where she and the driver loaded the luggage into the vehicle.

'Good riddance,' Emily muttered as the motor drove away. Angry tears stung the backs of her eyes and she blinked hard.

'Not all passengers are like that,' came Mr Buckley's voice from behind her.

Emily turned round. 'You followed me.' At once she felt better.

'Of course I did. I wouldn't leave you alone with the likes of him.'

'It was my own fault in the first place,' Emily said honestly. 'I didn't stack the trolley properly and he was so impatient that I didn't like to do it all over again.'

'Well, that's a mistake you won't make a second time, isn't it?' Mr Buckley said kindly.

Emily smiled at him. 'That's the nicest telling-off I've ever had.'

'I don't believe in rubbing folks' noses in it,' said Mr Buckley. 'People learn more if you're nice to 'em. That's what I think, anyroad.'

'It was foolish of me,' Emily admitted, 'and I won't do it again. I made Mr Hathersage's impatience worse by what I did. Not that that's any excuse for him to be rude,' she added, 'and I didn't like the way he suggested the problem happened because I'm a girl.'

'Aye, well, there are plenty of men who think they're better than women.'

Emily had heard about how a lot of railwaymen, and presumably men in other industries too, didn't like working alongside women because they thought women weren't up to the job, but the other porters she met while she worked with Mr Buckley were all pleasant to her and told her to ask if she needed to know anything.

Then she went to her first meeting in the buffet. It felt good to take her place alongside the others. They all smiled warmly at her and Mabel and Margaret budged up to make room. Mummy had warned her about the rule that said staff in uniform weren't allowed to be seen sitting in the buffet, so Emily had put on her coat and swapped her uniform cap for her felt hat before she entered.

'How are you getting on, chick?' asked Mrs Green, and Emily explained that the other porters were treating her nicely.

'It's a bit of a relief, actually,' said Emily, 'after what I'd been told.'

'I'm pleased to hear it,' said Mrs Green. 'There are plenty of decent fellas who have no objection to working with women.'

'Or perhaps by this time, men in general have learned that women and girls are every bit as capable as they are,' said Emily.

There was a pause around the table, then the others laughed.

'Trust me, Emily,' said Alison. 'Some blokes will never realise that.'

'Thanks for inviting me here to join you all,' said Emily. 'You made me feel wanted.'

'Of course we want you,' Margaret exclaimed.

'You're one of us now,' Mabel added.

'We've lost Joan after a fashion now that's she's a house-wife and mother,' said Mrs Green. 'I mean, we haven't lost her really, but she doesn't come here to the buffet any more. And we'll be losing our Mabel when she ties the knot. But we're gaining you.'

'That's a lovely thing to say, Mrs Green.'

'Now then, you're going to have to call me Dot. We all use first names when it's just us together.'

'I don't know if I could.' Emily shot her mother a look. 'It wouldn't be polite.'

'Don't worry,' said Persephone. 'It felt strange for all of us to start with, but you'll get used to it.'

'As long as you don't start calling me Cordelia,' said Mummy in a dry voice, making everyone laugh.

Emily laughed too. It felt good to be accepted as one of this group in her own right and not because of being Mummy's daughter. Everyone had been polite to one another at Daddy's office, but Emily had never felt she truly belonged, not like her lovely colleagues around the two tables squashed together were making her feel now. An eager, fluttery feeling filled her chest, only to vanish as suddenly as it had appeared, her chest tightening as guilt pounced on her.

'I don't think I've ever seen a smile drop off somebody's face so fast,' said Mrs Green. Would Emily ever be comfortable calling her Dot? She couldn't imagine it. 'What's the matter, chick?'

Should she say? It wasn't the done thing to wear your heart on your sleeve, but everyone had made her feel so welcome. It felt good to be accepted. Everyone was looking at her, waiting to hear what she had to say and they were really interested. This group had been instrumental in saving her mother's life, for pity's sake. Of course she could talk to them.

Colette reinforced Emily's thoughts when she said, 'Don't tell us if you'd rather not, but it's important you understand that you can tell us anything. We only want to help you.'

Emily drew in a breath. No wonder her mother thought so highly of her railway friends. 'It's Raymond. I feel guilty all of a sudden. It seems wrong to feel happy without him.'

'Grief's like that,' said Alison.

'He's not dead,' said Emily, surprised.

'It's still a kind of grief, though, isn't it?' said Alison. 'You've lost an important relationship. You've lost the future you thought you were going to have. It takes a lot of getting used to.'

'It's a hard thing to go through,' said Margaret, 'but sometimes a happy moment creeps up on you and you can't help smiling – even if you feel like a rat afterwards.'

'Or in this case,' Mabel added, 'a group of friends has crept up on you.'

Emily couldn't help but smile at that. Her heart felt full as gratitude blossomed inside her. She still loved Raymond and always would. Her heart was red-raw from missing him, but it seemed there could still be good moments, especially with these friends by her side to support her.

It was the strangest thing. Although Emily lay awake at night in a state of despair because of being rejected by Raymond, a different part of her seemed to take over during the times she was working in her new job. Her emotional confidence might have been shattered, but her day-to-day professional confidence was soaring now that she was in a job she enjoyed. What would her old school chums think if they could see her now, doing manual work? Mind you, heaps of people were working in roles they would never have given a thought to before the war.

Part of Emily's confidence at work came from being watched over by Mr Buckley.

'He doesn't hover over me – thank goodness,' she explained to her mother while they were on fire-watching duty one night beneath clear, cold skies.

'Why "thank goodness"?' Mummy asked.

'He doesn't make it obvious to the passengers that he's keeping an eye on me. That would be a bit humiliating.'

'It sounds like he's good at teaching new recruits the ropes.'

'He's definitely that,' Emily enthused. Would she have been happier at Wardle, Grace and Masters if Mrs Beswick had demonstrated the same attitude as Mr Buckley?

Emily was quite accustomed by now to ferrying luggage around the station to wherever the passengers needed to go and she had no qualms about setting sail in a completely different direction to that taken by Mr Buckley.

'I think it's time you had a go with a flatbed,' Mr Buckley told her. 'Your job as station porter involves the use of a sack trolley, but it's as well to be able to use a flatbed an' all.'

Emily nodded, pleased to be considered competent enough to try something new. The flatbed trolleys were large and could carry simply masses of luggage and boxes. Emily knew that part of Mrs Green's job as a parcels porter on the Southport train was to manoeuvre one of these big flatbeds from the parcels office, through the station and to her train to load up the guard's van before the train set off. During the journey, as well as parcels being put off at the correct stations, new parcels would be received and when the train reached Southport, Mrs Green had to sort them all, load them onto a flatbed and deliver them to the Southport parcels office.

'The thing you need to remember about a flatbed,' said Mr Buckley when he and Emily stood in front of one, 'is that when you're pushing it, if you want it to go *that* way, you have to pull the handle *this* way. That's because the steering is done through the rear wheels. Have a go with this empty one and see if you get the hang of it. Then we'll see about you having the chance to work a full load.'

The flatbed was surprisingly awkward to manage. The porters who pushed them around the station made it look so easy. But Emily was determined to master it and prove herself. It wasn't like her not to be good at something and she didn't like the feeling, but under Mr Buckley's guidance she persevered and grew more proficient, laughing out loud when at last the trolley consistently did what she wanted it to.

'Ten minutes ago, I'd have sworn it had a mind of its own,' she told Mr Buckley, who was smiling and nodding in approval, just like Emily imagined a real grandfather would.

'We'll see about you doing the real thing,' said Mr Buckley.

The next time they saw a porter with a flatbed trolley, Mr Buckley asked if Emily could try pushing it. It was harder pushing a full trolley than an empty one, but Emily took her time and managed without mishap.

'You'll be after my job next,' said the porter with a grin, even though all Emily had done was go in a straight line.

After that, Mr Buckley made sure Emily had a few goes at working a flatbed, her confidence increasing with each short journey.

'I learned to go round corners today,' she laughed to her friends in the buffet.

Next day, Mr Buckley announced, 'It's time you tackled going through the barrier onto a platform.'

'That sounds easier than navigating corners,' said Emily.

'Ah, but it's very public.'

'I don't mind that,' said Emily. 'I appeared in plays at school.'

'You fetch the Blackpool trolley and I'll see you on the platform.'

Emily was pleased. Meeting her on the platform meant he trusted her not to crash the flatbed. In the parcels office, she quickly ascertained which of the loaded trolleys was for Blackpool. Then she nipped off to the Ladies. Mr Buckley was the loveliest man imaginable, but the one disadvantage of being with him was that Emily felt self-conscious about going to the Ladies. Being left on her own gave her the perfect opportunity.

When she returned, she grabbed the trolley's long handle and set off. The concourse was busy and she was careful not to go too fast. Manoeuvring through the open barrier proved to be a piece of cake. Seeing Mr Buckley waiting for her up ahead next to the guard's van, Emily couldn't resist putting on a spurt, though she took care to slow down in plenty of time so she didn't overshoot.

'Well done, lass,' said Mr Buckley.

Emily felt her face glow with delight until the train guard said, 'Hang on a minute. These aren't the Blackpool parcels,' and then Emily's face glowed for a different reason.

She was about to apologise, but Mr Buckley stepped in.

'We'll fetch the Blackpool trolley now. This was by way of a practice run.'

Seizing the handle, Mr Buckley expertly turned the trolley in a circle and set off down the platform with Emily trotting alongside, her face hot with embarrassment. Even her eyes felt hot.

'I'm so sorry,' she said. 'I saw where the trolley was, but then I – well, I had to excuse myself and when I went back, I took the trolley from the same place.'

'Without checking,' said Mr Buckley.

'I know. I'm sorry. I feel a proper twit.'

Did Mr Buckley's silence mean he thought her a proper twit too? If he did, it was only what she deserved.

'Mr Buckley,' said Emily. 'Thank you.'

'What for?'

'For covering up for me. For pretending I'd brought this trolley on purpose. For calling it a practice run.'

'It's my job to look after you until you find your feet. I wouldn't make you look small in front of someone else.'

No, he wouldn't. He would always have her best interests at heart. Emily knew that. Secure – that was how Mr Buckley made her feel. Secure.

CHAPTER EIGHT

Mabel kept feeling all tingly with self-consciousness as Mrs Grayson showed her how to make meat rissoles. What would Mrs Grayson think of her if she knew what Mabel would be doing later that day?

Mrs Grayson had started giving her cooking lessons so that she was ready for married life.

'Doing our own cooking isn't what we were prepared for at private school,' said Mabel. 'The closest we came to preparing a meal was organising the flowers and the seating plan.'

'Usually you'd need egg to bind everything together for rissoles,' Mrs Grayson explained, 'but dripping does just as well as long as you stir it in briskly. I add a dot of Marmite along with it to give more flavour.'

After that, they went on to make paradise pudding.

'What you need to remember is that you leave the dried egg dry,' said Mrs Grayson, 'and go easy on the vanilla essence.'

'Is that because it's easy to use too much?' asked Mabel.

'No, it's because once it's run out, we might not be able to get any more.'

The meal was a success and Mrs Grayson made sure Mabel received her share of the praise at the table. It was Mabel's day off and Margaret was here for dinner too because of doing the shift that started in the middle of the afternoon. When she set off for work, Mabel ought to have travelled into town with her, but she couldn't because she couldn't risk letting anyone know about her appointment. Instead, she waited for Margaret to leave, then gave her a head start before going to the bus stop.

Mabel arrived for her appointment by the skin of her teeth. She ran up the steps and dived through the doorway, then stood for a moment to compose herself before announcing her arrival to the receptionist, who offered her a seat. The waiting room had elegant furnishings beneath a lofty ceiling and there were magazines on a long coffee table. Mabel picked one up, then put it down again. She wanted to get this over with. She felt wretched and embarrassed – but it was exciting too, in a way. She wished she could have confided in someone what she intended to do, but something like this was intensely private and not at all the kind of thing you talked about.

A door opened on the other side of the room and a well-dressed lady appeared. She wore a hat with a little veil attached that cast a haze over the upper half of her face. Fashion – or discretion? Mabel looked away, not because she didn't want to look at the lady, but because she didn't want the lady to look at her. Or should she be proud to be here? There was nothing wrong in what she was doing. It was just that it being a taboo subject made it feel wrong.

Well, it jolly well shouldn't. Surely women were entitled to make decisions like this without being frowned upon.

Another young woman arrived and took a place in the waiting area. Was she here for the same reason as Mabel? Or did she have a medical complaint and the wherewithal to pay for the very best treatment?

After a minute or two, the receptionist stood up and opened the door.

'Miss Bradshaw, Doctor will see you now.'

Mabel got up and went in, trying not to look self-conscious. Dr Yelland's consulting room looked more like a drawing room at first glance, with a handsome desk inlaid with burgundy leather, and scallop-edged lace curtains blurring the sight of the anti-blast tape that criss-crossed the long windowpanes. The silver frame around the wall mirror was all swirly and leafy and even boasted an attached pair of candle branches with holders for three candles on each side.

Dr Yelland didn't retreat behind his desk, but guided Mabel to a pair of balloon-backed armchairs upholstered in gold damask. He was good-looking in a Douglas Fairbanks kind of way, but with glasses.

'Now then, my dear,' he said as if they had been acquaintances for ages, 'how may I be of assistance? Don't be shy. You may say anything to me. Some ladies become very embarrassed about matters of gynaecology and there's really no need.'

For a moment, Mabel thought he might pat her hand, but he didn't. Taking heart from his encouragement, she said in a steady voice, 'Thank you, Doctor. I've come to ask you about . . . about birth control.'

'Birth control? I beg your pardon. I thought you were Miss Bradshaw, not Mrs Bradshaw.'

'I am – Miss Bradshaw, I mean.'

'Then I really don't think I can help you, not if you're single.'

Mabel hastened to clear up the misunderstanding. 'I'm Miss Bradshaw now, but I'm going to be Mrs Knatchbull and I – well, I should like some information, please, about how to . . . to delay having children.'

'That is not a suitable conversation for me to have with an unmarried girl, Miss Bradshaw.' Dr Yelland rose to his feet. 'I don't know what sort of person you think I am. Come back to me when you are married and not before. Good afternoon.'

*

Not sure whether she should be hopping mad or utterly humiliated by her so-called consultation with Dr Yelland, Mabel returned to Chorlton. She would have to pull herself together. She had a meeting planned to discuss the work that needed doing to improve the Extension in order to make it suitable for its new purpose, but her mind was too full of Dr Yelland's uncompromising dismissal for her to concentrate on anything else just yet. Fancy being sent away with a flea in her ear for daring to ask a perfectly reasonable question. She was engaged, too. It wasn't as though she was asking for . . . immoral reasons. 'Immoral' didn't seem quite the right word, but it was the only one she could think of, especially after the way Dr Yelland had spoken to her. Odious man.

It was annoying and frustrating to think that there were things she needed to know, but that the knowledge was denied to her. And there was nobody else to ask. She couldn't approach her own doctor in Chorlton. Heavens, no! Talk about embarrassing. That was why she'd found a private clinic in town. She needed to keep this enquiry well away from home territory.

Yet why should she feel this way? Why were girls kept in ignorance and made to feel that there was something shameful about going in search of information? There were books about birth control. Mabel knew that much, but how did one go about getting them? You could hardly put in a request at the library or pop into W.H. Smith's and ask in front of a queue of people standing there with their newspapers.

Could she have a word with Joan? But she knew she couldn't. Much as she loved her, she could never ask this for fear of losing Joan's good opinion. It was one thing to tell her that she didn't want a family right away after getting married; it was quite another to ask how to go about not having one. Joan and Bob had had Max in less than a year of marriage. Were they deliberately not having another baby yet? Or was it simply that it just hadn't happened so quickly second time round? If the former, then Joan could help Mabel, but if the latter, then Joan might not know the answer to Mabel's questions anyway.

As the bus passed the local shops, Mabel prepared to get off. She pressed the bell and stood up, edging past the person sitting beside her and stepping into the aisle, taking care as she walked down the bus towards the back and stepped down onto the platform. She got off before the terminus and headed for the estate agency run by the Hayter brothers. They looked up and smiled at her, rising politely as she entered the office.

'What a pleasure to see you again, Miss Bradshaw,' said Mr George.

'How may we help you today?' asked Mr Anthony.

The gentlemen's quietly spoken charm had a soothing effect. Mabel hoped that nothing about her demeanour gave away anything about the nature of her previous appointment.

'I've come to collect the keys to the Extension,' she reminded the Hayters. 'I'm going to meet a builder and an electrician to discuss the work that needs doing. One of you is going to come with me, I think.' She knew this was the case and was surprised that neither of them had said so immediately.

Mr George and Mr Anthony looked first at one another and then at her.

'I'm sorry, Miss Bradshaw, but it's all been cancelled,' said Mr George.

'Cancelled?' Mabel repeated. 'Why?'

'We thought it was done with your agreement,' said Mr Anthony, his kindly face taking on a puzzled expression.

'It's the first I've heard of it. Can you please explain?'

'We were told that the project isn't to go ahead,' said Mr George.

'Who on earth gave you that idea?' asked Mabel.

'A lady called Miss Brewster,' said Mr Anthony. 'She's from the Corporation. She showed us her credentials.'

'She said the project was unsuitable,' his brother added. 'She was most emphatic about it.'

Persephone spent the morning putting the pots of overwintered dahlia tubers under glass and then repotting the various container plants under the eagle eye of the head gardener. Not that he had many people left to be the head of these days, just another chap as old as himself and a boy who'd left school last year. With practically all the grounds given over to crops, the flowering plants that had been allowed to remain were precious. After a night of rain, the air smelled earthy and bright.

It really was silly of her to feel so wretched. Nothing had changed. Before this, Forbes had only ever seen her as the younger sister of the Trehearn-Hobbs boys and now it turned out that he still saw her the same way. Everything was precisely the same.

Except that it wasn't. That letter of his, that dashed letter asking for a visit, had raised her hopes as never before. Fool that she was, she had allowed herself to imagine that being injured had opened Forbes's smoky-grey eyes to the loveliness he had never previously appreciated. What rot! What an idiot she was. A twerp of the first water.

After she'd come home, Forbes had, with perfect manners, written to thank her for taking the trouble to come, and the sight of his handwriting on the envelope had caused a flutter of wild hope, making words appear inside her head – *and it wasn't until after you'd gone that I realised what a blind fool I've been all these years* . . . Utter madness. Never again would she be so stupid.

Well, at least nobody else knew what a twit she'd made of herself. That was something. Or was it? She remembered the kindness and understanding the others had shown Emily in the buffet when she'd mentioned Raymond. Persephone had been glad, of course, for Emily to receive comfort, but she had also felt a yearning that had startled her, a sudden need deep inside herself for that same sort of compassion from her friends. She remembered Colette saying, 'We only want to help you,' and Alison's words, 'You've lost an important relationship.' Hearing those words as they were all squashed together around the table had made Persephone long for the same sympathy and warmth to be directed towards her.

But she had never told anyone how she felt about Forbes. Never. No one. That was how it was when you had fallen head over heels for your brothers' chum. You kept your feelings as a gigantic secret, because what else were you to do? And thereafter it kept on being a secret, because . . . because it just did.

Looking back, she could perhaps have told her railway friends a couple of years ago, after she'd engineered that brief meeting between them and Forbes. She had wanted the meeting to take place because it was important that Forbes be introduced to these special friends of hers and that they should meet him, but as for telling her friends the truth of the situation, frankly it had never occurred to her that she might. She was so accustomed to it being her secret. Besides, she had been brought up not to discuss personal matters. ('One keeps one's troubles to oneself, Persephone.')

But witnessing the caring way the others had spoken to Emily had made Persephone realise what she had missed out on. Well, it was too late now, so she had better stop thinking about it.

Adjusting her thoughts, she instead dwelled on Emily, poor kid. Or maybe not so poor. She had taken steps to try to turn her life around and that was highly admirable. Leaving a job where she was miserable and getting taken on by the railways showed her mettle. She could have stayed put and wallowed in her unhappiness, but instead she'd chosen to improve things for herself. Maybe her lovely cornflower-blue eyes would regain their shine, given time.

And maybe it was time for Persephone to take a leaf out of Emily's book.

No, not maybe. Definitely.

CHAPTER NINE

Attending a fundraising evening of puzzles and card games with her parents, Emily found herself the centre of attention among Mummy and Daddy's friends, who all wanted to ask her about her new job.

'I love everything about it,' she enthused and then felt a flash of embarrassment when her listeners laughed.

'Steady on, Emily,' said Mr Horsfall, chuckling. 'Being so keen on the railways isn't very flattering to Wardle, Grace and Masters.'

'We're delighted Emily has settled in so well,' said Mummy and that was a bit embarrassing too, because Emily didn't want her riding to the rescue. That was what you did when you were keeping an eye on a child.

A little later, Emily overheard Mrs Horsfall telling Mummy how pleased she was that Emily liked her new job.

'But I imagine the gloss will wear off in the end,' she said. 'Portering is just portering after all.'

But it wasn't and it was all Emily could do to hold herself back from leaping in and saying so. People in general thought portering meant meeting passengers from the train or the taxi rank and taking their luggage to wherever it needed to go, but there was so much more to it than that. Porters on evening duty often had to help load the Perisher, which was the name given to the night train that ferried perishable goods out of Manchester, while the porters who were there early in the morning might be assigned to do the road boxes, which meant sorting out all the parcels, luggage and other items that were to be delivered to the various stations along every line. You had to know which destinations were on which route and also the order of all the stations, so that the road boxes were put in the correct order for the parcels porters to load them onto the trains. All sorts of things were sent by train, not just suitcases, trunks and wrapped-up parcels, but also boxes of groceries, even livestock, though not bouquets of flowers, or not at the moment, anyway.

'The powers that be stopped allowing bouquets of flowers on trains last month, for some reason,' Mr Buckley told Emily. 'Passengers can't even take them as hand luggage now.' He shook his head. 'I think the railways have made a mistake with this one, I'm afraid. People have put up with so many rules and regs, but there's been a real backlash over this.'

Then there was all the unloading that had to be tackled. Long lines of freight wagons drew in at all times and had to be dealt with promptly. Most wagons had dropsides and Mr Buckley warned Emily to keep her wits about her.

'I've seen more than one person get their foot crushed when they weren't looking and someone else pulled out the pin and the bar came down.'

'Aye, that'll put an end to your dancing days,' added another porter and a shiver went through Emily.

She enjoyed working alongside Mr Buckley. He took good care of her without making her feel like a child. He expected her to pull her weight, but he was never bossy. Emily realised she was learning a lot from him in the course of ordinary conversations, into which he dropped useful information and anecdotes. It was a good way to learn. It was certainly a big improvement on sitting silently at a desk while a teacher droned on or waiting in increasing desperation to be handed one or two crumbs of responsibility, as had happened to her in Daddy's firm.

Emily's birthday came and her parents gave her an amethyst on a pretty silver chain. She tried it on at the breakfast table and Mummy fastened it at the back of her neck before both her parents admired it.

'It's time you began gathering good pieces of jewellery,' said Mummy.

'Though nothing showy,' said Daddy, 'not at your age.'

'My age?' Emily pretended to be outraged. 'I'll have you know I'm seventeen now.'

'Ah, but you'll always be my little girl,' chuckled Daddy and Emily groaned, though deep down it was nice to feel loved and protected.

Before she went to work, as she put away her new necklace in her bedroom, her heart seemed to slow down and her lungs tightened, making it difficult to breathe properly. She'd received a piece of jewellery for her seventeenth birthday, but not the engagement ring she had once dreamed of. She forced herself to breathe in – forced her lungs to do their job. The first few snatches of breath felt thin and for a moment she felt giddy, but then everything returned to normal. Whatever her private sorrows today, she refused to put the mockers on it for her parents, who loved her so much and worried about her.

Emily didn't know how – perhaps Mrs Green had told them – but the porters knew it was her birthday and she received lots of good wishes. Mr Buckley gave her a new comb, a very simple little gift, but it was terribly sweet of him.

That evening, when they and some other porters had been told they had to stay on an extra hour or so because of the workload, Mr Buckley said, 'That's a shame, lass, with this being your special day.'

'It's all right. I expect everyone ends up working extra on their birthday these days. Besides, two of my friends, Margaret and Alison, have the same day off as I do this week and they're taking me to the pictures and then my parents are having a little tea party for us and other chums after the film.'

'So today isn't party day?' Mr Buckley smiled at her. 'That's good.'

'What about you?' Emily asked. 'Will Mrs Buckley mind you being late home?'

Mr Buckley's smile stayed in place, but his eyes lost their crinkle and he looked sad. 'I wish she was still here to mind, lass, I really do.'

'Oh . . . I'm sorry,' said Emily. 'I didn't know.'

'No harm done. She's been gone some years now, but at least she missed having to live through our son's death at Dunkirk. That's something to be grateful for, at any rate.'

Was it? Was it really? Wouldn't it have been better if they had both been there to cling to one another and comfort each other in their shock and grief? Emily had been thinking quite a lot about death recently because Mummy had told her that Lizzie, Mrs Cooper's late daughter, had been a lad porter at the start of the war.

'I'm only mentioning it because Mrs Cooper might – well, who knows what she'll feel about you being a lad porter? She won't be off with you or anything like that. You know how kind she is, not to mention how sensible I'm just mentioning it because . . .'

'Because you just want me to be aware,' said Emily. 'How old was Lizzie?'

'A little older than you are now. She was already seventeen when she became a lad porter.'

Seventeen. Imagine dying at seventeen. Poor Lizzie – and poor Mrs Cooper.

Emily had given it some thought and then gone round to Wilton Close one evening. She had tried to plan in advance what to say, but in the end had trusted that the right words would magically appear when the time came. In the event, she'd hardly had the chance to say anything. She only got as far as 'Mrs Cooper, I know that Lizzie used to be a lad porter—' before Mrs Cooper put her arms around her and gave her a hug.

'Dear little Emily, what a sweet girl you are. Are you worried that it's going to upset me that you've got the same job as my Lizzie? Well, it doesn't, but bless you for thinking of it. I'll tell you summat. My Lizzie loved her job and I hope you love yours.'

'I do,' Emily assured her.

Having been brought up to keep her hands to herself, Emily was surprised by the hug but found she liked it. She wouldn't have liked it once upon a time. Back when she first knew Mrs Cooper, she would have taken it as a sign of how ill-bred she was, but these days Emily knew it to be an indication of this dear lady's warm, generous heart.

Now, with Mr Buckley being grateful that his wife had been spared the heartbreak of losing their son, Emily thought that he must be the same sort of person as Mrs Cooper, a kind person who put others first. How lucky she was to have him as her mentor.

The reason for the compulsory overtime was that a freight train had come in.

'So it's all hands on deck,' said Mr Buckley. 'Everything has to be unloaded and sent on its way, though when things arrive at this time of the evening, often they aren't sent on until the early hours of the next morning. We can't hang on to things for very long here, because we haven't got the space. Keeping things moving is how we manage.'

Pushing her sack trolley, Emily accompanied Mr Buckley and a squad of porters to the wagons that were waiting to be unloaded. The line of wagons was so long that it had taken two massive locos to pull it on its journey. Down at the back of the line, another loco was reversing along the track into position to link up.

'Is it going to take the wagons away once they're empty?' Emily asked.

'No,' one of the porters told her. 'The half-dozen wagons at yon end are all full of coal, so they'll be uncoupled and taken to the coal yard.'

Everyone set to unloading the freight, the sack trolleys and flatbed trolleys going to and fro. Like ants, thought Emily. It was satisfying to feel part of the important job of keeping the country running.

A lot of what was unloaded was food. Mr Buckley showed her how to lift a sack of flour correctly and place it on her trolley.

'You have to be careful,' he said. 'We can't have sacks getting split.'

A porter passing by laughed. 'That's right. We can't have sacks getting split, can we, lads?'

A couple more men laughed. Emily smiled too. It was pleasing that even though this overtime had been dropped on them at the last minute, everyone was in good spirits.

'There's dried fruit over here,' said a porter.

There were sacks with SULTANAS and RAISINS stamped on them. Others said SUGAR or TEA. There were crates of tins and packets. Such a lot of food . . . but it wasn't such a lot when you thought how it had to be shared out between so many.

Emily made her way from the platform to the stores and back again. In the stores, there were long rows of tall shelving units and some empty areas marked out with chalk, where crates and large boxes were stacked. The porters worked quickly and efficiently and there was plenty of banter.

On her way out of the stores, Emily heard a man ask, 'Got your penknife?'

Ought she to equip herself with a penknife? It was the sort of thing boys had, not girls, but she was doing a man's job, so maybe one would come in handy. She made a few more trips to and fro and then the wagons were empty. Most of the porters dispersed, but there were still a few in the stores. Emily didn't like to leave without Mr Buckley. She ought to wait for him. It was the polite thing to do.

She hung about for a minute or two near the entrance. Then some porters walked past her on their way out and after that she saw Mr Buckley.

'You're a good lass,' he said, 'and you've worked hard.'

'Thank you.'

'Have you got a clean hanky?'

What a strange question. 'Yes.'

'A clean one, mind,' said Mr Buckley.

'Yes. Why?'

'Hold it out – no, I mean unfold it first. That's right. Here we go.' And Mr Buckley tipped tea leaves into it.

Emily's mouth dropped open.

'Nay, don't take on, little lass. You've earned it,' said Mr Buckley. 'A sack got split, see? You can't send it on its way with its contents pouring out all over the show, so we all take a bit home with us. No harm done. Fold your hanky over, there's a good girl.'

Emily did as she was told, returning the now bulging hanky to her pocket.

'Don't look so scared,' said Mr Buckley. 'Everyone does it.'

Leaving the stores, Emily walked alongside Mr Buckley. Soon she was collecting her things to go home. She was about to transfer her hanky from her jacket pocket into her handbag when she hesitated and glanced round to make sure nobody was watching. She bit her lip and then stopped doing so in case she looked guilty.

'Everyone does it,' Mr Buckley had said. If it had been going on for years, then it was part of the system . . . wasn't it? And it was only a bit of tea in her hanky. But if the whole sack had been emptied of its contents, that was a lot more than one hanky's worth. It was tea that was meant to be rationed out to the general population.

But if the bag had got split accidentally, then it couldn't be sent on with the rest of the stock or everything would end up covered in loose tea leaves, and that wouldn't bene-fit anybody.

'*Got your penknife?*'

Emily went cold inside. What if . . .?

'No harm done,' said Mr Buckley's voice in her head.

No harm? No harm! If what she urgently hoped she was wrong about had actually happened, then she, Emily Masters, daughter of a highly respectable solicitor, was a receiver of stolen goods.

CHAPTER TEN

Persephone stared at Miss Emery in astonishment. They were sitting in Miss Emery's office in Hunts Bank, where all the administration for LMS took place. It was a bit of a stretch to call it an office when it was really a three-sided alcove with no fourth wall where a door would be. Should be. How were Miss Emery and the ladies she helped supposed to have any privacy? Persephone knew that Miss Emery often had to arrange to borrow a real office when she needed to speak to one of the many women and girls under her care as assistant welfare supervisor.

The best one could say for the alcove was that it was the size of a small office and it was appropriately furnished with a desk and a separate table for the typewriter. Further back in the space were a coat stand and a tall cupboard.

'I'm not quite sure what your silence means, Miss Trehearn-Hobbs,' said Miss Emery in her usual calm way. 'Aren't you pleased with your new job? I ought to make it clear that when I offer someone a post, I am simply being courteous. This "offer" is actually an instruction. In other words, this is the post you have been appointed to.'

'I understand that,' said Persephone. 'It's just such a surprise. Here I am, coming cap in hand to seek a new post, and it turns out you already have one for me.'

Miss Emery smiled her polite, professional smile. 'I feel like the genie of the lamp. Your wish is my command.'

'It feels a bit like that,' Persephone agreed.

'Serendipity,' said Miss Emery. 'You had already been selected for promotion.'

Promotion! She had wanted a change from standing at her ticket barrier on the station, checking tickets as passengers entered the platform and collecting them as people left, and now she was going to be a ticket inspector, travelling on the trains, checking passengers' tickets. She would be out and about all the time. It was just what she wanted, what she needed. A change for the better.

'When will I start?' she asked.

'More or less immediately. You'll wear a different jacket and naturally you'll receive training,' said Miss Emery. 'But we've just lost a couple of inspectors, both of them lady inspectors. One applied to transfer to a different railway company for family reasons and the other is going to be off for some time because of needing a lady's operation. So you may well feel we're throwing you in at the deep end, Miss Trehearn-Hobbs, but I am confident that you shall cope splendidly.'

When Persephone told her chums in the buffet, they echoed Miss Emery's confidence.

'If anyone can step into a new role and be perfect at it, you can,' said Dot. 'You always know how to make things happen.'

Persephone was touched by the compliment, though she wasn't sure she deserved it. Yes, she was good at getting things done, but that was purely because she thought them through and then asked the relevant people if they would be kind enough to help. It was all down to good manners, really, and she could hardly take the credit for that. She smiled to herself. It was Nanny who deserved the credit if it was all down to good manners.

A letter came from Forbes, saying he was being discharged from hospital and heading home for a bit of convalescence time, *though my mother will be too busy organ-ising the WVS and the knitting circle and heaven knows what else to spend time wiping the fevered brow.* Clamping down on a powerful feeling of despair, Persephone wrote back to him care of his parents' address, telling him about her pro-motion. She resolved not to give in to her sense of loss. The whole point of her new job was to keep her occupied and get her through a difficult spell. Besides, she had no busi-ness feeling it as a loss when she'd never had a relationship with Forbes in the first place.

But it still felt like a loss.

Fortunately she then had a madly busy few days. It wasn't just that she was getting used to her new role at work. With the Wings for Victory Week coming up, she and Mabel had masses to organise, helped, of course, by their friends. Persephone had volunteered for the job of going around the local schools, sharing ideas so that the children would feel fully engaged with the week's events when they took place. The children made bingo cards, but with hand-drawn pictures of little Spitfires, Hurricanes, Halifaxes and Lancasters instead of numbers, and they prepared Battleship grids but with German planes to be shot down instead of ships to be sunk.

Persephone and Mabel had arranged for an ATA girl to visit a couple of schools to give talks about her work and then there would be a competition to see who could write the most exciting story about flying a plane or the most atmospheric poem about flying above the clouds. And one enterprising science teacher created a game of releasing 'bombs' onto a target from an electromagnet, which, when he demonstrated it, Persephone found every bit as thrilling as she was sure the children would.

'The boys will love it,' said the teacher.

'So will the girls,' said Persephone.

'It isn't really a girl type of thing.'

Although she longed to lay down the law about girls' capabilities and possible interests, Persephone said simply, 'At least let them have the chance. They might surprise you.'

Meanwhile, at work, she was settling into her new role as ticket inspector.

'I don't want to seem big-headed or anything,' she told Miss Brown, 'but I was brought up to have confidence and that goes a long way in a new situation.'

Her friends arranged an extra meeting in the buffet so they could hear all about how she was getting on.

'We want every detail,' said Alison.

'First of all,' said Colette, 'are you enjoying it?'

'I love it,' Persephone said frankly. 'Don't get me wrong. I liked being a ticket collector, but it was very samey.' She thought for a moment. 'I suppose being an inspector is pretty samey too, when you think about it, but being out on the trains makes a big difference. It makes it feel as though the work is full of variety.'

Dot laughed. 'There's definitely nowt samey about working with the public.'

'Tell us a bit about it,' Mabel urged.

'Well, today I was on a train packed so full that practically every passenger had another sitting on their knee, as well as people standing in the aisles. I'm supposed to go through the entire train before I get off and wait for my next train, but in this case I didn't even manage to get halfway. I wasn't sure whether to stay on until I'd finished or get off where I was supposed to, ready for my next train.'

'What did you do?' asked Margaret.

'I got off – rather reluctantly, I might add, because it was one of those really jolly trains where everyone's in a good mood in spite of everything, but I thought it best to stick to the list of duties I'd been given.'

'You can only do your best,' said Dot.

'Have you done any night work yet?' asked Emily.

'Not in the sense of an all-nighter,' said Persephone, 'but I've worked until midnight. There was one station where I was waiting for my next allocated train to come along and it was hideously late. I don't know how long the passengers had been waiting, but there were civilians and servicemen asleep all over the waiting room, in the chairs and seated around the table with their heads on their folded arms, like little children at school.'

'I expect the walls still had their colourful pre-war posters of all the lovely holiday destinations,' Cordelia commented.

'Let's hope they gave everyone sweet dreams,' said Colette.

As the huge knots of passengers crowding round the doors started to board the train at Victoria, Persephone offered her assistance to an elderly lady whose straight back, large brooch of jet and amethyst and old-fashioned hat with a wide brim bedecked with rosettes and feathers made her look like a duchess. Persephone certainly felt the need to treat her like one. The lady had a Scottie on a lead with her.

'May I take the dog for you, madam?' Persephone enquired. 'He'll be quite safe in the guard's van and I'll make sure he has a bowl of water.'

'Thank you.' Although the lady had a plummy voice, she wasn't anything like as haughty as she looked. 'Something tells me that Oscar will have a more comfortable journey than I will.'

Persephone immediately inserted herself into a group of young servicemen weighed down by kitbags, packs and belts with pouches. 'I've got a special job for you, boys.'

'Anything for you,' said one of them, immediately responding to her smile.

'Please can you make sure this lady gets a window seat and look after her during the journey.' Persephone smiled around the group. 'It would be such a kindness.'

Leaving the 'duchess' in the care of the cheerful young men, she took Oscar to the guard's van, where the parcels porter helped to make a little pen for him with some suitcases. Presently, after the usual rigmarole of door-slamming and whistle-blowing, the train started to pull away. Persephone gave everyone a few minutes to settle and then began to make her slow progress through the coaches, doing a swift little almost dance step to counteract the sharp swaying motion each time she moved through the part connecting one carriage to the next.

Although she would sometimes be sent here, there and everywhere according to staffing needs, the railway line she was on today was going to be one of her regular ones, so she had learned the names of all the stations in order to help any passengers who weren't sure when they should get off.

'It's the same for me,' Emily had told her. 'I have to learn all the stations on all the lines out of Victoria.'

'At least I only have to learn the ones I'll be on regularly,' Persephone had said. 'Railway journeys can be a real mystery tour without station names on display.'

She'd thought briefly of her own mystery tour to visit Forbes, but pushed the memory away. No use dwelling on that. Forbes didn't love her, never had and never would, and the whole point of taking on this new job was to give herself other things to think about.

And there were plenty of those. At one stop, a family of grandmother, mother and a girl no older than Persephone climbed aboard, half lifting, half dragging a pram through the door with them.

'Pop the pram over here,' said Persephone.

For a wonder, there was space for it in the corner next to the opposite door, which wouldn't be opened during this journey. More passengers crowded on and Persephone squeezed herself back against the carriage wall so she wouldn't get swept away.

'Have your tickets ready, please,' she called when the train was on its way again.

She examined and clipped some tickets belonging to the passengers clustered nearest to her, then she wriggled through them to the family with the pram. They had four tickets between them, one each plus one for the pram.

'Thank you.' Persephone was about to clip the tickets and give them back when she glanced inside the pram, ready to make a complimentary remark about the child within, only to find that the pram was full of luggage and there was no sign of a baby. 'I'm sorry, ladies, but pram tickets are for the benefit of mothers travelling with babies or small children.'

'You aren't going to make us get off, are you?' The girl's eyes filled with tears. 'How else are we supposed to manage with all our stuff?'

'We've lived in digs ever since we were bombed out a couple of years ago,' said the grandmother, 'and now my other daughter has offered to take us in. This is everything we've got left in the world.'

Persephone made a decision. She didn't know whether it was right or wrong – she might look it up in the regs later – but she chose it because it was the correct thing to do in the circumstances.

'The pram ticket is fine for this journey.' She clipped it along with the others. 'But if you'll be joining another train, I suggest you put it in the guard's van.'

'Thanks, love,' said the mother. 'You're a gem.'

Maybe – or maybe she was a soft touch. The railways wouldn't look kindly on that.

Persephone continued making her way along the train, keeping an eye on the time and making sure she looked out of the windows at every station to familiarise herself with what each one looked like while whispering its name to herself over and over again. She must sound mad to anyone who could hear her.

'It might sound unprofessional,' she told Mrs Mitchell that evening, 'but at the moment, while I'm still learning all the routes, I much prefer the shorter journeys, like the one from Chester. Much less to learn!'

At the moment, she was working on the Manchester to Leeds line, including offshoot local branch lines. She had an early start, went halfway to Leeds, then got off and caught the next train back to Manchester. One of the pleasures of the work for Persephone was that she sometimes saw the same passengers at either end of the day. She liked the idea of having regulars with whom she could have a bit of a chat. She'd had plenty of regulars when she was on the ticket barrier, but there was never any time for more than a swift 'Morning' or 'Lovely day' or 'Awful weather' when passengers were pouring through the barrier, intent upon hurrying towards their various destinations.

Now, though, there was ample time for a friendly word here and there. Innately good-mannered, she always started her shift by walking along the platform to the front of the train to call 'Good morning' up to the driver and the fireman on the footplate of the locomotive. She didn't hang about demanding attention, because they were busy with their preparations to get under way, but she thought it was the courteous thing to do. Like everyone who worked on the railways, she had tremendous admiration for the engine drivers and firemen, who worked long shifts day and night through all weathers. True, there wasn't so much danger from the air these days as there had been earlier in the war, but that didn't mean that Jerry had altogether stopped flying over, and railway tracks were always a target, as were the engine sheds, marshalling yards and bridges. Being an engine driver was skilled work and being a fireman was also a highly responsible job. In peacetime, the demands and responsibilities of the work included having to know every inch of their route intimately, not just all the signals and junctions but also all the landmarks. Now, in wartime, they had to know their routes every bit as closely, every change in the gradient, every area where there was a speed restriction, but now in the pitch-dark of the blackout too. In Persephone's book, engine drivers and firemen were every bit as heroic as the servicemen fighting for King and country.

One morning, getting off halfway as usual and crossing over the railway bridge to make her return journey in the company of a large number of commuters, she joined the passengers awaiting the Manchester train, though she kept to the back of the crowd. She often got into the guard's van rather than an ordinary carriage and started her walk up and down the train from there.

A few passengers nodded to her. Three gentlemen in pinstriped suits, all with silver watch chains, raised their bowlers to her and she smiled politely in return. The train drew in and everyone got on. One of the men in pinstripes stood back from the door, looking back questioningly at her, but she shook her head.

'Thank you, sir, but I'll get on at the other end.'

Walking quickly along the platform, she asked the guard for permission, then climbed aboard. Once the journey was under way, she made her way gradually through all the coaches, calling 'Have your tickets ready, please,' as she entered each one. Although the train was busy, it wasn't one of those days when she simply couldn't make it from one end to the other in the time.

Entering one of the front coaches, she saw that the WC was engaged and her heart sank a little. She hated doing this – it barely seemed polite – but it had been made clear to her that it was one of her duties.

She tapped discreetly on the closed door. 'Ticket inspector. Excuse me, but could you pop your ticket under the door, please?' As it appeared, she picked it up, clipped it and slid it back again. 'Thank you.'

Soon the train was coasting along next to the platform at Victoria. Persephone pulled down the window in the door, ready to lean out and turn the handle. There was a press of bodies behind her and she could feel the combined willpower urging her to get the dratted door open, but she didn't open it until the train had come to a halt, no matter that all the other doors had already banged open and passengers were hurrying on their way.

Persephone stepped down onto the platform, taking a few steps away so as not to block the exit from the train. Turning, she watched as passengers poured out, all intent on getting to wherever they had to go next. An elderly gentleman dropped his newspaper and Persephone picked it up for him. As the travellers streamed past her, she noticed the three gentlemen in pinstripes, which made her realise that she hadn't checked their tickets. But she must have, because she'd had time to go through the entire train. She'd just forgotten doing it. After all, with a packed train, how was she to remember clipping every single ticket?

She dismissed it from her mind as she answered some anxious questions put to her by passengers. By the time she had seen the last of them on their way, the crowd on the platform had thinned out, most people having vanished through the ticket barrier at the other end. Persephone glanced at the clock further along the platform. She had a few minutes before she had to board her next train and she needed to get to the platform at the far end of the concourse, preferably after having fitted in a visit to the Ladies.

'Morning,' said a cheery voice and she looked round to see a man in a grubby, loose-fitting jacket with his peaked cap pushed to the back of his head, showing off a squarish face streaked with grime that made his eyes look extra blue. The driver or the fireman? The fireman, presumably, as Persephone thought of drivers as being older. Besides, this chap's physique, though slim, was muscular and you had to be jolly strong to be a fireman, keeping the ravenous engine topped up with coal.

'Good morning,' she said with a smile. 'I'm sorry. I don't want to appear rude, but I've got to dash to another train.'

The fireman lifted his fingers, touching his temple in a mock salute as she hurried on her way. After walking along the platform to the engine whenever she could so as to say a polite hello to the men on the footplate, it made a pleasant change for one of them to make the effort to greet her, and it was a shame she couldn't have stayed a minute or two to chat, but never mind. She was due to be on the same train again at the same time the day after tomorrow, so maybe there would be another opportunity then.

Hurrying away, she dashed to the Ladies, slipping into the cubicle with the Out of Order sign on the door that an enterprising railwaywoman had hung there so as always to have a lavatory available for staff to use. Honestly! This far into the war, you'd have thought the powers that be would have provided proper facilities for their female staff instead of expecting them to share with the general public.

Even though she got tired during her long days on duty, Persephone kept a smile on her face and was often rewarded by an answering smile from the person she was dealing with. ('A little charm goes a long way, Persephone.')

'I've been hearing about a new ticket inspector on the trains,' Dot said in the buffet that evening. 'What was it I heard?' She pretended to think about it. 'Oh aye. "The beautiful ticket inspector with the lovely smile." I can't imagine who they were talking about. Can you?'

The others laughed and Persephone shook her head at Dot.

'You're naughty to tease,' she said.

'Actually,' said Dot, 'I felt proud. I thought: that's my friend, making a good impression. One of my daughters for the duration.'

It warmed Persephone to know that Dot was proud of her – and how good of her to say so. Ma and Pa would never have said anything of the kind. They expected their children to do whatever was required of them, and why would you praise someone for doing that? Something her wartime experiences and friendships had taught Persephone was that it was good to praise people. It made them feel valued.

Happy knowing that her 'mum for the duration' was pleased with her, Persephone sailed through the job until she once more found herself on the same platform as the three men in pinstripes. She greeted them with a smile and they raised their bowlers to her. Soon after that the train drew up alongside the platform and Persephone helped an old woman in a shawl to lift her bags aboard before she hurried down to the guard's van and climbed in.

Once again she had ample time to make her way all down the train. She even had time to chat with a few passengers. One of the lavatories was engaged and she had to knock and ask for the ticket to be pushed under the door.

'Thank you,' she called, slipping the clipped ticket back underneath, adding 'Sorry,' because it must feel so undignified to the person inside.

When the train pulled into Victoria Station, Persephone was one of the first to get off and she stood back as everyone alighted – and there they were again, the three pinstriped men, and this time she knew, she knew for a fact, that she hadn't set eyes on them as she'd made her way through the long line of carriages. Somehow they had evaded her.

'Morning,' said the voice she remembered from last time. 'Oh,' added the fireman. 'Sorry. Am I interrupting? You look . . . annoyed.'

Persephone turned to him. 'Do I? I apologise. I don't mean to be rude to you. I've just realised that . . .' She hesitated. She was about to make an accusation and maybe that wasn't wise, but what the heck. She knew she was right. Moreover, it was part of her job to nab people who tried to avoid paying for their tickets. 'I've come across a trio of men who I have reason to believe are dodging paying their fares, but I'm not sure how they've managed it.'

'What happened?' The fireman's blue eyes were fixed attentively on her.

'I saw these gentlemen get on. They boarded at the same station I did. They even said good morning to me and tipped their hats. But when I went through the train checking all the tickets, they weren't there. I know how silly that sounds – how impossible. But now I've just seen them get off. And it isn't the first time this has happened.'

'Fare-dodgers, eh? Unfortunately, it happens.'

Something inside Persephone relaxed. 'Thank you.'

'What for?'

'For not saying "Are you sure?" I know what happened, though I can't begin to explain it.'

For a mad moment, Persephone wondered if the men had tucked themselves away inside the net luggage racks above the seats – though surely the other passengers would have said, and anyway, she would have noticed.

The fireman's mouth shifted into a crinkly line for a moment, making him look both good-humoured and thoughtful. Then he said, 'Was the, um, the WC engaged? And did you ask for the ticket to be pushed under the door?'

Persephone's eyes widened. 'Yes. Is that how they did it? By all cramming into the WC?'

'You sometimes hear of people trying it.'

Persephone wrinkled her nose. 'I think I'd rather pay the fare. What a way to travel.' Three of them too – in one lavatory! 'And they look so well-to-do.'

The fireman grinned. 'Maybe that's why they're well-to-do – because they manage to hang on to their money.' The smile dropped from his face. 'I'm not making light of it. Fare-dodging is a serious matter.'

Persephone pictured the men's courtesy to her before they boarded the train. 'They've made a monkey out of me.'

'Well then,' said the fireman, and now there was a distinct twinkle in his blue eyes, 'let's see if we can make monkeys out of them, shall we?'

CHAPTER ELEVEN

It was a blustery, wet evening and the buffet felt cosy, the atmosphere warm with voices as passengers in damp mackintoshes snatched a few minutes to relax before continuing their journeys. Tobacco smoke hung in the air, its smell mingling with the tang of the coal in the fireplace beside which Persephone's friends had bagged a table to cluster around, sharing seats with one another because the room was full. Wearing her wool overcoat over her uniform, with a scarf wound round beneath the coat's oversized collar and dangling down the front, Persephone, carrying her cup of tea, made her way between the tables, taking care not to knock into any of the bags on the floor.

It wasn't long before she was telling her friends about the pinstriped fare-dodgers, though she kept her voice low so as not to be overheard at nearby tables.

'Rogues,' said Dot in disgust. 'There's no excuse for not buying a ticket.'

'It's not even as though they looked down on their luck,' said Persephone. 'They appear to be prosperous.'

'That makes it worse,' Alison declared. 'You're going to report them, of course.'

'Yes, but Mr Franklin – that's the fireman who guessed what they were up to – had an idea about how we could teach them a lesson as well.'

'I'm not sure I like the sound of that,' said Cordelia. 'It's your duty to report them and that's all there is to it.'

'I know,' Persephone agreed, 'but I'd like to get my own back. Does that sound childish?'

'No,' said Mabel. 'It sounds understandable to me. It's like you said. They made a monkey out of you. You deserve to have the last laugh – as well as reporting them through the correct channels, of course.'

'What's the idea this Mr Franklin came up with?' asked Emily.

Persephone hesitated. Had she given it too much of a build-up? 'Please don't imagine something dramatic. It's very simple. He suggested that when they put the ticket under the door, I should hang on to it. That'll give them something to worry about.'

'It'll probably be needed as evidence anyway,' said Colette.

'But what if they burst out of the WC and try to escape?' asked Alison. 'I know they can't go anywhere when the train's in motion, but they could push their way through to the nearest door, ready to leap out when the train slows down.'

'Mr Franklin and I wondered about tying the WC's door handle to the handle of the door into the carriage, so they can't get out. Or piling some luggage in front to barricade them in. Whatever it is, it has to be something I'm happy to do on my own, because of course he won't be with me. He'll be busy keeping the train running. I have to keep the men inside the lavatory until I can call for help when we get to Victoria.'

'May I make a suggestion?' said Colette. 'There's a man called Mr Gordon who works in the ticket office here at Victoria. I don't know exactly what his job is, but I've heard he's someone who looks into problems with tickets, by which I mean situations like this one, where someone is trying to get away with something. I think you ought to tell

119

him, Persephone. He's a good egg – so I've been told. He'll know what has to be done.'

'By which you mean he'll make sure I don't go too far and end up in trouble myself,' Persephone said wryly.

'Colette has a point,' said Cordelia.

'Aye, chick,' said Dot. 'We don't want you getting carted off to prison for barricading passengers in the lav – no matter how much they deserve it.'

'We could pop along to the ticket office after this,' said Colette, 'and see if he's there.'

After they had all finished their tea and said their goodbyes, Persephone followed Colette in the direction of the long, elegant sweep of gleaming wood panelling that formed the outer wall of the ticket office. Colette led her round the side to a door. She knocked and waited for it to be opened.

'It's kept locked on the inside,' she explained.

'How come you know that?' asked Persephone. It wasn't something she would have expected Colette to know, her job on the railways being that of chaperone to passengers who needed assistance because of infirmity or vulnerability.

Colette shrugged. 'I've been inside once or twice to collect tickets for the people I look after.'

The door was opened by a lady clerk.

'Is Mr Gordon available, please?' Colette asked.

They were shown to a small office set into the corner, where a good-looking man probably in his forties, with a high forehead and thinning golden-brown hair, politely rose to his feet.

'Good evening, Mrs Naylor. What can I do for you?'

'I hope I've done the right thing by bringing my friend to you,' said Colette. 'This is Miss Trehearn-Hobbs. She's a ticket inspector and she has something to report.'

'Please sit down.' Mr Gordon waved Colette into a chair before disappearing for a few moments to fetch a second chair for Persephone.

While she explained what had happened, Mr Gordon listened attentively and made notes on a pad. He had a serious, clever face and thoughtful eyes. He looked tired and Persephone wondered if she had just added yet another hour's work to an already long day.

'You did right to come to me, ladies,' said Mr Gordon. 'This is what we're going to do. Tomorrow, Miss Trehearn-Hobbs, you'll board the train as usual, if you please, and do everything in the same way as normal, with one exception: when the ticket is pushed under the door to you, you won't push it back. It will form part of our evidence.'

'That's what you said would happen,' Persephone said to Colette.

'A lucky guess, that's all,' Colette said modestly.

'But there won't be any tying up of door handles or barricading of the door,' said Mr Gordon. 'Instead, when the gentlemen emerge, they'll be met by a policeman and me. We'll join the train at the last stop before Victoria. The matter will be referred to the magistrates' court and you'll be called upon to be a witness, Miss Trehearn-Hobbs. For now, please could you make a short statement to my secretary about what has happened thus far and she will type it up for you. Please be specific as to dates and times – and there's no need to mention barricades,' he added in a wry voice, which made Persephone realise that in spite of his serious demeanour, he had a sense of humour.

Before she left the ticket office, Mr Gordon told her not to mention a word to anybody of what was going to happen and Persephone felt a small dip of disappointment. She would have liked, of course, to tell Mr Franklin if she'd had the chance. They could have had a laugh about their barmy idea of trapping the miscreants in the WC. Maybe they still could, after the event.

Everything happened just as Mr Gordon had said it would. He climbed aboard the train accompanied by a uniformed officer and they placed themselves outside the WC door, where Persephone was waiting for them.

'Do you have the ticket?' asked Mr Gordon. 'Good. Keep it safe.'

When the train arrived at Victoria Station, those passengers who had made it to the doors first jumped out, leaving those still inside to shuffle along the aisle, clutching their bags, but every single one of them who passed the closed WC looked twice at the sight of the burly bobby. After a minute or two, the door opened and Persephone glimpsed the three pinstriped gentlemen in their cramped quarters. As the first man started to emerge, he saw the policeman and stopped dead, only to be bumped from behind, whereupon he lurched out into the corridor, followed by his friends.

'What have we here?' asked the policeman.

With five men in the small bit of corridor, there was no room for Persephone and she had to descend onto the platform, where she waited. She could hear the three men's voices. They sounded as if they were blustering, though she couldn't make out the words.

Mr Franklin appeared beside her. 'Is everything all right? How did it go?'

'Not quite as we envisaged it,' said Persephone, 'but I don't think they'll try their trick again after this.'

Led by Mr Gordon, the men, their expressions a mixture of mutiny, vexation and shame, left the train, followed by the policeman.

'I'll be in touch with details of your court appearance,' Mr Gordon told Persephone before the little group walked away.

Persephone explained to Mr Franklin what had happened.

'And it'll go to court?' He whistled. 'They face hefty fines, I expect.'

Mr Franklin was correct. Persephone had to attend the court a couple of days later, where the three men were each fined a staggering but entirely deserved twenty pounds each because they had clearly given much thought to how to get away with their fare-dodging.

Persephone had to hurry back to Victoria afterwards to return to work. She had just passed the station's beautiful war memorial and was about to enter the concourse when Emily came running up to her.

'I've been watching for you. Today was the court day, wasn't it? What happened?'

'They were fined.'

'How much?' asked Emily and then gasped when Persephone told her. 'As much as that?'

'What they did was theft,' said Persephone, then excused herself with a smile and hurried on her way.

Her morning at court, waiting for the case to come up, had led the inspector who sorted out the work rotas to change her work round a little, not just for today but for the next two weeks at least. It was a shame if this meant that other ticket inspectors were put out because of the knock-on effect, but Persephone couldn't have been more pleased because for the next fortnight she would be starting her day on the same train as Mr Franklin, going all the way to Leeds and back.

Accordingly, the next morning, when she went to say good morning to the men on the footplate, she had the pleasure of seeing Mr Franklin's surprise. He jumped down onto the platform to have a word.

'I've only got a minute. What happened yesterday? I've been wondering how you got on.'

'They got hefty fines. Twenty pounds each.'

'Twenty? To plenty of blokes, that's a month's wages.'

'It's somewhat more than a month's wages if you're a woman,' said Persephone.

'Thanks for telling me what happened,' said Mr Franklin. 'I appreciate it. I thought maybe – well, I didn't take it for granted that you'd bother.'

'Of course I bothered,' Persephone exclaimed. 'You were the one who helped me in the first place. I appreciated the support.'

Mr Franklin smiled. 'So now we've appreciated one another . . .' He glanced towards the train's cab.

Persephone immediately took the hint. 'I'll leave you to it. I must get on as well. Thanks again.'

She walked away. What an agreeable chap he was. But it niggled at her that he had thought maybe she wouldn't have troubled to tell him the outcome. Did he think her upper-class voice meant she looked down on the likes of him? She didn't want to leave him with that impression, so she looked for an opportunity to instigate another chat. It wasn't possible at the Leeds end of the journey, but later on, when the train returned to Victoria, the men on the footplate were due for a meal break. Knowing how important it was for them to have a sit-down and something to eat, Persephone kept her distance, but she made sure she was on the platform when they were likely to return.

Although they walked onto the platform together, the engine driver stopped for a chinwag with a pair of porters and Mr Franklin left them to it.

Persephone went up to him. Not wanting to waste his time, she came straight to the point. 'You said something earlier and it's been on my mind. You said that you didn't necessarily expect me to tell you the outcome of the trial, and if I made you think that, then I apologise. When someone does me a good turn, like you did, I'd never brush it aside and walk away. I'm grateful for the help you gave me.'

The strong lines of Mr Franklin's lean face softened as he smiled at her. 'It's gradely of you to say so.'

Persephone smiled back. 'You're welcome.' Then something made her ask, 'Have you got to get straight back into the cab?'

'Have you got to get straight back to checking tickets?'

They both laughed.

'Actually,' said Mr Franklin, 'I sometimes take a few minutes to read some poetry before I have to start work again.'

'Poetry?' asked Persephone, then pulled a face. 'I'm so sorry if I sounded surprised. I don't mean to suggest . . .' Her voice trailed off. What a mess she was making of this – a right pig's whisker, Dot would have said. It wasn't like her at all. What had become of her unflappable good manners?

Mr Franklin laughed. 'Steady on or you'll end up wanting to apologise all over again. It's all right. No offence taken. I know folk find it unusual, shall we say, that a railway fireman enjoys poetry.'

'It's all too easy to think in stereotypes,' said Persephone, starting to feel comfortable again. 'What sort of poetry do you like?'

'I find myself drawn to nature poems these days. Things like "Spring" by Gerard Manley Hopkins and "Snow in the Suburbs" by—'

'Thomas Hardy,' chimed in Persephone, finishing the sentence along with him.

'In wartime, with all its difficulties and worries, it helps me to feel close to the natural world, even if it's only inside my head.'

'I can understand that,' said Persephone. 'I think we all need something to take us out of ourselves. That's why so many people flock to the pictures or go dancing. But poetry gives a different kind of solace, something quiet and deeply personal.'

'Do you read poetry?' asked Mr Franklin.

'Here we go again,' said a new voice in a sort of jovial groan. 'Not more poetry.'

Persephone turned to see the engine driver, a middle-aged man of chunky build with bags under his eyes.

'This is Mr Gibson,' Mr Franklin told her.

'How do you do,' said Persephone.

'This is Miss Trehearn-Hobbs, one of the ticket collectors.'

'By, that's a fancy-sounding name,' said Mr Gibson, 'but a pretty girl like you deserves a fancy name if anyone does. Come on, Byron,' he added to Mr Franklin. 'Let's be having you.'

As Mr Gibson headed towards the cab, Persephone asked the fireman, 'Is your name Byron?' How appropriate for a man who loved poetry.

He grinned. 'No, that's just what Mr Gibson sometimes calls me.'

'Because of the poetry,' said Persephone.

He left her and Persephone went on her way, glad to have had the chance of a chat, glad, too, that for the next fortnight she would be on Mr Gibson's train to Leeds and back every morning. It was good to have colleagues one got along with.

She had the chance of a few chats over the following days with both Mr Franklin and Mr Gibson, though Mr Gibson preferred to talk with long-time railwaymen. That suited Persephone, because she enjoyed talking to Mr Franklin.

'Do you come from a railway family?' she asked him as they sat on a bench at the station in Leeds, nursing mugs of tea.

'No. My dad's a policeman. When I was a lad, I wanted to be a train driver.' He laughed. 'The same as nearly every other boy, I suppose. But in my case, I never grew out of it. My parents sent me to grammar school, which was a big thing in our family. They had to sign something agreeing to keep me at school until I was fifteen, and there was the uniform to pay for and all sorts of things. But it wasn't where my heart lay and in the end my parents let me leave school at fourteen. They had to pay a penalty for the wasted grammar school place. I started on the railways with a privileged apprenticeship.'

'What does that mean?' Persephone asked.

'I got two days a week off work to go to technical college.' Mr Franklin pulled a face. 'Two unpaid days, which was another blow to the family finances.'

'But it obviously worked out for you in the end,' said Persephone. 'Look at you now, a fireman.'

'I think my parents have forgiven me,' he said with a warm smile that suggested his love for his family. 'What about you? I've heard you have a title. Is that right? Are you a Lady with a capital L?'

'Not quite. I'm an Honourable.'

'And here you are doing your war work on the railways. Good for you.'

'Good for me?' Persephone questioned. 'Are you suggesting that an Honourable with a double-barrelled surname is doing the country a favour by sullying her hands in this way?' She kept her voice light and teasing, but it needed saying.

'No,' said Mr Franklin. Then he laughed. 'Well, yes, maybe I did think that – but now that I've heard myself say it, I definitely don't think it any more. I'm sorry. Please don't be offended.'

'I'm not. I apologised to you once in case I'd given the wrong impression and now you've apologised for making assumptions, so that makes us square.'

'Fair enough,' Mr Franklin agreed readily. 'Seriously, what does your family think of you doing this job?'

'Everyone has to do their bit. They know that.' Persephone felt comfortable enough in Mr Franklin's easy company to confide: 'If they worry about anything, it's my wish to be a journalist. That's my ambition and it always has been.'

He asked about her writing and she told him about the articles she wrote on spec that were sometimes accepted for publication.

'I've done quite well with a magazine called *Vera's Voice*,' she said.

'That rings a bell. I think my mum gets that. Maybe she's read some of your pieces.'

Persephone liked the thought of that, though she didn't mention her pen name in case it sounded as though she was hinting to Mr Franklin that he should make sure his mother read her articles.

But on another occasion, the subject of pseudonyms came up in the context of the Brontë sisters.

'I use a pen name as well,' said Persephone, because this time it felt natural to say so. 'Not that I'm comparing myself to the Brontës, of course.'

'What's yours?'

'Stephanie Fraser. Stephanie because sometimes when I'm introduced to somebody and they've never heard the name Persephone before, they hear it as Stephanie. And Fraser after a character in a book.'

'The heroine?' he asked.

Persephone smiled. 'The baddy, actually.'

She enjoyed her chats with Mr Franklin, taking pleasure in what they had in common – a love of the railways, reading and poetry, and was it fanciful to say they shared a sense of personal striving too? He'd had to push for his career and she was forever working towards her own ambition.

One afternoon when she was on the Southport train with Dot, who was a regular parcels porter on this line, she mentioned Mr Franklin and what they had in common.

'You don't have to be out of the same drawer to be the same sort of person,' said Dot. 'Look at me and Cordelia. The first time I met her, I knew that if we'd come across one another before the war, it would have been because I was her charwoman and that was the only way we'd have met. But look at us now. Mates for life. It's not about what school you went to or who your parents are. It's about what you're like on the inside.'

How wise Dot was. Mr Franklin was a decent sort of fellow and he was good company. Good-looking too. Persephone couldn't help feeling inspired by his enthusiasm for his work. Best of all, she felt she had made a friend.

CHAPTER TWELVE

Indulging in a good old rant down the telephone to Harry about the disagreeable Miss Brewster made Mabel feel heaps better, not just because Harry shared her outrage but because his belief in her gave her a real boost.

'If this Miss Brewster thinks she's scuppered your plans for creating a nursery in the Extension, she's going to find she's made a serious mistake. I know my girl,' Harry declared, 'and I know you'll come up with a way to trounce her.'

Afterwards, Mabel lifted her chin and pushed back her shoulders every time she remembered Harry's staunch words of support. Unfortunately, though, battling with Miss Brewster would have to wait until after Wings for Victory Week, which was due to start on Saturday and run until the Saturday of the following week, which was when the dance at the Claremont would be held.

With what she and Persephone had organised on a local level, Mabel was in for a busy week and she couldn't wait for it to get under way, but she and Persephone had been adamant about one thing. Whatever they organised, it mustn't clash with the parade that was to take place in the middle of Manchester on the first Saturday. Many such parades were to be held all over the country. Down in Trafalgar Square, according to the proud reporting in the newspapers, a Lancaster bomber was going to be on display, providing the backdrop to the parade of servicemen that was to start after thirteen hundred pigeons, some of them previously used as carriers of wartime messages, had been released into the air to symbolise the thirteen hundred local committees countrywide that had worked tirelessly to organise the numerous events it was hoped would raise one hundred and fifty million pounds. One hundred and fifty million!

To Mabel's profound delight, Manchester also had a Lancaster on display. It stood proudly in Piccadilly, bearing the dings and dents of wartime fighting. Mabel was ready to burst with pride, because her Harry, her darling cheeky blighter, her soon-to-be husband, had flown so many missions as the bomb aimer in a Lancaster, risking his own life every single time.

THE BOYS IN BLUE LOOK TO YOU proclaimed all the banners and Mabel's eyes filled with tears, emotion swelling inside her because she knew herself to be part of the national salute to the courageous men of the Royal Air Force, the Fleet Air Arm and Allied air forces.

In common with parades all over the country throughout the week, it wasn't just the columns of men and the marching bands that the crowds applauded. Essential equipment was displayed on open-topped lorries, with bombs bringing up the rear, the 'little' ones weighing five hundred pounds on show alongside their considerably bigger and more deadly brothers, some of them weighing as much as eight thousand pounds. Mabel stood tall with pride on behalf of her Harry, her love so strong that her flesh barely seemed able to contain it. Was it wrong of her also to feel desperately grateful that he wasn't currently on a tour of duty? So many RAF boys never came home and it was often said that the bomb aimers had the most perilous job of all.

After the parade, people flocked to buy wartime savings stamps to contribute to the fundraising drive. Most people wrote messages on their stamps before sticking them to the bombs, things like *This one's for you, Hitler* and *If this doesn't blast Jerry, nothing will*. Others signed their names or wrote the names of loved ones who had lost their lives in air raids at home or in service overseas. Mothers encouraged their little ones to write on the stamps before sticking them onto the deadly bombs. On her stamp, Mabel wrote *Harry & Mabel, June 1943* because that was when they were going to get married. If only she could be by his side during this important week – but she had her own Wings for Victory commitments locally.

As well as long days lifting railway sleepers and levelling the ballast on the permanent way, Mabel was out and about every evening, and on her day off, willingly lending a hand at simple events such as the jumble sale and at more formal occasions, like the auction of promises. All the while, she looked forward to the dance this coming Saturday at the Claremont, which promised to be a wonderful occasion, just like Cordelia's War Weapons Week dance had been the summer before last.

To Mabel's delight, Joan and Bob were going to attend. The girls didn't see as much of Joan now that she was a housewife and mum, which was a shame, though it was understandable because her place was in the home now.

Mabel got off the bus early on Thursday evening on her way home from work to pop in and see Joan for a chat. Joan was special to her because of the closeness that had developed between them when Mabel had first lived in Wilton Close and the two of them had shared a room.

Joan led Mabel to the top of the stairs, then turned and put a finger to her lips. In the sitting room, two toddlers were flaked out on the sofa with a blanket over them.

'They look cosy,' Mabel said quietly, her heart softening at the sight.

Joan smiled. 'They're lovely when they're asleep.'

'But not when they're awake?'

'I don't mean to grumble. They're perfectly sweet children and they adore Max. But looking after three, and all of them so young, is a big job.'

'But think of the two mothers you're helping.'

'I do think of them,' said Joan. 'I think of them going out to work and – and it makes me realise how much I miss being at Victoria Station. I loved my job.'

'I know you did.'

'How's young Emily getting along? Does she like being a porter?'

'Seems to. She was pretty bored at her father's place.'

'That's one thing you can guarantee about being a station porter. It's never boring.'

'But being stuck at home is?' Mabel ventured.

'Don't get me wrong. I know how important it is for these children to be properly cared for. And I love every single minute I'm with Max. But I can't help wondering about working part-time – instead of childminding, I mean. Does that make me a bad mother?'

'You – a bad mother? Don't be daft. Max couldn't have better parents.'

'I'm sorry. Am I putting you off motherhood? That's the last thing I want to do. I've never been happier in my whole life. Anyway, you shan't be having children for some time, shall you?'

Mabel hadn't intended to say a word about Dr Yelland to anyone, but it felt right to share it now with Joan.

'So unless I nip out of my wedding reception for an hour to see a gynaecologist and get fixed up, I might end up falling for a honeymoon baby. You don't think I'm unnatural, do you, for not wanting a baby right away?'

'I think the war has changed all sorts of rules,' said Joan. 'Who am I to criticise you when I think all the time about leaving my baby so I can go back to work? There is one thing I will tell you, though, from my position as an old married lady. I know you're not meant to say these things to single girls, but here goes. Before I got married, I had no idea where babies came from and I thought that, however they were made, that was the sole purpose of a husband and wife . . . getting together, as it were. But it isn't. It's enjoyable for its own sake. It's rather wonderful, actually.'

They looked at one another and then laughed.

'Enough of that,' said Joan. 'Let's have some wedding talk. I've heard of some brides carrying a lace hanky instead of flowers.'

That made Mabel laugh. 'Over Mumsy's dead body.'

'I've never met your mother,' said Joan, 'but from everything you've said, I suppose the lace hanky idea wouldn't do the trick.'

'Especially not while she has roses in the garden,' agreed Mabel. 'I swear that when the lawns were dug up for vegetables, she preserved the rose bushes just in case of a wedding. Good old Mumsy.'

'What about the dress? Persephone popped round the other evening and she said that some girls who have had a London Season are now using their presentation dresses for their weddings.'

'Over *my* dead body,' Mabel retorted at once. 'What a thought! I loathed my London Season.'

'Persephone said there's a lady called Barbara Cartland who has gathered together a stash of wedding dresses to lend out on request – lend, mind you, not hire – so that brides in the forces can have their dream wedding.'

'What a gorgeous idea.' Mabel laughed. 'Maybe I should donate my presentation dress. I'd be glad to see the back of it. As for my wedding dress, Mumsy admitted after

I got engaged that she bought the fabric before the war, just in case.'

'She didn't!'

'She did. When everyone else was stockpiling toilet rolls and tinned salmon, she was rushing around all the draperies for miles around in search of the perfect material. And to give her her due, it is beautiful. White taffeta striped with silver.'

'It sounds lovely.'

'Mumsy's seamstress took all my measurements after Christmas and I'll have to go on a flying visit at some point to have a fitting.'

Joan sighed. 'I'm enjoying all this wedding talk.'

'It's not all nice, though,' said Mabel. 'I'm not going to be able to have all the bridesmaids I wanted. Persephone and Emily can't get the time off because of colleagues having already booked their leave in June.'

'That's a shame.'

'I've got Alison and Margaret, though – and you and Colette as matrons of honour.' Mabel bit her lip. 'Do you think Colette would prefer to be a bridesmaid? I mean, with her being separated.'

'Tricky,' said Joan. 'Why don't you ask her? Who else can and can't come?'

'Mrs Grayson can't, but that's not a surprise, of course. Mrs Cooper's coming. I told her I couldn't get married without her. Miss Brown was invited, but she had to refuse.'

'That's a shame. Is Mrs Mitchell coming?'

'Of course. She's family. Dot and Cordelia can't come, which is a huge shame.' Mabel made herself smile. 'But I'll have you, Colette, Margaret and Alison.'

'And Mrs Cooper and Mrs Mitchell.'

'I have to give Mumsy the final list. She's been after me for numbers, but I've been putting off telling her. Obviously she's sent out invitations and has been receiving replies, but of course people down here are telling me personally before they write to her. I know how daft this sounds, but when I talk to her about who's coming, that means the others definitely aren't.'

'Oh, Mabel,' said Joan. 'You know how much they'd love to be there.'

'I know they would. I'd love nothing better than to scoop up every single one of my precious friends and take all of you with me to my wedding.'

'I know.' Joan gave her a hug. 'It makes me realise how lucky I was to have all of you there at mine.'

'Your wedding was lovely,' said Mabel. 'Even the church hall getting flooded turned out for the best, because you got to have your reception in the station buffet.'

'It doesn't sound like anything special,' said Joan, 'but it was perfect. And you caught my bouquet, so I'm taking the credit for you and Harry getting married.'

That made Mabel laugh. 'Oh, you're the one to blame, are you?'

'The one who deserves all the credit, you mean,' Joan retorted. 'And I know it's disappointing that not everyone can come, but those of us who are there will make sure you have a wonderful time. Just wait and see.'

Persephone and Mr Franklin had taken to sitting tucked away in a relatively private and sheltered corner in Leeds Station to eat their midday meal together. Mrs Mitchell always provided Persephone with a flask of one of her delicious soups, along with a sandwich or a cold rissole. Mr Franklin always had a flask too, courtesy of his mum. The two of them had taken to sharing their meals, which felt very chummy.

'What have you got today?' Mr Franklin asked as they unscrewed their flasks.

'Chunky vegetable and chickpea.' Persephone sniffed it as she lifted off the top, feeling the heat touch her face.

'Mine's gravy soup,' Mr Franklin told her.

'I've never heard of that,' said Persephone.

'It's got leeks, carrots and tinned tomatoes in it.'

If Persephone's soup sounded more substantial, neither of them mentioned it – not out of self-consciousness, but because it honestly didn't matter. Being friends, getting along so well and so naturally, meant that they didn't judge one another's backgrounds – or the contents of one another's flasks.

'Did you go and see *Casablanca* with your friends?' Mr Franklin asked.

'Yes. It was wonderful. We're going to go again.'

'My sisters have been enthusing over the romance.'

'It's much more than a love story,' said Persephone, 'though that's an essential part of it, obviously. I'm sure you'd enjoy Humphrey Bogart in it.'

'He was very good in *High Sierra* and *The Maltese Falcon*. Did you know his middle name is DeForest?'

'I've never heard that name before.'

'One of my sisters read it in her film magazine. So you see, you aren't the only one with a highfalutin name,' Mr Franklin added with a chuckle.

Seeing she had emptied her cup of soup, he took the empty cup from her and topped it up with soup from his own flask. Persephone poured some chunky veg and chickpea into his cup.

'This is good,' he commented.

'I can get the recipe for your mum, if you think she'd like it.'

'I'm sure she would. She's always on the lookout for new ideas. She reckons the secret to cooking in wartime is finding new ways of serving up the same old things.'

'And making meals look attractive on the plate, too,' said Persephone. Both Mrs Mitchell and Mrs Grayson did this.

'You mean not just flinging the mash on from a distance?'

They laughed. There was a server in the station canteen who was famous for doing precisely that.

When the soup was finished, they split their sandwiches without having to ask. Persephone's were herring and horseradish and Mr Franklin had shrimp paste.

'What sort of a morning did you have?' he asked her.

Persephone grinned. 'Crowded. Or should I say overcrowded? By the time we were halfway, I could barely manage to get from one end of the train to the other.'

'Our locos have to work jolly hard these days.'

'So do our engine drivers and firemen,' said Persephone. 'I know what long hours you put in.'

Mr Franklin shrugged. 'It has to be done. There's a war to be won.'

'Do you mind working on passenger trains?' Persephone asked. 'Would you prefer troop or munitions trains?'

'To feel more like I'm helping to win the war, you mean? I'll work on whichever line and whichever train they put me on. I have driven munitions sometimes, as it happens, but providing passenger trains is essential too. As far as possible, people need to feel they can live normal lives. I know the government encourages folk to take their holidays at home, but having worked on the Blackpool train when it was crammed with families going to the seaside, including mums who were heading off to visit their evacuated kids for the first time since I don't know when, I can assure you that the atmosphere that day was in itself a huge morale booster.'

'And just think of those mothers and children being reunited,' Persephone added.

'So I'm perfectly happy on passenger trains,' said Mr Franklin, 'because in their own way, they contribute to winning the war.'

Persephone breathed a quiet sigh. She admired Mr Franklin as well as liked him. It felt good to have a friend to be proud of.

CHAPTER THIRTEEN

Persephone reined in her smiles, fearing that she might well be grinning like an idiot. Her eyesight had been blurred by tears when her sister stepped out of the taxi outside Darley Court. Fudge looked gorgeous, as always, and evidently the taxi driver had thought so too, if the expression on his face was anything to go by.

Persephone drew Fudge inside, the driver following with her suitcase. Miss Brown and Mrs Mitchell both appeared in the grand entrance hall. How good of them to form a welcoming committee. Taking Fudge's hand, she led her forward for introductions.

'May I introduce my sister, Mrs McLean Grey. Fudge, this is—'

'Fudge!' said Miss Brown and Mrs Mitchell in one voice.

'I know,' said Fudge. 'Ridiculous, isn't it? Almost as ridiculous as Iphigenia Clementina Honoria. Persephone couldn't say Iphigenia when she was a tot. She called me Fidge and that became Fudge.'

Persephone completed the introductions. 'This is Miss Brown, who owns Darley Court, and this is Mrs Mitchell, the housekeeper.'

'How do you do, Miss Brown? How kind of you to put me up. And Mrs Mitchell.' Fudge shook hands with them both. 'I've brought my ration book, so I'll hand it over. Persephone has told me what a splendid cook you are.'

'I see you have all the Trehearn-Hobbs charm,' Miss Brown said wryly.

140

Fudge smiled at her. 'Something tells me you're immune to it.'

Mrs Mitchell turned to Persephone. 'Would you like to show Mrs McLean Grey to her room?'

Fudge paid off the driver and Persephone led her upstairs. 'You're next to me – well, with a bathroom in between.'

It was the bedroom Colette had stayed in after she had left Tony. Persephone had been glad to think of providing her friend with a safe refuge after everything she had been through and all the secrets she had felt forced to keep, and she'd missed Colette when she left to return to the house in Seymour Grove. But now she'd have her sister instead, even if only for a few days. It felt like a huge treat. She hadn't seen Fudge in ages.

'Sweet room,' said Fudge, looking round at the beautiful walnut furniture that glowed almost golden with polish.

'I'm glad you were able to come,' said Persephone.

'I wouldn't miss your Wings for Victory dance for the world. We'll have a grand time together. And shall I tell you what will make it even grander?'

'What?' Persephone asked, ready to agree to anything.

'Let's drop the Fudge, shall we?'

'Oh. I thought you liked it.'

'I do, darling, but not so much now that you're grown-up.'

'Iphigenia it is, then, though it'll take a bit of getting used to.'

Or maybe not. With her blue-grey eyes and her silvery-blonde hair, she looked far more like an Iphigenia than a Fudge.

'After all,' said Iphigenia, 'I know you asked the boys to stop calling you Percy.'

'I did,' said Persephone, 'but that's because it turned out to be an insult from the Great War. Fudge was a nursery name.'

'And very lovely it was too in its day,' said Iphigenia. 'When you have children, you can make them roar with laughter at it, but for the time being I'd like to be – well, actually, I'd like to be Lorna or Caroline or Lavinia, but unfortunately I'm stuck with Iphigenia. But at least it's an improvement on Fudge,' she added, wagging a slender finger at Persephone. 'But I shan't mind being Auntie Fudge to your children. Aunt Iphigenia makes me sound a hundred years old.'

Persephone unlocked the suitcase and started to take out her sister's clothes.

Iphigenia half laughed, half groaned. 'You've no idea what a temptation it is to throw myself on the bed, lie back and leave you to get on with it. One is permitted either a cook or a lady's maid these days, but not both, so I opted for the cook.'

Persephone dug out a slipper and threw it at her. 'Come and help, you lazy beggar. Oh, what a lovely dress.'

Carefully she drew out and held up a dusty-pink silk gown with a fitted bodice, short sleeves and a flared, full-length skirt.

'That's my dress for your Wings for Victory dance,' said Iphigenia. 'There's a little headdress of tiny pink wax flowers that's worn on the side of the head. It's wrapped up in tissue.'

Persephone found a tissue-wrapped item. Opening it, she burst out laughing. 'This will look very glamorous worn on the side of the head.' She held the jar of Bovril above her own ear and struck a pose.

'A little gift for my hostess,' said Iphigenia. 'I've brought some dainty muslin bags of potpourri as well, though having met Miss Brown, I'm not sure she's a potpourri kind of person.'

Persephone removed some farming periodicals from the bottom of the case. 'She'll appreciate these.'

They finished putting the clothes away and Iphigenia took her sponge bag into the bathroom.

'What's on the cards for tonight?' she asked.

'Dancing at the Ritz,' said Persephone. 'We're going with some chums of mine. Before that, though, would you mind if we dropped in at the Claremont?'

'That's where you're holding your dance, isn't it?'

'Yes. Mabel will meet us there. She's the other organiser. We want to go through all the details with the manager.'

'Suits me.'

Persephone spent the afternoon showing her sister around the house and grounds, introducing her to the land girls and other staff. They chatted and caught up on family news as they went.

'I'm looking forward to meeting the friends you're always mentioning in your letters,' said Iphigenia. 'Who's going to be at the Ritz this evening?'

'Mabel – you'll meet her at the Claremont first. Then there'll be Margaret and Alison and Alison's boyfriend, Joel. He's a doctor.'

'Engaged?'

'No.'

'I'm only checking so I don't put my foot in it. So many couples are engaged nowadays.'

'Joan won't be there. She'll be at home with her family. And Colette won't be there either.'

'She's the one who left her violent husband.'

'That's it. She comes to the flicks sometimes, but she doesn't come out dancing, though she'll come to the Wings for Victory dance because it's a special occasion for the war effort.'

'And you mentioned a girl called Emily,' said Iphigenia.

'She won't be there tonight. This is a fire-watching night for her, though I imagine she wouldn't come anyhow. She's busy nursing a broken heart.'

'Poor kid.'

'Yes,' said Persephone, 'though she loves her new job as a porter on Victoria Station and that's given her a bit of a lift.'

Oh yes, it was amazing how a new job could give you a much-needed boost when you were feeling blue. Persephone had felt utterly crushed after seeing Forbes in hospital, but her new job had been a tonic that had helped her through. It hadn't taken away the emotional bleakness, but it had kept her busy and interested; it had provided challenge. Without it, the ache in her chest would have been much harder to bear.

After discussing the forthcoming Wings for Victory dance with the manager at the Claremont, Persephone, Mabel and Iphigenia went to the Ritz Ballroom, blinking to adjust their eyes as they left behind the pitch-darkness of the blackout and entered the glittering, magical world of music and dancing. After queueing for a minute or two to hand in their coats, they entered the ballroom and Persephone was aware of her sister looking all around, taking in the pillars and art deco features, as well as the balcony where some people chose to sit at tables and watch the dancers below.

'The stage revolves,' Persephone told her. 'There'll be another band on the other side and both bands play the same piece of music as it goes round, so the dancing never pauses.'

The ballroom was packed, which came as no surprise.

'There's Alison,' said Mabel and they threaded their way around the edge of the ballroom towards the table where Alison and Joel were sitting.

Persephone performed the introductions, then Alison stood up.

'No offence, but Joel and I can go and have a twirl now that you've arrived. Margaret and I have been taking turns to guard the table – well, not so much the table. People don't tend to bag tables that are clearly in use, but they do walk off with chairs.'

Iphigenia sat down. 'I'm an old married lady, so you two must dance every dance.'

Persephone laughed. 'Are you our chaperone?'

'Not a bit of it. I'll chaperone the table and make sure no one tries to make off with any of our seats.'

'I'm nearly an old married lady,' said Mabel. 'Does that mean I shouldn't dance?'

'It means, my love,' said Iphigenia, 'that you wave your beautiful engagement ring around and dance your socks off in perfect safety. If anyone gets a bit frisky, cut him dead and leave him standing.'

'Goodness,' said Mabel. 'Are you related to the person who wrote my mother's etiquette book?'

A fellow in uniform approached their table and asked Iphigenia for the pleasure.

She declined with a smile. 'But my sister would love to.'

Before she knew it, Persephone was slow-slow-quick-quick-slowing into the mass of dancers. She had several dances with various strangers and then the crowd parted for a moment and she glimpsed Mr Franklin. Had he seen her? Might he ask her to dance? She'd like that. One of the reasons she had loved her London Seasons so much was that she'd known so many young men and it had been fun dancing with them. Here, in a public ballroom, one inevitably danced with strangers.

A while later, when she was sitting at the table with Iphigenia and Margaret, she looked up to find Mr Franklin standing there, smiling down at her.

'Would you like to dance?' he asked and there was something appealingly shy in his manner.

'Thank you.'

Accompanying him onto the floor, she went into his arms for the foxtrot.

'It's a surprise to see you here,' she told him.

'A good one, I hope.'

'Yes. I was thinking earlier on that it's always a pleasure to dance with a friend instead of a stranger.'

'I'm glad you think of us as friends. I think so too.'

'You're a good dancer, Mr Franklin,' said Persephone. 'Would you think it forward of me to ask your first name? After all, we've established that we're friends – and we do share our sandwiches,' she added with a laugh.

'I'm Matthew – Matt,' he told her.

'And I'm Persephone.'

'Persephone,' Matt repeated. 'You mentioned it when you told me about your pen name.'

'It's a bit of a mouthful.'

'A very beautiful mouthful.'

'Thank you, kind sir.'

When the dance ended, Matt took Persephone back to her table, though he didn't hang about waiting for introductions. A touch of that shyness she had sensed earlier?

Persephone took the seat next to Mabel, who leaned towards her. 'Just think. Next time we're dancing, it'll be at our Wings for Victory dance. Won't that be something? Best of all, I'll have Harry with me.'

Mabel's eyes sparkled with joy and Persephone couldn't suppress a pang of envy. How lucky Mabel was – and Alison – and Joan. Persephone was never going to find happiness like that. She didn't even have her dreams of Forbes any longer.

*

'When I had my first Season,' said Iphigenia, walking through from the shared bathroom into Persephone's room as they got ready for the Wings for Victory dance, 'Ma watched me like a hawk. But when I had my second, she let me off the leash a bit, though I had strict curfews and when I got home, I had to open Ma's bedroom door and slip my dancing shoes inside as proof that I was back.'

'Yes, I had to do that too.'

'Ah, but did you have a second pair of dancing shoes, little sister? I did and I used to sneak out again.'

Persephone laughed. 'I had no idea you were so wicked.'

'I'm a reformed character now. Fasten this for me, will you?'

She held out a dreamy blue aquamarine on a silver chain, turning her back and lifting her hair for Persephone to fiddle with the dainty clasp. Iphigenia wore her dusty-pink silk dress with the rather darling little hair-ornament of tiny matching wax flowers. Persephone was in a lilac dress with a close-fitting, ruched bodice that went down to her slim hips, from where it flared and flowed almost to the floor.

'You don't mind having to go early, do you?' she asked.

'Of course not. You have to be there to keep an eye on everything. I hope you're going to have time to enjoy yourself as well.'

'I hope so too, but it's more important that everything goes smoothly.'

'You know what Ma would say. Everything must run like clockwork, but if it doesn't, the more frantic you feel, the most composed you should appear.'

'Have you got your corsage?' asked Persephone.

They each had a white carnation surrounded by curling red and blue ribbons. Persephone had a box of them for her friends, which she carried carefully to the waiting taxi.

In these days of shortages and making do, the Wings for Victory occasion was in some ways a repeat of the War Weapons Week dance Cordelia had organised. Outside the Claremont, the front steps were protected by the same dark blue awning, its underneath decorated with silver stars. Inside, across the lofty, pillared foyer, the ballroom's double doors were surrounded by an archway of rosettes in red, white and blue. There was even a table over to one side of the foyer where, just like last time, Mrs Cooper was ready to sell raffle tickets. Beside her sat Colette.

'Are you sure you're happy to spend the evening out here, you two?' asked Persephone.

'No, we've changed our minds,' said Mrs Cooper. 'You plonk yourself here at the table, Miss Persephone, and Colette and me will go and dance the night away. Of course we don't mind. We wouldn't have offered if we did, would we?'

Mabel arrived, looking radiant on Harry's arm. He was as handsome as ever in his RAF uniform.

'Honestly,' Persephone whispered to Mrs Cooper and Colette, 'we could sell tickets to dance with Harry and all the lady guests would queue up round the block to buy them.'

'I think our Mabel would have something to say about that,' said Mrs Cooper.

Alison and Joel came over.

'Would you like to come with us and we'll find our table?' Alison asked Iphigenia. 'I'm sure Persephone has lots of last-minute things she wants to check. We've got two big tables next to one another for all our friends and their partners and families.'

Persephone smiled to herself. That was the same as Cordelia's War Weapons Week dance as well. All they needed now was for tonight to be as big a success as Cordelia's dance had been and that would be splendid.

Everything went well. Persephone and Mabel circulated, keeping an eye on things.

'You ought to spend this evening with Harry,' Persephone instructed Mabel after the first hour. 'You see so little of one another.'

'But that's not fair on you,' said Mabel.

'It's entirely fair on me because it'll stop me feeling guilty,' said Persephone. 'Now be off with you and claim your dashing fiancé.'

Mabel didn't need telling again. Glowing with happiness, she hurried away.

Persephone watched with pleasure as people went to a table beside the stage to request favourite pieces of music, paying for the privilege. The gentlemen also had to pay each time they wanted to dance with a lady in the gentlemen's excuseme. As well as the ideas that Persephone and Mabel had shamelessly copied from Cordelia's fundraising dance, there was also a game of penny on the drum, which people were familiar with from the wireless. A drum was placed in the centre of the dance floor and players had to guess the titles of popular tunes from clues. Giving a wrong answer meant putting a penny on the drum. Persephone was delighted that everyone put on rather more than a penny to pay for their mistakes, and those who had given the right answers celebrated by pulling their own coins on the drum too.

'Darling, it's nearly midnight,' said Iphigenia when Persephone sat down beside her. 'It's high time you relaxed and had a dance or two before you turn into a pumpkin.'

She was right. Persephone gladly accepted several offers to dance – including one from Matt.

'I didn't know you were here,' she said.

'On the other hand, I *did* know *you* were,' Matt replied. 'I've seen you flitting here, there and everywhere.'

'That's because I'm one of the organisers.'

'Really? Congratulations. It's a first-rate occasion.'

'Thank you.' It felt good to receive an honest compliment from a friend.

At the close of the song, dancers all around them broke ballroom hold and clapped. Matt thanked her for the dance and escorted Persephone back to her seat. The group's two tables were both empty.

'Would you like me to stay with you until your friends come back?' Matt offered.

'Sweet of you, but no thanks.'

Some girls felt awkward and self-conscious sitting alone, but Persephone wasn't one of them. Matt disappeared into the crowd just as some of the others returned to their places. Iphigenia was escorted to her place by an older gentleman with a craggy face and a row of campaign medals from the Great War.

Sitting beside Persephone, Iphigenia watched Matt disappear. 'Who was that you were dancing with? No uniform. Is he in a reserved occupation?'

'He's a fireman,' Persephone told her.

'Brave fellows, firemen.'

'He's not the sort of fireman you're thinking of. He works on the railways. I met him at work, actually.'

'Well, he's good-looking. Nice smile. A good dancer too.'

'Yes, he's a very good dancer,' Persephone agreed.

'He scrubs up well, your fireman.'

'He's not *my* fireman. He's just a colleague.'

'Not yours?' Iphigenia gave a tiny shrug. 'I'm tempted to say "More fool you", my love.'

'Does that mean what I think it means?' Persephone asked in surprise. 'You're suggesting I might go out with him?'

'It's wartime, darling. The usual rules don't apply.'

'Anyway, I like him, yes, but not in that way. If you must know . . .' Persephone's heart started to beat more quickly ' . . . there's someone else, but *he* doesn't like *me* in that way.'

'Then stop thinking about him,' Iphigenia said at once. 'Easier said than done, I know, but what better way to get over a broken heart than by having a fling with a handsome fireman?'

'Fudge, don't – I mean, Iphigenia. I'm being serious.'

'As am I, poppet. Have some fun. Let your heart mend.'

'And then?'

'What d'you mean, and then? This is wartime. You said yourself one should make the most of every moment. Why not let your fireman help you feel better about yourself? Where's the harm? He'll enjoy it too.'

'But what about afterwards? After the war?'

Iphigenia laughed. 'Don't be an idiot. I'm not suggesting you marry him, for pity's sake. Sweetie, I know girls who are going through men like a dose of salts, but after the war, they'll know exactly whom to marry and live happily ever after with. We all know whom we can and can't marry. War doesn't change that. It's just that before marriage comes along, the war has given all you single girls this marvellous opportunity to enjoy yourselves. What's wrong with that? Grab it with both hands, little sister, that's what I say. You'll have years and years to be a respectable married lady afterwards. And I promise not to tell tales on you.'

CHAPTER FOURTEEN

At the end of her shift, Emily put her nut-brown coat on over her uniform and exchanged her porter's peaked cap for her felt hat, ready to meet up with the others in the buffet. She felt more than a little awkward about going. It was embarrassing and shameful to think of the frightful mistake she had made in accepting the purloined tea from Mr Buckley. By spending time with her friends and pretending everything was normal, she would be sullying their friendship. Ought she to cry off? But then she'd be asked why, and even if she could evade questions from the group in general, it wasn't as though she would be able to escape Mummy's questions at home. Besides, she wanted to be in her friends' company. Even though being with them made her aware of how stupid she'd been, she also felt the combined strength that emanated from the group and there was comfort of a sort in that. Then again, what would they think of her if they knew? What would her parents think?

'What have you been up to today, Emily?' asked Margaret.

For half a moment, Emily panicked. Up to? Did that mean . . .? No, of course it didn't. It was just a turn of phrase.

'I've been on the station all day,' she said.

'Which do you prefer?' asked Mabel. 'The station or the back-room stuff, emptying the supplies trains and so forth?'

'The station,' Emily said at once and she must have sounded emphatic because the rest of them laughed. 'I like helping the passengers,' she added, feeling the need to explain.

'I expect getting tips is nice too,' said Alison in a jokey voice.

'I put all mine in Brizo's collecting box,' said Emily. 'I know there are some porters who really appreciate the tips because their personal circumstances are a bit stretched, but it's not like that for me, so I like to do some good with mine.'

'And you get to give Brizo a hug every time, don't you?' her mother added, making her sound about five years old.

'I'm not surprised you enjoy being on the station,' said Colette. 'Being with other people is always interesting and the time flies.'

Emily made herself smile. Colette was right on both counts, but the real reason Emily preferred working on the concourse and the platforms was because she felt safe there. Yes, safe. Who could say what might happen if she had to venture into the stores again? She'd had to go back in there a few days ago and she couldn't get out fast enough.

Then, later, Mr Buckley had asked her, 'What happened to you earlier on, eh, Emily? You missed out on some dried fruit. I bet your mum would have liked that.'

That had allowed Emily to say, 'Do you . . . do the porters often, um . . .?'

'Help themselves to a bit here and a bit there?'

'Well, yes.'

'Don't fret about it, my lass. It's always gone on.'

Emily had wanted to say, 'That doesn't make it right,' but the words had stuck in her throat. She wanted to say, 'It isn't "helping themselves". It's . . .' But even if she'd been able to force the words out, she wouldn't have known what to call it. Pilfering? That didn't sound as bad as stealing, the same way that scrumping didn't either, but in her heart she knew that stealing was the real word.

She still went hot and cold when she thought of the tea she'd been given. She had been utterly stumped as to what she should do with it. At last, after much agonising, she'd added it to the tea caddy at home, but then, seeing how much fuller the caddy looked, she'd tipped some out.

'How strange,' Mummy had frowned when she next opened the caddy. 'I didn't think we'd got this much left.'

'You haven't been buying on the black market, have you?' Daddy said in a joking voice.

'Certainly not. Don't say it even in jest.'

And Daddy had put his arms around Mummy and held her to him. They had been affectionate towards one another recently. They had never been lovey-dovey before, but now Emily sometimes saw a look or a smile pass between them. At other times, it showed itself in a humorous way of speaking to one another. The old, formal atmosphere in the house had relaxed. Mostly Emily liked the new order of things, but there were times when it hit her hard and made her feel even more dumped than usual.

Oddly, the problem of the pilfering had to an extent taken her mind off Raymond, because dwelling on her bruised heart felt like a cowardly way of trying to avoid facing up to the situation at work and the part she had played in it. She had been so fond of Mr Buckley before this; she had looked up to him. She was still fond of him, which in itself came as a revelation. She hadn't realised previously that you could carry on caring about somebody who had done wrong, but evidently you could. On one occasion, Emily listened to a conversation between Mabel and Mrs Green – Dot – in the buffet, about a girl called Louise who used to work on the railways. Emily soon gathered that Louise's father had been a rogue, and a violent one at that, yet Louise had never stopped loving him.

And Emily *was* fond of Mr Buckley, who had been very good to her. He had lost both his wife and his son. Not only that, but he'd told her his son had been an only child. The last thing Emily wanted was to get dear Mr Buckley into any kind of trouble, yet how could she turn a blind eye? She was a railway employee and she had a duty. She was also a solicitor's daughter and what would her father say? But if 'everyone' was doing it, how could she possibly object? Whenever she passed another porter in the station, she asked herself every single time, 'Is he part of the pilfering gang? . . . Does she accept goods from sacks that have split open accidentally on purpose?' It was horrid to have these thoughts and at times her cheeks burned with shame.

'A packet of twenty has gone up to one and nine,' said one of the porters as he lit up a cigarette to have with his tea.

'Extortionate,' agreed another, blowing a stream of smoke into the air.

Did that mean a crate of cigarettes would get 'dropped' from a height in the stores?

'Tinned peas and tinned tomatoes are both points rationed now,' said Mummy when she arrived home from the shops.

Did that mean these items would also find their way into pockets and bags in the stores?

If only she hadn't accepted that tea! But even if she'd had the presence of mind to refuse it, she'd still be in a pickle now, agonising over what to do for the best. It wasn't just that she'd accepted the tea, it was that she'd let time slip past without doing anything.

What a coward she was. She still loved Raymond with all her heart, but he was undoubtedly better off without her.

Mabel and her bridal attendants sat together in Mrs Cooper's front room, eating toast on the hearthrug.

'I'm going to do the same as Joan and ask you to choose a nice dress for the wedding,' said Mabel.

'Do you want us to wear something different to what we wore for Joan?' asked Alison.

'It's up to you,' said Mabel, knowing full well that Margaret possessed only one really good dress, which Joan, a former seamstress, had originally made for her own late sister.

Joan laughed. 'I take it you'd prefer me to wear something different to what I wore at my wedding.'

Mabel laughed too. 'You're not allowed to compete with the bride.'

'I found some pretty rose-pink material at the market,' said Joan, 'so I'll make myself a dress out of that. If anyone wants to buy some fabric, I'll be happy to make dresses for them.'

'That's decent of you,' said Alison. 'I might take you up on that.'

'What about you, Colette?' asked Margaret. 'Shall you wear the same as last time or something different?'

'You wore that lovely blue dress,' said Mabel, 'but we'll all understand if you'd prefer to choose something else.' Really and truly, it was because of Colette that she had decided to give her friends the choice. If it hadn't been for that, she would have loved them to wear what they'd worn to Joan's wedding.

'Actually, I'd like to wear the blue dress,' Colette said after a moment or two. 'I love its bluebell colour and I'd like to have the chance to enjoy wearing it without the worry of what might be said and how I might be made to feel. Tony . . . well, I never knew whether I was going to get a compliment or a criticism. Everything he said mattered so much. I teetered along a tightrope all the time, trying to please him.' She glanced at Mabel. 'I'm sorry. This isn't the kind of thing you want to hear when we're discussing your wedding.'

'Yes, it is,' Mabel replied at once. 'I care about anything that affects my friends. Please do wear your bluebell dress, Colette. I remember how lovely you looked each time I've seen you in it.'

'Wear it as your matron of honour dress,' said Alison, 'so you can start having happy memories of it.'

That reminded Mabel. 'There's something I wanted to ask you, Colette. I automatically asked you to be a matron of honour because you're married, but I'd understand if you would prefer to be a bridesmaid.' Seeing Colette's eyes brighten under a sheen of tears, she added quickly, 'I'm sorry. The last thing I want to do is upset you.'

'You haven't,' said Colette. 'I'm just touched, that's all. It's kind of you to think of it.'

'It doesn't matter which you are,' said Mabel. 'What matters is that you're there.'

'I'll stay as a matron of honour, if you don't mind,' said Colette. 'Not because I consider my marriage to Tony to be something I'm going to resume after the war.' She shivered. 'Absolutely not. But I've had time to think about things since Tony went and I've decided to carry on being Mrs Naylor. I know there would be gossip and bad feeling if I went back to being Miss Davis, especially without being divorced. It might be cowardly, but it's easier to carry on being known as Mrs Naylor.'

'It's not cowardly,' her friends exclaimed at once.

'Anyway,' Colette added with a smile, 'if I'm Mrs, I get to walk immediately behind the bride while you poor single girls trail in our wake.'

That lifted the serious tone and they all laughed.

Mabel felt warm inside. Yes, it was disappointing that not all her friends could attend her wedding, but the ones who would be there were going to add to how special it was.

CHAPTER FIFTEEN

Now that the Wings for Victory Week was over, and Mabel and Persephone had written all their thank-you letters to the many people who had helped them in their endeavours, Mabel was determined to make headway with the Extension. She intended to go over Miss Brewster's head and prove to the Corporation that her project was viable. Harry's voice popped into her mind, saying 'You'll come up with a way to trounce her,' and this was it. She would begin by amassing detailed quotes for the work that was needed. That would lend authority to her plan and, she sincerely hoped, make the powers that be in the Corporation listen to her and not just to Miss Brewster.

When she was on first-aid duty at St Cuthbert's, Mabel took advice from some of the Heavy Rescue men and then arranged to take a general builder to look at the place and discuss the work that was needed to bring it up to scratch.

The builder, Mr Tennant, met her outside the estate agency.

'I'll pop into the tobacconist's and get some ciggies while you fetch the key,' he said.

Both of the Mr Hayters were out of their office and their secretary, Mrs Rushton, was on the telephone. Mabel knew by now where the keys were and with a polite wave to Mrs Rushton, she took the Extension key from its hook on the board. Mrs Rushton, still engaged in her conversation, waggled her fingers at Mabel, who smiled back and quickly made a note on the pad under the board. *Extension. M Bradshaw.*

Mabel took Mr Tennant along High Lane. Her spirits were buoyant. She was certain she could get the Corporation to take her project seriously. Yes, the building needed work, but it had the makings of a fine nursery, she was sure. A big room for playing, learning and eating, and another of equal size for resting or quiet activities.

When they got there, the door was already unlocked, which came as a surprise. Mabel pushed it open and led the way. Entering the lobby, she heard voices in the first of the big rooms. She walked in – and stopped in her tracks.

'Miss Brewster!' she exclaimed. 'What are you doing here?'

Miss Brewster turned round, as did the two men she was with. Miss Brewster breathed in sharply, which made her nostrils flare.

'Miss Bradshaw, how very . . . unexpected.'

Mabel felt stumped. Was this what Mrs Rushton had meant by that wave? Not that Mabel must sign for the key, but that she should hang on for the end of the telephone call and be warned of what to expect?

'What brings you here?' Miss Brewster enquired. 'Oh yes, I see you have Mr Tennant with you.' She shook her head, then turned to her companions. 'This won't take a minute.' To Mr Tennant she said, 'I fear that Miss Bradshaw has dragged you here under false pretences, Mr Tennant. She has no authority over these premises. As you can see for yourself, I, a Corporation official, am here with Mr Grimshaw and Mr Cummings.'

'Why?' Mabel demanded.

Miss Brewster's glance skimmed over her in a way that was positively insulting. 'What a shame, Mr Tennant, having your valuable time wasted in this manner. Is that a key

I see in your hand, Miss Bradshaw? Perhaps you would like to give it to me so that you aren't tempted to act in such an inappropriate way again.'

'Certainly not,' said Mabel, but Miss Brewster wasn't listening to her.

'Gentlemen, shall we spare the girl's blushes? Perhaps you would kindly step outside for a minute while I explain matters to her – and you can be on your way, Mr Tennant. You shan't be needed.'

'Yes, you shall,' Mabel said at once. 'As for sparing my blushes, you needn't bother. I'm quite happy to have this conversation in public. The Corporation is well aware of my wish to investigate the suitability of this building as premises for a nursery and I'm entitled to be here.'

Miss Brewster smiled the tiniest of smiles, conveying condescension and amusement. 'Dear me. "Entitled", she says. Yes, Miss Bradshaw, the Corporation is aware of your interest, amateurish as it is, but as I took pains to explain to you on a previous occasion, this building is not going to be a nursery. I thought I had made myself clear, but apparently not.'

'You made yourself very clear,' Mabel replied, fighting to maintain a civil tone.

'I thought so. Then you shouldn't be here, should you?'

'Are you telling me that the Corporation has rejected my idea for the Extension once and for all?'

'Naturally, my advice carries weight.'

'And your advice was to have a new Scout hut here?'

'Scouts do war work, you know. They can use this front room for their regular meetings and activities and the back room for storing all the things they collect for salvage.'

'They must collect an awful lot of salvage if they're going to fill that room,' Mabel said drily.

Miss Brewster lifted her chin. 'I don't care for your tone, young lady.'

Much as she wanted to retort 'Hard cheese,' good manners forced Mabel to say, 'I'm sorry. I didn't mean to be rude.'

The men's tight expressions said they weren't impressed by her sarcastic remark and her apology didn't entirely mollify them. They probably thought her a brash young woman who didn't care how she spoke to her elders. She couldn't afford to alienate the local builders. Was it time to back down? Much as it rankled, Miss Brewster had clearly won the day. There would be another building for her nursery – oh, but never one as perfect as this. Never mind the work it required; it had captured Mabel's imagination and her heart.

Time to let go, she told herself.

'I think I'd better get in touch with the Corporation again, but I'll make an appointment to call in this time instead of just telephoning.'

'No, don't do that,' said Miss Brewster.

'But I'll be able to have a thorough discussion in person,' said Mabel. 'That isn't really possible on the telephone.'

'Even so, I don't see the need.'

'I've learned a lot through seeing the Extension,' Mabel persisted. 'It's helped me shape my ideas. I wouldn't be wasting anybody's time at the Corporation, if that's what you're worried about.'

'I'm sure you wouldn't,' said Miss Brewster, 'but if I might make a suggestion, why don't you and I meet again next week and put together a list of requirements for the premises you seek.'

'That's a handsome offer, Miss Brewster,' put in Mr Cummings.

Miss Brewster bowed her head graciously. 'What do you say, Miss Bradshaw? There's really no need for ill-feeling. I can be of great assistance to you.'

What could Mabel do but agree? It felt odd, though, when she recalled how dead set against the nursery Miss Brewster had been. Or maybe Miss Brewster had accepted that Mabel was resolved to set up a nursery and it would be better to give advice than to leave a novice to her own devices? That must be it. But it was a great shame that Miss Brewster's change of heart didn't run to letting Mabel have the Extension.

As Mabel left, she couldn't help turning back for a last, lingering look at the building she had pinned her hopes on. She was due to telephone Pops this evening, as he expected regular updates in return for his agreement to fund the project, and she had started the day anticipating the excitement of telling him everything that Mr Tennant had said. Instead, she was right back where she had started.

'It's a rotten shame, Pops,' Mabel said that evening as she stood in the telephone box. 'Not that I'm an expert in these matters, but I truly felt that the Extension was exactly the right building. Anyway, at least I'm now going to get the benefit of Miss Brewster's experience, so at least there's that.'

'Yes, it's funny that she did such a complete turnaround,' said Pops.

'I know,' Mabel agreed. 'She hadn't got a good word to say about nurseries the last time I saw her, but now she's prepared to help me.'

'And what's your gut reaction to that?' asked Pops.

'What do you mean?'

'Exactly that. Does it feel right, Mabs? Did she seem sincere?'

'Sincere? Yes, I think so,' Mabel answered. 'She said there was no need for ill-feeling.'

'And you say this sudden wish to help you didn't happen until after you'd said you were going to go to the Corporation offices?'

'Yes. What difference does that make?'

'What did you feel when she made this offer?'

'I thought—'

'Not what did you *think*, Mabs. How did you *feel*? Gut reaction.'

'Well, I was surprised, obviously.' Mabel considered. 'It felt . . . strange.'

'That was your instinct talking, and mine says the same. I wonder if she was trying to stop you going to the Corporation. I think you need to get down those Corporation offices right away. Always listen to your instincts, Mabs.'

It might be less then good-mannered not to make an appointment, but Mabel decided it was worth it. If Pops was right, and there was some reason why Miss Brewster wanted to keep her away from the Corporation, then she didn't want to risk Miss Brewster finding out that she was expected. Not having an appointment meant she had to sit for ages in a waiting room, but she was determined not to leave until she'd had the chance to speak to somebody, even though she wasn't entirely sure what she needed to speak to them about.

At last a young clerk with a Dorothy Lamour hairstyle came and perched beside her on the next chair. 'I'm sorry you've been kept waiting, but you're meant to make an appointment. If you could give me some details, I can find the right person to help you.'

'My name is Mabel Bradshaw and I telephoned the Corporation a while ago to discuss the possibility of my funding and setting up a new nursery in Chorlton.'

'On-Medlock or cum-Hardy?'

'Chorlton-cum-Hardy. I found what I thought could be appropriate premises, but that now appears to have fallen through, so I'm here to ask for advice.'

'Wait here, please, and I'll fetch your paperwork.' The clerk disappeared but soon returned. She held a sheet of paper against her chest as if determined to keep it from Mabel. 'Somebody should have been in touch with you before now, Miss Bradshaw.'

'Yes, they have.' Mabel's heart sank. She'd been hoping not to have to mention Miss Brewster's name. 'Miss Brewster,' she said, at the same moment that the clerk said, 'Miss Brewer.'

'No – Miss Brew*ster*,' said Mabel.

The clerk glanced down at the sheet. 'Wait here, please.'

She vanished again and this time there was a protracted wait, then the door opened and this time in walked a young woman a few years older than Mabel, with striking good looks. Her hair, which she wore scooped away from her fine-boned face and smoothed into a plump victory roll at the nape of her neck, was a gorgeous deep red and her eyes were hazel.

'Mabel Bradshaw?' she asked, coming forward and thrusting out a hand. 'I'm Fay Brewer.'

'I remember now,' said Mabel. 'I was expecting a Miss Brewer to come to the Extension, but Miss Brewster came instead. I thought I'd heard the name wrong on the telephone.' She shook hands warmly.

'No, there's been a ghastly mix-up, I'm afraid. Someone gave your details to Miss Brewster in error.' Fay Brewer pulled a face. 'I shouldn't call it "ghastly", should I? That's dreadfully disrespectful to Miss Brewster.'

On the contrary, it seemed precisely the right word, but Mabel forbore saying so. Instead, she beamed at Miss Brewer.

'Come through to the office. It's a bit cramped, but we make do. This way.'

Mabel followed Fay Brewer into what would have felt a spacious room if it hadn't been so full of desks and cupboards. All the other desks were arranged in such a way that the people at them sat with their backs to the wall, but Fay Brewer headed for a desk the other way round, so that when she grabbed an empty chair from another desk and set it down for Mabel, she could turn her own chair around and they faced one another in a comfortable, confiding sort of way.

'I can't imagine Miss Brewster sitting like this with a member of the public,' Mabel couldn't help remarking.

'I prefer it this way,' said Miss Brewer. 'My mother has written for a women's magazine for years and she's interviewed plenty of people. She says you shouldn't have a barrier, not even something as ordinary as a desk, between you and the person you're talking to. And people speak to her pretty freely, so it shows she's right.' Sitting sideways to her desk, Fay Brewer crossed one knee over the other and pulled a sheet of paper towards her across the blotter; Mabel recognised the paper the clerk had held earlier. 'You're interested in setting up a nursery, I gather? I've got the provisional application here.'

'I didn't put in an application, provisional or otherwise,' Mabel said, puzzled. 'I only made a telephone call to discuss it.'

'Well, someone in the office filled in the paperwork on your behalf.' Miss Brewer scanned the sheet of paper. 'You spoke to Mrs Eckersley on the telephone, is that right?'

'Yes, she was most helpful.'

Miss Brewer smiled. 'So helpful, in fact, that she wrote out a provisional application on your behalf.'

'I wasn't aware of that.'

'It means your proposed nursery is already in the system,' Miss Brewer told her, 'which makes things simpler. Less red tape. It's a good job you came here today to talk about it, because your application is due to lapse the day after tomorrow.'

Mabel's senses went on full alert. 'Really?'

'Provisional applications only last a certain amount of time, for obvious reasons.'

'Miss Brewster suggested that I meet her next week to discuss how I can set up a nursery.'

'You must do what you deem best, Miss Bradshaw,' said Fay Brewer in a neutral, professional voice, 'but I must warn you that if you wait to do that, then your provisional application will vanish in the meantime.'

Which Miss Brewster was perfectly well aware of – and indeed was what she had intended. She wanted Mabel's provisional application to fall by the wayside so that she could step in to have the Extension for the Scouts. What a sneaky plan. No wonder she had suddenly turned all helpful when Mabel said she would go to the Corporation in person. *Thank you, Pops!*

'You say your chosen premises might have fallen through,' Miss Brewer prompted.

'I'm not so sure about that now,' said Mabel. 'I'm prepared to put in a formal application quickly, but I still need advice and costings beforehand.'

Fay Brewer reached across her desk for a diary, its open pages covered in writing. 'Then I'd better come and see your proposed building as soon as possible.'

CHAPTER SIXTEEN

Persephone's work rota had changed. What a relief not to be on the Manchester to Leeds run any longer. It would feel jolly awkward seeing Matt at the moment. Remembering what Iphigenia had said made her go all prickly with self-consciousness. Thank goodness Iphigenia had gone home – and without saying anything else ridiculous about Matt's potential as a fling to help Persephone get over her unrequited love. But her sister's absence didn't make it any easier for Persephone to face Matt. If she saw him, she wouldn't be able to think of anything other than what Iphigenia had said, and what if Matt realised she was uncomfortable and asked what she was thinking about? She couldn't put the pair of them in that position. Would it be best to forget all about him and the fledgling friendship that she'd been enjoying so much? Drat Iphigenia a thousand times over. Her saucy little dart of 'I promise not to tell tales on you' had made Persephone feel she was doing something wrong.

The trouble was that Iphigenia's startling suggestion of a wartime fling had made Persephone see her friendship with Matt through fresh eyes. As Iphigenia had pointed out, he could never be marriage material, but he was prime fling material. Was that the way others viewed their friendship? Persephone felt a tightening inside her chest. Were whispers even now going round about the Honourable ticket collector slumming it with a fireman from the lower ranks of life? She couldn't bear the thought of their honest relationship being sullied like that – but was it a reason to call a halt to the friendship that was rapidly coming to mean so much to her?

Maybe it was. She had been brought up on a diet of duty and responsibility and doing the right thing no matter what. She fully appreciated now, for the first time, how much the war had interfered with social rules. Look at her precious and deeply valued friendship with working-class Dot. That would never have happened in the old days. This new friendship with Matt would never have happened either. They would simply never have met. Even if by some extraordinary accident they had met, nothing would have come of it. Iphigenia had spoken of enjoying wartime flings and then marrying the right person after the war. That showed exactly how she saw Matt.

Persephone questioned whether she ought to take a step away from her new friendship. Was that the right thing to do? But she knew in her heart that this friendship was sound and honest and real. It hurt her to think that maybe others saw something grubby in it. Even so . . .

Oh, this was ridiculous. She was going round in circles. She tried not to dwell on it so much, but casting Matt from her mind was easier said than done. Working on the railways meant she had reminders every way she turned. She only had to see two locomotives working together to haul an extra-long line of carriages or goods wagons to make her remember what Matt had told her about the poorer quality of the fuel reducing the performance of locos. He'd also told her how engines often had to wait longer for maintenance work to be done.

Then there was the occasion when she was working on the night shift and she had walked into a carriage that was almost completely dark. The whole train was dark because of the dim blackout bulbs, but this carriage was even darker. It turned out that a group of revellers travelling together had removed every bulb in the carriage in order to try to fob her off with dud tickets. Naturally she'd had her torch with her, so they hadn't got away with it, and she was pleased with herself afterwards for the calm but decisive way in which she had dealt with the miscreants. But, of course, the incident brought Matt to mind, together with the moral support he'd given her on that other occasion. Recalling the idea they'd had of trapping the pinstriped men in the WC, Persephone couldn't help chuckling. What a lark that would have been.

She chided herself for having such thoughts, but couldn't prevent them from leaking through.

She had wanted a new job to help her stop thinking about Forbes and now here she was, plagued by thoughts of Matt. Two completely different cases, of course, one of unrequited love, the other a simple friendship. The new job had helped distract her from her hopeless feelings for Forbes, so she certainly didn't intend to wallow in thoughts of Matt. All it would take was a few more distractions, like going dancing or to the pictures.

Alfred Hitchcock's *Shadow of a Doubt* was on, and so was *In Which We Serve*, both of which she was keen to see. Alison and Margaret were too. Perhaps Emily would like to come with them. It would be nice to take the younger girl out a few times. It would help her feel part of their group. Might Emily like to go dancing with them, or would that be too painful a reminder of losing Raymond? As well as that, there was the land girls' party this weekend to celebrate one of their number officially becoming the future Mrs Hank Wainwright the Third.

'Honestly, it makes it sound as if Hank Wainwright has had two previous wives and she'll be number three,' said Miss Brown in her wry way, 'but don't tell her I said so.'

Persephone went dancing a couple of times with her friends – and she was right about Emily not wishing to join them.

As Persephone, Mabel, Margaret and Alison walked together across the Ritz's glittering ballroom and found a table beneath the balcony, Margaret asked, 'Does being here beside the dance floor make you wish you could be back at the Wings for Victory dance?'

Persephone and Mabel looked at one another and laughed.

'Nope,' said Mabel.

'It's lovely to be in a ballroom where someone else is in charge of everything,' said Persephone.

'The only thing I'd go back to that evening for,' said Mabel, 'is to have Harry with me as my partner.'

'It won't be long before you're together all the time.' Alison gave Mabel a nudge. 'Mrs Harry Knatchbull-to-be!'

'Don't wish it away,' said Margaret. 'We want to make the most of having you here with us until the last minute.'

They'd hardly had a chance to sit down before they started receiving requests for dances. Mabel made sure that every prospective partner spotted her engagement ring.

'You never know who's here to try and pick someone up and who's here because they love dancing,' she said.

A few dances later, when Persephone was escorted back to the table by a spotty young lad in uniform who looked like he should still be at school, she saw Matt approaching. Her breath caught as her mind flooded with everything Iphigenia had said, but then she smiled. Civil but not encouraging. That was the way. She still felt deeply conflicted about the best thing to do.

Matt smiled at her and his blue eyes crinkled at the edges. He was some years older than she was, she guessed. Well, he must be to be a fireman. He must have ten years on her.

'Would you like to dance?' he asked.

She wanted to say yes, but that might not be wise. Instead, she shook her head. 'I'm sorry. My next few are booked.'

'Oh. Well, that's hardly surprising when a girl has your looks. Maybe later?'

She couldn't say no to that, could she? She simply smiled and made a show of pretending to look behind him as if expecting her next partner to arrive. Now she really would have to carry on dancing. As Matt walked away, she caught the eye of a fellow she'd danced with before and moments later they were waltzing.

Persephone had never had a problem attracting partners and it was no trouble to make sure she stayed on the dance floor. She adored dancing, but not like this, not as a means of keeping away from somebody, especially Matt. Frankly, there was nobody here she would rather dance with. What a waste of a friendship.

Then a gentlemen's excuse-me was announced and there was a ripple of laughter around the room. Everyone loved an excuse-me. They were always fun. Persephone's first three partners were excused and then Matt tapped her current partner, an army man, on the shoulder.

'Excuse me.'

The soldier let go and Matt drew Persephone into a ballroom hold.

'It seems this is the only way I can have a dance with you,' he remarked.

For once in her well-bred, well-mannered life, Persephone was lost for words. Please don't let him have realised that she was avoiding him.

Matt executed some nifty footwork and avoided a chap who was approaching with a purposeful look in his eyes.

'Have I offended you?' he asked bluntly.

'Goodness, what a question.'

'Have I?' he repeated. 'I have the feeling you aren't keen to dance with me and I'd like to know why, so I can apologise if I've done something wrong.'

'You haven't done anything wrong,' Persephone assured him.

'Then why do I feel as if I have? Or am I being oversensitive? Only I thought we were friends – or at least that we were becoming friends. We seemed to have a lot in common – in spite of the differences in our backgrounds, I mean.'

'We did – we do.'

'Is that what the problem is? The social difference?' Matt asked. 'I'm sorry to press you, but I'd appreciate the truth. Is it that I'm not good enough? Someone pointed out your sister at the Wings for Victory dance. Did she object to you dancing with a lower-class railwayman? Did she warn you off?'

Warn her off? Oh, if only he knew!

Matt shifted his gaze away from hers. Embarrassment? Frustration? Then he looked straight into her eyes. 'I can see there's something. I wish you'd tell me. It's not like you to be tongue-tied. But if you can't bring yourself to say the social difference is too great, I suppose I can understand that. You're a kind person. You don't want to hurt my feelings.'

The music ended and all around them couples drew apart and applauded, laughing, as people often did at the end of a busy excuse-me. Matt let go of Persephone and she stepped back, trying desperately to come up with something to say and failing utterly. Then someone bumped into her from behind, sending her straight into Matt's arms. Little bolts of lightning darted all through her, rendering her dazzled and breathless.

Making sure she was steady on her feet, Matt stepped away from her.

'I think it's pretty clear that you've changed your mind about being friends. Fair enough. Maybe it's for the best if we don't see one another again after this.'

CHAPTER SEVENTEEN

At the end of a long shift, Emily was on her way to the buffet, weaving her way between the many passengers filling the concourse. Some, like her, were creating their own paths towards where they wanted to go; others stood at the timetable board or in front of the platform notices beside the ticket barriers, studying the information. Some stood with a companion, chatting as they waited, while others were alone, reading folded-over newspapers. There wasn't a space left on any of the benches.

'Emily!' Persephone called, catching up with her a moment later. 'Had a good day?'

'Yes, thanks. You?'

'Yes, thanks.'

Emily looked at Persephone, who was the most beautiful girl she'd ever seen. She couldn't imagine Persephone having a day that was anything other than good. She was so lovely to look at, and so charming with it, that people must fall over themselves to oblige her. Of course, there had been that nasty business with the pinstriped fare-dodgers, but she hadn't had to face that alone, even though she was in a position of responsibility. The train's fireman – the fireman, for heaven's sake – had waded in, wanting to help her.

If only somebody would wade in offering help to Emily, how much better everything would be. As matters stood, she was completely on her own and didn't know what to do. Or rather, she knew what she ought to do, but how was she supposed to do it when it would cause such frightful trouble for Mr Buckley?

'Good evening,' said Persephone to a man walking past.

'Oh – good evening, Miss Trehearn-Hobbs,' came the reply. He was an older man; if not as old as Daddy, then certainly as old as Mummy. Emily barely took any notice.

As they walked on, Persephone said, 'That was Mr Gordon, the man who dealt with the fare-dodgers.'

Emily wished she had paid more attention. She looked over her shoulder, but to no avail. The crowd had swallowed him. Drat – though why was she disappointed? It wasn't as though she could have run after him and poured out her woes.

In the buffet, they waved across the room to where Colette was already at a table. For once there wasn't a queue and Emily and Persephone soon joined her.

'We've just seen Mr Gordon,' said Persephone as they sat down.

It was only a throwaway remark, but Emily pounced on it. 'I've been thinking about the fine those men got. Such a lot of money.'

'It was what they deserved,' said Persephone.

'I know. What I mean is, the way you described them, with their smart suits and their watch chains, it made them sound well-to-do. I was wondering if someone less well off was fined, would they get a smaller penalty?'

Persephone and Colette looked questioningly at one another.

'I don't know,' said Colette, 'but I wouldn't think so. I imagine the penalties are laid down and the magistrates simply follow them.'

'I think there might be scales of penalties,' said Persephone, 'and individual penalties are at the magistrate's discretion. One does hear of magistrates who are tougher than others. But I don't know for certain, so don't quote me.'

All of which was of no help to Emily.

'I do know they could have been given a prison sentence,' said Colette. 'Mr Gordon told me that one of them tried to get well in with the authorities by telling tales on the man whose idea it was in the first place. Apparently, they'd been using their ruse for months.'

Prison. Emily swallowed hard, more of a gulp, really, that almost blocked her throat. She definitely didn't want to be responsible for having Mr Buckley sent to prison. He was such a dear man, like a storybook grandpa. Emily's only grandparent was Granny, Daddy's mother, who was a thoroughly formidable lady. If people did as Persephone asked, it was because she was so polite and charming, but when people did as Granny wanted, it was because they were too scared to do otherwise. Emily loved her, but she most definitely was not a sweet old grandma, dispensing cuddles and sweeties and bedtime stories.

Mr Buckley, on the other hand, was patient and kind and had provided her with no end of help. Not only had he taken pains to explain all aspects of the job to her, but when a couple of porters had teased her, he had immediately put a stop to it.

A few days ago, Emily had seen Miss Emery on the concourse and Miss Emery had stopped to ask her how she was getting on.

'Fine, thank you,' said Emily, because what else could she say? And in all respects except one, it was true.

'Is Mr Buckley taking care of you?'

Her feelings suddenly welled up and Emily blurted out, 'He's a complete sweetheart.' Trying to make up for her lack of professionalism, she added, 'I mean, he makes sure I don't put a foot wrong.'

'Good. He was recommended to me as the right person to guide you through your early weeks as a lad porter.'

But he hadn't made sure she didn't put a foot wrong, had he? Quite the opposite. He had more or less pushed her into going wrong – into doing wrong.

Becoming more unsettled by the day, Emily tried to find relief and distraction in small things, like taking Mrs Grayson to her hairdressing appointment on Saturday. She had grown fond of Mrs Grayson and liked to give her the support that helped her leave the house and get out and about.

When they returned to Wilton Close, Colette was there, along with Mabel and Margaret. Emily smiled. There was often a houseful on Saturday or Sunday. Mrs Green was there too, but there was no need for Emily to worry about what to call her, because here at Wilton Close she was always Mrs Green.

When it was time for Colette to leave, Emily said, 'I'll walk with you to the bus stop.'

'Are you sure?' asked Colette. 'It's the wrong direction for you if you're meant to be going home for tea.'

'It'll only take me a few minutes out of my way,' said Emily.

They said their goodbyes and set off. It wasn't far to the bus terminus, which was good because it meant Emily had no option but to launch into what she wanted to say.

'I keep thinking about the fare-dodgers on Persephone's train.'

'Why is it on your mind so much?' Colette asked. If only she would add, 'Is it because you're in a tricky situation involving wrongdoing? Do you need help?' But of course she didn't.

'It just worries me that these things are going on.'

'Unfortunately, they do,' said Colette. 'I once saw some railwaymen in the act of pilfering.'

Emily was so surprised she actually stopped walking. Colette did, too, turning to look at her. Pulling herself together, Emily started up again and they walked on side by side.

'Railwaymen? What happened?'

'It was not long after I became a chaperone,' Colette told her. 'I was sitting on a platform one day and some goods wagons arrived. I watched as they were unloaded and then I realised some sacks were being shoved about. I didn't think anything of it at first, but then a sack split open. I still didn't think anything of it. In fact, I was about to get up and walk away, but then a hand reached up from the gap in between the wagons and, one by one, some containers were passed up and the men on the platform quickly took them away. I told Miss Emery and she said that whatever was in the split sack – probably sugar – would have poured through the gaps in the boards on the wagon floor, straight into the containers underneath.'

'You went to Miss Emery?' asked Emily. Her heart beat quickly. 'Why her?'

'Oh, I think I had to see her about something else, so I told her at the same time.'

'What happened to the men?' Emily asked, trying to hide her eagerness to know.

'I don't know. Miss Emery mentioned the possibility of in future stationing inspectors there when goods wagon arrive, so that it couldn't happen again.'

'So the men didn't go to court?' Oh please let this be a possibility for her own situation.

'I don't know,' said Colette.

'You didn't have to give evidence?'

'No.'

'So the men weren't punished. They were just prevented from doing it again.' Emily could have wept with relief.

'Emily, I honestly don't know,' said Colette. 'Maybe the ringleaders were prosecuted. Maybe there were disciplinary interviews. Or maybe the matter was dealt with by making it impossible for it to happen again. I've really no idea. Why are you so interested?'

And there it was: her chance to speak up.

'No reason,' said Emily.

No reason? That had been her chance to speak up – not just a chance, an actual invitation. And she hadn't taken it.

CHAPTER EIGHTEEN

Persephone surprised her friends by suggesting the Ritz the next couple of times they wanted to go dancing. Normally, they chopped and changed, going to different venues. Not that returning to the Ritz did any good. Matt wasn't there on either occasion.

The next time the girls met up in the buffet, partly in order to make arrangements to go out together, Alison raised her eyebrows in Persephone's direction. 'The Ritz again?'

Persephone didn't need to glance around to know that all eyes were on her. Had she been that obvious? She looked at her friends – Alison, Margaret, Mabel and Colette, though Colette only came out with them if they went to the pictures. How dear they all were to her. She'd always had a lot of friends; she came from that type of background, where everybody knew everybody else and one expected to see all the old familiar faces around candlelit dining tables, in boxes at the opera and at hunt balls. Knowing the right sort of people was an essential part of the way they lived. Becoming friends – real, true friends – with women and girls from lower down the social scale had come as a revelation to Persephone. Who could have predicted that such a thing could happen? She'd been far too well bred to let her surprise show, but honestly, the eye-opener had almost knocked her socks off.

Persephone's heart swelled with love and appreciation as she looked around the table at them now. Mabel, her glorious dark brown waves every bit as gorgeous as Rita Hayworth's in *Blondie on a Budget*, had shown such courage during the Christmas Blitz. Alison, who had been singled out for some sort of special job that she was being trained up for by working in all sorts of areas, had overcome desperate heartbreak to find happiness with Joel Maitland. Next to her was Margaret, who had changed her surname to honour her beloved late mother and, since putting her family troubles behind her, seemed more secure in her own skin. Completing the group around the table was buttermilk-blonde Colette, who had suffered in silence for years at the hands of a cunning, manipulative husband for whom the rest of the world had had nothing but admiration. She was now, in her quiet way, finding her own feet as she embarked upon this new and, Persephone sincerely hoped, much better phase of her life. If anyone could be said to deserve happiness, that person was Colette.

Then there were the friends who weren't present this evening. Joan, lovely, sweet-natured Joan, so happy with the little family she adored. Cordelia had seemed so cool and even remote when the others had first known her, but Persephone knew better now and saw Cordelia for the warm-hearted person she truly was. And Dot, dearest Dot, everyone's mum, everyone's friend, with a heart the size of Lancashire and always ready to dole out a dollop of common sense. Not forgetting, of course, their newest member, Emily. She was still in the shadow of her recent heartbreak, and possibly in her mother's shadow too, but time and the support of her new friends would help her to blossom as she was meant to.

'Are you going to tell us?' asked Alison. 'I'm sure something's up.'

Well, why not? If she couldn't tell these staunch friends, who could she tell?

Persephone laughed. 'As a matter of fact, there is something – or someone, I should say. I don't know why I laughed. It's all a bit of a muddle, really.'

'Someone?' Mabel instantly picked up on the most important word. 'You've met a chap?'

'About time too!' Alison exclaimed.

Persephone had never shared her feelings for Forbes and now Alison's words rubbed in how very alone she'd been all these years in her secret longing. It was time to end all that. If she wanted her friends' support, if she wanted the relief and, yes, the pleasure of confiding in them, then she had to tell the whole truth. It was the only way.

So she talked about Forbes and how she'd loved him for years.

'He's the one you went to see in hospital,' Colette recalled.

'And now he's finally seen sense and realised what a catch you are,' said Alison, jumping to conclusions.

'No, it's not that,' Persephone explained. 'I just wanted you to know about Forbes because . . . well, just because. The man I've met, the one I've been hoping to see again at the Ritz, is somebody else. It's Matt Franklin. You know, the fireman.'

'The one you told about the men in pinstripes,' said Margaret.

'That's him. We've seen quite a bit of one another since then – not in a going-out way, just as colleagues, and then we became friends. We seem to have a lot in common. And then, one evening at the Ritz—'

'So that's why you keep wanting to go back,' Mabel said archly.

'I've danced with him there a couple of times,' said Persephone. 'Things didn't end well, you might say, the last time I saw him there. I'd like to have the chance to put them right.'

'An Honourable and a fireman?' Alison said bluntly. 'I'm sorry.' She looked round at the others. 'I'm only saying what everyone else will say.'

'Not quite everyone,' Persephone replied, surprised to hear a note of challenge in her tone. 'My sister said I should have a fling with him.'

'She didn't!' and 'She never!' said her friends.

'It's wartime and single girls should make the most of it, apparently. Plenty of time to settle down and be respectable afterwards.'

It was tempting to add that she wondered now about Iphigenia's marriage, which had started with a glittering wedding, a dozen bridesmaids, a towering cake covered in tiny sugar roses, and everyone else's mothers pouring congratulations on Ma. Persephone was sure Iphigenia loved Hugo, but now that she saw so many girls having a high old time during the war, did she sometimes wish she'd had the chance for unrestricted fun on a grand scale instead of being steered firmly in the direction of an engagement ring? Was that why she'd encouraged Persephone to have a fling?

'Speaking as someone who's about to settle down,' said Mabel, 'I think it's all about feelings, not about going all out to have fun. If you like this chap and he likes you, then where's the harm? Two people caring about one another matters all the more in wartime. I'd never have met Harry if it hadn't been for the war, because the war brought me to Manchester.'

'And Joan wouldn't have met Bob,' said Colette, 'because neither of them would have learned first aid.'

'Without the war,' said Alison, 'there'd have been no War Weapons Week dance, and Paul would never have met Katie and thrown me over, and I wouldn't now be with Joel and happier than I've ever been.'

Margaret reached across and laid a gentle hand on Persephone's arm. 'You can't control who you're attracted to. If the two of you were friends with things in common before you realised you'd fallen for him . . .'

'Yes, we were. I remember thinking how much I valued him as a friend.'

'Then I for one,' said Margaret with quiet decisiveness, 'can't think of any better foundation for a relationship.'

Talking to her friends strengthened Persephone's resolve. She gave up on the idea of bumping into Matt at the Ritz. If she wanted to see him, the obvious thing to do was to seek him out at work.

During her meal break, she positioned herself near the ticket barrier, waiting for the Leeds train to arrive. She chatted with Mr Thirkle, the ticket collector on duty. She'd always liked him. He had assisted when the group of friends had worked together to trap a thief who'd been stealing regularly from a food store in the early part of the war. Mr Thirkle had been a big help to them, because he'd known about the communication system between the signal boxes and the line controller. Mr Thirkle seemed to have faded into the background since then, which was a shame, but sometimes things just happened that way.

'How are you getting on in your new elevated position?' Mr Thirkle asked her with a kindly twinkle in his eye.

'Fine, thank you. I love being out on the trains.'

'Are you inspecting on the next Leeds train?'

'Here it comes now.'

Persephone deftly avoided answering the question as the train appeared and coasted alongside the platform, heading for the buffers. As passengers poured out and headed towards the ticket barrier, Persephone stood out of the way until most of the crowd had passed through onto the concourse, then she walked up the platform and sat on a bench, keeping an eye on the driver's cab.

When Matt descended, climbing out backwards and jumping down, Persephone waited for him to turn and spot her. She wanted to wave, but shyness swept over her, a new sensation for her. Matt came down the platform. Would he stop? Ought she to stand up to make it clear she wished to speak to him? Or would he simply give her a nod and carry on?

He stopped. Persephone rose to her feet. Her knees felt wobbly.

'I know you need to get something to eat, but could we talk later?'

'I'm not sure that's a good idea,' said Matt.

'Please. I'm sorry about . . .' She searched for the right words.

'About snubbing me at the Ritz? There's no need. I understand. It's a matter of class, which is fair enough.'

'This has nothing to do with class,' she stated.

'Oh.' Matt looked taken aback. 'Is that meant to make me feel better? I could accept it if it was because you're from an important family, but,' and his voice caught on a humourless laugh, 'if it's because you don't like me . . . I thought we were friends. I shouldn't have presumed.'

'You didn't presume anything. You were completely right about us. We get along well.'

'Then it *is* the class difference that's put you off.'

'No. Look, if you'll stop putting words into my mouth and listen, I'll tell you. I was hoping to talk to you later, when you might have more time.'

'Spit it out, will you? Sorry,' Matt added. 'My mum would give me a thick ear for saying that to a lady.'

Persephone's wits deserted her. Even though it was all she'd been able to think about previously, now she simply couldn't think how to explain herself. How ridiculous. She was a writer, wasn't she? She dreamed of earning a living from her words and her ideas. Yet now she didn't seem able to string two words together.

Matt shifted uncomfortably. Was he about to walk away and leave her stranded?

Persephone jumped into the silence. 'Matt, please, this is important – more important than anything has been for a long time. The reason I gave you the brush-off was because somebody said something that made me feel embarrassed to be in your company.'

'Embarrassed to be with me? Thanks very much. It was your sister, wasn't it?'

'Please let me finish.'

'It was the class issue.' He didn't make it into a question.

'Yes, in a way, but since then I've realised how very much I enjoy your company. I'm the one who should apologise. I want us to be friends. We seem to think the same way and that's very special.'

The hardened lines of Matt's face softened a little. 'I'd like to carry on being friends.'

Persephone drew in a shaky breath. 'What I really want to say is that I'd like us to be more than that. More than friends.' She looked up at him, willing him to understand, longing for him to want the same thing.

Matt frowned. 'Does that mean what I think it means?'

'It means, Matt Franklin, that I liked you enormously as a friend, but I also like you in a romantic way and – and I hope you feel the same way about me. I hope . . . I hope I can persuade you to give us that chance. What d'you say?'

Matt looked at her for a long moment. 'I don't think I'll need much persuading.'

CHAPTER NINETEEN

On this sunny April morning, the Extension looked tired, its windows grimy, but Mabel imagined it with a fresh coat of paint on the window frames and doors, and with rays of sunshine making the windows sparkle. On the waste ground to the side were clusters of field forget-me-nots forming clouds of light blue while the richer blue of ivy-leaved speedwell made mats on the ground. There was common chickweed too; Mabel recognised the tiny white flowers. You were supposed to be able to eat chickweed in salad, but Mabel thought it too bitter. Some people boiled it and added it to the veg.

Turning, she saw Fay Brewer approaching. She wore an olive-green jacket and knee-length skirt and carried a leather satchel under her arm. Her suede shoes had high tongues and she wore a hat with a feather.

They exchanged greetings and Mabel admired Fay's hat.

'My brother bought it for me,' said Fay. 'I think he liked the feather rather than the hat. Shall we go in? Show me around and I'll listen to your ideas before I stick my oar in.'

'Fine by me.'

How different to Fay Brewer's almost namesake, Miss Brewster. Mabel felt an instinctive liking for Fay. She wasn't a jolly-hockey-sticks type, but there was something about her that suggested the great outdoors – or maybe that was just the impression Mabel had formed because Fay's attitude came as such a breath of fresh air.

As they walked around inside the building, Mabel shared her vision.

'Of course, it all needs sprucing up,' she concluded.

'Paint can only be used for protective purposes these days, not for decoration,' said Fay, making notes, 'but I can put in a request so that you get what you need, assuming everything goes ahead. What hours will the nursery be open? We have what we call hostel nurseries that open at six in time for breakfast at six thirty and stay open until nine in the evening, with supper at eight thirty. It's the only way to accommodate the twelve-hour shifts so many women work. You'll require aprons, slippers and toys for all the children, kitchen equipment, though these days you can ask the mothers to send their children with their own crockery if you need to, and towels. You could try writing to local laundries to ask if they have any unclaimed linen you could have. They're often a good source, assuming nobody else has got there first. You'll also need some spare clothes.'

Mabel busily scribbled notes. 'I thought of enlisting the WVS's help to organise some clothes-making. Ladies' nightgowns can be turned into vests and baby clothes, and any worn-out coats that aren't good enough for the clothes exchange can be made into boys' shorts and girls' skirts.'

'Good idea,' said Fay. 'But be aware of the possibility of mothers sending their children in tatty clothes. You do occasionally get a mum who takes advantage. Why should she bother clothing her children decently if the nursery or the WVS will do it for her?'

'Do people do that?' Mabel asked, dismayed.

'There's always one,' Fay said matter-of-factly. 'As for toys, I have contacts at a couple of ambulance depots where the chaps make toys now that they're no longer busy every night.'

Mabel nodded. 'It's the same at the place where I do first-aid duty. One of the men there is a joiner and he's made some cots. He even made a rocking horse.'

'You'll need to get on the Food Office list for cod liver oil and orange juice. I can organise that for you.'

'Thanks,' said Mabel.

'Lavatories?' said Fay.

'Outside.' Mabel led the way. 'Not very impressive, I'm afraid.'

'Don't tell me. Old earth closets. They won't do at all, I'm afraid. We need proper sanitation. Have you the where-withal to provide that?'

'I'll get somebody to quote for the work, but I'm sure it won't be a problem.' Mabel mentally crossed her fingers.

'I'll give you a list of approved companies,' said Fay. 'Have you written a statement in support of your application for permission?'

'Not yet,' Mabel admitted. 'There wouldn't even be a provisional application if Mrs Eckersley hadn't put one in without my knowledge.'

'I'll give you some pointers. You must make sure you include a list of what the children will be taught: hygiene, nutrition, good manners, good habits. You'll need to give a good idea of the daily timetable, including times for sleep.'

'You've given me lots to think about,' said Mabel, writing furiously, 'as well as lots to do.'

'I'm here to help,' said Fay. 'Don't forget that.' She glanced at her wristwatch. 'I must go now. I need to visit a child who's being watched over by the welfare department. She was taken to hospital yesterday.'

'Nothing too serious, I hope.'

Fay smiled. 'Suspected appendicitis – but then it turned out she had just eaten her first ever orange and she didn't know she was supposed to peel it. Hence the stomach pains.'

'Poor kid,' said Mabel. 'I hope it hasn't put her off oranges for life. Thank you for coming today. You've been a big help.'

Fay left and Mabel hung on for a few minutes, walking around inside the building before she locked up. It had been a useful and satisfying meeting and she looked forward to getting on with the work. Then a wave of nostalgia and sorrow washed over her at the thought of leaving the area that had come to mean so much to her, but it would be good to leave something behind – something tangible and lasting.

Going out with Matt made Persephone feel all fluttery and excited. Although she had received heaps of attention when she was in London, she'd never had a proper boyfriend before. It had always been Forbes or nobody for her – which had meant having nobody. That had been the normal state of affairs for her for such a long time that being with Matt now made her feel extra awake and alert as her heartbeat drummed inside her chest.

Dot and Cordelia got Persephone on her own.

'We're delighted that you're going out with Matt,' said Cordelia, 'but we want to be sure you aren't on the rebound.'

'There wasn't anything to rebound from,' Persephone said ruefully. 'Forbes never so much as spared me a glance of that kind.'

'Happen he didn't,' said Dot, 'but you carried a torch for him for years, so you might be on the rebound. Cordelia and me want to be sure that you're certain of what you're doing, so don't mind us sticking our motherly noses in.'

'We only want to know that Matt is the right one for you,' said Cordelia.

'You mean compared to Forbes?' Persephone took a moment to choose her words. She didn't want to say anything against Forbes, but she dearly wanted to convince her friends. 'Matt is easy to talk to and he really listens to what I say.'

'Didn't Forbes?' asked Dot.

'Not in the same way. Forbes was all charm and good manners, but we never had a truly personal conversation, no matter how hard I tried to steer us into one. Forbes was a chum, someone I could have rung up in London and asked to take me out for tea and he'd have dropped everything and done it and been the most marvellous company – but he'd have done exactly the same for any other girl of his acquaintance.'

'You weren't special to him.' Dot nodded. 'But Matt makes you feel special.'

Alison invited Persephone and Matt to go out with her and Joel. The four of them went to see *For Me and My Girl*, a wonderful Busby Berkeley musical starring Judy Garland and Gene Kelly. Persephone loved being out with another couple. For so long, she'd been one of the single girls tagging along and she had never minded because she wasn't the wallflower type, but still, it was fun and exciting to be half of a couple. A proper couple too. She might have spent years hankering after Forbes Winterton and his smoky-grey eyes, but there was nothing second best about Matt. She loved his company, his enthusiasm for his job and the fact that he had pursued his dream. She valued his being well read, while his good looks and ability to dance were the cherry on the cake.

But she couldn't forget what Iphigenia had said and it niggled at her, refusing to go away. Iphigenia had made it sound so simple, but it really wasn't. Persephone wasn't the sort to indulge in flings and if this lovely relationship blossomed, then what would happen after the war?

'The last thing I want is to lead Matt on and then end up letting him down,' she explained worriedly to her friends one evening in the buffet.

'Of course you don't, chick,' Dot agreed. 'You wouldn't do something like that.'

'Never on purpose,' said Persephone, anxious for the matter not to be swept aside in the current of her friends' good opinion of her. 'But I'm trying to think ahead.'

'There are plenty of people who don't take the time to do that these days,' said Cordelia. 'The general motto seems to be: live for the moment.'

'It's understandable in wartime,' said Margaret.

'Everyone is so aware that they might not have a future,' said Colette, 'or at least not the future they thought they were going to have.'

'I know how that feels,' said Alison. 'I was in utter despair when Paul left me. I felt as if I'd lost not just my boyfriend but the whole of the rest of my life.' Her eyes clouded. Was she remembering the old future she had once looked forward to so much, living in Paul's mother's house after she and Paul got married? Alison gave her head a little shake. 'Being dumped by Paul taught me that you never know what's going to happen to you – and then meeting Joel taught me the same lesson all over again but in a different way. A happy way, a hopeful way.' She looked at Persephone. 'If you're happy now, that's what matters.'

'But Persephone wants to think about the future,' said Cordelia. 'In so far as anybody can in these uncertain times.'

'Well, one thing's certain,' said Dot, with the air of one getting down to business. 'You and Matt would never have met before the war, Persephone. However happy you are together, you both know that. If you decided to split up because of the ructions it'll cause after the war, nobody would blame you. Everyone would understand.'

'That's just it,' said Persephone. 'I don't want to split up. I don't want that in the slightest – but I still worry about the future. Am I trying to have my cake and eat it?'

'So what if you are?' asked Mabel. 'All sorts of unlikely friendships spring up in wartime.'

'I think you shouldn't agonise over the years ahead,' Alison declared. 'Who can say what's going to happen? Look at Lizzie. Look at Letitia. Think of the thousands and thousands of people who have lost their lives – civilians as well as servicemen. When you've got the chance to be happy, you should grab it with both hands. That's what I think.'

Persephone very dearly wanted to think so too. She couldn't imagine giving up Matt now that they were getting to know one another, but she just didn't have it in her to follow Iphigenia's breezy advice and have a mad wartime fling, something to look back on with secret smiles in the years to come. It flew in the face of the way she'd been brought up. Duty and responsibility and all that. On the other hand, she risked spoiling things if she kept fretting over possibilities way outside her control.

It might not be in her nature to live for today, but maybe it was worth giving it a try.

Mabel sat on the train. Other passengers were reading books or newspapers, knitting or striking up conversations with strangers, but she was happy with her own thoughts. She was on her way home to Annerby for a fitting for her wedding dress. Just thinking of it made her feel fluttery inside and she realised it had also drawn a wide smile on her face because the man sitting opposite was sitting up straighter, apparently imagining the smile meant his luck was in. Mabel quickly smoothed her features and looked away, directing her gaze out of the window.

The journey wasn't too bad in terms of keeping to time and the train pulled into Annerby only forty minutes late, the rhythmic chuffing sound ceasing as the mighty loco drew its long line of coaches alongside the platform. The brakes squealed and then there was a clunking noise as the train came to a stop. As eager as she was to disembark, Mabel stayed put. Even if she'd got to her feet, she would have had to wait while the passengers standing in the aisles shuffled along and disappeared.

When she stepped down onto the platform, she saw Mumsy and they hurried to one another for a hug, then Mumsy held her at arm's length.

'Let me look at you. It's so good to have you home. I can't wait to see you in your wedding dress. Are you looking after your hands? And creaming your elbows?'

Mabel gave Mumsy another hug. It was wonderful to see her again. She couldn't wait to see Pops, but he would be at work until this evening.

'When we get home, we'll have something to eat and you can have a bit of a rest,' said Mumsy, linking arms as they made their way towards the ticket barrier. 'Miss Wooding, the seamstress, is coming later for the fitting.'

Mabel laughed, excitement bubbling up. 'A rest is the last thing I need. I'm dying to see the dress and put it on.'

When she saw her dress for the first time, Mabel's eyes filled with tears of pure happiness. The white taffeta with silver stripes was utterly beautiful. The gown had a sweetheart neckline, cap sleeves and softly gathered shaping beneath the bustline. The fabric had been cut without a seam at the waist and the material flowed into a full-length skirt that was longer at the back.

When the time came to try it on, she cried all over again.

'I hope those are happy tears,' Miss Wooding said with a smile.

'Couldn't be happier,' said Mabel, taking the hanky Mumsy offered.

'Walk over there to the door,' said Miss Wooding, 'then turn round and walk back to the mirror. That's right. This is what you'll look like as you walk up the aisle.'

Mabel walked from the door to the mirror a dozen times and even then she would gladly have done it a dozen more.

'Have you a veil?' asked Miss Wooding.

Mumsy stepped in. 'I want to talk to you about that, Mabel.'

Mabel assumed Mumsy must want her own veil to be used, but later on, after Mabel had reluctantly been helped out of her dress and Miss Wooding had departed, Mumsy had a different suggestion.

'Now you must say right away if you aren't happy with this, darling, but I did wonder . . .'

'What?' asked Mabel, curiosity piqued.

'It's about your veil.'

'Would you like me to wear yours?'

'No – well, yes, obviously, but I've had a different idea.' Mumsy reached for Mabel's hand. 'It's to do with Althea. I know how you two always said you'd be one another's bridesmaids when you grew up, so I wondered whether you might like to ask Mrs Wilmore if you could borrow her veil – assuming she still has it, that is. I haven't said a word to her about this, so if you'd rather not, she'll never know I thought of it.'

The world seemed to slow down as a thousand memories and regrets came flooding back, but more than anything what Mabel felt was a rush of love and nostalgia for the girl she used to call the sister of her heart – that, and a deep pride in Mumsy for being so thoughtful and selfless.

'I think that would be perfect,' Mabel said softly. 'Thank you for thinking of it.'

'Then we'd better go over there now,' said Mumsy, 'because you've got to go back to Manchester tomorrow.'

On the way over to the Wilmores', Mabel fretted about whether it would hurt Mrs Wilmore to be asked. Would it rub in Althea's loss all the more?

When Mabel asked her, Mrs Wilmore caught her breath and closed her eyes, placing a splayed hand on her chest.

'I'm sorry,' Mabel said immediately.

'Don't be.' Mrs Wilmore opened her eyes and looked straight at her. 'I think it's a lovely idea. I just feel over-whelmed, that's all. But I'd be delighted and honoured. It's so kind of you to think of Althea – and me – in this way.'

As Mrs Wilmore dabbed her eyes, Mabel shot a warm look at Mumsy. *Thank you*, she mouthed.

CHAPTER TWENTY

When Persephone had a day off from her job on the railways, it was seldom a day off work. She was expected to
pull her weight at Darley Court, helping to ensure that
everything went smoothly for the visiting groups that were
holding their meetings and training events on the premises. This morning, Light Rescue and Heavy Rescue were
coming for a training day, while contingents of policemen
were arriving each day this week to refresh their first-aid
training. The boardroom had also been made ready for an
important meeting. Pre-war this had been a grand drawing
room known as the saloon, but these days it contained a
long table surrounded by chairs and the groups that made
use of Darley Court had equipped it with noticeboards.

Today the Fire Guard was booked into the boardroom.
The Fire Guard Plan had been announced a few weeks ago,
following last year's terrible Baedeker air raids, when the
Luftwaffe had targeted some of Britain's most beautiful cit-
ies in reprisal for the RAF's devastating assaults on Lübeck,
Rostock and Cologne. This month, the Fire Guard had
become a separate service within each local authority and
today's meeting was about the revised personnel structure
and the newly laid-out geographical divisions.

Persephone helped get the rooms ready. Gone was the
lovely old furniture, or at least as much of it as it was possible to store away, but nothing could disguise the elegance
and generous proportions of the rooms. When everything
else had been done, Persephone placed a crystal vase of

blue and yellow hyacinths on the table in the boardroom, their delicious scent mingling with the aroma of Mrs Mitchell's home-made lavender polish. This might be a venue for wartime meetings, but touches of traditional beauty remained and were regarded by Darley Court's inhabitants as important, even by Miss Brown, who was quite possibly the most practical person Persephone had ever met.

At the end of the morning, everything stopped for lunch. The various delegates had brought their own sandwiches and barm cakes, though tea and cordial were offered by Darley Court. Mrs Mitchell had a special tea allowance to provide refreshments, though it never stretched as far she would have liked.

'There's an awful lot of secret business discussed under this roof,' she said wryly to Persephone, 'but the biggest secret of all is the number of times I have to reuse the tea leaves.'

The other downside to offering tea was that they had had to watch the cups and saucers like hawks ever since the day, when shortages had first started to bite hard, the gold-rimmed service of a dozen settings had been used to serve tea to a crowd of bigwigs and only eleven cups had made it back to the kitchen. A steely Miss Brown had personally written to each of the bigwigs requesting the return of her teacup and several months later it had miraculously reappeared, although because of who was present in the house on that particular day, it was impossible to say who the culprit was.

After the cup went missing, Miss Brown had vowed never again to use 'the good stuff' for people attending meetings and had bullied the powers that be into providing crates full of plain white crockery and plates, which had been in use ever since. Persephone understood why and fully agreed with it, but still, it was a shame that their visitors didn't get to see the pretty china.

Pushing a loaded tea trolley along the corridor – never an easy task on carpet – Persephone headed for what was now designated the common room, a spacious room where visitors were invited to eat their sandwiches. She backed into the room, pushing the door open with her behind and manoeuvring the trolley over the threshold towards an urn that was already steaming away on a table over to one side, with two of the local women who came in to do the cleaning standing ready.

There was a contingent of police officers in the room, as well as men in civvies, but not a single female visitor to be seen, which was depressing, though not unexpected. As the tea was poured and handed round, Persephone chatted pleasantly with the guests, asking them if their meetings had gone well.

'Excuse me, Miss Trehearn-Hobbs,' said one of the cleaners and Persephone turned to answer her question. When she turned back, a policeman approached her. He was tall, with thinning hair and a beaky nose.

'Miss Trehearn-Hobbs? I think my son knows you – Matthew Franklin.'

'You're Matt's father,' Persephone said in surprise.

'Sergeant Michael Franklin.'

'How do you do, Sergeant Franklin? It's a pleasure to meet you.'

They shook hands.

'Nice to meet you too, miss. Our Matt said you live here, but I didn't expect to find you working here too, not with you having your job on the railways.'

Persephone glanced at the empty tea trolley and laughed. 'I can turn my hand to most things if I need to. We all have to in wartime, don't we?'

'We do indeed, miss.'

There was a short silence, which Persephone was about to fill. ('Never permit a silence to become awkward, Persephone.') Sergeant Franklin spoke first.

'It's a beautiful old building, this, isn't it?'

'Yes, it is,' Persephone agreed readily. 'It's a shame you're seeing it in its wartime clothing, with so much of its beauty hidden away. How has your morning gone? I hope everyone found it useful.'

'Yes, thank you, miss. It was a first-aid refresher course.'

'Of course it was. I remember now.'

They talked for a while about first aid and policing and shift patterns. Persephone had been brought up to be able to make small talk about anything at all and to think up sensible, relevant questions on the spur of the moment and Sergeant Franklin was clearly able to keep up his end of a conversation too. He had a pleasant manner and she liked him. Although he seemed unassuming on a personal level, Persephone sensed a quiet authority about him that must serve him well in his work.

Later, she told Miss Brown about meeting him.

'Well, what a coincidence,' said Miss Brown. 'I hope it wasn't awkward.'

'Not at all. We chatted for a while.'

'Good manners prevailed. I'm pleased to hear it. There's a lot to be said for good manners.'

'You sound like my old nanny.'

'I'll take that as a compliment,' said Miss Brown.

Persephone was pleased to have met Matt's father in that unexpected way and for the situation to have felt easy and natural. She felt buoyed up by it. In fact, it gave her an idea. What about a piece on good manners for *Vera's Voice*? She made a few notes, then thought about it at various times over the next couple of days before writing a jolly little piece extolling the virtues of good manners and how important they were in wartime when nerves were stretched, rationing was tight and everyone was worried about loved ones on the front line. When it was finished, she examined it with a critical eye. It was good as far as it went, but it lacked something. There were plenty of morale-boosting articles these days. Hers needed something extra, something different, to make it stand out and be chosen for publication. But what?

Persephone was scheduled to do some trips on the South-port train, which gave her the huge pleasure of travelling with Dot, even if their respective duties meant they would barely see one another on the journey. As parcels porter, Dot had to load up all the parcels – and a parcel could be anything from a punnet of fruit to a wooden leg or a small flock of sheep – into the guard's van, taking care to keep together everything that had to be unloaded at a particular station. Even then it wasn't as simple as opening the van's double doors at each station to unload the relevant things. No, she had to make sure that all the parcels for dropping off were taken through the train to exactly the right carriage door to match up with where the station staff would be standing ready to accept them.

'Easier said than done when the trains are packed solid with passengers,' Dot said cheerfully.

In between a couple of journeys, when they had forty minutes spare after Dot had got her new lot of parcels ready for the return trip, they nipped out onto Lord Street and found a little tea shop so they could treat themselves.

'A letter from Forbes was waiting for me when I got home yesterday,' said Persephone as Dot poured the tea. 'He's fit again and returning to the fighting.'

'And how do you feel about that?'

'I've got mixed feelings, the same as anybody who knows someone who's being sent back overseas,' said Persephone. 'Glad he's fully recovered, but worried about him going back. Though there is one difference in how I feel. This time when he leaves, he won't be taking my heart with him. Great fondness and friendship, but . . .' She shook her head.

'How are things going with you and Matt?' Dot asked.

'We don't see as much of one another as we'd like.'

'You both work long hours, and then you've got your compulsory overtime and your Darley Court duties.'

'We're more likely to snatch a few minutes together on a station platform than we are to go out for an evening,' said Persephone.

'You're lucky to have the chance to bump into one another at work,' Dot pointed out.

'Believe me, I do know that.' Persephone hesitated before adding, 'Quite honestly, it startles me how much I want to be with him. I've always been so self-sufficient. Years of not being of interest or importance to Forbes made sure I learned to have an independent social life.'

'Well, I'm glad for you, chick. I wish you and your Matt all the best.'

'Thank you. I met his father, you know.'

Dot glanced at her in surprise. 'Oh aye?'

'Groups of policemen have been coming to Darley Court on first-aid courses and he was at one of those. Matt had told him I live there and he heard someone say my name, so he introduced himself.'

'And how did the two of you get on?' asked Dot, taking a sandwich from her plate.

'Fine, though of course we only spoke for a few minutes.'

Dot nodded. 'Now that his dad's met you, his mam won't rest until she has an' all. You mark my words, chick.'

'D'you think so?'

'I know so,' Dot said firmly. 'Have you told your parents yet?'

'No, not yet,' Persephone admitted. 'It doesn't feel right putting it in a letter, because . . .'

'Because?'

Persephone started to lift her teacup, then realised it might look like she was trying to hide behind it, so put it back in its saucer. 'Because it'll come as a shock,' she said honestly.

'The class difference?' Dot's tone was shrewd but kind. 'Well, they didn't flaunt you all over London and take you to court to curtsey to the Queen so that you could take up with a lowly fireman.'

Persephone flinched inwardly, but Dot was right. 'Precisely.'

'You need to tell them, love, especially as you'll soon be going to his mam's house for tea.'

'I'm not going there for tea.' Persephone couldn't help laughing. Where had Dot acquired that idea?

Dot nodded. 'You will be.'

'My mum asked me to invite you round to ours for tea,' said Matt.

Persephone had volunteered to work extra hours tonight so as to finish shortly before the last train was due in from Leeds. Matt looked tired and strained after his long shift, all the more so because of spending the final hours in the pitch-dark as he and Mr Gibson concentrated doubly hard to drive the train safely without any of the visual reminders they would have received had there been no blackout to contend with.

Persephone and Matt were now spending a few minutes in one another's company. Persephone was well aware that Matt longed for more time together every bit as much as she did, but she also knew he needed to go home and get his head down while he could.

They sat together on a bench on the platform. The air was filled with the tang of smoke and steam and oil.

When Matt issued his mother's invitation, Persephone couldn't help laughing.

'What's so funny?' he asked.

'Nothing. It seems one of my friends has a crystal ball, because she said your mother was going to ask me.'

Matt nudged closer to her. 'Been talking about me, have you?' he asked in a teasing voice.

'Who, me?' Persephone retorted. 'Someone's got a fine opinion of himself, hasn't he?'

'So what do I tell Mum?' asked Matt. 'Would you like to come?'

'Yes, please. I'd love to.'

'Mum suggested Easter Sunday, if you're free.'

'Would you mind if I make another arrangement first, before replying to your mother's invitation?'

'Replying to Mum's invitation?' Matt grinned. 'All you have to do is say yes or no. What is it you want to do first?'

'I'd like to arrange to travel down and see my people. The thing is, your family knows about me, but mine doesn't know about you. I'd like to put a firm date in the diary for going home and when I've done that, I'll feel comfortable about saying yes to your mother's kind invitation.'

'So you don't need to visit your family before meeting mine?'

'No, I just want to make the arrangement. It feels more appropriate that way. I know it probably sounds silly to you.'

Matt hooked his arm around her shoulders and drew her to him for a moment, planting a tender kiss on her temple. 'It's not silly. Well, actually, yes, it's plain daft, if you ask me, but it's also kind-hearted and respectful of you to want to do things in what feels to you like the right order.'

They slid apart again. With Persephone in uniform, they mustn't be caught canoodling in public.

'Thanks for understanding,' she said. 'I'll see about booking leave first thing in the morning. I might not be allowed any yet, with this being a fairly new job. And now, Mr Franklin, it's high time you went home and grabbed some shut-eye.'

'There's just one thing before I go,' said Matt.

'What's that?' Persephone felt a little burst of happiness. Another kiss?

'That friend of yours with the crystal ball – can she foretell the football results?'

CHAPTER TWENTY-ONE

'You could have some time off in May,' Persephone was told, 'as long as you steer clear of Whitsun. Busy time, that.' Persephone chose days early in the month. Having done that, she felt able to accept Mrs Franklin's invitation.

'I can't see the difference myself,' said Mrs Mitchell when Persephone helped her fill pasties in Darley Court's spacious kitchen. 'You're saying it's all right for you to meet Matt's folks now that you've got arrangements in hand to go and see your own family.'

'It's a fine distinction, I know,' said Persephone, 'but this makes me feel I'm doing things the right way round.'

'As long as you aren't getting yourself in too deep too soon.'

'What d'you mean?' asked Persephone.

Mrs Mitchell gave her a shrewd look. 'You know perfectly well what I mean. When a fellow asks a girl to meet his family, that's an important step.'

'I like Matt. I care for him. His family want to meet me and I want to meet them.'

'Don't forget you've got a family of your own as well. That's all I'm saying.'

Persephone couldn't pretend not to understand. The social implications of her relationship with Matt were more than she cared to examine in detail. Even so, she was filled with happy anticipation and she loved every moment of her new relationship.

When she wrote to her mother to tell her about the forth-coming visit, she hesitated over whether to add *I'll have something special to tell you* and then didn't say it.

Instead, she concentrated on the pleasure of meeting Matt's family.

'Easter Sunday will be a nice time for the visit,' said Mrs Cooper when Persephone called in at Wilton Close, bringing a knitting pattern for Mrs Grayson from Mrs Mitchell. 'The church bells are allowed to ring. It'll be a special day.'

'Meeting Sergeant Franklin at Darley Court has made this happen rather sooner than it might otherwise have done,' remarked Mrs Grayson.

'True,' Persephone agreed, 'but I don't mind.'

'I think it's good that you're meeting them early on,' said Margaret. 'It shows there's a lot more to this relationship than just being dance partners.'

'Does that mean you wouldn't go out with a chap if he wasn't happy to take you home to meet his parents?' Alison asked Margaret.

Colour flushed Margaret's cheeks. 'All I'm saying is it gives Persephone's relationship with Matt a solid foundation.'

Persephone liked the sound of that. She was entranced by the idea of being welcomed into a new family. It made her think of Joan and the Hubbles. Bob's family had been quick to take Joan to their hearts. According to Joan, Bob's parents said there was no such thing as in-laws in the Hubble household and she was another daughter to them. Remembering that made hope bubble up in Persephone's heart. Meeting Matt's family would go well, of course it would. They all had one thing in common: they cared about Matt.

Persephone smiled to herself, thinking of how she and Sergeant Franklin had made conversation quite easily. There was no reason to imagine the rest of Matt's family would be any different, and if there was one thing

Persephone excelled at, it was behaving impeccably in company and making an occasion run as smoothly as possible. Good manners could carry you a very long way.

She loved the way her friends were all so interested in the forthcoming Sunday tea, their pleasure adding to her own.

'Where do they live?' Alison asked her in the buffet.

'Ordsall,' said Persephone and noticed Cordelia glance Emily's way. Emily looked down, studying her hands with what was obviously pretend nonchalance.

A little later, when they were all about to go their separate ways, Emily drew Persephone to one side.

'I hope you enjoy having tea with Matt's family. I don't want you to think I'm not interested.'

'You seemed deep in thought.'

'Ordsall is the place where the fire-watchers' party was held, where Raymond was trapped after the bombing. He might have been killed.'

'And that was when the two of you fell in love,' said Persephone, understanding at once.

Emily nodded, pressing her lips together so hard her chin wrinkled. 'Don't worry I shan't make a spectacle of myself just because you mentioned Ordsall.'

Persephone leaned closer and said quietly, 'I know what it is to grab hold of every possible connection, however tenuous, and use it to indulge in thoughts. I did it for years with Forbes, for all the good it did me.'

'I know it's foolish,' said Emily, 'but I can't help it. Sometimes a memory sneaks up and jumps out when I least expect it.'

As Emily fastened her coat, moving out of the way a little as she did so, Cordelia spoke quietly to Persephone.

'I heard what she said,' Cordelia murmured. 'The poor child.'

'It's so hard not to tell her that her heart will heal in the end,' said Persephone.

'I agree, but it's not what she wants to hear at the moment. I just hope and pray that one day she'll feel ready to open her heart again. She's such a lovely girl, though I do say so myself. I dearly want her to find happiness. I want her one day to be as happy as I am with her father.'

Persephone felt deeply touched by those words. Surely this was what every loving parent wanted, for their children to find true and lasting contentment. It made her look forward all the more to meeting Matt's family. She wanted them to see how right she and Matt were as a couple. They would see that, wouldn't they? And they would be glad Matt had met her?

Tears sprang into Persephone's eyes as the church bells pealed on Easter Sunday. Glancing around, she saw others also wiping away tears as the symbol of hope touched their hearts, no doubt making them think of beloved servicemen far away, just as Persephone was thinking of Roddy and Giles – Forbes, too. He was always in her prayers, in her heart. She pictured him tucked away safely in a corner of her heart, inside a box labelled NOSTALGIA.

Now she had tea with Matt's family to look forward to. She had chosen a pretty apricot-coloured dress with a V-shaped neckline and panelled skirt, together with a wide-lapelled cropped jacket in ivory linen, topped off with a simple felt hat.

The head gardener gave her a bunch of yellow tulips in frothy greenery to take as a gift for Mrs Franklin, and Persephone had saved up her sweets ration so she could take a few bars of Cadbury's Whole Nut. Mrs Mitchell produced a length of red ribbon with which to tie them together.

Persephone allowed plenty of time for her journey. Matt met her off the bus at the other end and she stepped down from the platform at the rear of the bus, uplifted to be in his company.

He smiled at the sight of the tulips. 'Are those for my mum? She'll love them.'

'I hope so,' said Persephone.

They walked down a long road of large semi-detached houses whose front doors were set inside porches, most of which contained the ubiquitous buckets of sand and water. Persephone was about to ask if the Franklins lived along here, but she and Matt were chatting about other things and she missed the opportunity, and then she was glad she'd missed it because they left that road, turning into a narrower one with runs of six or eight terraced houses with side roads in between. Each house had a small front garden and a big window, criss-crossed with anti-blast tape, next to the door.

It was into one of these that Matt ushered her. Persephone formed a hasty impression of stairs on the right and two doors on the left, with a glimpse of the kitchen straight ahead before Matt took her into the front room, where a Bakelite wireless set stood on a low table next to the tiled fireplace and a standard lamp with a tasselled shade stood behind one of the armchairs. In pride of place on one wall was a glass-fronted display cabinet with a pair of tureens on the bottom shelf and a collection of cream jugs on the top. The two middle shelves were empty, suggesting that the best tea service would be in use this afternoon.

Matt introduced Persephone to his family.

'You've already met my dad,' he began, and Sergeant Franklin shook hands gravely. 'And this is my mum.'

Mrs Franklin wore a shirtwaister dress in narrow stripes, plain dark brown alternating with lines of tiny brown flowers, with a brown belt. Her salt-and-pepper hair was rolled neatly at the back of her neck; her drawn-on eyebrows showed what her original colouring had been. Her dark eyes took in every detail of Persephone, but that was only to be expected when her son brought his new girlfriend home for the first time.

Persephone presented her with the flowers and the chocolate and there were murmurs of delight from the rest of the family.

'I love tulips,' said Mrs Franklin. 'I'll go and put them in water. We can each have a couple of squares of chocolate after tea. That'll be nice, won't it?'

Matt had two sisters. Peggy looked as if she was the same sort of age as her brother; she had the same colouring too, but whereas Matt got his height from their father, Peggy was shorter and fuller-figured like her mother. Persephone knew that Peggy was married and had her own home, so she must be here to give the new girlfriend the once-over.

Jill, the younger sister by some years, was nearer to Persephone in age. She wore her fair hair beautifully curled, like Greer Garson in *Mrs Miniver*, and her light blue dress was patterned all over with tiny white leaves. Instead of shaking hands with Persephone, she held up both hands, showing their backs, the skin red and angry-looking.

'It's all right. You won't catch anything. It's from the munitions. They moved me into a different section and I had a bad reaction to something or other.'

'It looks painful,' said Persephone.

'I can't go back until it clears up.'

'She's keeping busy, though,' said Mrs Franklin after everyone sat down. 'She's working for the WVS, mainly helping take care of women who have been in hospital and who need a bit of a rest when they come home.'

'It keeps her out of mischief,' said Matt.

Jill was looking at Persephone's clothes. 'That's a swish rig-out. It's definitely not Utility.'

'No. I've had it for a while,' said Persephone. 'The housekeeper helped me take up the skirt to make it a fashionable length.'

'That would be the housekeeper at Darley Court,' said Sergeant Franklin.

'Yes,' said Persephone, adding for the benefit of Mrs Franklin and her daughters, 'That's where I live,' even though she felt sure they must already know. It was all about keeping the conversation flowing pleasantly.

'Aren't you the lucky one?' said Peggy with a smile.

'Yes, she is,' said Sergeant Franklin. 'It's a beautiful place.'

'So how did you meet our Matt, then?' asked Jill.

Persephone described her job as a ticket inspector, ending with, 'Matt helped me with a sticky situation when some men were trying to get out of paying their fares.'

'They weren't just trying to,' said Matt. 'It turned out that they'd succeeded at it for quite some time.'

'They all got fined, didn't they?' remarked his father.

'Don't get him started or he'll go on about lawbreakers until the cows come home.' Mrs Franklin waved a mock-stern finger at her husband.

Persephone looked at Peggy. 'Do you go out to work?'

'I work in a home for old soldiers. I first went there because they let me work around school hours, but since the kids were evacuated, I do whatever hours they need.'

'And you're an ARP warden,' Mrs Franklin added. 'That keeps you busy, doesn't it, Peggy?'

'Meanwhile, I'm stuck at home while my hands get better,' said Jill.

'Is it taking a long time?' asked Persephone.

'Longer than I thought,' Jill told her.

'We've just got to hope it won't happen again when you go back,' said Mrs Franklin.

'It shouldn't. Touch wood.' Jill brushed a hand against her brother's head. 'But if it does, I'll run away and join the Land Army.'

'Knowing your luck, you'll be allergic to horses too,' teased Matt.

A big black and white cat strolled into the room, tail erect, and made a beeline for Persephone, who extended her fingers for him to sniff.

'Don't let him jump up,' Mrs Franklin said at the same moment as the cat leaped onto Persephone's lap. 'I'm so sorry. You'll be covered in cat hair.'

Persephone stroked the cat, scratching behind his ears, which had him pressing harder against her hand, wanting more. 'It doesn't matter in the slightest. I grew up with animals and I love them, though I'm not sure what Miss Brown's dogs will think when I go home smelling of cat. What's this fellow's name?'

'Alf,' said Jill. 'He's a teddy bear in cat's clothing.'

'And he's our own personal air-raid alarm too,' added Sergeant Franklin. 'At every single air raid we've had, before the siren starts up, Alf ups sticks and goes to sit in the garden beside the Anderson's door.'

'Clever boy,' Persephone crooned into the cat's soft fur.

Mrs Franklin stood up. 'Time to put the tea on the table. Peggy, lend a hand, love. Jill, put the cloth on the table, will you?' As Persephone made a slight move to signify her willingness, Mrs Franklin added, 'Certainly not. You're our guest.'

As they left the room, Matt murmured, 'You can help next time, but Mum has to make a fuss because it's your first visit.'

So Persephone stayed, cuddling the cat, who did indeed shed fur all over her while she chatted to Matt and his father. Out in the hallway, Mrs Franklin hissed, 'Not *that* cloth, the best one,' and Persephone pretended not to hear, smiling instead at Matt's father and keeping the conversation going by asking him about his work. It was all about showing consideration and respect for others by applying good manners to every situation.

And that was when it all fell into place. She hadn't known how to improve her article for *Vera's Voice* before, but now she knew. There was a standard piece of advice that was handed out to writers, wasn't there? Write about what you know, and one thing that had been brought home forcefully to Persephone recently, and especially this afternoon, was the value of good manners between the classes. There was far more interaction across social boundaries these days and it wasn't just the necessities of wartime that made this successful and acceptable, it was pure good manners.

Yes. That was exactly what her article required to make it perfect.

CHAPTER TWENTY-TWO

It was a good thing Raymond had got tired of her. Now he would never know what a dithering, dishonest fool Emily was and that she wasn't worthy of him. If he had still been her boyfriend, though, would it have made a difference? As Raymond Hancock's girlfriend, would she have held her head high as she reported the pilfering? Oh, if only she still had Raymond to talk to. But even if they had still been a couple, they wouldn't have been able to discuss anything because he was away fighting.

Where was he? Was he safe? He must have finished his basic training by now. Sometimes Emily had an all-consuming temptation to go round and ask his mother, but that would be a huge mistake.

At other times her throat dried up and she felt hot all over as envy scorched through her when she saw Persephone looking radiant with new-found happiness, her skin glowing and her violet eyes dewy. Not so long ago, Emily had looked like that, but now her appearance was lacklustre. When she was Raymond's girl, she used to look at herself in the mirror and it had been rather like looking at a photograph of a film star in one of those posed pictures where the light was angled just so in order to make her as lovely as possible; but whereas it was artificial light for the actress, it had been an inner glow for Emily. She had never felt happier or more confident.

Strangely, she still felt confident. Raymond had given her that. By loving her, he had made her feel self-assured, and bizarre as it might sound, that feeling was still there even though her heart was in tatters. It had been partly because of this that she had been able to insist on leaving her boring old job to start on the railways.

And look where that had got her! Into a right old pickle – although 'pickle' made it sound as if it wasn't a serious situation. Should she confide in Daddy and ask for his advice about what she ought to do? But if she was going to do that, she should have done it ages ago when this had all started.

Every time she examined her new rota at work, her heart was in her mouth as she silently begged God not to let her be on stores duty. Mostly she wasn't, because her official role was as a station porter, a job she loved. She also enjoyed tasks that did not take place on the station but were well away from the stores, such as salvage work.

'And what does that entail?' her father asked, lighting his pipe in the sitting room.

'Mostly ferrying trolleys loaded with bundles of paper to the wagons to be taken away to paper mills. It's not very exciting, but it matters.'

'It's important work, I agree,' said Daddy, 'but—'

'I know,' put in Emily. 'It's not going to help me find a job after the war.'

'I was going to say, "not at all what I imagined for you when you were a little girl." Anyway, darling, after the war you'll have no need to work. Naturally, you shall live at home until you marry.'

'But I have to work!' She couldn't imagine not working.

Her father smiled indulgently. 'Of course you don't. Mummy won't work either.'

After that Emily knew she couldn't possibly tell him about Mr Buckley. Daddy was far too protective. What if he used the pilfering as an excuse to stick her back into a 'suitable' job, as befitted her position as a young lady from an upper-middle-class background. Or would that be a good thing? A safe thing? Like working on the station felt safe. Emily suddenly felt vulnerable. Imagine feeling safe all the time.

No. Changing jobs wasn't the answer. She was in a tight spot and it was up to her to do something about it. That was the grown-up thing to do, the self-respecting thing to do. It was high time she stopped all this internal waffling and acted in a proper manner.

There was nothing for it. She must tackle Mr Buckley – well, maybe not tackle, exactly, but talk to him about it and tell him how worried and upset she felt. He was such a decent man. Emily had no doubt about that, even though he was on the receiving end of goods dishonestly come by. That left her feeling conflicted and she experienced a sinking feeling inside. How could she know what she knew and yet still feel she could trust him? It didn't make sense . . . except that deep down inside her heart, it did.

Having finally made up her mind to speak to Mr Buckley, Emily was deeply frustrated by how difficult it was to find the right opportunity. Finally, the chance arose when they were waiting on the Blackpool platform for the next train to arrive, so that they could offer their services. They had to keep out of the way because the train's next lot of passengers were waiting up and down the platform.

'Keep an eye on my trolley while I nip to the Gents, will you?' asked a porter, who had parked his flatbed trolley beside a pillar.

'Let's take the weight off us feet,' said Mr Buckley, sitting on the edge of the trolley.

Emily perched further along, ready to leap up when she heard the train coming. How long would the porter be? Was there time to raise her all-important worry? At the very least, she needed to open the subject or she would kick herself afterwards.

'Mr Buckley, may I ask you about an important concern I have?'

'Goodness, that sounds serious.' Mr Buckley turned his kindly face towards her. 'Is it to do with the job?'

'Yes, I'm afraid so.'

'Well then, let's hear it.'

Panic streaked through Emily, then she stilled as calm unexpectedly descended. 'It's to do with what sometimes happens in the stores.' She spoke carefully. She didn't want to sound as if she was pointing the finger – even if she was.

'The stores? Everything in there is pretty straightforward. What's the problem?'

'It's not to do with the stores as such,' Emily went on. 'It's the – the way that some of the porters sometimes . . . well, help themselves.'

'And you've been fretting about that? Bless you, my lass. There's no need to get into a frap about it. I told you. It's always gone on. A perk of the job, you might say.'

Oh, crikey. Emily proceeded with even greater caution. She couldn't bring herself to speak outright about theft. Instead, hating herself, she found a way around it. 'But not in wartime, surely? I mean, with rationing and everyone tightening their belts, it's hardly fair, is it, if some people have a means of getting something extra?'

'That's a fair point,' said Mr Buckley, 'but we're not talking about the black market here. Now, that really is bad. Marking up prices sky-high and selling for huge profits – that's downright wrong, that is, whichever way you look at it.'

'My parents say the same. They would never buy on the black market.'

'I'm reet glad to hear it,' said Mr Buckley. 'It's a crying shame what goes on. Why, I was in the pub t'other night and a chap came in – you know the sort, well dressed and shifty-eyed – and he was trying to flog—'

'Excuse the interruption, Mr Buckley,' said Emily, 'but that isn't what I wanted to talk about. I know that what happens in the stores isn't linked to the black market.'

'Dashed right it isn't. It's just a few hard-working men taking home a little bit extra to make life easier for their wives and families. Where's the harm in that?'

Put like that, it sounded reasonable and for half a moment Emily was in danger of getting sucked into that way of thinking, though it would only have lasted as long as her conversation with Mr Buckley.

'I'm sure nobody intends any harm,' she said. It took a surprising amount of resolution to talk in this way. Standing up to Mr Buckley made her feel ashamed of herself. He was so sure he was in the right, and not in an arrogant way, but in a quiet, rather casual way that was strangely compelling. 'But it does mean that there is less to go round when it comes to measuring rations for the local population.'

Mr Buckley chuckled. 'A sack here and there, or a few tins, won't make any difference.'

'But it's the principle of the thing,' Emily exclaimed.

'Oh well, if you're going to talk about principles,' said Mr Buckley and now his voice was stronger than his usual softly spoken tone.

'Yes, I am,' Emily retorted. Then her voice dropped to a whisper. 'Dear Mr Buckley, it's *stealing*.'

'Is it?' Mr Buckley shook his head, sadness filling his eyes. 'What d'you imagine I do with the bits and bobs that come my way? Do you picture me feasting on a bag of dried fruit in my kitchen with the curtains drawn? Let me tell you what I do – well, I'll come to what I do with it *now* in a moment. First off, let me tell you that, yes, I used to take stuff home, but I also helped an old widow up the road. She lost her sons in the last war and hadn't got sixpence to scratch herself with, as the saying goes. I used to slip a bit of this and that her way and she was grateful until the day she died. As for what I do with stuff now – you remember I said my son copped it at Dunkirk? Well, my daughter-in-law, his wife, was killed in the Christmas Blitz later the same year, leaving my grandchildren, Philip and Norah, as orphans. It was up to me to take them in and look after them. There was nobody else to do it – and I wanted to do it. More than anything else in the world, I wanted to do it. Only I couldn't, could I? Not with me being out at work all hours, and a widower to boot. You need a woman in the house if there are kiddies needing looking after. So I had to put them into the railway orphanage. How do you think I felt that day, eh? I'd let everyone down, that was how I felt: my son, his wife, my wife, the children. I'd let all of them down. I was so ashamed I could barely breathe.'

'That's so sad,' whispered Emily.

'Aye, that's one word for it.' Mr Buckley's voice was gruff. 'I'd never felt so desperate in my life. It's a bad business when you lose people because they die, but losing them because you have to send them away . . .'

'You couldn't help it,' said Emily. 'The children had to be looked after.'

'I know, but it's the principle of the thing. Isn't that what you called it? In principle, kiddies are meant to be with their families, with their flesh and blood. It doesn't matter how many times you tell me it's not my fault. It doesn't take away the principle, does it?'

'You did the best you could for them. That's a principle too.'

'Yes, and I'm carrying on doing the best I can for them an' all. When I get a few tins of tomatoes or pears, or a bag of sugar, I don't hoard them for my own use. I knock on the back door of the orphanage, where the cook has no scruples about receiving extras. She'll grab anything she can to make the food stretch that bit further. You might want to call it stealing and you're entitled to your opinion, but I call it doing my very best for my son's kiddies. It might not be a very good best, but it's all I can manage. It breaks my heart that this is what my family has come to. We were a man and wife, with a son and beautiful daughter-in-law and grandkiddies we thought the sun shone out of. And what are we now? A few tins of peas or jars of fish paste at the back door, a couple of tins of salmon if we're lucky. That's not much to have left of a family, but it's all I've got and it's the best I can do. Do you know something? I'm scared of dying.'

'Oh, Mr Buckley.'

'What happens when I meet my son and his mother in the afterlife? What am I supposed to tell them?'

Distress clogged Emily's throat, making it impossible to speak. Not that she could imagine what to say. What answer could there be to a question like that?

CHAPTER TWENTY-THREE

It was early evening when Persephone arrived at Meyrick House, a happy smile forming on her face at the sight of the dear old Georgian building bathed in sunshine. Before she could open the door and step out of the taxi, the driver had opened it for her and was all set to carry her carpet bag, but she hung on to it as she paid him and added a tip. He had automatically brought her to the grand front entrance, where columns stood tall along the terrace, and Persephone hadn't corrected him even though the family hadn't used the front doors since war broke out. This part of the house, indeed most of the house, now belonged to the RAF.

Carrying her tapestry carpet bag, Persephone walked round to the side door, next to what had once been the parterre, where every year the gardeners had laid out thousands of colourful annuals in intricate geometric designs. Now, though, the parterre had been replaced by a salad garden.

Persephone went up the steps and pushed open the door to the bootroom. This at least hadn't changed – well, not much. It was a large lobby with benches along both sides that used to have umpteen pairs of shoes and wellies crammed underneath, but there were only a few pairs now. Likewise, every coat hook had once been in use for mackintoshes, overcoats and shabby old jackets, but most were now empty.

Passing through the inner door, Persephone entered the corridor leading to the sitting room that had taken on the role of her mother's drawing room for the duration. Outside the bootroom stood a table with a small brass bell on it. This was what passed for a bell pull these days. Dumping her bag, Persephone rang the bell to announce her presence.

Dawkins appeared, their lovely old butler, dressed in Home Guard khaki.

'Evening, Dawkins.' Persephone experienced a rush of pleasure at seeing him, though it felt odd, too, seeing a man in uniform moving with the stately grace of a butler.

'Good evening, Miss Persephone. Welcome home. Did you have a good journey?'

'Long,' Persephone answered cheerfully. 'It's good to see you.'

'And to see you, if I may say so. I've no wish to hurry you, but I rang the dressing gong ten minutes ago. Dinner will be served in twenty minutes.'

'Then there's just time for me to change,' said Persephone.

But first things first. Before going to her own room, she ran upstairs to the second floor to find Nanny. Nanny Trehearn-Hobbs had been with them ever since Roddy was a twinkle in his father's eye. After Persephone had left the schoolroom, Nanny had stayed on, officially to do the household mending and watch over visiting children, but just as important, if not more so in Persephone's view, was the interest she took in her old charges and the way she could be relied on for late-night cocoa.

'You'll look after me and be my lady's maid while I'm here, won't you?' asked Persephone.

She put on her most pleading face. Was Nanny fooled by it? Probably not, but she would adore having a chick to fuss over.

'As a matter of fact,' said Nanny, 'I've had a look through your wardrobe and picked something out for this evening, just in case you needed a hand.'

'You're a darling. Shall we go and look?'

She slid her hand into the crook of Nanny's fleshy arm and together they went downstairs into the bedroom Persephone had moved into before leaving for Darley Court. She couldn't have slept in here more than a dozen times since then.

As long ago as 1936, Meyrick House's grounds had been identified as a suitable place for the RAF to have an airfield. Persephone had dismissed the very idea at the time. Far too many trees. But after the house and land were requisitioned, six hundred acres had been cleared for the airfield and its temporary buildings and a long line of ancient horse chestnuts had been felled to provide the necessary visibility for the runway.

The family had been permitted to retain the south wing. Before the RAF took up residence, Pa had arranged for all the best furniture and paintings and the most valuable objets d'art to be carried into the ballroom to be locked away for safe keeping.

'Honestly, Daddy,' Persephone remembered saying. 'It's the RAF that's coming, not the marauding hordes.'

'Don't you believe it,' had been the gruff reply.

Indeed, ever since Persephone had arrived in Manchester, her mother's letters had occasionally contained a line the gist of which was *Those high-spirited boys had another go at the locks last night.*

Persephone's real bedroom was at the front of the house, overlooking the fountain that sat in the centre of the carriage circle, as well as the rose-lined driveway beyond. Now she had a room at the side of the house and the grand driveway was vegetable-lined – apart from the shrubbery, inside which Pa had had a gun turret constructed, declaring, 'If Adolf thinks he's going to walk up the drive and through the front doors of Meyrick House, he's in for a surprise.'

On Persephone's bed, Nanny had laid out a dinner dress in fine wool crepe in the softest of pinks. The sight of matching shoes on the bedside rug gave Persephone a little jolt. The importance of matching shoes had slipped her mind. On the dressing table, with its shield-shaped mirror, lay a glittering aigrette with a dainty puff of pink feathers for Persephone to wear in her hair. It was like travelling back in time.

'You are a darling to do all this for me,' said Persephone.

'I'll help you dress,' said Nanny.

'But first . . .' said Persephone and walked into the old lady's arms. One of the great certainties of childhood had been Nanny's hugs. Persephone might have forgotten about matching shoes, but she had never forgotten Nanny's hugs.

Soon she was ready to go downstairs – not down the grand staircase as in former times, but down a side staircase. She entered Ma's temporary drawing room and there was her mother seated on the sofa, looking elegant in midnight blue with gleaming bands of gold beading around the collar and cuffs. She'd had her silvery hair cut short and styled flat across the top of her head, with flattened rolls of curls down the sides, a version of the Liberty hairstyle.

'Persephone, my dear, how splendid. You've arrived in time for dinner.'

Persephone crossed the room to brush a light kiss against the cheek Ma presented to her. Ma smelled of fresh air and violets with just the tiniest hint of gun oil.

'Stand on the rug, Persephone, so I can look at you. Yes, you're looking well. We're dining à deux this evening. Pour yourself a cocktail.'

'That's rather a whopper of a drink you've got there, Ma,' observed Persephone, going to the huge sideboard, where a crystal jug and glasses were arranged on a silver salver. 'Bad day?'

'It's not alcoholic, silly girl,' said Ma. 'If only . . .'

Persephone sat down before taking a sip. 'Goodness, that's sharp.'

'That'll be the rhubarb.'

Dawkins appeared and announced dinner. Persephone and her mother rose to their feet.

'That's all Dawkins does at dinner time now,' Ma remarked. 'He rings the dressing gong and announces dinner, then he goes on duty.'

They went through to the wartime dining room, previously the billiard room. The long, gleaming table was set for two at the far end with the third-best china, the best and second-best having been packed away in paper and straw in the cellars. A competent middle-aged maid placed tureens on the table and withdrew.

'We serve ourselves these days,' said Ma.

They had devilled fish and there was wine to go with it.

'And this really is wine,' said Ma. 'Apparently, the country has received a shipment of it from Algeria that is going to be released gradually into the shops. I bought three boxes.'

'Three!' Persephone exclaimed. 'That's not exactly fair on all the other customers.'

'It's not all for me, silly child. I still give dinners and it's such a relief to be able to do things properly and offer wine. I donated a couple of bottles to a raffle and I sent four bottles down to the village hall for the WVS. I imagined them sipping it in a genteel fashion and saving the rest for later, but they knocked back the lot and spilled out onto the village green to deliver a rousing rendition of "There'll Always Be an England". Rather sweet, really.'

'I suppose people aren't as accustomed to alcohol as they used to be,' said Persephone.

'Try it,' said Ma. 'It's not bad at all.'

'I think we should start with a toast.'

'Good idea.' Ma raised her glass. 'To all the boys fighting for us. There'll always be an England.'

Persephone raised her glass in response. 'There'll always be an England,' she echoed.

Of all the places to find herself, Persephone lay in a ditch the following morning beside her mother, flinching and hunching each time a bomb landed.

'Oh well,' said Ma. 'If we get blown to kingdom come, at least we'll go in a shower of pretty petals. That's something, I suppose.'

One bomb had been jolly close – close enough for dirt and gravel to pepper them. Every time a shell hit the ground, Ma groaned.

'God, what have they hit this time? This is how we lost the garage roof, you know, because of bally silly trainee airmen who couldn't aim for toffee. Most people spent the phoney war swanning about, carrying on more or less as usual. I spent most of it hiding away from being bombed by our own side because the boys were incapable of hitting the practice targets. Then it stopped, presumably when the airmen got the hang of what they were meant to be doing, and it didn't happen for ages. Then the Yanks turned up and here we are all over again, sheltering in ditches and wishing we'd changed our wills when we had the opportunity.'

'You don't need to change your will, do you, Ma?'

'Certainly not. I'm just making a point. You should appreciate that, a bit of lively exaggeration making a story more interesting, you fancying yourself as a writer.'

'I don't just fancy myself as a writer, Ma,' Persephone said in the light, civil tone she had perfected years ago. It was the tone she was obliged to use almost every time a relative brought up her ambition. 'I am a writer. I've had articles published.'

She shifted position in an attempt to make herself more comfortable, viewing the situation in the way she so often saw things that happened around her. Could she make an article out of it? A publishable one? A ditch at the edge of a meadow, the dainty lilac blooms adorning the lady's smock, the rich yellow of the buttercup and the long, ribbed leaves of the ribwort . . . Put together, they would all create an appealing picture – but not the bombs from the Allies, even though it was the Yankee trainees' lack of skill that made this situation interesting. Persephone smiled to herself. Interesting. Was this what they referred to as great British understatement?

'Old Mr Hardman over at Redroofs Farm makes his POWs carry on working when this happens,' Ma added. 'Poor blighters. He reckons that at least some good will come of it if the Yanks inadvertently kill a few Jerries. Whenever he gets a new POW, he goes right up to him, toe to toe, and examines his face closely to see if he looks like any of the Germans he glimpsed in the Great War. Mrs Hardman reckons he's looking for the son of the man who killed his brother. They were twins, you know. How much longer is this going to go on? We've got guests coming for dinner, including Grandmama. This really is a confounded nuisance. I'm due at a village meeting in half an hour.'

'To give a morale-boosting talk?'

Her mother's face expressed a mixture of incredulity and disdain. 'Is that what you think I do? You imagine yourself to be modern because you write for women's magazines and have a man's job on the railways, yet you still think all my position as headman entails is shaking hands and saying "Good show" to the peasants. I thought better than that of you, Persephone, I really did.'

'I'm sorry if I've given offence, Ma. What shall you be doing?'

'What I've done all through the war – be in charge, make decisions. Being the official headman of the village is an important position. I oversee all our civil defence and I would remind you that we're very near the south coast here. I was sent an official letter at the start of the war. It was sealed and it said on it: *Not to be opened until the enemy is within 10 miles.* I opened it immediately.'

'You didn't,' Persephone breathed.

'I jolly well did. I didn't want tactical orders to be sprung on me in a crisis. I wanted time to consider and make plans.'

'What did it say?'

'Can't tell you that, silly child. But I went over to see Mrs McKenzie, who is the next headman along to the west, to see if she'd opened her letter.'

'And had she?'

'No, she'd put it straight in the fire. She didn't want it falling into enemy hands if there was an invasion. Shame, really. It would have been good to compare notes.' Ma sat up, looking at the sky. 'There hasn't been one for a while and I can't hear the aircraft engines. Let's take our lives in our hands, shall we, and assume they've landed?'

They scrambled out of the ditch.

'At least the bomb that fell in the field didn't land in the middle and destroy the crops,' said Ma, scrutinising the scene before them. 'Shame about that tree, though.'

Marking the adjoining corners of four surrounding fields, a mountain ash, previously tall and graceful, was now half gone and what remained curtsied to the ground in a mass of creamy-white flowers in a wide crater.

'It'll have to come down, of course,' said Ma.

'A job for the POWs?'

'No, this land is considered too close to the airfield for them.'

'It has certainly felt a bit too close to the airfield this morning,' said Persephone.

'We'll have to cut short our walk. I've got to get the village meeting.'

'I'll come with you.'

Ma looked at her. 'There's no reason why not, I s'pose,' she said and they set off. 'Did you sleep well?'

'Yes, thanks.'

'I imagine the train journey was tiring. But you'll need to stay up late tonight and tomorrow night. Some of the chaps from the airfield come round most evenings – later on, you know, so as not to interrupt dinner. I told them to stay away last night so you and I could have a bit of a chinwag and I could send you to bed early.'

'Do they stay horrendously late?' Persephone gave a laugh. 'Are these the same lads who occasionally try to pick the locks and invade the ballroom?'

Ma stopped and turned to face her as Persephone, too, halted. 'They need to talk. Mostly we have a jolly time, but quite often – far more often than one would like – one can see that there's a fellow, hardly more than a boy often as not, who's feeling the pressure and, of course, they can't say a word to their colleagues about their fears.'

'So they come to you.'

'I suppose I'm a sort of mother figure, but a mother whom they don't need to keep sheltered from the truth.'

'Ma, that's a wonderful thing to do for them.' Persephone longed to reach out and touch her mother's arm, just touch her arm, nothing more, to show her sense of pride and compassion, but that wouldn't be appropriate.

'Don't be silly, Persephone. It isn't wonderful at all. Don't romanticise it. It's heartbreaking but necessary. It provides some boys with the boost they need so that they can carry on.' Turning, Ma continued walking. 'I've lost a lot of boys in this war. My two sons are alive as far as I know, but I've lost a lot of boys. It's been . . . hard.'

CHAPTER TWENTY-FOUR

Persephone slipped her feet into strappy silver kid evening sandals. Nanny had picked out a silk-taffeta evening dress in periwinkle blue with no waist seam, the short-sleeved bodice with its square-cut neck flowing into a sleek skirt with the most discreet of flares. It was a dress that used to belong to Iphigenia, who had raved about its 'devastating simplicity', and there had been much discussion when she wanted to pass it on to Persephone as to whether a younger, single girl could wear it and be respectable. But honestly, if Nanny thought it suitable, then suitable it most certainly was.

Persephone had mixed feelings about this evening. She was longing to see Grandmama, natch, and it would be enjoyable to see familiar faces around the dining table as well as meet new people. But after the conversation in the ditch earlier on, followed by seeing Ma as headman, running the busy meeting with brisk efficiency, Persephone wondered how Ma could bear to step back into her other role as lady of the manor. Did it feel trivial compared to her important war work? It must do.

Today Persephone had seen her mother in an entirely new way. Oh, she'd known about her being the headman, of course, but she'd never really experienced it before and she was both astonished and deeply impressed. Ma was so very different to the Mummy she had known all her life. As a child, she had worshipped beautiful Mummy from afar. As she grew up, she had seen Mummy as the perfect lady whose elegance and social grace she aspired to emulate in all ways. When she had decided to drop the 'Mummy' and use 'Ma', she had thought it was because she wished to sound more grown-up, but had at least part of the decision been some kind of subconscious recognition that there was much more to Mummy than met the eye? Did the casual-sounding 'Ma' better reflect the confidence of the guiding hand and the strong backbone that had come as such a revelation to Persephone?

She felt confidence burst into life inside her. Ma – modern, determined, forthright and eminently sensible – wouldn't be shocked by Persephone's relationship with Matt. Mummy would have been appalled, but Ma would take it on the chin. Ma would understand.

She met Ma downstairs before the guests started to arrive. Grandmama was the first and Persephone had to quell a childish urge to run into her arms. Grandmama's hair had been snow-white for years, but beneath the faintest dusting of face powder she had more lines than she used to. Her eyes hadn't changed, though. They were still lively and bright.

Ma had evidently decided to cram as many as she could around the dining table and Dawkins must have been busy all afternoon polishing the silverware. The main course was officially referred to as pork fillets when really it was sausage meat mixed with mashed potatoes and crispy breadcrumbs and fashioned into the appropriate shape, accompanied by plentiful vegetables, with a tangy lemon tart afterwards, not to mention the Algerian wine.

The guests included county people and bigwigs from the RAF and the American Air Force. When the party repaired to the drawing room after the meal, some evening guests arrived, the ones Ma had earlier referred to as 'chaps from the airfield' and Persephone cast her eye over them, wondering if later tonight one of them might pour confidences into Ma's ear or even into her own. There might be one who would respond better to a sister figure than to a mother figure. If so, she would be ready.

'Ah, so you're Persephone,' said the wing commander when they were introduced. 'You're the one who works as a ticket inspector and writes for that women's paper. What's it called? *Someone-or-other's Voice*. My wife reads it.'

'Vera,' said Persephone. '*Vera's Voice*.'

'That's it. And you won the point-to-point trophy when you were a little girl even though you were two years younger than all the other riders. That was you, wasn't it?'

'How on earth do you know that?' The job and the writing, yes – but an ancient pony-riding triumph?

'I go up to London to the War Office sometimes,' he told her, 'and I've had the pleasure of meeting your father.'

Persephone looked at him. It still didn't make sense.

'He talks about you all the time,' said the wing commander. 'He's so proud of you.'

It was all she could do not to exclaim, 'Really? I had no idea.'

Pa? Proud of her – of *her*? Always talking about her? That didn't fit in at all with Persephone's experience. She hadn't known Pa was even particularly aware of her existence beyond paying compliments when she dressed her best, and even those compliments had always been prompted by her mother. But apparently he talked about her to other people – and showed pride in her.

After having to revise all her ideas about Ma, was she now also required to see Pa through fresh eyes? But she couldn't be as happy about this new version of Pa as she was about the way she now viewed her mother. If Pa loved her and was proud of her, why had he never told her?

*

232

Emily and her mother had spent the evening at the knitting circle that was held in St Clement's church hall, about halfway between where the Masters family lived on Edge Lane and Mrs Cooper's house in Wilton Close. Sometimes Emily blushed as she remembered the very first time she had attended and how deeply unimpressed she had been at having to hobnob with Mummy's lower-class friends, one of whom, as she discovered during that evening, was, of all things, a cleaner. How horrified she'd felt – and how differently she felt now. She'd been a self-satisfied little snob back then, but she'd grown up a lot and had learned to value people according to their personal merits. As for the cleaner – well, Mrs Cooper was someone she now loved dearly and had all the time in the world for.

Colette came to the knitting circle too. She could have joined one much nearer to home, but she enjoyed seeing Mrs Cooper and Mrs Grayson, so she came on the bus from Seymour Grove.

As the evening neared its close, Miss Travers approached the table around which Emily sat with her mother, Colette and the ladies from Wilton Close. Mrs Grayson, an expert knitter, was churning out squares for baby blankets and the rest of them were working on various garments for children. Emily's knitting had come on no end since she'd met Mrs Grayson, who had patiently taught her heaps of new stitches and calmly undone all Emily's mistakes, encouraging her to try again.

Emily smiled up at Miss Travers. She was Mrs Grayson's hairdresser and sometimes Emily accompanied Mrs Grayson there and back because she had a fear of being outdoors and benefited from the moral support provided by a sympathetic companion. A flash of memory struck her – being asked for the first time to assist Mrs Grayson in this way and feeling outraged by her mother's manipulation. Lord, what a little horror she had been.

'We've got a large quantity of finished items in the back, far more than we normally have,' said Miss Travers. 'I need a volunteer to pack them up and label the boxes. Any takers?'

'Let me finish my row and I'll do it,' said Colette. 'I won't be a minute.'

When Colette glanced around the table, Emily expected her to ask Mrs Cooper to help with the packing, because the two of them were very close, but instead Colette's gaze fell on Emily.

'Care to lend a hand?'

Emily was pleased to be asked. It was nice to think that Colette wanted her company. She finished her row and carefully folded the little jumper she was making. A minute or two later, she and Colette were in the small side room, looking through the garments, baby blankets and baby shawls that had been sent in by women who knitted every day. How enjoyable it was to be engaged in something that didn't involve worrying herself silly about other people's questionable conduct. Emily gave her head a slight shake. Even when there was no need to think about what was happening at work, it was still there, ready to creep out and distract her and make her tummy feel fluttery.

It was so hard living with her secret. She stole a glance at Colette, who was putting the clothes into piles. Colette of all people knew everything there was to know about living with a secret. How had she managed it for all those years?

In the next moment, it seemed that Colette had read her mind, because she remarked, 'You seem preoccupied, Emily. I don't mean just this evening. I mean in general. It seems to be every time I see you.'

'Has my mother put you up to this?' The question spurted out of her mouth before Emily could prevent it.

'No,' Colette said quietly.

'I'm sorry if that sounded tetchy,' said Emily.

She felt as though she was hovering on the brink. Should she speak up? And just like that, the words appeared in her head. *If ever you want to talk to somebody . . .* Colette's words, Colette's kind offer back at the start of the year. Of course, Colette had meant that they could talk about Raymond, but might this be the moment to share those dark worries about the pilfering? Colette was such a caring person. She wouldn't tell Emily off for not having spoken up sooner. She wouldn't despise her for her silence. She would understand that the situation was more complicated than that.

Emily had a sudden feeling of ease and calm that had been missing from her life for a long time.

'You're right,' she told Colette. 'I do have something on my mind.' She waited, but to her surprise, Colette didn't press for details. After a moment, Emily added, 'Aren't you going to ask?'

'Not straight out, no. I'm always ready to listen and I won't ever let my own opinions cloud what you say. If you want help or a shoulder to cry on, I'm here, though I'm sure you've got plenty of friends your own age who are more than ready to support you.'

'Not that I could talk to about this,' said Emily.

Colette frowned. 'Does that mean it's something other than Raymond? Sorry – I shouldn't pry.'

They carried on sorting the knitted clothes into piles.

'May I ask you a question?' said Emily. 'When you lived with Tony and he was so horrid to you, how did you manage? It went on and on and you never told a soul.'

Colette stopped with a couple of pinafores in her hands. 'I managed because I had to. I managed because I thought it was the right thing to do. I was so scared and ashamed.'

'You had nothing to be ashamed of,' Emily exclaimed and when Colette smiled at her, she realised what she'd said. 'That was what you said you wouldn't do if I confided in you. You said you wouldn't try to make me feel better; you'd just let me feel what I feel. And here am I telling you how you should have felt before I even met you.'

'When everyone else thinks things are as they should be, and you know how wrong and tasteless it is to wash your dirty linen in public, you feel stuck with matters the way they are. That was how it was for me. I believed the rest of my life was going to be that way, but eventually Mrs Cooper overheard Tony when he was showing his true colours and that was the beginning of my way out of an impossible situation, though that makes it sound as if it was resolved easily, which it certainly wasn't.'

'But if Mrs Cooper hadn't overheard . . .' Emily mused.

'But she did overhear.' Colette spoke with quiet firmness. 'And I'm eternally grateful she did, because otherwise I'd never have breathed a word.' She touched Emily's hand. 'I just hope you can be braver than I was.'

'What?' Emily might have jerked her hand away, but in that moment she was frozen.

'I'm sure there's something wrong,' said Colette. 'Maybe having kept my own secret for so long has made me sensitive to the existence of unhappy secrets in other people. If you want to tell me, Emily, I promise I'll do all I can to help you.'

CHAPTER TWENTY-FIVE

Lying in bed, Persephone struggled to come to terms with the picture of her father that the wing commander had painted. All she could think was what a terrible waste it was if Pa felt like that about her without ever letting on. If only she had known . . . but she never had, so there was little point in dwelling on it. Even so, she spent much of the night doing precisely that, her thoughts going round and round and always ending up back in the same place. What a waste.

It was better, surely, to concentrate on Ma. Much more positive. Persephone relaxed as tension she hadn't even been aware of melted away. What a fine person Ma was, a real brick, truly admirable. She had taken her position at the head of her community and proved what she was made of. Forget the lady of the manor. Lady Trehearn-Hobbs was the headman through and through. Persephone had witnessed for herself at the village meeting how much everyone looked up to her and how her every word counted. If anybody had entertained doubts and fears at the outbreak of war when the General had announced he would be spending most of the time in London, those worries wouldn't have lasted long, not with Ma at the helm, proving her worth on a daily basis.

Having spent ages before this visit wondering exactly how she was going to tell her mother about her relationship with Matt, Persephone now had no fears at all, not now she'd seen Ma in charge of the area, not now she under-stood what a strong, independent woman Ma was.

The next day, Ma was out all morning, 'on business' she said, and Persephone spent the time calling on local people and hearing all their news. Ma was due to chair a meeting in the afternoon, but she would have a free hour after lunch and this was the time Persephone chose for telling her about Matt.

Ma had kept a small flower garden going and after lunch the two of them strolled through drifts of columbines and forget-me-nots, admiring the bright greeny-yellow of the euphorbia at the back and the dainty violets sprawling at the front next to the path.

'If one sat out here for long enough,' said Persephone as they settled on the wooden bench, 'one might forget the war existed.'

'Silly child.' Ma turned her face up to the spring sun-shine.

'Ma, I've got something to tell you.'

'What's that?'

Persephone's heart beat a little harder. 'It's to do with a man.'

'Oh, darling,' Ma exclaimed, turning to her and looking full into her face. 'I've been agonising over whether to men-tion it ever since you said you were coming.'

'What d'you mean? How did you know?' Crikey, Iphigenia hadn't blabbed, had she?

'I've known all along, ever since you were a young girl. You had stars in your eyes every time you looked at him. Don't worry. I was the only one who noticed. Your brothers never had an inkling and Forbes, stupid male that he is, was utterly clueless.'

Forbes! Persephone stared at her mother.

'You knew about Forbes?'

'Haven't I just said so? I've known ever since the first time the boys invited him here to stay in the hols. I always hoped he'd finally see what was in front of him, but he never seemed to, not even when you were so ravishingly lovely in your first Season. That was why I finally took matters into my own hands when he was laid up in hospital at the start of the year. I wrote to him, sending commiserations and such, and suggested he ask if you might be able to travel down to see him. No one was more delighted than I was when you did. I felt very much the matchmaker. I hope you don't mind, darling. I wasn't interfering – well, not exactly – but he was being such an oaf, you see, and he needed a shove in the right direction.'

'That was you?' A chill rippled through Persephone. 'It was your idea?'

And she had travelled with such hope in her heart, certain that at long last Forbes had realised what a peach she was and couldn't wait to tell her. But he'd only asked for the visit because Ma had suggested it. Undoubtedly, left to his own devices, he wouldn't have thought of it.

'Don't blame Forbes, darling,' said Ma. 'He just needed a teeny push, that's all. I've been waiting ever since for you to tell me the good news. When you never wrote about him, I feared maybe it had gone horribly wrong, but when you told me you were coming for a visit, I felt sure Forbes was the reason. I've been biting my tongue ever since you got here. Much as I longed to dive in, I knew I had to let you speak first. Tell me, child. Are congratulations in order?'

What a fiasco. Persephone stared at her hands as if they might contain all the answers. Imagine it – Ma had known about Forbes all this time and never let on. Then, determined to do the pair of them a good turn, she had engineered Persephone's visit to Ashridge, whereupon not only had matters not resolved themselves as Persephone had longed for at the time, but they hadn't worked out as Ma had intended either. Persephone cocked her head, her gaze drifting out of focus. Ma had known the whole time. It was difficult to take it in.

The conversation with Ma in the flower garden had descended into profound embarrassment on both sides when Persephone had admitted that Forbes remained utterly uninterested her romantically.

Then Ma had said, 'Oh well, it's best that you know. No point in keeping on with hopeless dreams. You've dreamed for a very long time, child.'

And if she had said it kindly, softly, if she had put an arm around Persephone when she said it, if she had kissed Persephone or stroked her arm, if she had gently expressed her sorrow . . . then Persephone might have felt able to say that her own feelings had moved on from her youthful love and she'd met another man. But instead Ma had uttered the words in a sensible voice that verged on the bracing, which had somehow prevented Persephone from mentioning Matt. In any case, she was too taken aback.

But now, some hours later, with Nanny helping her to dress for dinner, she cursed herself for not leading the conversation in Matt's direction – but she'd been so thoroughly astonished.

One thing was certain. She had to tell Ma about Matt today. It mustn't be left any longer. Ma had been busy right up until Dawkins rang the dressing gong and there were to be more guests this evening, so that meant telling Ma after everyone had left. Persephone hoped that there wouldn't be an unhappy airman this evening in need of moral support into the wee small hours.

'There.' How proud Nanny sounded. 'I'll just move the mirror a fraction for you.'

'There's no need.' Goodness, had she really once upon a time lived in a world in which, instead of her being required to take a step to the side, someone had discreetly adjusted the position of the cheval glass?

This evening Nanny had chosen a primrose-yellow full-length gown with wide shoulder straps and a panelled skirt. The very first time Persephone had worn it, she had hoped her appearance would give Forbes the jolt he needed to fall for her charms. How many times had she dressed for an evening with that precise aim in mind? Now she had a new man in her life and the difference was that Matt really was a part of her life in every sense. Not like Forbes, who, while being of paramount importance to her, had only ever existed on the fringes.

She couldn't wait to tell Ma. All right, so Ma wouldn't gush about it and be thrilled and start talking about hats. She wasn't that sort. But she would be glad that the Forbes situation hadn't caused prolonged unhappiness. And the wider vision with which she viewed the world as headman of the community and confidante of airmen johnnies in need of moral support would ensure her ability to accept Persephone's relationship with a man who was from a different part of society. Gone was Mummy, to whom good manners, perfect appearance and the social round meant everything. Ma was a different and far more interesting kettle of fish.

The evening passed pleasantly and Persephone did her duty as daughter of the house, ensuring that every guest felt included. After a dinner of tomato and bean pie followed by a pudding of apple rings with honey and walnuts, Ma asked her to play the piano as a gentle background to drawing-room conversation. When Ma's after-dinner airmen pitched up, the music soon turned into a singalong, starting with 'Whispering Grass' and ranging through the likes of 'I, Yi, Yi, Yi, Yi (I Like You Very Much)' and 'Hey Little Hen' to the heart-tugging strains of 'The White Cliffs of Dover' and, of course, 'We'll Meet Again'.

The evening ended on an uplifting note and the guests took their leave, smiling and offering best wishes all round.

Having exchanged the final farewells, Ma turned to Persephone as the drawing-room door shut for the final time.

'I think we can count that as a success. Thank you for playing for everyone.'

'Pleasure,' Persephone murmured.

'Shall we go up?' Ma suggested just as Persephone was about to take a seat. 'Another busy day tomorrow.'

'Before we do,' said Persephone, 'please could we have a bit of a talk?'

'Honestly, hasn't there been enough conversation without a late-night chinwag? I'm not really in the mood.'

'No, not a chinwag,' said Persephone. 'A proper talk. I have something I want to tell you.'

'And it can't wait until the morning?' said Ma. 'Oh, very well, if you must. I'm sorry not to sound more gracious, but I'm tired.'

It was hardly the opening Persephone had hoped for, but she persevered. 'Come and sit over here. Would you like another cushion?'

'I'm not an invalid, Persephone.'

'I didn't mean to suggest you were.' Persephone sat down opposite her. 'I'm simply trying to make a little fuss of you. You work jolly hard.'

'I'm hardly alone in that. Everyone works hard at the moment. It's called the war effort. Pass me a cigarette, would you?'

Persephone picked up the carved ivory box from the rosewood table that stood between them. Removing a cigarette, she slotted it into the long cigarette holder that Ma referred to as her barber's pole because of its red and white spiral pattern. Giles had given it to her as a joke present one Christmas and much to everyone's surprise, she had adopted it for everyday use.

Ma held it to her lips and inhaled strongly, lifting her chin to exhale. 'That's better. What did you wish to say?'

'I want to start by saying what an eye-opener it's been seeing you in action, Ma. You're amazing. You're in control of everything and you project such an air of confidence and efficiency. I can see how sincerely everyone looks up to you and how deeply you deserve it.'

'Don't gush. You sound like a schoolgirl in love with Clark Gable.'

'I only want to express my admiration. You're simply marvellous as the headman. And then you have to come home and change for cocktails, non-alcoholic, of course. Is it galling to do such sterling work all day and then have to be the lady of the manor again?'

'Galling? What an odd word to choose. It's all about appearances, Persephone. Appearances are important. When people look to one to set the right example, naturally one must be seen to do the right thing.'

'I don't mean to suggest that appearances are irrelevant,' said Persephone, 'but they can be shallow compared to what really matters.'

'What are you saying?' There was a sharp note in Ma's question. 'Kindly come to the point. Where is this leading?'

Persephone drew in a breath, confidence riding high. 'I was never more astonished in my life than when you told me you'd known all along about Forbes. When we went into the flower garden, it was my intention to talk about what I'm going to tell you now, but you took the wind completely out of my sails. I've been waiting since then. The fact is,' and a tingle of anticipation swept across her skin, 'it wasn't Forbes I wanted to discuss. It was . . . Matt.'

'Matt?' Ma had been about to place her cigarette holder to her lips again, but instead she jerked it away, or rather it was her chin that jerked away. Her brows drew together.

'Short for Matthew,' said Persephone.

'Are you telling me you've met somebody else? Already?'

'Don't say it like that, Ma. Presumably you'd rather I didn't spend the rest of my life pining for Forbes. And if you're surprised that I could meet another man so soon, well, it took me by surprise too.'

'You're on the rebound,' Ma stated.

'No, I can assure you my feelings are real.'

Ma let out a breath that contained a small laugh. 'This is the last thing I expected you to say. Obviously, I'm glad if you're happy.'

'Thank you,' said Persephone. 'I'm very happy. Matt is – well, he suits me. We seem to see the world in the same way.'

'Did you meet him at Darley Court?'

'At work, actually.'

Now Ma gave a genuine laugh. 'Did you have to check his ticket? Which branch of the services is he in? I hope he's good at writing letters, because that's one of your strengths, always has been. A solid correspondence between a couple parted by war is a good foundation.'

'When I said I met him at work, I meant he works on the railways.'

'Exempt from active service, is he? On what grounds? I hope you haven't taken pity on a weakling, Persephone.'

'He isn't there because he's exempt. He's always worked on the railways. He's a fireman.'

'I beg your pardon – did you just say he's a fireman? Are you saying you've taken up with a man who stokes fires for a living?'

'It's highly skilled work,' said Persephone.

'Skilled? He's a *fire*man. He works with his hands. Good grief, Persephone. What were you thinking?'

'I was thinking that, with your experience of wartime life and responsibilities and the way your horizons have widened, you'd accept it. After all, you've well and truly left behind the lady of the manor.'

'Left behind . . .? For your information, Persephone, I perceive no difference between the headman and the lady of the manor. Both positions are essential in wartime and I make no distinction between them. You speak as if the headman is the real me and as Lady Trehearn-Hobbs I'm acting a part. That's pure drivel. I am one person, capable of many things. Who are you to suggest that my life as the lady of the manor is some sort of sham? How dare you imply that I did not become my real self until war was on the horizon and I resolved to undertake my patriotic duty to the best of my ability? Through my patriotic duty, I became the headman of the local community and I have worked tirelessly in that capacity. At the same time, as lady of the manor, I have organised competitions for who can grow the potato plant with the biggest yield and the most vegetables relative to the size of their garden. I have organised every single type of fundraising event you can imagine, from beat-the-clock crosswords to whist drives to tennis tournaments and make-do-and-mend fashion shows. I may be a Lady with a capital L, but I'm also – no, not "*but* I'm also" – *and* I'm also a strong-minded, intelligent, capable woman and a deeply patriotic one, who has worked hard to be worthy of the title of headman. I also firmly believe that no man could have made a better fist of it than I have.'

Persephone started to speak, but Ma cut her off.

'If Herr Hitler walked through my drawing-room door one evening, I would jolly well keep him talking so that all my guests had a chance to get away, and then I'd slit his throat from ear to ear, with my fingernails if I had to. That's how I see my patriotism. And where has your patriotism led you, might I ask? You have your war work on the railways and I'm proud of you. But what about your backbone? Where's your loyalty to the family? Patriotism means working all hours to keep the country in one piece, working towards returning it to the way it used to be, the way it's meant to be. Patriotism does not mean consorting with the lower orders and potentially giving them ideas.'

'But it isn't like that, Ma,' Persephone said eagerly. 'Take the Franklin family.'

'And who might they be?'

'Matt's people. Yes, they're not landed or titled, but that doesn't mean they can't be decent and respectable.'

'Of course it doesn't. Everybody should strive to be decent and respectable, regardless of their status in life.'

'Exactly.' Persephone pounced on this. 'And doesn't that make everybody the same? Aren't personal values more important than whether somebody went to public school?'

'I see. We're descending into the realms of philosophy now, are we? Of course personal values matter – as you are perfectly well aware, because if they didn't, you wouldn't have brought them up.'

'The point I wished to make was that, yes, there is a social gap—'

'A social chasm,' Ma murmured.

'—a social gap,' Persephone repeated, 'between this family and the Franklins, but when I went to meet them—'

The colour drained from Ma's face. 'You've met them?'

'At their house, yes. I was invited for Sunday tea – and before you make any comment, please let me finish. I only want to say that good manners saw us through. It's something I've been thinking about for a while, actually. As a matter of fact, I had started to write an article about it, taking the view that in these days of wartime, when social boundaries are blurred in a way they never have been before—'

'I'm sorry, Persephone. I have to stop you there. I refuse to listen to such twaddle. "Social boundaries are blurred" – no, they most definitely are not, you foolish girl. Do you imagine I have less dignity because I am headman? Do you imagine I am treated with less respect?'

'That isn't what I meant. I meant that these days we are all meeting people whom we would never previously have come across—'

'It certainly seems to be so in your case.' It was a disapproving mutter but more than loud enough to be heard.

'The point being,' Persephone stated, 'that it's simple good manners that make this happen in a reasonable and acceptable way. And then,' she hurried on before Ma could interject with another put-down, 'I met Matt's family and we had a pleasant afternoon, and it was all possible because we knew how to behave. We were all polite. We paid attention to one another and made sure the conversation flowed. In fact, it was because of the success of that Sunday tea that I extended my article and used the tea as an example. I don't mean I named names or anything of the kind, but this is how articles are often written. One makes one's point by creating a little fiction out of it, though it is presented as the real thing to the reader. "Allow me to tell you about my friends Mary and Harold, who are struggling to cope with missing their sons . . ." "A young friend confided in me how much she wishes her parents would permit her more freedom . . ." That kind of thing.'

'And so you used your personal experience to write an article. I see.' Ma looked thoughtful. 'Why didn't you say so in the first place?'

Persephone took heart. 'It's a jolly good piece. *Vera's Voice* bought it immediately. Normally articles don't get published for a while because magazines are planned way in advance, but they're going to make space for my article quite soon. I'm jolly proud of that.'

'So when you met these people,' said Ma, 'you were conducting research for what sounds, if I may say so, like a deeply ill-advised article, in the course of which you have fallen into an unsuitable relationship with a lower-class man who probably can't believe his good fortune. Not only are you on the rebound from Forbes—'

'Ma, I've already told you I'm not.'

'—but in the pursuit of your so-called writing career, you have indulged in a social experiment that has now gone hideously wrong for you. Oh, Per*seph*one, you foolish child.'

CHAPTER TWENTY-SIX

Having slept fitfully, Persephone awoke early to azure-blue skies and a dew-sprinkled lawn. It was the perfect spring morning, except for the planes flying overhead on the way back to their various bases. How many of them ought there to be? How many brave boys would never come home again? How did Mabel stand it when Harry was flying missions? Thank goodness he was based on terra firma, for the time being at least.

That thought put her own woes into perspective. She wasn't entirely sure how she was to face her mother this morning. Oh well, better get it over with. Later on, she would pour out the whole story to Nanny, who would be every bit as shocked as Ma, of course, but would be a great deal kinder about it.

She put on a skirt and blouse with a lightweight jumper on top. Downstairs, she paused outside the dining room to take a breath and pin on a smile before walking in.

'Good morning, Persephone.' Ma looked up. 'Did you sleep well? I can't say you deserved to after last night's horrors.'

'I did feel a bit unsettled,' Persephone said lightly.

'So did I, to start with – more than a little. Then I decided that you're a level-headed girl, not normally given to ludicrous flights of fancy, so I'm sure you'll see sense in due course. Moreover, I have no intention of letting this spoil your last day at home. After that, I slept like a top.'

'Ma, if you'd just let me tell you about Matt—'

'No, thank you. I'm sure he's the salt of the earth, exactly what we need to keep our railway network running – and we have already established that his family has beautiful manners. Now then, I shall be busy all morning and I'd like you to accompany me. I assume you'd prefer that to remaining at home in a sulk.'

'You assume correctly and I dislike being called a sulker.'

Before Ma could respond, the door was more or less flung open and Dawkins practically sprang into the room.

'Your Ladyship, the Dowager Lady Trehearn-Hobbs is—'

And that was as far as he got before Grandmama marched in, all but bowling him aside.

'Mama,' Ma exclaimed.

Grandmama froze in position. 'That will be all, thank you, Dawkins,' she said without looking at him. When the door shut behind him, she swished across the room and slapped a folded-open newspaper onto the table. 'There!' She glared at Persephone. 'What *have* you done?'

Persephone's insides trembled. It was hard to believe this was actually happening, but there it was in black and white in Clarinda's society column. Even though by now she knew it word for word, she couldn't stop reading it.

In March, the Honourable Persephone Trehearn-Hobbs, who is residing in the north for the duration, organised a splendid Wings for Victory dance at the prestigious Claremont Hotel, where guests danced the night away while raising funds for this most essential of causes. Since then the Honourable Miss Trehearn-Hobbs has been seen out and about on the arm of her handsome new escort, Mr Matthew Franklin, who is a train driver. Miss Trehearn-Hobbs is visiting her ancestral home and the proverbial little bird has whispered in my ear that on the occasion of her next visit, Mr Franklin may accompany her.

'It's the last word in absurdity, of course,' Grandmama declared, shuddering. 'Tell me it's absurd, Persephone. We shall have to demand a full apology from the newspaper and they must sack Clarinda, whoever he or she is.'

'We can only demand an apology if it's untrue,' said Ma, giving Persephone a meaningful look. 'Isn't that so? Well, go on. Tell your grandmama.'

'The only bit that's untrue,' said Persephone, 'is calling him a train driver. He's a fireman.'

'There is a second untruth,' said Ma. 'The suggestion that I would countenance receiving the likes of a fireman under my roof.'

Grandmama's hand flew to her silk-clad chest. 'Do you mean to say that this is basically the truth, Persephone? That you are in fact . . . I cannot bring myself to say it.' She gave another shudder, a more elaborate one.

Persephone felt as if the heavens had fallen on her head. Her sister would now think she was engaged in a fling. Her mother already thought she had undertaken a social experiment that had backfired on her heart. The world in general would think she was slumming. Nothing could be worse than this.

The door opened and Dawkins appeared.

'The General is on the telephone, Your Ladyship.'

By the middle of the morning, Persephone was on the train bound for London to explain herself to her father – and he wasn't the only one she intended to see, though she hadn't shared this with her mother and grandmother. Before Pa had the opportunity to eat her up and spit her out, she must hotfoot it to the newspaper offices to confront Mr Bunting. She would barge in if she had to. She needed to find out who Clarinda was. She had to know who had done this to her.

Every single person she or her family had ever met must be lapping up the juicy details. People who didn't know Persephone but who loved the Clarinda column must have read the piece with fascination. She felt a dark chill right to the centre of her being. Oh, it didn't bear thinking about. It was intolerable. Tears blurred her vision, but she blinked them away. She had to be strong.

Arriving in London, she rushed to see Mr Bunting in his offices.

'My dear Miss Trehearn-Hobbs,' he began, coming to his feet as she was shown in and waving her towards a seat before he resumed his own. 'To what do I owe the pleasure?'

'Not so much "to what" as "to whom", Mr Bunting. Who is Clarinda these days?'

'Why, you of all people know perfectly well that Clarinda's identity is a closely guarded secret.'

'Not necessarily as closely guarded as all that. I seem to recall that my grandmother knew who the Clarinda before me was.'

'That doesn't mean I'm going to divulge the identity of the current Clarinda.'

No, of course it didn't. Persephone breathed out a soft huff of frustration. And after all, what difference did it make? Actually, it felt as though it made a very large difference. She felt as if . . . no, she was being silly and oversensitive. No, she wasn't. Someone – Clarinda – had seen her with Matt, presumably more than once. That someone had dug about and found out information about

Matt – not merely his name but his job. Persephone felt as if she'd been spied upon. It made her skin crawl.

'Why do you wish to know anyway?' Mr Bunting enquired.

'Have you seen what Clarinda has written about me?'

There was a short delay while Mr Bunting called for the relevant piece and it was brought in and put before him. A way of playing for time when really he already knew exactly what it said? Persephone couldn't tell.

Mr Bunting read the lines. 'Are you saying that this is untrue?'

'No, but—'

'And Clarinda starts by positively admiring your remarkable contribution to the Wings for Victory Week.'

'Yes, but—'

'You will, of course, recall from your own days in Clarinda's chair that the two rules for the society column are truth and tone, the tone being flattering. Has either of these rules been broken?'

'That sentence at the end—'

'I don't need to tell you, Miss Trehearn-Hobbs, that the house rule is that if Clarinda links a lady's name with that of a gentleman, it has to be done in such a way as to suggest the respectability of the matter. Here,' and Mr Bunting waved a hand over the top of the paper in front of him, 'by suggesting that Mr Franklin might be introduced to your parents, Clarinda is clearly showing the world that this friendship is all that it should be and not some grubby little hole-and-corner affair. Come, my dear, you're a modern young lady doing your bit for the war effort, which is entirely admirable, and you've made some new friends outside your own class, which I venture to say is entirely normal these days.'

'But the implication is that Mr Franklin will come to Meyrick House.'

'Is that not the case? Well, Clarinda hasn't stated it as a fact. Look, a "little bird" has told her. If I may say so, perhaps it is the little bird's identity that you should pursue rather than Clarinda's.' Mr Bunting's manner was still avuncular but his eyes were shrewd as he asked, 'Are you saying that this . . . speculation in the final sentence harms you?'

Persephone opened her mouth to reply, to retaliate, and then shut it again, cutting off her response. She gave herself a moment, then smiled charmingly at Mr Bunting, her whole manner exuding good-natured calm. 'I'm not suggesting that at all, though I will admit to being disconcerted, shall we say, by Clarinda's hint.'

'Disconcerted,' said Mr Bunting. 'That's understandable.'

There was nothing to be gained by prolonging the interview. Persephone stood up and Mr Bunting did likewise.

'Thank you so much for your time,' said Persephone. 'It was most kind of you to see me.'

'Always a pleasure, Miss Trehearn-Hobbs.'

They shook hands and Mr Bunting walked round his desk to open the door for her.

As Persephone went on her way, Mr Bunting's questions echoed in her thoughts.

Are you saying that this . . . speculation in the final sentence harms you?

To her eternal shame, when he had put the question to her in his office, she had been about to say yes. Was that because of Ma's influence and Grandmama's outrage? No, she absolutely wouldn't try to lay the blame elsewhere. Where had that 'yes' sprung from? Not from her heart, she knew that more certainly than she had ever known anything. Then where?

From social convention, that's where. From the age-old rule that required one to keep to one's own class. From the social law that meant a lady derived her status from the man whom society deemed to be her lord and master, namely her father to start with, and then her husband. From the social code that said a girl could rise in the world through a prosperous match, but she could also damn herself by a foolish one.

But Persephone's relationship with Matt had nothing to do with social convention. It was based on sincere friendship, on warmth and humour and being like-minded. It had grown out of having similar ideas, from each of them having dreams that they had followed. It had come from honest liking and admiration, from the way they instinctively smiled at one another without a word needing to be said. It had come from . . . from a feeling of rightness. That was it. Rightness.

And yet – and yet for Persephone to say those lines in Clarinda's column hadn't caused harm would not be true, because harm had indeed been done. The world would now see her as a posh girl defying both her family and every social expectation by enjoying a bit of rough, which was sort of all right if one did it in secret but was an absolute no-no in public. And Matt would be denounced as an upstart.

Persephone's eyelids fluttered and closed for a moment as again she saw Grandmama stalking into the dining room and flinging the open newspaper onto the table with a cry of 'There!'

Grandmama had caused a scandal in her day as the Gaiety Girl who had married a title. But that had ended up being an acceptable sort of scandal because she had done everything she could to learn the ropes and had never put a foot wrong. Now, when people recalled her career on the stage, the word 'scandal' was spoken with affection and even a chuckle of admiration.

But it would never be that way for Persephone and Matt. And didn't that thought contain within it a huge assumption? It suggested something long-term. They had hardly known one another five minutes and it was far too soon for ideas of that sort. Yet it wasn't an idea Persephone wanted to turn her back on.

But this piece in Clarinda's column might well put paid to any relationship at all, even to the most basic friendship.

Another thought. It was newspaper readers from her own rank in life who were the most likely to see and be dismayed and disgusted by the revelation, not people in Matt's circle, because wouldn't they prefer different, less grand newspapers? If that was the case, then the harm might be solely on her side. Did that matter? She certainly didn't want Matt to be hurt in any way whatsoever. But if his family and friends were to remain unaware of Clarinda's assumption simply because they bought a humbler newspaper, was this just another way of highlighting the differences between them?

The more she thought about it, the more fiendishly complicated the matter became. Why did it have to be this way? All Persephone wanted was a warm, loving, trusting relationship, the sort that Joan had with Bob, Alison with Joel, and Mabel with Harry. Was that too much to ask? After years of hopelessly loving the eminently suitable Forbes, was she now to have Matt wrenched away from her because their friendship was socially undesirable?

If only she could have more time to think things over before she had to see Pa, but that was out of the question. She had been instructed to go to the family's London house and wait for him. Goodness knew how long he would be if there was any kind of emergency going on at the War Office. Persephone smiled wryly to herself. Well, she had hoped for more thinking time, hadn't she?

She hadn't set foot inside the London house since before the war and things had changed considerably, which she had known about, of course, but it still came as a bit of a shock to see the downstairs rooms now given over to offices. Pa lived on the first floor and a great deal of moving around of furniture had evidently been undertaken to accommodate this.

She had to wait a couple of hours before voices on the stairs alerted her to Pa's arrival. The door was opened by a military aide and the General walked in. Knife-edge smart in his uniform, he was tall and well built, with a clever, distinguished face and all the self-confidence that came from a privileged background, which had only been increased by his military service and experience.

'Thank you,' he said to the aide. 'That will be all. Leave that,' he added, and the aide put down a polished briefcase before, with a curious glance at Persephone, quitting the room and softly closing the door.

Persephone stepped forward. 'Pa,' she said. In spite of everything, she felt the old familiar rush of childish eagerness at seeing him.

He talks about you all the time. He's so proud of you.

The eagerness dissipated. How come he had never shown her that pride? How come she had never known? Why had he never given her the opportunity to bask in the glow of his appreciation? Didn't he know how much it would have meant to her? Or was she supposed to know without being told?

In any case, she had probably forfeited that pride now.

'You idiot,' he said. 'You little idiot. Talk about letting the side down. Just when the country is feeling proud and hopeful because of the breaching of the dams in the Ruhr by the RAF, our family has to face this . . . horror.'

'Pa, if I could just explain—'

'I'm sure he's a perfectly decent fellow in his own way, this railwayman you've taken up with, and certainly the railways are providing an essential contribution towards the war effort. Indeed, we couldn't manage without them. But the fact remains that he's not one of us.' With a sudden bark of displeasure, he declared, 'You've let everyone down. Can't you see that? You've turned our family into a laughing stock.'

'Pa, I'm sorry. I never intended—'

'It's a bit late to be sorry,' he flung back at her. 'I'll tell you what else you've done. You've played into the hands of everybody who thinks women haven't got what it takes to do a man's job.'

'What? That's ridiculous.'

'Is it? You're helping to keep the country going by doing a man's job, which is an entirely laudable thing for any female to do. But what else have you done? You've taken up with a lower-class worker. In other words, you've shown the world that girls can't be trusted to remember their proper position in life. You've shown that the pressure of war work has made you lose respect for your upbringing and everything you've ever learned. Not only have you brought shame on your mother and me and the whole family, but you've also shown that doing a man's job has addled your brains. You've let down every right-minded woman in the country.'

CHAPTER TWENTY-SEVEN

The atmosphere at St Cuthbert's had changed, sharpened; the furniture repairs and toymaking had ceased for the time being. When Mabel was sent to grab some sleep, she simply lay awake, her senses alert and primed, and others said the same when they returned to the main hall after spending a couple of hours lying on the cots. Mabel's thoughts had resumed their old focus. Would she soon be called upon to exercise her first-aid skills once more? Would the Heavy Rescue team be needed? Would the gas and electricity men be summoned to one emergency after another?

Everyone had been on heightened alert since 617 Squadron's daring attack on the dams in Germany, using the bouncing bomb. What a breathtakingly clever idea that bomb had been. The mission represented a huge success to the Allies and had given everybody's morale a tremendous boost, Mabel's as much as anyone's, but even so, she couldn't help thinking of the eight Lancasters that had been shot down in the course of the mission. Anything to do with Lancasters was inextricably linked with Harry in her mind and her heart.

She was glad to be seeing her friends in the buffet this evening after work. Dashing into the Ladies, she freshened up. As she stood in front of the mirror, she unfastened her hair and shook it loose before delving in her knapsack for her comb. Then she headed across the busy concourse towards the buffet. Joining the queue to get herself a cup of tea, she looked across the room and spotted Alison and Dot at a table. Alison waved and she waved back. Soon she joined her friends and it wasn't long before the others arrived. Alison and Dot had pushed two tables together to accommodate them all comfortably, but as the buffet filled, they stood up and moved one of the tables away to be used by other passengers, squeezing themselves around just one. Emily and Colette shared a chair, as did Alison and Margaret.

Cordelia brought in her newspaper from home to show the others in the buffet – not an article about 617 Squadron, but a piece about Persephone.

'Who's this Clarinda when she's at home?' asked Dot.

'Nobody knows,' Mabel explained. 'It's a pretend name used by the person who reports on high society.'

'I'd hardly call Matt Franklin high society,' said Dot.

'When I had my London Season,' said Mabel, 'there were girls who were dying to be mentioned by Clarinda. They pretended to take the whole thing as a huge joke, but really they saw it as a feather in their caps.'

'Were you ever mentioned by Clarinda?' asked Alison.

'Crikey, no,' said Mabel. 'With London swarming with the daughters of dukes and viscounts, she had far bigger fish to fry than the likes of me.'

'Don't do yourself down,' said Colette.

'I'm not,' Mabel answered. 'It's just the way things were. The Bradshaws are new money. I never felt comfortable among all those families who could trace their ancestry right back to the dawn of time.'

Margaret was examining the newspaper column. 'So it's a good thing for Persephone to be featured here – at least, if you take out the final sentence, it would be.'

'That final sentence is rather cheeky,' said Dot.

Alison shook her shoulders in a tiny shiver. 'As much as Joel means to me, I wouldn't want our business mentioned in the newspapers for all to see, and I'd have particularly hated it if it had happened back when we were first getting to know one another. Imagine being placed in that position.'

'It isn't just that, though, is it?' said Cordelia. 'Though goodness knows, that on its own would be bad enough.' She looked around at the rest of them, as if expecting them to understand.

'I know what Mummy is referring to,' said Emily. 'It would be one thing for Clarinda to say "the Honourable Persephone and Lord Humphrey Christmas-Tree", but it's quite another to match her with an ordinary railwayman.'

'There's nowt wrong with being an ordinary railwayman,' Dot said stoutly, 'but I know what you mean.'

'It's Cinderella but the other way round,' said Emily.

They all looked at one another.

'Poor Persephone,' Colette said quietly.

Mabel looked at her. Colette had endured her fair share, or her unfair share, of being written about in the local paper when Tony had had his day in court and had cunningly used it to push the blame for his violence onto her. Mabel hated him for that. He had been given a choice between being sent to prison or going into the army and he'd opted for the latter. Mabel still seethed when she thought of it. As far as she was concerned, the authorities should have hurled him into prison and thrown away the key.

'Do you think Matt knows about this?' Alison indicated the newspaper on the table.

'There's no knowing,' said Cordelia.

'Let's hope this is just a storm in a teacup,' said Dot.

'That remains to be seen,' said Cordelia, 'but I think we've exhausted this subject for the time being. We'll see how Persephone feels about it and take our lead from her.

She might want sympathy and support or – you never know – she might laugh it off.'

'Let's talk about Max's party while we're all here,' said Colette. She laughed. 'For someone so small, he's doing ever so well for parties.'

'It's just a shame he won't remember them when he's older,' said Alison. 'Not many people get to have three in one go.'

There was a change in the atmosphere at the table they were all crushed around as everyone cheered up. Max was indeed having three parties for his first birthday, the lucky little fella. He'd already had one with his Hubble family during the previous weekend, while on his actual birthday Joan and Bob, together with Joan's gran, had had a little celebration at home. Mrs Cooper was going to host another party this coming weekend.

'Mrs Cooper does love giving tea parties,' said Margaret with an affectionate smile.

'And we all like going to them,' said Dot. 'Cordelia and I are each going to bring a plate of something. So will our Sheila and our Pammy. Joan has asked them and the children to come too. Wasn't that kind?'

'Joan isn't the sort to move on and forget people,' said Mabel. 'She and Bob lived with Sheila for quite a while and Bob had a lot of time for Jimmy.'

'And she wouldn't leave out Pammy and Jenny,' Margaret added.

'Jenny can't wait,' said Dot. 'She's longing to see Max. The rest of us will be lucky to get a look in.'

'I must admit,' said Cordelia, 'I'm looking forward to all the baby talk.'

'Don't forget the wedding talk,' Alison added. 'As soon as Max's birthday celebrations are over, it'll be full steam ahead to Mabel and Harry's wedding.'

Pleasure swept through Mabel as she saw her friends' smiles. No matter what was happening to any of them, no one was forgotten, no event overlooked. They all cared for one another and showed it in so many ways. Oh, how she was going to miss these dear friends when she moved away.

CHAPTER TWENTY-EIGHT

Persephone told herself it was good to be back at work. It would keep her mind off her troubles. When her colleagues asked her the usual question of 'Did you enjoy your time away?', their expressions showing they were ready for her to say how lovely it had been, she smiled back and said, 'Yes, thanks,' because what else was she to say? The truth was that she felt battered and bruised.

She was anxious to see Matt again, but his shifts didn't immediately permit it. If things had been different, she might have cycled over to his parents' house – but how was she ever to face his family again after the things her parents had said about him? And that was before Clarinda's bombshell was added to the mix. Oh cripes. It was all such a colossal mess.

Mabel, Margaret, Emily and Joan cycled over to Darley Court to welcome Persephone home.

'You're so sweet to come,' said Persephone, hugging them. 'Dump your bikes over there. It's such a fine evening. Shall we sit outside on the terrace at the back of the house? Mrs Mitchell said she'd bring us some of her cordial.'

Soon they were settled on chairs on the terrace, turning up their faces to the lingering sunshine.

'Who's looking after Max for you?' Persephone asked Joan.

'His great-gran,' Joan answered. 'She loves him. It's good for her to have him to herself for a little while and then give him back. She brought up Letitia and me single-handed from when we were babies and she had to shoulder all the responsibility. I think she is able to enjoy Max in a way she could never enjoy us.'

'It was a lot for her to take on,' said Mabel. 'When you think about it, she missed out on being a grandparent. She had to be the parent to you and Letitia.'

'She's enjoying being a great-grandmother,' said Joan, 'and Max has made things easier between her and me as well. He makes a good focal point.'

Persephone laughed. 'He's certainly a focal point. Three birthday parties!'

'I'm glad you're back in time for the one at Mrs Cooper's,' said Joan.

'I wouldn't miss it,' said Persephone.

'Did you tell your mother about Matt?' Mabel asked.

'Mabel!' Margaret exclaimed. 'That wasn't exactly discreet.'

'It's all right,' said Persephone. 'It was pretty rough.'

'Was it?' Mabel's hand closed over hers. 'I'm sorry to hear that. We aren't here to pry.'

'I know that,' Persephone assured them. 'I'll be glad to talk about it, actually. I feel as if it's weighing me down.'

She thought for a few moments, putting everything in order in her mind before she started on her tale. The others murmured sympathetically and didn't interrupt her until she got to the part about her father.

'But he was so charming to Gran and me when we met him,' said Joan. 'I'm astonished that he'd speak to you so fiercely.'

Persephone shrugged. 'He has very fixed views about behaviour and he doesn't give an inch, even with his own children – especially with his own children. He was glad to help you and Mrs Foster last year. You deserved his assistance and he was pleased to send that dreadful man packing. Anyway, he wasn't just angry with me about Matt. He said – he said that I'd played into the hands of everyone who thinks women aren't up to the task of keeping the country running effectively.'

'How so?' cried Mabel indignantly.

'Because by mixing with people from different backgrounds, I've ended up neglecting the niceties of what one might call social expectations.'

'That's unfair,' said Emily. 'You and Matt care for one another.'

'Yes, we do, but that isn't supposed to happen when people are from different backgrounds. Or at least, if it does,' Persephone added, thinking of Iphigenia encouraging her to indulge in a fling, 'it's meant to be strictly on the QT.'

'How horrid to think of needing to keep it secret,' said Joan. 'Mind you, I'm not one to talk. I did my share of sneaking around behind everyone's backs with Steven.'

'That's different,' Mabel said staunchly. 'That was after the pair of you lost Letitia. It was grief that threw you together.'

Emily leaned towards Persephone. 'So not only is your father against your relationship with Matt, he also thinks you've committed a – a social crime.'

'More or less.' Persephone spoke as lightly as she could.

'Here's a thought,' said Margaret. 'Which is worse, the disgrace of getting together with a man from the wrong class, or the disgrace of it being made public?'

'Good question,' said Persephone.

'I'm sorry you have to face this situation,' said Margaret. 'Having your private business flaunted in public must be horrid. Privacy matters so much.'

'You are going to carry on seeing Matt, aren't you?' Emily's blue eyes were bright with an inner fire. 'You must. You can't let this stop you. I know you love your father and respect him and all that, but – but this is your heart we're talking about. I know what it's like to have parents who disapprove. Actually, that's not fair. Mummy was always perfectly sweet about it. I'm talking about my father and what he was like when I was going out with Raymond.'

'He disapproved?' asked Joan.

'With bells on,' said Emily.

Persephone glanced at Mabel, Joan and Margaret before saying softly, 'Do you want to tell us, Emily? If you do, we'll listen and give you our understanding and support, but you need to be sure. Don't forget that your mother is our friend too, and we all know your father.'

'Persephone isn't saying that to put you off,' said Mabel. 'It's just a gentle reminder not to say anything you'll be sorry for later.'

Emily thought for a moment. 'It won't damage your opinion of Daddy, because you'll understand his point of view. It fits in with what's happening to Persephone and that's why I want to tell you.'

'Go on,' said Margaret.

'Daddy hated me seeing Raymond. He thought Raymond wasn't good enough because his family were grocers.' Emily looked at Persephone. 'I know the gap between Raymond and me wasn't as vast as the gap between you and Matt, but it's the same principle. And then,' she went on, tilting her face so that she wasn't looking at her companions, 'Raymond thought better of it and ditched me and I thought Daddy was going to be jubilant, but he wasn't. I expect he was pleased deep down, but he didn't show it. He was kindness itself to me and I can't tell you how much that meant.'

'I'm glad of that,' Margaret murmured.

Emily turned in her chair and faced Persephone. 'What I mean to say is, no matter how dead against you your father seems to be right now . . . well, fathers can surprise you sometimes.'

Persephone's heart melted. 'I'm delighted that yours provided the love and support you needed at such an unhappy time.' She couldn't imagine her own father doing the same, but this wasn't the time to say so. 'In my situation, it isn't just that I've committed the sin of jumping the class barrier. I've also set a bad example to women in general, apparently, because my behaviour might be seen as a highly undesirable side effect of women working in wartime – and my bad example has been picked up by Clarinda and published for all to see.'

'I'm sure no harm was intended,' said Mabel. 'Not that that's of any comfort, I know, but the Clarinda column is always so polite about the people that are mentioned. Well,' she added, 'I don't need to tell you that, do I? You used to contribute to a society column yourself. You told me that right back at the start of the war when I lived here.'

Persephone hesitated, then resolve took shape inside her. 'That's right. What I didn't tell you was that for a time *I* was Clarinda.'

The others stared at her.

'*You* were Clarinda?' Margaret repeated, hazel eyes widening.

'Yes. So I know all about the way the column is written. It isn't just meant to be polite, Mabel. The intention is to flatter, to show the ladies and gentlemen in their best light, to make them glad to appear, and absolutely not to be fearful of the possibility.'

'Who is Clarinda now?' Joan asked.

'No idea,' Persephone told her. 'It's always kept secret.'

Mabel gazed into the distance. 'I'm thinking of all the girls I met in London and wondering if it's one of them.'

'It could just as easily be a man,' said Persephone, and might have laughed at the others' surprise if the matter hadn't been serious. 'Don't be fooled by the name. "Clarinda" is just a posh-sounding byline. I don't know how many Clarindas there have been. My predecessor was a man.'

'Who?' her friends asked at once, immediately followed by Joan saying, 'We wouldn't have heard of him anyway – though Mabel might.'

'Actually, you'd all have heard of him,' said Persephone, 'which is why I'm not going to tell you his name. I gather he didn't have as much money as one might think and he used Clarinda as a means of earning a few extra bob. He belonged to what my mother calls her LUG. That's her List of Useful Gentlemen, chaps who can be called upon at the last moment to make up numbers if someone drops out, as they're good at conversation and fitting into any social situation.'

Mabel pulled a comical face. 'I must tell Mumsy. On the other hand, maybe not. She has enough ideas as it is.'

'Does your father really think you've let everyone down? I mean, everyone. Women everywhere,' Margaret asked. 'Or did he say that just to hammer his point home?'

'He meant it,' Persephone said quietly. 'He's not the sort to exaggerate. If he didn't mean it, he wouldn't say it.'

'Crikey,' said Mabel.

That was the moment when the enormity of Pa's accusation hit home. Persephone inhaled deeply and made sure she was smiling. 'Let's just be grateful that it was Clarinda who blabbed and not the Pathé News. Now that really would have been annoying.' But she couldn't keep up the pretence of lightness. 'The one thing we haven't talked about is the most important of all. What am I going to say to Matt?'

*

Persephone and Matt sat together on the stairs. Everyone else was inside, watching the Abbott and Costello comedy *Pardon My Sarong*, but Persephone and Matt, as they went up the stairs, had walked more and more slowly and the rest of the audience had overtaken them, some with impatient mutters. Finally, the two of them had made it to the head of the staircase, where an usherette was waiting beside the door to look at their tickets, but instead of going towards her, they had looked at one another and, without needing to say a word, headed back downstairs.

Halfway, they had stopped and Persephone tucked her linen skirt under her as they sat down. They sat close together, not snuggling up, but near enough to lean against one another if . . . if what? If the need arose?

Matt pulled his tweed cap off his head and dangled it between his fingers. 'I'm sorry if you wanted to see the film. I know you like Abbott and Costello.'

'You do too,' said Persephone, 'but neither of us could have concentrated. It makes more sense to talk about what's happened and try to get to grips with it. I'm so sorry that my parents aren't keen on you. It's nothing personal. It's – well, as I said before, it's because of the class difference, not because of you.'

'That seems pretty personal to me,' said Matt.

'I know. What can I say, other than I'm sorry?'

Matt slipped an arm around her shoulders, drawing her to him. He ducked his head past her hat and kissed her temple. 'There you go apologising again. It's not your fault.' He let go of her.

Persephone edged closer. 'I feel awful about it, especially after the way your parents were so welcoming to me.'

'Of course they were welcoming.' Matt angled a smile at her. 'Who wouldn't welcome a beautiful girl like you? As for your parents, it was only to be expected, I suppose, given your family background.'

'I wish it didn't matter so much,' said Persephone. 'It *shouldn't* matter. It should just be about how much we like one another and how well we get along. Surely that's what counts.'

'In an ideal world.'

'Isn't that what we're fighting for? The best possible world?'

'I don't want to come between you and your family,' said Matt. 'You're in an impossible position.'

'Please don't say you want to back out.'

All at once, Persephone's mind was full of Emily and how Mr Masters had heartily disapproved of Raymond, but ended up showing what a loving father he was. She couldn't imagine Pa behaving like that. She knew for a fact he wouldn't. But even if he would do it, even if he scooped her up in a hug for the very first time and made a fuss of her because she was heartbroken, that wasn't what she wanted. Matt was what she wanted.

'The war has made changes to all our lives,' she said, 'and this is one of the changes it's made to mine.'

'Is that what I am?' Matt asked, a teasing note in his voice. 'A change?'

'A change for the better,' she answered with spirit.

'What are we going to do?' Matt asked. 'I know I ought to do the decent thing and walk out of your life—'

'Never mind the decent thing!' said Persephone.

'It isn't what I want, but it doesn't seem right to go against your parents' wishes.'

Persephone sighed. 'I know. I can't bear to hurt them and let them down, but if they knew you as I do . . .'

'I'd still be the unsuitable railway fireman.'

'There's something I haven't told you yet.' Persephone went on to explain about the Clarinda column. 'To my parents, that makes it even worse. My friendship with you is bad enough without the rest of our set knowing about it.'

Matt stiffened. 'At least we needn't worry about "my set" finding out about it that way.'

'Please don't be like that. We knew from the start the different backgrounds we come from.'

'Sorry,' said Matt. 'It's come as a shock to know that I've appeared in a newspaper.' Then he sat up straighter. 'If this Clarinda only writes flattering things, isn't it good that she linked us together? Doesn't it mean she sees us as a decent sort of couple?'

'That's what makes this so strange,' said Persephone. 'Clarinda's column is about high-society people who enjoy reading about themselves and feeling they're getting hold of the latest social titbits. Clarinda doesn't stir up trouble, so naming us as a couple should be a good thing – but it isn't. Families like mine won't see it as a good thing. So why did Clarinda say it in the first place? I just don't understand.'

'Well, that puts me firmly in my place,' said Matt. 'That was meant to be a joke, so don't start apologising again. Never mind this Clarinda and why she said what she said. What it comes down to is this: what are we going to do? We both know what we ought to do. We ought to split up.'

Persephone's heart took the next few beats at top speed. 'Is that what you want?'

'No, absolutely not,' said Matt.

'Good.' She felt almost giddy with relief.

Matt nudged closer to her. She could feel the length of his body next to hers. 'Was that the right answer?' he asked.

'Yes,' said Persephone.

'I think we should carry on as we are for now. I think that's the best we can hope for.'

CHAPTER TWENTY-NINE

Mabel sat on the stool in front of the dressing table while Margaret and Alison, standing one on either side, did her hair, alternating between working on the style and peering at Mabel's reflection. They were trying out the 'three dots and a dash' style, which was a version of the victory roll. This was worn as a striking fringe, with three small curls of the same size, then a wider curl to represent the dot-dot-dot-dash for V in Morse code.

'What do you think, Mabel?' Margaret asked. 'Do you like it?'

'I do, but it's quite different to the way I usually have my hair. Normally, I brush my fringe right away from my face.'

'That's why we're practising now,' said Alison, 'so you have lots of time to think about it before the wedding.'

'There are plenty of other ways of having a victory roll if you don't fancy this one,' Margaret reminded her. 'But this one would look really good in the photographs.'

'Something to point out to your children in years to come,' said Alison, adding cheekily, 'and your grand-children!'

Grandchildren? Crikey! But Alison had a point. This was a wartime wedding, with the groom in uniform and a V on top of the cake, which, according to Mumsy, was going to be a spectacular tower of four layers – made of cardboard, naturally. In these days of shortages, the real cake would be modest, to say the least.

'I do like it,' said Mabel, 'but I need to get used to it. Let's see what everyone thinks of it this afternoon.'

'I hope you aren't intending to upstage the man of the moment,' Margaret teased, 'or should I say the Max of the moment. As one of the godmothers, I won't stand for that.'

This seemed like a good moment to drop it into the conversation.

'Before the party, I must pop out for a short while,' said Mabel, leaning towards the mirror and fingering her hair, but this was just a way of looking casual and not meeting their eyes. 'It's a nuisance, but it won't take long and I'll be back before you know it.'

Now that work on the new nursery was under way, it was getting harder all the time to keep it a secret. Mabel hated making excuses and telling fibs, even if the result was going to give all her friends a wonderful surprise. She had to keep a tight rein on her tongue at home, especially when there were difficulties, such as the time the wrong timber was delivered, not to mention all the hoops she had to jump through to be allowed to have paint. The Messrs Hayter and Mrs Rushton, their secretary, took messages and dealt with as much as they could, but Mabel knew that as the person in charge, her absence didn't help matters.

She was deeply grateful to Fay Brewer, who was assisting with all the paperwork and had provided useful contacts. Mabel wanted to heap praise on her and shout from the rooftops what a marvel she was, especially compared to the awful Miss Brewster, but evidently Fay wasn't interested in compliments.

'Just doing my job,' she said.

With Max's party about to start, it was hardly the best time for Mabel to have to deal with matters at the Extension, but it was unavoidable.

'I'll be as quick as I can,' she told Margaret and Alison. 'If anyone asks, say I'll be back soon.'

Putting on her cream jacket over her peacock-blue linen dress, she positioned her felt hat on her head. It had a peter-sham rosette on the hatband. For half a moment she wondered whether a plain hat would be better, so as not to draw attention away from her dot-dot-dot-dash, then she told herself not to be so vain and left the house, heading for the Hayters' estate agency, where Mrs Rushton was on her own in the office.

'The water pipes have come,' Mrs Rushton informed her. 'I looked in the back of the delivery van and they were all there. I gave the delivery man the key to the Extension.'

'Good. Thank you,' said Mabel. 'That means the plumbing can be put in for the lavatories.'

Mrs Rushton frowned. 'It was a bit odd, actually. You'd best pop over and check that all's well. The delivery man returned the key as normal, but then he came back a while later and took it again.'

'He must have left some of the pipes in his van,' said Mabel. Her heart sank a little. An inefficient delivery man was the last thing she needed.

'I know. It doesn't exactly inspire you with confidence, does it?' said Mrs Rushton. 'You'd better cut along and see what's what, Miss Bradshaw. Here's the key. The driver brought it back.'

'Did you ask him what the problem was?'

Mrs Rushton gave her a steady look. 'No, Miss Bradshaw, I did not. As you can see, I'm on my own in the office today and I had three couples in here at the time, all looking for somewhere to live. The driver just left the key on my desk. Here, you'd better take Durrell's telephone number as well, just in case. They're the builders' merchant.'

Mabel walked along to the Extension and let herself in, smiling as she inhaled the tang of fresh paint, which was an unusual smell these days, with paint only being used for essential purposes, not decorative ones. There was no sign of the water pipes in the first room, so she went through to the back. They weren't there either. Mabel stuck her head back round the door to look into the front room again, as if she might have missed seeing them the first time, which, of course, she hadn't. Letting herself through the side door, she searched outside. No delivery man would have left them there, especially not when he had the key, but she had to check all the same.

It was a good thing she had Durrell's telephone number. She went to the nearest telephone box and put through a call.

'I'm very sorry,' said the woman who listened to her query, 'but the driver had to take the pipes to a building site instead.'

'Do you mean he took my order, which he'd already delivered, and gave it to someone else?'

'I'm afraid so, but you're top of the list for when we get the next consignment of water pipes.'

'I'm not interested in the next consignment. I want *my* consignment. Without them, work on my project has to stop and I can't afford to lose the time.'

'I'm very sorry,' the woman said again.

'Why has this building site taken priority?' Mabel asked.

'Well . . .' There was a pause and then the woman said, 'I can only apologise. It's just one of those things.'

Just one of those things? Mabel pictured how Pops would have exploded if someone tried to fob him off with those words. And that was the point, wasn't it? This woman was trying to fob her off. Mabel's spine stiffened. She was about to say something sharp, but then she held her tongue. Whatever had happened, it wasn't the receptionist's fault.

'Where is this building site?' asked Mabel.

There was a pause at the other end of the line.

'Listen,' said Mabel, polite but firm. 'I know this isn't your fault. You're just the person who has the nasty job of giving me the bad news, and I'm supposed to accept it and creep away like a meek little mouse. Well, believe me, a meek mouse is the last thing I am, so please tell me what I need to know. On top of that, I expect your delivery man to meet me at the Extension on High Lane in twenty minutes to take me to the building site.'

It took more than half an hour for the van to arrive. The driver was grouchy, but Mabel summoned up all the lessons she'd learned from Mumsy's etiquette book and greeted him with a smile, thanking him for coming.

'I'm Miss Bradshaw and you are . . .?'

'Name of Hawkins, miss.'

'How do you do, Mr Hawkins? If you wouldn't mind taking me to the place where you delivered my water pipes . . .'

They didn't have to go far, just to a site on the Hardy Lane crossroads, over the road from Chorlton Park School, where there seemed to be a sports day going on in the playground. The sound of cheering floated across the road as Mabel climbed down from the cab. She and Mr Hawkins walked onto the site.

'I need to see the foreman,' said Mabel.

'That's the site foreman over there,' said Mr Hawkins, jerking his chin in the appropriate direction. 'And that's the big boss by that pile of bricks.'

'The big boss?'

'The builder. This is his site. He has projects going on all over the place.'

'Do you know his name?' Mabel asked.

'Jolly. Mr Jolly.'

Mabel went straight to him. He was a thickset man with a beer gut and heavy jowls. He looked anything but jolly.

'Mr Jolly?' Mabel asked pleasantly.

'Who are you?' he demanded. 'You can't come waltzing onto this site. It's dangerous.'

'I am Mabel Bradshaw,' Mabel answered, undeterred, 'and I believe you have acquired something of mine, namely water pipes from Durrell's.'

Mr Jolly's eyes widened, then narrowed. His lips narrowed too. 'Hard luck. They're here now and that makes 'em mine. Everyone knows possession is nine-tenths of the law.'

'I have a docket from the Corporation.'

'Don't we all?' Jolly sneered.

'That entitles me to those pipes.'

'To water pipes, yes, maybe,' said Jolly, 'but not to *those* pipes. Like I said, possession.'

'I'm willing to bet that my docket has an earlier date than yours,' said Mabel, 'which is why the water pipes were supplied to me in the first instance.'

Mr Jolly laughed. 'Hark at her! "In the first instance", if you please. Swallowed a dictionary, have you? The water pipes are mine. Now clear off.'

'On the contrary, Mr Jolly, the water pipes are mine and I'm staying put.'

Jolly thrust his face into hers. 'You'll get lost if you know what's good for you.'

Mabel couldn't help taking a step backwards, though she wished she hadn't. Did it look like a sign of weakness? Glancing round, she caught the expressions on the workmen's faces. Their boss might be lapping this up, but they weren't – well, a couple of them were, but mostly the men looked awkward and embarrassed. Would they help her?

Looking directly at them, Mabel said clearly, 'Those water pipes belong to me. I'm getting a nursery ready that will benefit the local community, possibly even some of your children if you have little ones.'

'Shut your trap!' bellowed Jolly.

Mabel turned to him, doing her best to appear unruffled even though her heart was beating hard. 'I can see how you persuaded Durrell's to let you jump the queue and take the water pipes.'

'It's in their interests to oblige me. I'm a good customer.'

'It's never in anybody's interests to oblige a bully,' Mabel retorted, 'because it makes the bully think he can get away with it again next time.'

'Who are you calling a bully? That's defamation of character, that is. I can sue you for that.'

'Feel free, but I would remind you that it's only defamation if it's untrue. I have a friend who's a journalist and she'd be very interested to look into how you do business, and don't kid yourself that she couldn't. Her father's in the War Office.'

Jolly's face had gone purple. 'Get off my building site or I'll have you for trespass as well as defamation.'

'I'll go with pleasure,' said Mabel, 'but only if I can take my water pipes with me.'

'Saints alive! How many times do you need telling? You're not having them, you bloody stupid harridan. Now get off my building site. I shan't tell you again.'

Mabel turned once more to the workmen. 'If you attempt to fit those pipes, you'll be flying in the face of the Corporation's rules, not to mention common decency. I take it you all believe in fair play.'

'They believe in the bloke who pays their wages,' gloated Jolly.

'You've got them right under your thumb, haven't you?'

Mabel's instincts pushed her to avert her gaze in disgust, but she quelled the impulse, regarding Mr Jolly steadily. What an odious man. What was she going to do? If she went for the police, they might well declare it to be a matter for the Corporation. At half past two on a Saturday, the Corporation's offices would now be closed. If the issue was postponed until next week, Mabel wouldn't put it past Mr Jolly to make his men fit the pipes before they went home today, even if it took them until midnight.

And then it came to her. Of course. It was the obvious solution. She had been determined to do this on her own and not tell her friends about the nursery until afterwards, but now she needed them. To her own surprise, she felt herself relax as the tension seeped away. She nodded to herself. That was how much she trusted her friends, how deeply she believed that as a group, they were strong and effective. Just deciding to bring them here was all it took to make her feel better and set her confidence soaring.

There was a roar of delight from the children over the road. Mabel glanced across. A race had just finished and some of the children were jumping up and down in excitement. She knew just how they felt.

To Mr Hawkins, she said, 'I need you to take me somewhere, if you please. Do you know Wilton Close?'

'I'm not a taxi service,' Mr Hawkins grumbled.

'No, you're the person who took my water pipes and gave them to somebody else.'

'I only did what I was told to by my boss.'

'And believe me, I shall be having words with him, as well as informing the Corporation that a builders' merchant on their list has acted improperly. It would be good for Durrell's if I could name you as the person who helped me sort out this mess.'

As the two of them headed towards the parked van, Mr Jolly's derisive laughter followed them.

'Bit off more than you could chew, did you, missy?' he called.

Mabel turned round to address him. 'Yes, I did, actually, just not in the way you mean.'

Mr Hawkins opened the cab door for her as if he was a chauffeur and she climbed in. He then walked round to climb in the other side and started up the vehicle.

Wilton Close wasn't far. As they turned into the cul-de-sac, Mabel said, 'Drop me outside the first house on the right. Then will you please turn the van round and wait for me to come out again.'

'Look, I really need to be getting on—'

'And could you please open the rear doors? We'll be taking some passengers with us when we go back.'

Mabel ran into the house, where Max's party was in full swing. Everyone turned towards her as she opened the door to the front room.

'There you are at last,' said Mrs Cooper.

'You said you wouldn't be long,' said Alison.

'I know. I'm sorry, everybody. I'm especially sorry, Joan and Bob, for barging in like this on Max's party.'

'You aren't barging in,' said Bob, mystified. 'You're a guest.'

'And I'm about to take all your guests away for a short while. Listen, please, everyone. I need help. I'm in the process of setting up a nursery on High Lane—' She was obliged to stop as she was bombarded with exclamations and questions. She held up her hands. 'I meant to do it alone as a surprise, a sort of parting gift from me, something for you to remember me by.'

'You didn't need to do that to make us remember you,' said Cordelia.

'Aye, that's right,' said Dot. 'You're one of us and you always will be, even when you're far away.'

Mabel's heart swelled with love in spite of the urgency of the situation. 'I know, but I still wanted to do something special. The thing is, I meant to keep it secret, but I've run into a problem and I need your help – all of you.'

She looked around the room at all her friends and the people they'd brought with them. As well as Bob, Kenneth Masters was here, and Joel was next to Alison. Dot had brought her husband and their two daughters-in-law, Pammy and Sheila, plus Pammy's daughter, Jenny, and Sheila's lad, the irrepressible Jimmy. Joan's gran was here too, which was in itself something of a miracle, as she wasn't exactly famous for being sociable. Miss Brown and Mrs Mitchell were here from Darley Court. And Mr Darrell, Margaret's father, was here, because Joan, lovely, kind Joan, hadn't wanted to miss out a single person.

Mabel explained about the water pipes.

'It's no good waiting for the Corporation to deal with it,' said Mr Darrell. 'They'll all have gone home by now.'

'I know,' said Mabel. 'That was when I thought of all of you – especially you,' she added, looking at Cordelia's husband.

Mr Masters stood up. 'Of course.'

'We'll all come,' Dot said decisively. 'There's strength in numbers. How far is it? Will it take us long to walk there?'

'I've a van waiting outside,' said Mabel.

'So we really can all go,' said Alison.

'Mrs Grayson,' said Bob, 'you stay here with Joan, Mrs Foster and Max.'

'Would you prefer to stay here?' Mabel asked Miss Brown.

'I hope you aren't suggesting my age is a barrier to being useful in a crisis,' said Miss Brown.

'I wouldn't dream of it,' said Mabel.

'Can me and Jenny come too?' asked Jimmy.

'No,' said Sheila and 'Yes,' said Mabel at the same moment. Mabel looked at Sheila, who shrugged.

'I'm not sure I want my Jenny caught up in any unpleasantness,' said Pammy.

'I want to go,' said Jenny. 'I'm a Girl Guide. We don't shirk our duty.'

It was a full van that set off back to Mr Jolly's building site. Mr Hawkins pulled up outside the school and everyone piled out, gathering to cross the road together. Even from this side of the road, Mabel could see the astonishment on Jolly's face, but this was quickly replaced by a sneering sort of amusement. The large group set off across the road, cheers from the playground behind them seeming to urge them on their way.

'Well, well, well.' Jolly made a show of being impressed. 'Brought the cavalry back with you, have you, Miss Bradshaw? Or it is more a case of Dan'l Whiddon, Harry Hawke, Old Uncle Tom Cobley and all?'

'Actually, it's Wardle, Grace and Masters,' said Mr Masters, stepping forward. 'Kenneth Masters – and I gather you must be Mr Jolly. I am here to represent Miss Bradshaw's legal interests in this matter.' Raising his voice so there was no doubt that the watching workmen would hear, he went on, 'I am a solicitor and I strongly recommend that none of you touch the water pipes in question until ownership has been formally established.'

'They're mine,' snapped Jolly. 'Ask Durrell's if you don't believe me.'

'I shall – and I'll also make enquiries as to how it came about that items that were destined for Miss Bradshaw's nursery, and indeed were originally delivered there, found their way instead to this building site. It seems very fishy to me.'

'You can fish as much as you like,' said Jolly, 'but by the time you can do anything about it, those pipes will be in position and no one with any sense will consider asking for them to be removed.'

Mr Masters raised his eyebrows. 'But will they be in position? Any workman who interferes with them might find himself on the receiving end of a lawsuit.' He smiled urbanely at the listening men. 'I suggest you consider that, gentlemen, and decide which you are more scared of – Mr Jolly or a visit to the magistrates' court.'

'You wouldn't,' snarled Jolly.

'I shan't need to if this matter is dealt with appropriately,' said Mr Masters.

'You don't scare me,' said Jolly. He addressed his workers. 'Pay no heed to this . . . gentleman. He's got no authority here. Just ask yourselves which you're more scared of: a lawsuit that friends of mine will make sure never happens, or losing your jobs.'

The men shuffled awkwardly, glancing at one another. Before this, they had been looking at Mabel's followers with interest; now they looked anywhere but.

Beside Mabel, Jimmy tugged Dot's arm. 'Nan, he's a bad lot, that man, isn't he? Why has he pinched the water pipes?'

'Because, as you say, he's a bad lot, love,' said Dot. 'He's muscled in to get his own way when everything's in short supply. It's unpatriotic, that's what it is.'

Jimmy looked up sharply to stare wide-eyed at his grandmother. 'Unpatriotic?'

'Aye, our Jimmy, that's what I said and I don't say things I don't mean.'

Jimmy's eyes narrowed as they focused on Mr Jolly. 'Traitor!' he hissed under his breath.

Mabel was about to step forward when Miss Brown spoke up in her grandest voice.

'I am Miss Brown of Darley Court and I take a personal interest in this matter.' Although her keen eyes were on Mr Jolly, her words were clearly also addressed to his unhappy workmen. 'My war work has brought me into regular contact with the chiefs of every form of Civil Defence and a great many Corporation departments. If it is your intention to remain on the list of approved builders, sir, you will heed Mr Masters' warning.'

'Are you threatening me?' Jolly demanded.

'Yes, I do believe I am,' said Miss Brown.

'For all the good it'll do you,' said Jolly. 'I don't care how many of you there are, and I don't care where you work or where you live. You could live in Buckingham Palace for all I care. It makes no odds to anything. Those water pipes are mine, full stop— *Ooof!*'

A huge breath streamed out of Mr Jolly's body as children appeared from nowhere at top speed and hurled themselves upon him with yells of 'Got him!' and 'Got the traitor!' and 'Take that, Hitler!'

As Jimmy Green sped by, Dot yanked him to a standstill by the scruff of his neck.

'Jimmy! Is this your doing?'

'Yes, Nan. You said he was a traitor, so I fetched the kids from over the road. I knew we could get him if we tried, and we have, haven't we?'

'But, Jimmy—'

'I had to do it, Nan. We never get to do owt, us kids, apart from collecting salvage, and I know that's important because scrap iron gets turned into Spitfires, but look at this, Nan. This is *real* war work. Me and these others – we've just nabbed a traitor.'

With Mr Jolly largely invisible beneath a seething mass of young bodies, one of his workmen stepped forward and spoke to Mabel.

'If you want them water pipes, miss, I suggest you get your friends to take 'em and get your van loaded. Like Mr Jolly said earlier on, possession is nine-tenths of the law. And with Miss Brown and that lawyer fella on your side, he won't come after you. We all know he gets his own way by strong-arming folk.'

Mabel smiled round at her friends. 'Shall we?'

The group returned in triumph to Wilton Close, having taken the water pipes to the Extension, locking them in a big walk-in cupboard for good measure. Joan, her grandmother and Mrs Grayson listened wide-eyed to the tale.

'In the end it wasn't legal threats or Miss Brown at her grandest,' said Alison. 'It was a bunch of kids determined to do their duty and nab themselves a real live traitor.'

'Please don't keep calling him that,' begged Dot.

'Yes, don't,' added Sheila. There was a steely glint in her eye as she looked at her mother-in-law. 'You should be more careful what you say in front of our Jimmy. You know what he's like.'

'But Jimmy did bring the problem to a successful resolution, don't forget,' Cordelia put in smoothly.

'I did what?' asked Jimmy.

'You sorted it out, Jimmy,' said Joan. 'Good for you.'

'Yeah, I did, didn't I?'

When everyone had settled down, Mrs Cooper said to Mabel, 'Tell us all about this nursery.'

Mabel explained her plans, including why she had wanted to act alone.

'I'm glad you turned to us for help when you needed it,' said Persephone. 'What a nasty piece of work that Mr Jolly was.'

'It's a good job you were all here,' said Mabel.

'We shan't forget this party in a hurry,' chuckled Bob.

'What I'd like to know,' said Mrs Grayson, 'is whether you intend to go back to organising everything all on your own?'

'There's plenty of help available if you want it,' said Margaret.

'I'd love you all to help,' said Mabel. 'For a start, I need lots of toymakers.'

'That's the kind of thing I can easily do,' said Mrs Grayson, pleased. 'I can knit teddies and dollies. I could knit some clothes for spare, too, in case a child gets dirty playing outside.'

'If we can get some old gloves off the market,' said Margaret, 'we can make miniature mice, one per finger. I remember my mum doing that when I was little.'

'National Dried Milk tins make good rattles with a few nuts and bolts inside,' Joan added.

'Is that where the nuts and bolts went?' teased Bob.

'If you could find some coloured pictures,' said Mr Darrell, 'I could glue them to plywood and cut them up to make jigsaws.'

'Rag dolls with buttons for eyes,' said Cordelia.

'Teddies and stuffed animals made out of old fabric or old clothes,' added Emily.

'The WVS ladies who come to Darley Court to make jam and chutneys and so forth can be roped in,' said Miss Brown. 'The land girls will want to help too, I'm sure.'

'Thank you all from the bottom of my heart,' said Mabel.

'And don't forget,' Alison added, 'if you need the cavalry to come rushing to the rescue again . . .'

'I'll remember,' said Mabel.

CHAPTER THIRTY

Emily, Margaret, Mabel and Colette went to the pictures together after work to see *The Talk of the Town*. Being in the company of girls in their twenties always made Emily feel grown-up and special. Standing at the bus stop after the film, they discussed which actor they liked more, Cary Grant or Ronald Colman.

'Cary Grant,' said Emily. 'He always seems so charming, but in a light-hearted way.'

When the bus came along, many of the seats were already taken and the four of them had to split up into pairs and sit in different places. Emily swung into the double seat first and looked out of the window up at the sky as Colette followed her and sat down.

'Looking at the stars?' Colette asked.

'Raymond was interested in astronomy,' said Emily. 'He taught me to recognise some of the constellations – the Plough, Orion's Belt.' She turned to look at Colette. 'That was the one thing Daddy liked about him.'

'I expect he liked other things as well,' Colette said mildly. 'I know your mother approved of him, so he must have been all right. It's just that your father wanted something different for you.'

'I know,' said Emily.

Was Raymond alive and well and still stargazing? She hoped so with all her heart. 'Before he dumped me, I dreaded his call-up papers arriving. I tried to comfort myself with the thought that even though we'd be miles apart, we'd still be able to look up at the same stars. At least, I did until I realised he might be sent somewhere that has different stars.'

'But it would have been a connection between you,' said Colette.

'Yes, it would.'

'Does it still hurt to think about him?'

'Not the way it used to.'

'That's partly because you're busy,' said Colette. 'It was good for you to change jobs and start on the railways. I know how much my job has helped me.'

Emily was touched by Colette's understanding, though it wasn't simply her job as a lad porter that was keeping Emily occupied. There was the constant worry associated with the pilfering. But things weren't all bad. It felt important to focus on that.

'It heartens me to see how everyone helps one another,' she said. 'Look at Mabel and how everyone piled in to help her when that horrid man pinched her water pipes. Piled in, literally – we all piled into the van.' She laughed. 'It still amazes me when I picture it, but it's the thought of how funny it must have looked that amazes me, not the fact of us all doing it. That just felt right and natural. Nobody questioned it.'

Colette nodded. 'Mabel needed help and we all gave it.'

'That's real friendship, if you please,' said Emily. She remembered, too, how she had spoken up when Persephone had talked about the General's reaction to her relationship with Matt; she had so wanted to give Persephone hope as well as immediate support. But she didn't mention that now, because Colette hadn't been there for that conversation and she didn't want to seem either to gossip or to blow her own trumpet.

'I've been on the receiving end of a lot of help too,' Colette remarked, 'some of it entirely practical.'

'Such as when Mrs Cooper helped you escape,' put in Emily.

'And when Mabel and Alison got me out of hospital,' Colette added. 'There's also been heaps of emotional support, of course. You and I are very lucky, Emily. We have such good friends.'

Colette looked at Emily and waited.

Emily felt her heart turn over, but at the same time something slotted into place, and that something was resolve.

She drew a breath. 'I need help,' she said.

Emily's heart beat hard as she and Colette made their way across the crowded concourse, passing along the front of the long line of smart wooden panelling, set into which were the small windows where passengers queued up to enquire about journeys and purchase their tickets. Colette led Emily round the side of the large ticket office and knocked on a door. As they waited to be admitted, Emily looked around. She had never been aware of this door before, but then she had never had occasion to notice it.

'We've come to see Mr Gordon, if he's available,' said Colette when the door opened, and the clerk stood back to allow them in.

Colette went over to a corner where there was a small office. The door was open and she leaned in slightly to knock. A man stood up. Emily remembered having glimpsed him before, one time when she was with Persephone.

'Good afternoon, Mrs Naylor. What can I do for you?' The man – Mr Gordon – glanced at Emily.

'Good afternoon,' said Colette. 'This is Emily Masters. She's a lad porter.'

'So I see.'

Colette turned to Emily. 'This is Mr Gordon. He helped Persephone when there was that nasty business with the fare-dodgers.'

Mr Gordon nodded to Emily, then his gaze flicked back to Colette. 'Have a seat, Mrs Naylor.' He edged past them and fetched another chair for Emily, closing the door before he returned to his own chair behind the desk. 'What's this about?'

'Miss Masters has something important to report,' said Colette.

'I'm listening,' said Mr Gordon.

Colette gave Emily a nod of encouragement and Emily quietly drew a breath. She had prepared what to say. She explained what she knew of the pilfering in the stores.

'And you've known about this for how long?' asked Mr Gordon. 'But you're only now bringing it to my attention?'

'I think it's brave of Miss Masters to speak out,' said Colette. 'She's only seventeen and new in the job. Most people would have kept quiet.'

Mr Gordon appeared to consider this. 'Maybe. She's here now, that's the main thing. But this really isn't a matter for me, Mrs Naylor. My work concerns passengers and the staff who work on the trains, not station staff. I will take this matter to—'

'But don't you see,' Emily exclaimed, 'that's what makes you the right person to deal with this. If it goes to the – the real right person, the consequences would be far more serious. If you deal with it, you could – I don't know – make less of an issue out of it.'

'Less of an issue? This is theft we're talking about, young lady.'

Colette raised an eyebrow. 'Excuse me, Mr Gordon,' she said mildly, 'but if Emily is old enough to go out to work, then she's old enough to be addressed as Miss Masters.'

'Of course. I apologise. No offence intended.' Mr Gordon rested his elbows on the edge of his desk and clasped his hands, leaning forward a little. He had a serious face, but he was good-looking too, considering how old he was. 'Let me put this in context for you, Miss Masters. Theft is a serious matter and there's a good case for saying it is even more serious in wartime when everyone should be pulling together. I'll give you an example. This wasn't a railway matter, but the principle's the same. Last year, a case of mass pilfering from a paint factory in Hackney was uncovered. The matter went to court in January and the ringleaders were fined and imprisoned.'

Emily's mouth had gone dry. She had to swallow a couple of times before she could say, 'But the matter here is just ordinary men taking a bit here and there.'

'And that's all right with you, is it, Miss Masters?' Mr Gordon didn't raise his voice. 'Also, I might ask how you know it's "just ordinary men"? Let me tell you about an "ordinary man" at Paddington Station who was corrupted by a black market gang and went on to steal damaged parcels. If you think London is a long way away, allow me to tell you about a fellow right here at Manchester Victoria, a perfectly "ordinary man", as you would call him, who came across an unattended trolley of cartons of cigarettes waiting to be loaded onto the next train. He wheeled the trolley through the station unchallenged and took it home during the blackout. He was eventually caught because he drew attention to himself by trying to sell wholesale cartons.'

'Nothing like that is going on,' said Emily.

'Isn't it? If it isn't, I can assure you that makes Victoria the exception rather than the rule. It's a problem all over the country. There's a railway depot in South London where in just six months, they lost goods to the value of more than ten thousand pounds.'

Colette reached across and pressed Emily's hand for a moment before withdrawing her own hand. 'These issues are, of course, very serious, but as Miss Masters has explained, all she is aware of is men taking a few cigarettes or a tin of corned beef or a twist of tea. These are men who are topping up their kitchen cupboards, not involving themselves in organised crime.'

'You make it sound harmless,' said Mr Gordon, 'but if a number of them are doing it, you can't say it isn't organised. I do, however, take your point that this seems to be pilfering on a personal level and not for the black market.'

Emily's shoulders almost sagged as relief gushed through her. 'So it isn't as serious as it might have been?'

'No, it isn't,' Mr Gordon conceded in a measured voice, 'but it is still theft and must be dealt with as such. I require the names of those you know to be involved.'

'I – I couldn't,' said Emily. Hand over Mr Buckley on a plate? Never! But what would her father say if she didn't?

'Miss Masters has done her duty by coming forward in this way,' said Colette. 'Asking her to name names is unfair, because she only knows a few of those involved. There may be many more.'

Mr Gordon drew in a breath, looking thoughtful. 'Very well. I shan't press the question . . . at this stage.'

'Thank you,' Colette murmured.

Emily leaned forward in her chair, anxious to make Mr Gordon understand. 'I know for a fact that there is one . . . porter' – she deliberately used the word 'porter' instead of 'man' – 'who donates what they get to a worthy cause.'

'And by "get", Miss Masters,' said Mr Gordon, 'you mean "take", "steal". Please don't try to minimise the offence by using bland vocabulary.'

'Yes, all right, what they take,' cried Emily. 'Doesn't it count for anything that they aren't taking it for themselves?

That they are doing it for the good of others? That they are doing their best to . . .' She'd gone too far.

'Doing their best to what?' Mr Gordon asked.

Emily shook her head. 'I can't say.'

Colette stepped in, her voice quiet. 'There are times when someone does the wrong thing, but they do it with the best of intentions.'

Mr Gordon looked at Colette for a long moment. Emily held her breath.

'Thank you for bringing this to my attention, ladies,' said Mr Gordon. 'You can leave it with me now.'

'What are you going to do?' asked Emily.

For his answer, Mr Gordon rose from his seat and opened the door for them. 'Good afternoon, ladies.'

CHAPTER THIRTY-ONE

How time was flying past. Already it was the last full week of May. Next Monday would see the end of the month and Tuesday would be the start of June – the month Mabel was to get married. Sometimes it felt very far away and at other times she couldn't believe how close it was.

In the middle of the week, Joan came round to Wilton Close for the evening, leaving little Max at home with his great-grandmother.

'How are things going with the nursery?' Joan asked.

'Pretty well, thanks, I'm pleased to say,' Mabel told her. 'There's a lady at the Corporation who has been a marvel. She's dealt with the Ministry of Works for me and she's going to help with the staff interviews.'

'Is Mr Bradshaw paying for staff?' asked Mrs Cooper.

'It will be a mixture of paid staff and volunteers,' said Mabel. 'That seemed like the best way to organise it, given that I have to leave it in such a way that it can function on its own once I've gone. The volunteers will be WVS ladies. Oh, I meant to tell you,' she added, remembering. 'Miss Brewer – that's the lady from the Corporation – put me in touch with a professional handicrafts instructor, who has given me some patterns to use for making the toys.'

They talked for a while about the nursery, then the conversation moved on to the wedding.

'With everything being organised in Annerby,' said Alison, 'doesn't it bother you that you're missing out on all the fun?'

'I don't feel I'm missing out,' said Mabel. 'Mumsy writes two or three times a week with ideas and questions and plans.' She laughed. 'And changes of plan. Think of it this way. I'm not missing the fun. I'm missing the headaches.'

'I bet your mum is having a whale of a time,' said Mrs Cooper.

'She is,' Mabel agreed. 'The latest is that Louise and her mother – you remember the Waddens? They've said they'll organise the factory women to queue up early in the morning at the various bakeries and cake shops in Annerby to get their hands on as many cakes as they can for the reception.'

'So there'll be plenty of goodies to go round, as well as your wedding cake,' said Joan.

'It's just a bore that numbers are restricted to forty,' said Mabel. 'Pops is making jokes about getting me married off on the cheap.'

'He doesn't really mean it,' said Mrs Cooper.

'Of course he doesn't,' said Mabel. 'He's chuffed to bits. He can't wait to walk me up the aisle.'

'It's going to be a very smart wedding,' said Mrs Cooper. 'I hope my Sunday hat is going to be good enough.'

Margaret spoke up. 'Sally in the engine shed told me that she went to a wedding early in the war when we were still having air raids all the time. She bought a hat second-hand and the shop manageress kindly steamed it into shape for her, but apparently she'd barely got it home before a daylight raid started and part of the ceiling fell on it.'

'As long as your hat doesn't look like the Luftwaffe crushed it,' Mabel told Mrs Cooper, 'it'll be fine.'

'What about flowers?' asked Alison.

'Mumsy is lavishing care on her rose beds. According to Pops, you'd think she was entering them into a posh flower show.'

'I'm sure they'll be beautiful,' said Mrs Grayson. 'What colour shall you have?'

'To be honest,' said Mabel, 'it's a question of which blooms look best on the day, but the plan is to have red roses tied together with white and blue ribbons. I pinched the idea from the Wings for Victory corsages.'

'Perfect,' said Joan. 'It's lovely that they're coming from your parents' garden.'

'I'm very lucky,' said Mabel.

'A girl up the road from us got married last week,' said Joan, 'and the florist charged four shillings each for carnation buttonholes for the men.'

'Four bob!' Mrs Cooper exclaimed. 'That's daylight robbery.'

'I can't wait to see you in your wedding dress,' said Joan.

'I've heard all about the dress,' said Mrs Grayson, 'but what about the veil? I wore my mother's veil.'

Mabel's heart filled. 'I'm going to wear Mrs Wilmore's veil. That's my friend Althea's mother. Althea would have been my chief bridesmaid had she lived. We always promised one another we'd be each other's bridesmaids.'

The doorbell sounded and Alison left the room to answer it.

'I think that sounds lovely,' Mrs Cooper told Mabel, 'but,' she asked gently, 'doesn't your mother mind?'

'It was her idea,' said Mabel. She inhaled a deep, gratifying breath. She was proud of Mumsy for being so generous.

'Nothing will make up for not having Althea with you on your wedding day,' said Joan, 'but we'll all do everything we can to make your day perfect for you.'

The door opened and Alison came in with Persephone.

'You've walked into the middle of a wedding conversation,' said Mrs Grayson.

'That's very appropriate,' said Persephone. She addressed Mabel. 'I've had an idea for the wedding. Would you mind if we talked about it in the other room, just in case you don't like it?'

Mabel got up and they went into the dining room.

'You could have said it in front of the others,' said Mabel. 'I wouldn't have minded.'

'It isn't about the wedding,' said Persephone. She removed a newspaper cutting from her pocket and held it out. 'It's this. I'm so sorry, Mabel.'

Persephone watched anxiously as Mabel, her face serious, read Clarinda's words out loud.

'Oh – it's about me. *Miss Mabel Bradshaw, only child of the wealthy entrepreneur Mr Arnold Bradshaw of Annerby in Lancashire, is gamely doing her bit by working with a will out on the railway tracks in all weathers, her radiant beauty only enhanced by the fresh air.* "Her radiant beauty"! *Miss Bradshaw will make the perfect June bride—*' Mabel broke off. 'What's wrong with it?'

'You haven't finished it yet,' said Persephone.

Mabel carried on reading. '*What a fortunate fellow her fiancé is. The son of a humble pharmacist* – I'm not sure I like that word "humble". *The son of a humble pharmacist, brave bomb aimer Harry Knatchbull will soon acquire a delightful, patriotic wife, who is heiress to the Bradshaw fortune.*' Mabel's head jerked up and she stared at Persephone. 'Why didn't they just call him a gold-digger and have done with it?'

'I'm sorry. I know how much it must hurt.'

'You can say that again.' Mabel sounded breathless.

She read the piece once more, silently this time. Persephone wanted to urge her not to, but she knew from her own experience that it was impossible to look away from Clarinda's words.

'Is it . . .?' Mabel bit her lip. 'D'you think you and I are reading "gold-digger" into it because of what we know about Harry?' Her eyes blazed with hope. 'Maybe to an ordinary reader, there's nothing untoward. Maybe they'll just think "Lucky devil!" and that'll be that.'

'Well . . . possibly.' Persephone couldn't hide her doubt.

'But you don't really think so.' Mabel blinked away sudden tears.

'It's the clever juxtaposition of "humble" and "heiress" that does it,' said Persephone. 'Without the "humble", it wouldn't be anything like as bad.'

'But with it . . .' Mabel stared up at the ceiling for a moment, gathering herself, then she swung her gaze back to Persephone. 'One little word, but it tilts the meaning in a slightly different direction.'

'But only slightly,' said Persephone. 'That's what's so clever. I'm sure there will be people who read nothing at all into it, but there will also be those who do.'

'It's like a secret code,' said Mabel, 'but not so secret. And I can't complain because . . . because it's true. That was how Harry started out.'

'Even if you did complain and you got an apology printed,' said Persephone, 'you couldn't make all those readers forget what they'd read.'

'And a printed apology would simply draw further attention to it. I can't win.' Mabel's face had drained of colour. 'Besides, it's true. I shall deny it to all and sundry, of course, but . . . it's true.'

Her shoulders shook and she covered her face with her hand. Before Persephone could put her arms around her, she moved away.

'Don't be kind or I'll sob the house down.'

'We're the only ones who know that it's true – well, and Joan – but nobody else knows.'

'Harry's old friends know,' said Mabel, 'the crowd he used to kick around with.'

'They're not going to stir things up. Why would they?'

'They already have,' said Mabel. 'Where else could Clarinda have got her information?'

Mabel emerged from the telephone box with tears streaming down her cheeks. She had managed to hold her emotions in check while she talked to Harry and explained the situation. She had even uttered words of comfort, assuring him she was unfazed by what she referred to as 'this unpleasantness', and she must have been convincing because Harry admitted that he'd already been on the receiving end of a few sideways glances.

'Ignore them,' Mabel had said stoutly. 'If anyone says a word, don't dignify it by answering. You and I know how perfect we are together and that's all that matters.'

But as she had hung up and pushed open the door to leave the telephone box, she couldn't hold in her anguish a moment longer. Sobs juddered out of her. She was dimly aware of startled looks from people in the queue and a couple of voices expressing concern, but she was too overwrought to acknowledge them. She hurried on her way, not home to Wilton Close, but to Torbay Road to see Joan.

She rang the bell, hoping Mrs Foster wouldn't be the one to answer the door. To her relief, it was Joan.

'Who is it?' called Mrs Foster from the back of the house.

'It's for me,' Joan called back, standing aside to let Mabel slip past her and run upstairs.

In the doorway to Joan's sitting room, Mabel stopped for a moment as two toddlers looked up at her.

She turned to Joan. 'Sorry. I was forgetting you had these little ones to take care of.'

'They're happy playing together and it's good for Max to have company,' said Joan. 'As long as we're here to watch them, they'll be fine. I'll be glad of the distraction, to be honest.' She put her hand over her mouth for a moment. 'I'm so sorry. That was a dreadful thing to say. I didn't mean it the way it sounded.'

'Don't be daft,' said Mabel.

'Thanks for getting Persephone to tell me about the Clarinda column.'

'I couldn't face doing it myself,' Mabel admitted, 'but I wanted you to know. You and Persephone are the only friends I told.'

Joan pressed her hand. 'I'm glad you did.'

'I've just spoken to Harry. Some chaps at the base saw it in the paper and picked up its meaning.'

'Are you going to tell the others?' asked Joan.

'I know we generally share most things with one another,' said Mabel, 'but I can't tell them that Clarinda's broad hint is actually the truth. I just can't. The fewer people who know about Harry having been a gold-digger the better. The point is that it isn't true any more; it hasn't been true for a long time. That's all that matters.'

But it wasn't that simple, as Mabel very soon found out.

Cordelia, of course, had been the first to see it, just as she'd seen the piece about Persephone and Matt. Bless her heart, she caught up with Mabel on the way to the buffet and drew her aside to show it to her.

'I don't know whether you've seen this, Mabel.'

'Yes, I have.'

Cordelia's usually cool features looked troubled. 'It contains a rather unpleasant insinuation.'

'I know,' said Mabel. 'Let's go in and tell the others. I need them to know.'

Oh yes, she needed them to believe in Harry's goodness and honour, which meant not sharing the whole truth, but that was the way it had to be.

Nevertheless, it was hard to lie to her dearest friends. She told herself she had to, because Harry's reputation was at stake. Hers too, for that matter. Her friends would be appalled if they knew that the future husband she adored had started out firmly intending to marry money.

'This isn't like the piece about Persephone and Matt,' said Alison. 'That was true – apart from the mistake about Matt being an engine driver. But the unspoken suggestion here is that Harry is a cad. He deserves an apology in print. So do you, Mabel.'

'That would simply serve to keep the story alive for longer,' said Persephone. 'It would also bring it to the attention of more people.'

'I've talked to Harry about it,' said Mabel, 'and we'd rather let it die down of its own accord.'

'But it's such a horrible thing to say,' said Margaret.

'It isn't said outright,' Colette pointed out. 'It's hinted at, which somehow makes it worse.'

'That's because it takes a few moments for the meaning to sink in,' said Emily.

'You're right.' Colette smiled at Emily.

A mad urge to blurt out the truth surged up inside Mabel. She hated to deceive her friends, but on this occasion she had to. Her first loyalty lay with Harry and their future together. She would never say or do anything to compromise that.

'Has your mum seen it?' Dot asked. 'What does she say?'

'I have to telephone her this evening about the wedding. We can talk about it then.'

How casual she made it sound when really her skin was tingling all over. Mabel had no doubt Mumsy would have seen it, but would she have picked up on the hint it contained?

She didn't have to wait long to find out. As soon as the operator put the call through and Mumsy came on the line, Mabel knew that the worst had happened.

'Mabel, have you seen what Clarinda has written about you? Oh my goodness, this is shocking. What must everyone think? And so close to the wedding.'

'Mumsy, we just have to grin and bear it—'

'Wait a moment, Arnie,' said Mumsy.

'No, I won't wait,' said Pops. His voice became louder as he took over the line. 'Mabs, what's going on?'

'Nothing. It's just some unfortunate wording, that's all.'

'So I can write to the editor demanding a full apology, can I?'

Mabel shut her eyes.

'Mabs, are you still there?'

'I'm here, Pops.'

'Don't worry about anything. I'll have a full retraction printed.'

'But won't that just make people more aware of it?' Mabel tried the argument Persephone had employed on their friends.

'Aware of the apology – good thing.'

Mabel couldn't speak.

'Are you there? Is this a duff line?'

'I'm here,' said Mabel. 'Pops, you – you can't ask for an apology.'

Now it was his turn to fall silent. Then he asked, 'And why is that?'

'Because . . . because when I first knew Harry . . .' She got no further.

'Do you mean to tell me that Harry Knatchbull was after your money – my money?'

'Only at the very beginning, I swear. Then he fell in love with me. Everything since then has been real.'

'Is that so?' Pops said coldly. 'In that case, you're right. I can't demand a retraction. But I can go and see Harry and demand a full explanation from him.'

'Pops, *no.*'

'Mabel, *yes.*'

CHAPTER THIRTY-TWO

Emily's heart thudded hard in her chest. It was happening. Mr Gordon had decided upon a plan of action and today he was putting it into practice. The porters were full of it. No one could talk about anything else and feelings were running high. At the end of the previous shift, as the porters were finishing, they had been summoned to listen to Mr Gordon, who was flanked by senior members of station staff. He hadn't bothered to ask them to keep quiet about it; it would have done no good if he had. As soon as his talk was finished and the men and women were dismissed and sent on their way, they had flooded all parts of the station, seeking out the porters who had started the next shift.

Emily was sure her face must be in danger of giving her away. She tried to be invisible, leaving the talking to everyone else. At first she felt too panicked to listen, but then various comments filtered through.

'Laid the law down good and proper, he did. Said that if anyone is found pilfering in future, they'll be up before the disciplinary.'

'Who is he, anyroad, this Mr Gordon? He's not part of the portering staff. He shouldn't be giving us what for.'

'Damn cheek, talking to the whole lot of us like that, as if we've all got sticky fingers. A ruddy liberty, I call it. I've never done nowt wrong in my life.'

It was one heck of a shift. All the porters muttered to one another at every opportunity while Emily's thoughts whirled round and round. This was all because of her. She had made it happen. Ought she to be proud of having done the right thing? Instead, she felt terrified in case somebody found out. She dreaded being asked by Mr Buckley if she was all right.

As the day wore on, her tummy screwed up into ever-tightening knots. She was desperate for the shift to end so she could get the next bit over with, but at the same time she was scared of having to live through it.

At the end of the shift, all the porters congregated in a large, empty area at the back of the stores. A row of wooden crates had been placed at one end and Mr Gordon, along with a couple of others, climbed up and stood there. There were some grumbles from the waiting porters, but some voices sounded anxious. When Mr Buckley placed a gentle hand on Emily's shoulder, she thought her feeling of betrayal would overwhelm her.

The head porter, up on the makeshift dais, spoke first, looking serious. He introduced Mr Gordon.

'I'm pretty sure you already know why you're here,' said Mr Gordon, looking around at his listeners. 'I am going to deliver the same talk – and the same warning – to all of you as I gave your colleagues on the previous shift. That way, no one among you can say that you weren't spoken to. I am now going to read a statement to you.' Putting on a pair of reading glasses, he referred to a piece of paper. 'You'll see at the end why it is important that I read this.

'It has been brought to our attention that petty pilfering is going on in the stores and very likely also in other parts of the station. This pilfering is by no means new. As we understand it, it's been going on for years. Therefore I am here to inform you that pilfering, even on a small, personal scale, is theft and to give you due warning that in future anybody who is caught in the act of pilfering, or who is found with stolen goods about their *person, will face a disciplinary interview before being reported to the police.*

'A copy of this statement,' Mr Gordon added, removing his spectacles, 'will be included inside every porter's next wage packet. That is all, ladies and gentlemen. Thank you for your attention.'

'Aren't you going to ask for questions?' called a man's voice from near the back.

'Did you not understand anything in the statement?' Mr Gordon enquired. 'Did anyone not understand? No? Good. Then there is no need for questions.'

He and the other men climbed down from the dais and walked away, leaving the porters to burst out talking among themselves.

'Talk about all being tarred with the same brush!' said an indignant voice.

Someone else sounded shocked. 'Has that really been going on?'

'I wish I'd known,' another joked, but that was the only light-hearted voice Emily caught.

'Phew,' breathed someone else close by. 'We got off.'

'No, we didn't,' came the soft reply. 'Not really.'

'There was no harm in it,' said another.

'No harm?' chimed in a different voice. 'Who are you trying to kid? Haven't you heard of rationing?'

At that, a loud argument broke out and Mr Buckley ushered Emily away.

'Off you go, lass. It's time you went home.'

Emily was glad to leave. She felt cold and fluttery inside. What had she unleashed?

Emily got off the bus at Seymour Grove. She was pretty sure that today was Colette's day off and she hoped to find her at home, preparing her evening meal. She didn't know what she would do if Colette wasn't there. She had to talk to Colette before going home or there was a serious danger of her bursting into tears in front of her parents.

When Colette answered the door, Emily's legs wobbled. They actually wobbled.

'Come in,' said Colette, asking at once, 'What's happened? Come and sit down and I'll put the kettle on. You look rather ghastly.'

She drew Emily into the parlour and parked her in an armchair, but as Colette was about to go into the kitchen, Emily caught her hand and stopped her. Colette sank onto the arm of the chair.

'Did you know what Mr Gordon was going to do?' Emily asked.

'No. Why should I? He had no reason to tell me.'

Emily poured out all that had happened, including some of the remarks she'd heard from the other porters, while Colette placed her hand on Emily's back and made gentle circles.

'It's not your fault,' Colette said softly when Emily's words ran dry. 'I'm sure you know that, but you still feel rotten, don't you?'

'I'd no idea it was going to be so bad,' whispered Emily. 'It's not that I want to feel guilty, but I can't help it. I'm not wallowing, if that's what you're thinking.'

'I never thought that for one moment,' said Colette. 'I've told you before. I don't believe in telling others what they ought to feel or not feel. Life isn't that simple. You have to live with your own thoughts and feelings and come to terms with them.'

'Is that the voice of experience?' asked Emily and the hand making circles on her back stilled.

After a few moments, Colette said, 'When I left Tony, I was dreadfully ashamed.'

Emily twisted round to look up at her. 'You had nothing to be ashamed of, not after the way he treated you.' Then she realised what she'd said. 'That's what you mean, isn't it? I was telling you how to feel.'

Colette smiled. 'It shows you care. It means you don't want me to be hurt. I know that, but I also know from experience that being told how to feel doesn't actually help me. I was ashamed because – well, because decent people are ashamed when a marriage fails. The neighbours look at you differently afterwards. There will always be somebody who'll say that it couldn't have been all his fault, and that's hard to brush off.'

'It must be,' Emily agreed with a shiver.

Colette left Emily's chair and went to sit in the other armchair. Facing her, she perched on the edge of the seat, leaning forward and fixing her gaze on Emily.

'I know that my situation with Tony and your situation with the pilfering are different, but I can think of one similarity. The way Tony treated me was wrong and in the end I stood up to him and pressed charges. He had no choice other than to plead guilty and we all thought that he'd be sent to prison and I'd be free of him and that would be that. Instead, he was allowed to join the army without having a conviction on his record and there are people who see me as being not quite respectable because I'm the girl who left her husband, and never mind the reason why.'

'It's not fair,' said Emily.

'Life isn't fair, no matter how much you want it to be. Look at what's happening to you. The pilfering is wrong and you've done the right thing by reporting it, but now things are difficult for you because – well, you tell me. It isn't up to me to speculate.'

Emily thought before she spoke. 'I feel bad for all the innocent porters who have never taken anything. I heard one of them say something about being tarred with the same brush. But I couldn't have prevented this from happening to them without naming the guilty porters, and I couldn't bear to do that. Even if I'd wanted to, I only knew a handful of them and I'm sure there were more involved. But it turns out that the guilty ones are just as angry as the innocent ones.'

'That could well be fear talking,' said Colette. 'They know how close they've come to being hauled up before the magistrate.'

Emily nodded. That made sense.

Colette's lips twitched and she smiled. Emily thought how pretty she was; she hadn't really appreciated it before.

'I know I'm always saying I won't tell you how to feel,' said Colette, 'but maybe you could allow yourself to feel a bit better for having spared those porters from fines or prison sentences.'

Emily smiled back. That made sense too.

'I told you about the time I saw some porters syphoning off sugar,' said Colette. 'They were ordinary men trying to stock up their kitchen cupboards, not vicious criminals stealing wholesale and flogging everything at inflated prices on the black market. Pilfering is wrong, but there are degrees of wrongness.'

'And degrees of punishment,' said Emily.

'Exactly. You found yourself in a horrid situation and you did your best to resolve it. Today has been nasty and upsetting, but I hope you'll be able to put it behind you.'

'But . . . Look, I'm not wallowing, I swear, but it'll always be there, won't it? If the others knew what I did, they'd be appalled. They wouldn't trust me again. They might even send me to Coventry.'

There was sadness now in Colette's smile. 'I know. You have to keep reminding yourself why you did what you did in the way you did it.'

'You're a wise person,' said Emily.

'No, I'm not,' Colette answered with a laugh. 'I'm just someone who has had a lot to come to terms with.'

CHAPTER THIRTY-THREE

Persephone looked forward eagerly to the publication of her article about good manners. Tuesday was publication day for *Vera's Voice*, but that day Persephone had a double shift. Not to worry. When Mrs Mitchell bought her own copy, she would purchase an extra one for Persephone. Persephone felt a little flutter of excitement. She cut out every article of hers that made it into print, though the collection wasn't growing as quickly as she would have liked.

A copy of *Vera's Voice* lay on her bed when she crept in late that night. She switched on the light, knowing it was safe to do so because Mrs Mitchell would have done the blackout for her. Seizing the magazine, but careful not to tear the flimsy wartime paper, Persephone opened it – and her breath caught in a heady mixture of shock and delight. The inside front cover was, as usual, a page of advertisements. Opposite, on the first 'real' page, was her article – *her* article. It had received top billing. Out of all the stories and articles in this week's edition, hers was first. That had never happened before. She felt like waking up the household and throwing a party.

She couldn't wait to share her joy with her friends. She wasn't surprised to find that they already knew about her success because Dot and Colette both got *Vera's Voice* every week, as did Mrs Cooper, which meant that the Wilton Close girls had already been shown her article. Cordelia didn't read *Vera's Voice*, but Dot had told her.

'I'm going to buy a copy on the way home,' Cordelia said in the buffet. 'Congratulations, Persephone. It's quite a triumph for you.'

'We're all proud of you,' said Alison.

'Aye, we are,' Dot agreed. 'It's a feather in my cap an' all since you're my daughter for the duration.'

Everyone laughed at that.

'Your parents must be delighted,' said Colette.

Persephone kept the smile on her face. Her parents had never treated her journalistic ambitions as she would have wished. In former times she might have received a mild 'Good show' on having her piece in such a prominent position, but now, having let them down by starting a relationship with a mere railway fireman, they definitely wouldn't have any time for her *Vera's Voice* success. In fact, Ma would probably shudder at the memory of what she saw as Persephone's social experiment that had gone horribly wrong.

Persephone was careful not to let the side down by appearing to criticise her parents.

'They're not keen,' was all she said.

'I bet you always wanted them to be, though, didn't you?' said Dot.

'Well – yes,' Persephone admitted. She wasn't going to elaborate, but then she decided on the truth. 'I've never stopped yearning for parental approval of my writing, even though I know I'll never receive it.'

There were murmurs of 'I'm sorry' and 'That's a shame.'

Persephone smiled around the table. 'It makes your approval all the more important.'

'It's more than approval,' said Margaret. 'We're chuffed to bits for you.'

Her friends' support meant the world to Persephone. It wasn't just that they were pleased her article had been given the prime spot. They wanted to discuss it too.

And they weren't the only ones. On Friday, Persephone arrived home to find a flat parcel had been delivered for her that day. When she opened it, out tumbled three or four dozen letters.

'Readers have written in to *Vera's Voice* to say what they think of my article on good manners,' Persephone told Miss Brown in an awed voice.

'And what do they think?' Miss Brown enquired.

Persephone laughed in sheer pleasure. 'They agree with me and they give examples from their own experiences.'

'Well done,' said Miss Brown. 'Your piece has obviously struck a chord.'

'Yes.' Persephone wanted to hug the whole wide world. 'Isn't it wonderful?'

'It'll certainly give you something to talk about when you see Matt's family on Sunday.'

That put a bit of a damper on Persephone's happy mood. After everything her parents had said about Matt and their relationship, was she going to feel horribly self-conscious in front of his family? No. She mustn't let anything spoil her relationship with Matt.

'I'm sure Matt's family will be fascinated to hear about your writing,' Miss Brown said.

'I wouldn't dream of showing off,' said Persephone.

As it turned out, she had no need to, because Matt did it on her behalf. Best of all, Sergeant and Mrs Franklin had both admired the article before they knew who had written it.

Seeing his mother's copy of the popular magazine on the sideboard, Matt remarked, 'Persephone has had an article published this week.'

'Really?' said his father. 'Well done, dear. I must admit I wouldn't normally look twice at a ladies' story paper, but Nettie showed me a piece in this week's issue that she thought I should read.'

'It's about the importance of good manners,' said Mrs Franklin, 'and how common civility helps people in these dark times.'

'I wish some of the blokes I arrest had better manners,' her husband joked.

'Persephone wrote that,' said Matt, looking at her proudly.

'Persephone?' Mrs Franklin looked puzzled. 'But . . .'

'Stephanie Fraser is my pen name,' Persephone explained. 'Or my byline, I should say, since I write for the press.'

'You're Stephanie Fraser? I see.'

'Loads of readers have written to say they agree with the article,' said Matt. '*Vera's Voice* posted on all their letters to Persephone.'

'I'm not surprised they agreed,' said Sergeant Franklin. 'It's a jolly sound argument you make.'

Persephone felt as if she was glowing, but what mattered most to her was the special smile Matt gave her.

Matt's sisters weren't here today, so when Mrs Franklin stood up to make the tea, Persephone got up too. Unlike last time, when she hadn't been permitted to lift a finger, she was given the job of warming the pot and making the tea. It felt like a big step forward, a sign of true acceptance.

Hearing a soft click, Persephone turned to find that Mrs Franklin had closed the kitchen door.

'Can I ask you something?' said Mrs Franklin.

'Of course,' said Persephone.

'How long ago did you write that article?'

'Not all that long.'

'What I'm really asking,' said Mrs Franklin, 'is did you write it before you met my family?'

'Most of it, yes,' Persephone told her. 'I'd almost finished it before I came here.'

314

'Almost,' Mrs Franklin repeated in a flat voice. 'So you added to it after you met us.'

'Yes.'

'What did you add?'

'I beg your pardon?' Persephone was puzzled. What was going on?

'It's a simple question. What did you add to your article after you came here for tea? No, don't tell me. Let me guess. You added the part about good manners oiling the wheels between the different classes.'

'Well – yes.' Oh cripes.

'I see.' Mrs Franklin's face crumpled, but only for a moment; then she thrust out her chin and her features hardened. 'We were part of your research. That's very flattering, I don't think.'

'It wasn't like that,' Persephone answered at once. 'I didn't come here with an ulterior motive.'

'Didn't you?'

'No, I promise. But being here made me see what a difference—'

'What a difference it makes when the rabble kowtow. Is that it?'

'No!' cried Persephone.

'Now you listen to me, young lady.' Mrs Franklin's voice was low and steady, but her eyes were fierce. 'I don't appreciate having my family used like that.'

'I never intended '

'And while we're at it, I don't want you toying with my son's affections either.'

So far Mabel had kept to herself the subject of her conversation with Pops. It had seemed the only way to cope. At home, she couldn't, just couldn't tell Margaret or Alison about it. She couldn't bear for them to know the truth about

Harry. Even if his being a gold-digger wasn't the truth any longer, she didn't want to share it, especially so close to her wedding. Her wedding! Her happy anticipation had been swamped by a dark cloud.

But it was a mistake to hug her problem to herself, and she knew it. She only had to remember the support she'd received over the matter of the water pipes for the Extension to appreciate the value of sharing her troubles. Discussing her current situation wouldn't be a happy experience, but she needed her friends to help her.

Knowing that Bob was on nights, she arranged to meet Persephone at Joan's on Monday evening.

'You answered the door pretty sharpish,' said Mabel when Joan let her in. 'You must have flown down the stairs.'

'I was down here already,' said Joan. 'Persephone got here twenty minutes ago and we're in Gran's sitting room. Persephone came early so she could spend a while with Gran. She helped us with something this time last year, so she knows Gran from that.'

Joan took Mabel into the parlour where they spent a few minutes with Mrs Foster, then the three girls went upstairs to the Hubbles' rooms, where they whispered admiringly while gazing at Max fast asleep before settling down in the front room.

'Why did you want the three of us to see one another?' Persephone asked Mabel. 'I assume it must be to do with Harry.'

'With bells on,' said Mabel. She told her friends how she had telephoned Mumsy. 'Then Pops muscled in on the call. He was outraged by the suggestion, however vague, of Harry being after the family money. He was all set to demand an official apology from the newspaper, so I was forced to tell him he couldn't.'

Joan caught her breath audibly. 'You told him it was true?'

'I had to.' Panic fluttered through Mabel. 'Otherwise he would have been on to his solicitor first thing next morning. Can you imagine what would have happened after that? Believe me, if there had been any way, any at all, to avoid telling Pops, I would have seized it with both hands. The very last thing I wanted was for my parents to find out that my fiancé started out as a gold-digger.' She dashed away a tear. 'I've kept it secret all this time. I thought it was well and truly behind us. I *hate* Clarinda for doing this to us.'

'Oh, Mabel,' breathed Joan. 'Sweetheart.'

'That's not all,' Mabel continued. 'Pops says he's going to go down south and get the truth out of Harry.'

'No!' the other two exclaimed.

'Have you warned Harry?' Persephone asked.

'Pops made me swear I wouldn't,' said Mabel.

'When is he going?' asked Joan.

'I don't know exactly. He could be there now, for all I know. I keep having to stand up and walk about every time I think of it. It's as if I've got ants crawling about under my skin.'

'What a worry for you,' said Joan. 'If I could get my hands on that Clarinda . . .'

'Let's think this through calmly,' said Persephone. 'Harry is going to get the shock of his life when Mr Bradshaw turns up unannounced.'

'I can't allow that to happen,' said Mabel. 'I've got to warn him – haven't I? I know Pops said not to, but if I don't tell Harry in advance, it would feel like setting a trap for him. I can't do that. I just can't.'

'Your first loyalty should be to Harry,' said Joan. 'He's going to be your husband. That means you should tell him so he can be prepared.'

'But if Pops gets there and it's clear that Harry is ready for him, how will that look?'

'Tell Harry not to prepare anything to say.' As soon as she uttered the idea, Joan pulled a face. 'No, that wouldn't work. It would be impossible for him not to think about it – and your father would be certain to realise.'

'Think of it this way,' said Persephone. 'What do you want the result to be?'

Mabel pictured it. 'I want Pops to believe Harry. I want him to see Harry the same way I do. I want Harry to win Pops over.' She sighed. 'And that won't happen if Harry is forewarned.'

'Poor Harry,' said Joan. 'I think you have to chuck him to the wolves.'

'Looks like it.' Mabel curled her right hand around the fingers of her left one, covering the ruby ring she loved so much. Her heart had overflowed with hope and happiness when Harry gave it to her. 'But what about afterwards? What will Harry think when he knows I could have warned him but chose not to? What sort of future wife lets her husband-to-be face her father's wrath without a warning? What does that say about me?'

Joan took Mabel's hands in her own. 'It says you trust Harry. It says you believe he can win Mr Bradshaw over.'

'It also says you respect your father's point of view,' Persephone added. 'If you tell Harry beforehand, your father will know and that will muddy the waters. You want Mr Bradshaw to believe in Harry. The only way for him to end up doing that is to catch Harry unawares in the first place.'

Mabel swallowed hard. She knew Persephone was right.

'The meeting will be tough for Harry,' said Persephone, 'but speaking with unprepared, heartfelt sincerity is the only chance he has of impressing your father.'

Joan nodded. 'That's true.'

'So I just have to sit back and wait,' said Mabel.

Joan smiled. 'That doesn't sound much like you, does it?'

'Thank you both,' Mabel said. 'You've helped me think things through and see them clearly.'

Persephone smiled at her. 'It's easy to do when it's happening to somebody else.'

'That sounds like the voice of experience,' said Mabel. 'Do you mean your own situation with Clarinda?'

'Actually, I was thinking of my situation with *Vera's Voice.*'

Joan turned to her in surprise. 'What's happened?'

'Matt's parents read my piece about good manners. They didn't know it was by me because of the Stephanie Fraser name.'

'Didn't they like it?' asked Mabel. 'How could they not? It's sensible and uplifting and completely true.'

'They did like it,' said Persephone, 'but afterwards Matt's mother got me on my own and asked me when I'd written it and when I'd had the idea about good manners between the classes. It so happens I thought of that after I'd met the Franklins.'

'And you were honest and said so,' Joan finished for her.

Persephone nodded. 'It never occurred to me what was going to come next. She more or less accused me of using her family's Sunday tea for research purposes.'

'No!' said Mabel, the word emerging on a breath of dismay.

'That's not all,' said Persephone. 'She warned me against toying with Matt's feelings. She obviously thinks I'm only interested in him and his family for what I can get out of them for magazine articles.'

'That's unfair,' Joan exclaimed. 'You care about Matt.'

'And he cares about you,' Mabel added.

'As a matter of fact,' said Persephone, 'my mother said practically the same thing. Not the bit about toying with Matt's feelings, but she thought I'd made friends with him so as to exploit his family for journalistic purposes. Only she thinks I then went and spoiled it by developing feelings for him.'

'Oh, Persephone, I'm so sorry,' said Joan.

'She called it my "social experiment that has now gone hideously wrong". So now you know what my mother thinks of me.'

'Then it's a good thing you've got us and the others beside you,' Joan said staunchly. 'Do you remember how Gran threw me out of this house when she found out I'd been seeing Steven behind Bob's back? I ended up sitting on Dot's doorstep, waiting for her to come home. She was the one who thought of taking me round to Mrs Cooper's to stay with her. Not one of them judged me – not Mrs Cooper or Dot or Mrs Grayson. They were all so kind – and so was everyone in the buffet. Yes, you were all shocked by what I'd done, but you all stood by me and that meant so much. That's what you must cling to now, Persephone – and you too, Mabel, while you're worrying about your father seeing Harry. I know how upset you both are, but you have friends who think the world of you and that's what you must both draw strength from.'

'It's true,' said Mabel. 'I had good reasons for wanting to get the nursery set up on my own. I see it as a sort of legacy that will be here after I've left. But when things went wrong, I didn't need to think twice about turning to the rest of you.' To Joan, she said, 'It's because of you that I came up with the nursery idea in the first place.'

'Me?' asked Joan.

'Yes. A while back, you talked about how mothers doing war work need proper arrangements for their children.'

Joan smiled. 'Glad to have been of service.'

Speaking through a wave of emotion, Mabel said, 'We all look after one another. Goodness, but I'm going to miss you all when I leave.'

Tears started to fall and the other two moved to be close and put their arms around her.

'Don't cry or you'll set me off,' said Joan.

Mabel clung hard to her friends for a few more moments, then detached herself, scrabbling for the hanky up her sleeve and performing a mopping-up operation.

'I'll never forget you,' she said. 'I'll never forget any of the friends I've made here in Manchester.'

'We'll never forget you either,' Joan assured her. 'We'll write all the time.'

'And,' Persephone added, 'we'll think of you every time we pass the Mabel Bradshaw Nursery.'

That surprised a laugh out of Mabel. 'Don't be daft. It can't be called that.'

'Why not?' said Persephone. 'You said yourself that it's the legacy you're leaving behind. What else could it be called?'

CHAPTER THIRTY-FOUR

If Emily had hoped the pilfering and its consequences would cease to be a matter of interest to the porters, she was sadly mistaken. It seemed to be all they wanted to talk about. Every time it was mentioned, she experienced a creepy-crawly sensation under her skin.

She had arranged to share her dinner breaks with Colette, Persephone or Dot whenever she could, but this didn't go unnoticed.

'Eating with one of your chums again?' Mr Buckley asked just before they stopped for dinner.

'Yes,' said Emily.

Mr Buckley nodded. 'Much nicer for you than eating with an old codger like me.'

'You're not an old codger.'

'I'm an old something.' Mr Buckley's eyes twinkled, but then he turned serious. 'You might do well to make a few friends among the porters. You don't want to look stand-offish.'

'Is that what people think?' Emily felt a flutter of alarm.

'Not that I know of,' said Mr Buckley, 'but they might start to if you carry on like it, especially since Mr Gordon did his speechifying. Folk are feeling sensitive at present. There are them that, to listen to 'em, have never put a foot wrong in their whole lives and they resent being treated as if they're part of the brigade that's always helped themselves to the odd little summat here and there to help stretch the housekeeping a bit further. The thing is, my little lass, we're all in a delicate situation. Don't look so scared. Give it time and it'll blow over.'

How long would that take? Emily found a chance to talk privately to Colette.

'The trouble is,' Emily confided, 'it's hard to give it time. I keep expecting somebody to pounce on me because they can see in my face that I'm the one who gave the game away. I feel especially bad about Mr Buckley.'

'You did your best to stand up for him when we went to see Mr Gordon,' Colette reminded her.

'True. It just makes me uncomfortable knowing that he thinks well of me, but only because he doesn't know the truth.'

Colette thought for a moment. 'Do you feel bad because of everything that's happened or just because of Mr Buckley? I know he means a lot to you.'

'Because of Mr Buckley.' It was the first time Emily had realised this. It hadn't been true all along, but it was true now.

'Because you like him. He's been good to you.'

'What are you getting at?' asked Emily.

'Nothing. I'm simply trying to understand. It's not easy keeping a secret from somebody you like and respect. When Mrs Cooper found out the truth about Tony and me, I didn't exactly rush into her arms and pour out the whole story. It was some time before I felt ready to confide. Not that I'm suggesting you open up to Mr Buckley.'

That evening, Emily thought a lot about what Colette had said. Two words in particular rang out loud and clear. *Like* and *respect*. Emily both liked and respected Mr Buckley, in spite of what he had done, and she felt bad about having gone behind his back to put a stop to it. She knew he liked and trusted her too.

There was nothing else for it. She had to tell him what she'd done.

When would be the best time to talk to Mr Buckley? Emily thought things through. A tea break wouldn't be long enough. Perhaps she should ask him to stay on after the end of a shift – but that way, the two of them would have to work together all day with him wondering what was coming. No, it would be best to get it over with right at the start of the day, before they began work.

So determined was she to get to Victoria in plenty of time that Emily tried to skip breakfast, only her mother wouldn't let her.

'Honestly, Mummy,' said Emily, taking care not to sound whiny, 'you might let me grow up a bit.'

'Leaving the house on an empty stomach counts as grown-up, does it?'

Emily might have rolled her eyes, but Daddy was there and he wouldn't have put up with it.

At long last she arrived at Victoria and put on her peaked cap, patting her hair at the sides. Where was Mr Buckley? He was always early. Not like some, who dashed in at the last minute. Mr Buckley liked to have a cigarette and a chat with his cronies. Emily normally stayed out of the way until it was time to start the shift, but today she approached the group with a smile.

'May I have a quick word?' she asked Mr Buckley.

'Can't it wait?' asked Mr Buckley. 'I haven't had a chance to chew over last night's war news yet.'

Heat rose in Emily's cheeks. 'Please,' she said and he came with her.

'Everything all right, lass?'

'Well . . . no, since you ask. Please could we go somewhere less conspicuous? I need to tell you something.'

'Sounds mysterious,' Mr Buckley commented.

They entered the concourse. In with the all-pervading smell of tobacco, Emily caught a whiff of perfume as a lady walked past, heels tapping as she made her way confidently, unlike another lady, who was frowning as she looked around. A pair of black-clad nuns shepherded a crocodile of children, and two men with trilbies set at jaunty angles stopped to light up cigarettes, flicking the used matches to the floor.

'We won't exactly be inconspicuous here,' Mr Buckley commented.

Emily led the way onto a platform.

'Oh good! Just what we need,' came a man's voice, sounding relieved. 'Porters. Could you help with this luggage, please?'

Emily was about to say they weren't on duty, but Mr Buckley said, 'Of course, sir,' and picked up a suitcase in each hand, leaving two smaller bags for Emily. 'Where to, sir?'

When they'd seen the man to the taxi rank, Mr Buckley said, 'If you're on the station in uniform, you're on duty. Simple as that. Now then, let's find somewhere a bit more private.'

At the far end of the concourse were half a dozen empty flatbed trolleys. Mr Buckley walked round to the far side of them. Stopping, he turned to Emily.

'I've missed my ciggy and my chinwag. What's up?'

There was no time for a preamble. They would be starting work soon.

'Mr Buckley, the person who told on the porters for pilfering – I did it. I reported them.'

'You did? You? What were you thinking?'

'It's stealing. I know pilfering doesn't sound serious, but it is, and it's extra wrong when there's rationing.'

'Wait a minute,' said Mr Buckley. 'As I recall, I gave you something – what was it? And you took it.'

'Tea.' Emily had to avert her face for a moment in shame. 'I took it without thinking, though that's no excuse. So, yes, that makes me a wrongdoer as well. But I wish I hadn't taken it. I felt awful afterwards.'

'Then you only needed to say "No, thank you." That's all.'

'But it wasn't all. Please try to understand.'

'Try to understand?' Mr Buckley shook his head, his eyes clouded with thought. 'Me and the other blokes, we've always had a bit here and a bit there, and we weren't the ones that started it neither. The porters who trained us did it an' all. It's always gone on.'

'That doesn't make it right.'

'It's a perk of the job and I don't appreciate a young lass like you coming along and calling me a thief.'

'I'm sorry, Mr Buckley.'

'And after everything I've done for you. Taken you under my wing, I have.'

'I know. I'm sorry.'

'Being sorry doesn't butter any parsnips. I don't know what to make of this, I really don't.'

'You aren't going to tell the others, are you?'

'What? No. What d'you take me for? I wouldn't chuck you to the wolves like that, even though that's what you did to the rest of us. Eh, you seemed such a nice little lass, and then you go and do this.'

'I'm sorry,' said Emily.

'So you keep saying.'

'I mean that I'm sorry to have hurt you. You've been good to me and I appreciate that. It's thanks to you that I've settled in so well.'

'Aye. You got your feet so far under the table that you took it upon yourself to change things from how they've always been for as long as anyone can remember. You might have got a lot of good men into trouble, men whose only crime is to take a bit extra home for their wives to put on the table. Well, I don't know about you, but I've got a job to do.'

Utterly wretched, Emily dug in her pocket for her hanky as Mr Buckley walked away.

CHAPTER THIRTY-FIVE

Until now Mabel had been happily counting down the days to her wedding – literally. As soon as the date had been settled, Alison had worked out how many days away it was and made a numbered chart.

'You cross off each day and when you get down to one, that's your wedding-day eve,' Alison had explained. 'It's what I did when I was away in Leeds and desperate to come home.'

Mabel had been only too glad to cross off the days before now and her housemates had teased her about it, which had added to the fun. Now, though, she felt like tearing up the blessed chart and sticking it in the salvage box – except that she couldn't, could she? Not without answering lots of questions. She experienced an unexpected spurt of anger towards Harry for putting her in this position. It was bad enough that he had set out to marry money, but whatever had possessed him to tell his old chums? That was the root of the current problem, which had now escalated to the point where Pops was going to have it out with him. Perhaps he already had. Not knowing was turning Mabel inside out with nerves.

'Look at her,' Alison said at the tea table. 'She hasn't heard a word – have you, Mabel? You're in a world of your own.'

'Are you busy thinking about your wedding, dear?' asked Mrs Cooper.

Mabel pulled herself together. 'Sorry. What were you all talking about?'

She had to be careful or she would give herself away. She was desperate to telephone Harry, but she mustn't until after Pops had seen him. She didn't trust herself not to pour out what Pops intended to do.

If Pops fell out with Harry, what would that mean for Mabel's future? She treasured her position as her parents' daughter and only child and had been looking forward so much to welcoming Harry into her family. Could Mumsy and Pops ever feel the same way about him again?

But Harry was a reformed character and he didn't deserve all the question marks that now hung over his head. Could he convince Pops?

Poor Mumsy too. She had looked forward to being the mother of the bride for such a long time. Was it now to be irretrievably spoiled for her?

Mabel telephoned home a couple of times, hoping to speak to Pops, but Mumsy said he wasn't back yet. They did their best to discuss the wedding as usual, but it was hard with such a cloud hanging over them.

'Harry's a good man,' Mabel assured her mother.

Mumsy sighed. 'I certainly hope so.'

'I know he set out to marry money, but he really and truly did fall in love.'

'I know,' said Mumsy. 'That's what you said to Pops.'

'It's true,' said Mabel. 'He loves me and I love him.'

'I don't doubt you love one another,' said Mumsy. 'Nobody who saw you together on Christmas Eve after Harry's proposal could possibly think otherwise. Pops knows it too.'

'Then why has he gone steaming down to Bomber Command?'

'Because he loves you and he won't have you taken advantage of. Because he needs to hear it from Harry. And I'll tell you something, Mabel: Harry had better be jolly convincing or goodness knows how this will end.'

'It will end,' Mabel said stoutly, 'with Pops understanding that Harry is everything he could wish for in a son-in-law.'

'You sound so sure.'

'I *am* sure.'

She was too. She tried to work out when Pops would get home to Annerby. Had he really travelled all that way just to speak to Harry? Given that he conducted some secret war work in his factory, might he take the opportunity to go to London as well?

Mabel arrived home after a long day on the permanent way to be met at the front door by Mrs Cooper telling her that her father was there. Mabel felt a shiver of anxiety, but Mrs Cooper was too excited at having an unexpected visitor to notice.

'I've invited him to eat with us,' she said, 'but he says he has to get back to Victoria Station to catch the evening train.'

Mabel went into the front room. Even though she felt jumpy with nerves, she experienced a rush of love at the sight of her father. He was her lifelong hero – well, one of her heroes. She was in the privileged position of having two: Pops and Grandad. Pops was the man she looked up to and admired for having risen in the world, and also because of the social conscience that made him strive to improve conditions for the less fortunate; while Grandad, darling, much-missed Grandad, had always been the man she idolised for being true to his roots and for seeing everyone and everything through clear eyes.

She went to Pops and he hugged her, keeping hold of her to look searchingly into her face before he let her go.

'Well, Pops?' Mabel couldn't wait a moment longer.

'It's good to see you too, Mabs,' he answered drily, 'and my journey wasn't bad, all told.'

Mabel flushed, but she wouldn't be put off. 'I'm sure you can understand if my manners aren't all they should be. I'm glad you had a good journey. Now please tell me what happened with Harry.'

'He was most taken aback to see me, even more so when he heard what I had to say. I let him think I was there purely on the basis of having seen that wretched piece in the newspaper. I didn't say anything about what you'd told me of his original intentions.'

Mabel went cold. Please don't let Harry have tried to get away with it. Then she lifted her chin. She believed in him. Yes, he'd had caddish ambitions to start with, but that was a long time ago and he was a different person now.

'Don't ever try to play poker, Mabs,' said Pops. 'You'd lose all your money.'

'What happened?'

'I shan't keep you on tenterhooks. He coughed up the truth. He admitted he'd been after the money in the beginning, but then, as he got to know you, he fell in love. He seemed sincere.'

'He didn't just *seem* sincere,' said Mabel. 'He *was* sincere.'

'I'm sure you're right. All the same, I will admit to having been shaken up by this.'

'I'm sorry you had to find out,' said Mabel.

'Believe me, I'd rather know than not know, though I wish it had never been inflicted on your mother.'

'Poor Mumsy,' said Mabel. 'But she'll feel better when you reassure her. You did believe Harry, didn't you, Pops?'

'All I can say is I very much wanted to believe him – but I also need to tell you that I'm going to disinherit you.'

'You're . . . what?'

'I'm sorry, Mabs, but there's a lot of money at stake here and I'm too shrewd a businessman to take this kind of chance. You'll have your allowance, but you won't inherit the bulk of the money and you won't get the factory. I'll turn it into a cooperative. It's the only way I can be completely certain about the security of everything I've built up over the years.'

'Pops . . .' breathed Mabel.

'Seriously, Mabs,' Pops replied. 'What did you expect?'

Disinherited. *Disinherited.* Mabel's brain split in two. Half of her mind had been left stunned and disbelieving. It was such a huge idea to take in. But at the same time, the other part of her brain completely accepted it. There was something inevitable about it – or was she being dramatic? She didn't think so. It felt as if, in some horrible, unavoidable way, this was the wretched consequence of everything that had happened since the first moment Harry Knatchbull had contemplated marrying for money and had told his chums of his intention.

Mabel had never given a lot of thought to what one day would become hers. Some people did. Some people lived in expectation. That was what it was called. Mabel didn't know if it still happened, but in the old days, young men had been able to borrow vast sums against their future expectations. That was how much they depended upon receiving it, how much it must have occupied their thoughts.

Mabel had never dwelt excessively upon her own inheritance. Not because she was frivolous or empty-headed. Her inheritance was something that was there, something to be aware of without particularly thinking about it, something to be relied upon in an abstract kind of way. She had certainly never thought of it in terms of travelling the world or splurging on diamonds when she got her hands on the money.

It wasn't that her inheritance didn't matter to her. Financial security was important. Mabel shared her father's social conscience and she knew enough about the lives of the poor to be in no doubt as to which end of the social spectrum she wanted to be. She was well aware of how deeply money mattered and what a difference it could make, not merely in a practical sense but also to one's sense of personal well-being.

She knew, too, how very much Harry mattered to her and the difference he had made to her life and her happiness. He was an essential part of her life and if the price she had to pay was giving up her future wealth, then so be it.

'It won't make any odds,' she had said to Pops.

'I'm not doing this as a means of forcing you to leave Harry,' Pops had told her. 'I know you're going to marry him. That's the sort of person you are. Determined. Resolute. Strong. But I have to do what I believe to be the right thing and that means keeping my fortune and my business safe. That's *my* right thing. Your right thing is obviously to be Mrs Harry Knatchbull. Unfortunately, the two things don't go together. This is very far from being what I would have chosen, Mabs, but I hope you can understand my point of view.'

Yes, she could. Part of her wished she could rail against it, wished she could weep and rage and feel hard done by, but the truth was she understood exactly why Pops had made this drastic decision. She remembered only too clearly how shocked and distraught she had been when she had found out about Harry's past – so she knew exactly how Pops saw things now. She had left Harry and he had had to fight to win her back.

It was all about consequences, wasn't it? Harry's choice to seek out a wealthy wife had led to their all but splitting up for good. And now it had caused Pops to disinherit her. It wasn't losing the money that was so distressing – although she would be lying if she said it didn't matter. What was worse was the thought of the profound effect this was bound to have on her family. Mumsy and Pops meant the world to her and this would change things for ever.

Mabel had learned all about the pain of loss through Althea's death. This would be a loss of a different sort. She wouldn't lose her parents; they weren't going to cast her out into the snow. But their relationship would change. Even if they all worked hard to keep things as normal as they could, there would still be subtle changes. How was she to bear that? She adored her parents and they had always worshipped her. But no matter how deeply they loved her, they were bound to view her differently if she was no longer the Bradshaw heiress. That would represent the worst possible disappointment.

She loved Harry with all her heart and couldn't wait to be his wife and take her rightful place by his side. The price she would have to pay for this wasn't losing her inheritance. It was causing her beloved Mumsy and Pops a profound and lasting disappointment.

'The editor of *Vera's Voice* has indicated that she'd be interested in receiving more from me,' Persephone said to her friends in the buffet, 'so I'm on the lookout for fresh ideas.'

'That's wonderful,' said Margaret.

'Congrats,' said Alison and the others added their own words of praise.

'It's not the same as being commissioned to write a specific piece,' Persephone explained, wanting to put it into context, 'but it's very pleasing all the same.'

'Very pleasing?' said Dot. 'A whopping great feather in your cap, I'd say.'

'What sort of thing do you want to write about next?' asked Emily.

'Preferably something that will capture the public imagination,' said Persephone, 'and get lots of response from the readers.'

'What about a make-do-and-mend fashion show?' Alison suggested. 'You sometimes see them advertised as fund-raising events and you could pick up lots of ideas for updating older clothes. The readers might like that.'

'That's a good idea,' said Persephone, 'but it would really require photographs of a professional standard to go with it. Besides, *Vera's Voice* have their own writers covering fashion.'

'I suppose that as a freelancer, you mustn't step on any-one's toes,' said Cordelia.

'How about the importance of dancing?' said Colette. 'How good it makes people feel, and the way that strangers dance together.'

Persephone wrinkled her nose. 'Too similar to the mes-sage behind the good manners article, I'm afraid.'

'I know,' said Margaret. 'What about the ballroom as the perfect place to relieve all the strain and difficulties of war-time and everyday life.'

'Oh *yes*,' said Alison. 'Ballrooms can be magical places – the music, the lighting, the sense of everybody wanting to have the best possible time. It's as if the war is left outside when you walk through the doors.'

'That's a good idea, chick,' said Dot, 'but I'm sure I've read that once or twice before.'

'Which goes to show how true it is,' said Persephone.

'You need something original,' said Emily.

'If there is such a thing,' Persephone answered with a smile.

Cordelia looked thoughtful. 'How about the beauty of the ballroom?'

Everyone looked at her and Persephone felt the first stirrings of an idea.

Cordelia warmed to her theme. 'Take the ballroom at the Claremont. It has a certain amount of ceiling, of course, complete with chandeliers. But a lot of where the ceiling would be is empty and the diners on the first floor who are sitting on the balcony can look down onto the dance floor. Best of all, hanging from the topmost ceiling in the hotel, all the way down as far as the dining room's balcony level, is a vast chandelier with thousands of crystals, right above the ballroom. It's astonishingly beautiful.'

Dot nodded, understanding what Cordelia was getting at. 'You could write about the ballrooms themselves, Persephone, and what makes them special.'

'There's the revolving stage at the Ritz,' said Alison.

'I've never thought of it that way before,' said Margaret, 'but the beauty and elegance of the ballroom adds to the magic of being there.'

'That's a terrific idea,' said Persephone. 'Thanks, all.'

'Make sure you add our names as co-writers,' said Dot.

'Or we could have pen names, like you,' Emily added and they all laughed.

The group broke up shortly afterwards. Alison hurried off to Manchester Royal Infirmary to meet Joel at the end of his shift. Margaret was going to the pictures with Sally from the engine shed.

'All welcome, if you fancy it,' said Margaret. 'They're showing *Now, Voyager* again.'

'Bette Davis is such a wonderful actress,' said Cordelia.

Mabel nudged Persephone and discreetly tilted her chin to indicate that they should withdraw together. Saying goodbye to the rest, they walked away, leaving the station.

Persephone was sure she could guess what this was going to be about. 'Have you heard from your father?'

'Pops came to see me,' said Mabel. 'Harry admitted it. He told the truth.'

'It's a good thing he didn't try to hide it,' said Persephone.

'Yes.' Mabel sounded as if she was trying to convince herself.

'There's something more, isn't there?'

Mabel nodded. 'This is strictly between ourselves. You and Joan are the only ones I can tell.'

Persephone experienced a frisson of alarm. She instinctively linked up with Mabel, matching her step to her friend's.

Mabel drew in a deep breath. 'Pops is going to disinherit me.'

Shocked, Persephone stopped dead and turned to face Mabel, who wouldn't meet her eyes. After a moment, Mabel started walking again.

Persephone squeezed her arm. 'Didn't he believe Harry when he said how much he loves you?'

'He wanted to believe it. It sounds as if Harry was very convincing, but this business has shaken Pops badly. It has stripped away what he thought he knew about Harry.'

'I don't know what to say. Did Mr Bradshaw tell Harry he's disinheriting you?'

'No,' said Mabel. 'He's left that to me to do.'

'Will it . . .' Persephone began. 'Lord knows I hate to ask, but will it . . . might it possibly make a difference?'

This time it was Mabel who stopped walking. She pulled Persephone round to face her.

'Are you asking if it will make Harry change his mind about marrying me?' Mabel's voice was steady and low-pitched. 'If you are, I suppose I can't blame you, but I can assure you it will make no difference whatsoever. Harry loves me. He *loves* me – and this isn't me protesting too much. It's just the plain truth. I would trust him with my life. I know he was a bounder to start with, but we put that behind us long ago.' She shook her head and after a moment started walking again. 'It's so unfair to have it resurrected like this.'

'All the more so if your father disinherits you,' said Persephone.

'I'm not going to pretend it doesn't matter, because it would be idiotic to suggest that. But I want you to know, and I'll make sure Joan knows too, that I didn't waver for a single moment.'

'That doesn't surprise me,' Persephone assured her. 'I know how devoted you are to Harry.'

'Thanks for saying that. It means a lot.'

'Have you told Harry yet?'

'Not yet. He isn't going to be available at all today. I can telephone tomorrow.'

'He won't waver either,' said Persephone. 'He worships you.'

'If only Clarinda had kept quiet,' said Mabel, an edge to her voice, 'this wouldn't be happening. She has a lot to answer for. She's cast a cloud over my wedding and the way my parents view my future husband. To cap it all, I'm going to be disinherited. Whoever would have thought a society gossip column could have such far-reaching effects? I know I sound pretty self-obsessed at the moment, but I want you to know I haven't forgotten how Clarinda messed things up for you and made your parents so angry just when you and Matt were enjoying getting to know one another. Things would be very different right now for both of us if Clarinda hadn't stuck her oar in.'

*

Before it was time to go to the telephone box, Mabel went to see Joan to tell her about being disinherited. Joan was shocked, but Mabel was more interested in defending Harry.

'I think it goes back to when his father gave up his engineering research post. That ended up being lucrative work for his colleagues and meanwhile he was a simple country pharmacist. That hit Harry hard, I think.'

'The loss of status?' asked Joan.

'Yes, and the loss of money too,' said Mabel. 'I can't remember exactly what it was that Dr Knatchbull and his research colleagues were working on – something to do with motor oil. Dr Knatchbull left before the work was finished and tested and all the others did well out of it financially.'

'And you think that's what made Harry decide to marry money?'

'I don't know. It could be. It's not something I've ever wanted to discuss with him.'

'I can understand that,' said Joan.

'What matters is that Harry and I are a loving, trusting couple now.'

'Of course it is,' Joan agreed. 'Shall I tell you what I think? I think Harry must be a lot like his father.'

'How d'you make that out?'

'Dr Knatchbull thought that research work in industry was for him, but it turned out not to be, so he followed his heart and changed career. Harry thought he'd have a go at gold-digging, but in the end, his heart found him the perfect girl. They both made choices, but in the end they listened to their hearts.'

Mabel leaned over and kissed Joan's cheek. 'You're a good friend. I'm going to miss you.'

'We've been through a lot together.'

Mabel glanced at her wristwatch. 'Time to make tracks. Harry will be expecting my call and I need to allow time for queuing.'

'Give me a minute to pop downstairs and ask Gran to keep an eye on Max,' said Joan, 'and I'll come with you.'

'There's no need.'

'There's every need. We're friends and that means we do things together. Don't worry,' Joan added with a smile, 'I shan't come in the telephone box with you.'

Soon they were on their way.

'This reminds me of another occasion when you waited while I made a telephone call,' said Mabel, thinking back to the time when Harry's Lancaster didn't return with the rest and she had endured hours of waiting for news.

'This is different,' said Joan. 'That other time might have had an unhappy ending. This one won't.'

Mabel's heart filled. It meant the world to her that both Joan and Persephone harboured no doubts as to the strength of her relationship with Harry.

At the telephone box, they only had to wait for a few minutes. Then Mabel stepped inside, shutting the door behind her and placing her coins on the small ledge.

Soon she was talking to Harry. Her pulse raced, partly with happiness at the sound of his voice, partly because of what she had to tell him.

'Your father came to see me,' said Harry. 'Did you know?'

'He made me swear not to say anything in advance.'

'That's all right. It's for the best that I didn't know. It must have made my answers easier for him to believe. He did believe me, didn't he?'

'Yes, he did, but—'

She stopped. No matter how much thought she had poured into this, she still didn't know the best way of saying it. It was going to hurt Harry and make him feel rotten. There was no avoiding that.

'But what?' Harry asked. 'I can hear in your voice that it's something important.'

Mabel took a breath. 'Pops is going to disinherit me.'

There was silence at the other end. Mabel waited. She needed, oh how she needed Harry to be the next one to speak.

'God, Mabel, I'm so sorry. If I'd never . . . if I hadn't been such a cad . . . This is my fault. You don't deserve this. I thought, I really thought your father believed me.'

'He did. He told me he did.'

'Then why?'

'Because there was still an element of doubt, I suppose. I don't know. He said he wasn't prepared to take the chance.'

'Mabel, if you – if you want to call it off—'

'What?' cried Mabel. 'No! How could you even think it?'

'I don't want to be responsible for you losing your inheritance.'

'I'm not going to pretend it doesn't matter,' said Mabel, 'but it isn't more important than you and me. Nothing could ever be more important than us.'

'You're a wonderful girl.' Harry's voice was filled with warmth. 'I said it when I proposed to you and I'll say it again: I don't deserve you, Mabel Bradshaw, and I swear I'll work hard to give you the best life I can.'

Mabel closed her eyes as she listened to his words. 'That's what I wanted to hear. We'll be all right as long as we're together.'

'Guaranteed,' said Harry. 'I'm deeply sorry and ashamed to be the cause of this. I'm sorry if it's come between you and your parents. I know how much the three of you mean to one another. And I'm sorry if it's made them think badly of me. I'll do everything I can to win back their good opinion.'

Mabel felt her world righting itself. 'I love you, Harry Knatchbull.'

'I love you too, Mabel Bradshaw,' said Harry. 'Always.'

At the end of the call, Mabel found herself battling against tears as she stepped out of the telephone box straight into Joan's arms.

'Are those happy tears?' Joan asked.

Mabel nodded. 'Just like last time.'

As shocked as she was by Mabel's disinheritance, Persephone was delighted that Mabel and Harry had taken it on the chin. If anything, it seemed to have strengthened their commitment to one another. It also made Persephone wonder about her own future. Supposing she and Matt – and it was a very big supposing – wanted to marry, would she too face disinheritance? Not that hers would be on the scale of Mabel's, but might her father feel it was the only way to express the depth of his disapproval?

Was she silly to be thinking along those lines? After all, nothing had ever been said between her and Matt about the future. It wasn't because they didn't have feelings for one another. It was because they were still getting to know each other, and the Clarinda situation, followed so closely by the aftermath of the *Vera's Voice* article, hadn't exactly helped.

'Obviously there's a big social gap,' she said to Joan when they took Brizo for a long tramp across the meadows while Mrs Foster took care of Max, 'but it doesn't feel as if there's a personal gap. We never run out of things to talk about and it means a lot to me that he sacrificed a grammar school education to join the railways. It creates a connection between us, because my writing isn't what I was brought up to do.'

Joan smiled. 'There's a lot to be said for following your heart. I said the same thing to Mabel.'

'She and Harry seem to have emerged from the disinheritance business even stronger as a couple. I'm so glad.'

'Me too,' said Joan. 'Mabel has telephoned her mother and they've agreed that the disinheritance won't be mentioned again. The plan now is to have the most wonderful wedding possible. That was always the plan, of course, but you know what I mean.'

'So it's full steam ahead for Mabel's wedding.' Persephone smiled. 'I wish I could attend, but I just can't get the time off.'

'I wish we could *all* go,' said Joan. 'One of the reasons my wedding day was so happy was because all my friends were there.' She paused. 'Can I ask you something personal?'

'You can try.'

'Do you ever think about a future with Matt?'

Persephone was about to deny it, then decided on honesty. She could trust Joan to keep it quiet until such time as Persephone was ready to share her thoughts more widely.

'If I said no, I'd be lying, but the truth is it could never happen. It doesn't matter that Matt and I get on like a house on fire. The gap between us is far too wide. My family wouldn't stand for it and I don't think his would either. His mother isn't going to forgive me for that good manners article in a hurry.'

'I'm sorry to hear it,' said Joan. 'It must put a strain on you and Matt.'

'It does,' Persephone admitted. 'We truly care for one another, but . . . it just isn't that simple.'

'Oh, Persephone,' said Joan. 'I hope you end up as happy as I am, as happy as Mabel is. That's my wish for you.'

Unable to speak, Persephone laid a hand over her heart to indicate her gratitude. Joan was so kind. But then disappointment swelled inside her and she felt more like using her hand to cover her face. Honestly, what chance did she and Matt have?

CHAPTER THIRTY-SIX

Emily's parents were talking in quiet voices. Emily sighed to herself. They thought she didn't know what they were discussing, but she did. It was the Nazi brutality against the Jews. Did they really imagine she could be protected from knowing about such things? Did they really still see her as their little girl who shouldn't have to face the harshest of realities? Of course, it was a good thing to have parents who loved her and wanted to treasure her, she knew that, but it could be frustrating that they didn't seem to see that she was grown-up now.

Mummy and Daddy did quite a lot of talking in low voices these days and it wasn't always because of their concerns about the war. Sometimes these conversations seemed to be – well, intimate, even a bit flirty sometimes, though of course they couldn't really be flirting. They were far too old and had been married since the year dot. Nevertheless, Emily had glimpsed a few darting glances and shared smiles, and that wasn't like Mummy and Daddy at all. Now she thought about it, she realised that the way they had always spoken to one another at home had previously been the same as the way they'd spoken to one another in company. They had always been rather formal towards each other.

Now, though, they appeared to be more relaxed. An effect of the war? Like Daddy's attitude softening towards Dot Green and Mrs Cooper? Emily had the grace to blush. It wasn't only Daddy's attitude that had softened.

That made her think of Mr Buckley and his changed attitude towards her. Not that he was being in any way unpleasant, but the gentle good humour had vanished from his expression and she missed having a grandfatherly eye watching over her.

Sometimes she felt she would do anything to restore their working relationship to how it used to be, but then she would remember the worry the pilfering had caused her and she knew she'd done the right thing. She would have liked to discuss it with Colette, but she dreaded becoming a bore.

Mrs Cooper popped round to their house that evening with some wool from the knitting circle.

'I'm sorry, but I have to ask you to sign for it,' she said.

'New rules?' Mummy asked.

'Not exactly,' said Mrs Cooper. 'They had a bit of a hoo-ha at the knitting circle in Stretford, apparently. The garments they made didn't match up with the quantity of wool they'd been allocated. It looked like somebody might have filched some wool for her own purposes.'

'How unpleasant,' said Mummy.

'It all turned out right in the end,' said Mrs Cooper. 'Some balls of yarn had got mislaid. But it made me decide to keep a proper record of what I hand out.'

'I don't blame you,' Mummy said sympathetically.

'I can't stop,' said Mrs Cooper. 'I've got more wool to deliver.'

When Emily returned from seeing their friend out, she said to her mother, 'Poor Mrs Cooper. It must have brought back how horrid it was for her when she was under suspicion of theft last year.'

'Unfortunately, circumstances can sometimes be misleading,' said Mummy. 'It'll be a long time before she forgets how things turned sour for her.'

Sour. That was exactly the right word for how things had changed between Emily and Mr Buckley. He might have done wrong, but he hadn't hogged his ill-gotten gains to himself. He'd tried to help an impoverished neighbour and now he was helping the orphanage where Philip and Norah, his beloved grandchildren, his only remaining family, lived. Emily could never agree with what Mr Buckley had done, but she could appreciate what had made him do it and the last thing she wanted was for things to be sour between them.

Choosing her words with care, she asked, 'Mummy, if you'd hurt someone, how would you go about setting it right?'

'It depends on the circumstances, but generally speaking, if one hurts someone, then an apology is a good way to start.'

'What if it's not that simple? What if the other person has done something they shouldn't have and you'd stopped them from doing it again?'

'I assume we're talking about you, Emily. Perhaps you should just tell me what's happened.'

'I'd rather not, if you don't mind,' said Emily. 'It's just that I know I did the right thing, but I hate having upset this other person.'

'Even though they did the wrong thing,' said Mummy. It wasn't a question.

Emily nodded. 'Even though. It's turned things sour between us.' She didn't miss the small smile that flickered across her mother's face at hearing her own words repeated back to her.

'It's impossible to give advice without knowing the details,' said Mummy. Then she smiled, a real smile this time, and her grey eyes glowed with warmth. 'You aren't the only one who can talk in riddles, you know. I can too.

347

There was a time when I saw my life in a certain way and I couldn't imagine seeing it any differently. Then I did see things differently.'

'That really is a riddle,' Emily said with mock severity.

'I think you're looking directly at this problem. This other person did wrong and you put it right and that's all you can see. Try thinking about other things to do with this person and see where that gets you. Am I making sense?'

'You mean I can't see the wood for the trees.'

'Something like that,' said Mummy. 'Give it some thought.'

But Emily didn't need to. It was as if her mother's advice had unlocked her ideas. Instead of fixating on the current situation, she opened up to all kinds of other thoughts about Mr Buckley. And she knew exactly what she was going to do. On top of that, she wasn't going to be like Mabel, trying to do it on her own. No, she was going to rope in her friends right from the start.

Emily couldn't wait for the next meeting in the buffet. She felt excited every time she thought of her plan. Would her friends like it as much as she did? With their help, it could be a huge success. She couldn't wait to share it with Mr Buckley too. She wanted him to see how important it was to her that their old friendship was restored. But first she had to speak to her friends.

Standing in the queue, edging her way towards the counter, she heard the couple in front of her discussing the expected invasion of Italy while a trio of girls behind her shared their shock and sadness at the death a few days earlier of Leslie Howard and had an emotional discussion about his performances in *Gone With the Wind* and *'Pimpernel' Smith*.

Soon Emily was seated at the table with Margaret and Colette. After a few minutes, Mabel arrived and there was some general chit-chat while they waited for the rest to come.

There was some wedding talk to start with, then Emily judged it the right time to say her piece.

'I want to ask you for your help,' she said and that was all it took for everyone to focus their attention on her. 'I'd like to organise a special day for the railway orphanage. I've got the superintendent's permission to do it and I've got some ideas, but I'm going to need assistance because I'd like to do it quite quickly. I want it to take place before Mabel gets married.'

'What ideas do you have so far?' asked Colette.

'Races, skipping and hopscotch competitions, that sort of thing, but I want other activities as well.'

'An obstacle course,' said Margaret.

'Our Jimmy and his mates used to spend whole afternoons sending one another messages in Morse code,' said Dot Green. 'All you need for each team is a spoon and an empty tin can to bang it on.'

'Perfect,' said Emily.

'If we can get hold of a map of Germany,' suggested Alison, 'the children can plot aircraft missions.'

'A treasure hunt,' said Mummy. 'The treasure could be Hitler's secret plans.'

Emily was delighted. 'I knew I was right to ask you.'

'We'll help out on the day too,' said Margaret, 'if we're not working.'

'You're quiet, love,' Dot Green said to Mabel.

'I've been thinking,' said Mabel. 'I could contact that handicrafts instructor who gave me patterns for toys for small children. I wonder if she'd like to do a session of toy-making with the older children at the orphanage. I've gathered loads of materials, so I can tell her what we've got and she can plan what to do.'

'Sounds good,' said Alison.

'She had so many ideas,' said Mabel, 'that I wished nurseries could be for older children too.'

'Such as?' asked Colette.

'Using bottle tops or big buttons as whizzers on string.'

'I know,' said Alison. 'You pull both ends tight and the whizzer spins round.'

'That's right,' said Mabel. 'And old doorknobs as yo-yos.'

'If she ran a toymaking session,' said Mummy, 'the orphanage would end up with a new selection.'

'And that would be especially lovely,' added Colette, 'because those children might not have relatives who can provide toys for them.'

'You're so clever, all of you,' said Emily.

'That's us,' said Dot Green with a laugh. 'Next news, we'll be on *The Brains Trust* on the wireless.'

'It's not just your ideas I'm grateful for,' said Emily. 'It's the feeling I've got friends who rally round.'

'Of course we do,' said Alison. 'You're one of us.'

CHAPTER THIRTY-SEVEN

When Persephone explained about her proposed article, the manager of the Claremont Hotel was only too pleased for her to take a thorough look at the ballroom.

'Of course, I've been here on various occasions as a guest,' said Persephone, 'and seen the ballroom at its best when it's full of people, but I really need to see it empty. Would you mind if I had a look round on my own to start with, so I can soak it up?'

In the ballroom, she made notes in between walking around to take a closer look at the various features – the stage, the pillars, the alcoves, the fountain. Then an odd feeling made her look round – not just look behind her, but behind and up towards the dining room on the first floor. A young woman was there, standing quite still, her hands resting on the rail.

Persephone started to smile politely, then a delighted laugh broke forth and she waved.

'Davinia!' she called.

After a moment, Davinia called back. 'Persephone.'

'Wait there. I'll come up.'

A minute later, Persephone walked through the doors into the dining room, explaining, 'I've just seen an old friend,' to the maître d'. Davinia was still standing at the rail, her back to Persephone. Now she turned. Persephone went to her, hands outstretched, a gesture learned through copying Iphigenia. Davinia took Persephone's hands lightly in her own and they leaned towards one another for the tiniest of kisses on the cheek.

'How perfectly lovely to see you,' said Persephone. 'I can't remember the last time. Must have been yonks ago.'

'Before the war,' said Davinia.

'Shall we plonk ourselves down and have a natter?'

'If you like.'

An elderly waiter showed them to a table and Persephone ordered tea and scones.

'No scones for me, thanks,' said Davinia, adding, 'I'm meeting someone for afternoon tea.'

Persephone smiled at her companion. She was pleased to see her. They knew one another from London and the country house circuit and while they'd never been bosom chums, they'd always got along well enough. Davinia's mother had been presented the same year as Persephone's.

'What brings you here?' Persephone asked.

Davinia took a cigarette from a silver cigarette case and offered one to Persephone, who shook her head. She didn't care for the way some women and girls were now smoking in public. Davinia lit up, whereupon an ashtray appeared on their table as if by magic.

'Here, Manchester, or here, the Claremont?' Davinia asked.

Persephone laughed. 'Both, I suppose.'

'I'm a driver in the army.' Davinia glanced down at her poppy-red dress. 'Not on duty today, as you can see.'

'Hence the afternoon tea,' Persephone surmised.

'With my godmother. Mummy insisted that if I came this way again, I had to look her up.'

'So you've been to Manchester before? Recently?'

'Fairly,' said Davinia.

'What do you do as a driver?' asked Persephone.

352

'If you're imagining ambulances or lorries full of equipment, it's nothing like that. I'm a chauffeur. I drive Brigadier Allsopp, mostly around London, but he sometimes goes further afield.'

'Like here.' Persephone smiled. 'I'm on the railways, myself.'

'Yes, I know.'

'I started out as a ticket collector on Victoria Station. Earlier this year, I was made up to ticket inspector.'

'Congrats,' said Davinia.

'Thanks.'

Persephone related a couple of amusing anecdotes. Davinia smiled and chuckled at the right moments, but Persephone felt obscurely uncomfortable. This wasn't exactly the chatty catch-up she had envisaged.

'Iphigenia was up here for a visit a while ago,' she said.

'I see her around London occasionally,' said Davinia. 'I don't mean we go out together. It's more a case of smiling at one another across restaurants.'

Persephone asked after Davinia's family and Davinia returned the compliment, so Persephone gave her the edited version of her trip to Meyrick House.

'And what do your parents think of what you're up to?' Davinia asked. Maybe Persephone looked startled, because she added a moment later, 'About your job on the railways, of course. Why? What did you think I meant?'

'They're happy about my job, natch – just like I'm sure your parents are proud of you for doing your bit as a driver.'

'It's all about whom one rubs shoulders with, though, isn't it?' said Davinia. 'I've been introduced to heaps of bigwigs. Mummy has hopes of a high-ranking husband.' She blew out a stream of smoke, lifting her chin and giving her head a little shake, showing off her dark victory roll. 'Just imagine if I ended up with one of the other drivers.'

'Or the mechanics,' said Persephone.

'We look after our own vehicles.'

'Clever old you,' said Persephone, pleased that Davinia seemed to have relaxed into the conversation and was opening up. 'You might make a useful wife one day.'

Davinia gave a throaty chuckle. 'I don't intend to marry someone who needs to save money on the garage bills, but you never know. One comes across all sorts of people one would never previously have met – don't you find?'

'Yes, since you mention it. Through being on the railways, I've made some dear friends from various backgrounds. I say,' Persephone added, 'one of them is Mabel Bradshaw. Do you remember her from that Season we had?'

'New money. Father owns a factory.'

'She's a good egg,' said Persephone. 'I like her. She's getting married this month. The lucky man is in the RAF.'

'What about you?' Davinia asked. 'Do you have a chap in tow?'

Persephone experienced a momentary alarm, but it turned at once into resolve. She would have to get used to this sort of thing. She wasn't going to let Matt down by dodging the question. She wasn't going to let herself down either.

'I take it you didn't see what was written about me in Clarinda's column?'

Davinia crushed the remains of her cigarette into the ashtray. 'I don't need to read it. Did she have a pop at you?'

'Sort of. Not intentionally. She revealed that I'm seeing a railwayman.'

'Well, well,' said Davinia. 'How do you know it wasn't intentional?'

Persephone blinked. 'Of course it wasn't.' She could hardly say that she was thoroughly au fait with the column's rules because she had once been Clarinda. She settled for, 'Clarinda only ever makes flattering remarks.'

'Yes, but you never know what the result is going to be, do you?'

'That's true,' said Persephone.

'Did your parents give you a hard time?'

'As a matter of fact, yes.'

Davinia nodded. 'That's understandable. I expect Mabel's parents gave her a roasting too – after what was in Clarinda's column,' she added when Persephone frowned.

'How do you know about that?' Persephone asked. 'You said you don't read Clarinda.'

Davinia shrugged. 'One hears things.'

'Let's talk about something else,' said Persephone. This Clarinda stuff was getting a bit near the knuckle.

'Fair enough,' Davinia agreed. 'I've been trying to think when I last saw you. Was it at the Simmond-Ryalls' house party when Yvonne and Cedric got engaged? No, wait, it couldn't have been then, could it? You weren't there.'

'No, I wasn't. I heard all about it, though. It sounded like great fun.'

'Did it really?' Davinia leaned forward, her gaze sharpening. 'I know you heard all about it, because you then wrote about it in your wretched Clarinda column, didn't you?'

Persephone's mouth dropped open. 'You knew? You knew I was Clarinda?'

'Not at the time, no. At the time, all I knew was that dear Clarinda had dropped me right in the whatsit. I wasn't supposed to be at that party. My parents thought I was somewhere else. I'd spent ages persuading my cousin to cover for me. I went there to meet someone. Someone I shouldn't have been meeting. Someone married. It's no use looking shocked now, Persephone. You did your damage at the time. It's because of you that my parents found out. And you weren't even there,' she finished, her voice rising.

'I asked Gail Waterhouse about it. She gave me a few details.'

'Including my name, which you blabbed to all and sundry in the newspaper.'

'Davinia, I had no idea—'

'Of what? Possible consequences? But then why would you?' Davinia asked in a mocking tone. 'It's so flattering to be written about by Clarinda, isn't it? A big feather in one's social cap. Did you think you were doing me a favour by mentioning my name? Did you say to yourself, "Oh, she'll be so thrilled"? Did you feel you were really rather clever to write about an event you hadn't attended? Covering your tracks, keeping the secret of your identity.'

'I don't know what to say.'

'That's not a problem you had when you were Clarinda.'

'I'm truly sorry if I hurt you,' said Persephone, 'if I made things difficult for you.'

'Difficult?' Davinia repeated bitterly. 'That's one word for it. My father—' She stopped and pressed her lips together. Her eyes were pools of anger and pain. Then she drew a slow breath and her features underwent a subtle change. 'But you know all about the problems Clarinda can cause, don't you? You've been through it yourself, you poor thing.' Davinia's eyes were soft with concern as she reached across the table to place a comforting hand over Persephone's. 'You poor darling.'

'It has been rather grim,' Persephone admitted.

Davinia folded her hands in her lap. 'There's no need to be brave about it. "Rather grim"? I expect it was worse than that. At least,' she went on with a bright smile, 'I hope it was.' Now she leaned forward and dropped her voice. 'I hope it was pretty bloody devastating. Pardon my French,' she added with a smile.

Persephone was shocked to her core. 'You,' she whispered. 'You're Clarinda. That's how you found out I was your predecessor.'

'Full marks. Do you have any idea how many times I went over the guest list for the Simmond-Ryalls' house party? I knew that one of those people had to be Clarinda, but I couldn't imagine which one. I stopped speaking to Catherine, Leonie and Vanessa because they seemed the likeliest candidates. Then I got the Clarinda job and found out it was you – and you hadn't even been there. You caused havoc in my life and you did it based on pumping Gail Waterhouse for a bit of gossip. Were you proud of yourself for that? I'll tell you how it made me feel. I was stunned.'

'I can only apologise,' said Persephone. 'I had no idea I was putting you in a sticky position. If I'd known—'

'The whole point was that nobody knew,' flared Davinia, 'until you told the whole world.'

'And so you wrote about Matt and me, knowing it would cause an upset.'

'Revenge is sweet, Persephone darling, and don't ever let anyone tell you otherwise. Brigadier Allsopp was up here for meetings a while back. I had the night off and went dancing. I saw you and realised that the handsome chap with you was more than just a dancing partner, so I asked a few questions. Imagine my satisfaction when your beau turned out to be a fireman on the railways. I called him a train driver in my column because it sounded better. Not everyone knows what a train fireman is.'

'You wrote about me on purpose.' Persephone was struggling to believe it.

'I did to you what you did to me,' said Davinia.

'I didn't do it *on purpose*,' Persephone exclaimed. 'You wrote about Mabel too.'

'I couldn't resist. I saw her the same night I saw you. I was lucky enough to get talking to someone who used to know Harry Knatchbull in the good old days – or should that be the bad old days? It's a much more appropriate description when one is talking about a self-professed gold-digger, don't you think?'

Persephone sat back in her chair, feeling winded. 'I can hardly believe it. It was you. I know we've never been close, but we've known one another for ever. I thought you were my friend.'

'That's *precisely* what I thought when I found out you used to be Clarinda. Welcome to the club.' Davinia pushed back her chair and stood up. 'And now, if you'll excuse me, my godmother has just arrived.'

CHAPTER THIRTY-EIGHT

Mabel unlocked the Extension and went inside, feeling increasingly satisfied as she walked around. How different the place was to the tired old building it had been when she'd first seen it. She had brought Pops here after he'd told her she would be disinherited, partly because as its financial backer he was entitled to see it, but mainly because she felt it was important he saw that his decision to disinherit her wasn't going to make her behave differently towards him.

His approval of the building had meant a lot to her.

'You're a capable sort, Mabs,' he'd said. Coming from Pops, this was high praise.

'I've had plenty of support,' she told him. 'The Hayter brothers have overseen a lot of the work and there's a lady at the Corporation who's been an absolute brick.'

'It's important to have the right people around you.'

Mabel had slipped her arm through his. 'You're one of my right people – and so is Harry. You'll see that one day. You'll realise I'm right about him.'

Pops had hugged her, dropping a tobacco-scented kiss on her cheek. 'I hope so, Mabs. I truly hope so.'

This evening, Mabel was going to show off the Extension to Persephone, who had asked for permission to write an article, but when Persephone arrived, instead of peppering Mabel with questions, she was subdued.

'Can we talk about something else first?'

Mabel listened in astonishment as Persephone explained about Davinia being Clarinda.

'Are you saying she deliberately set out to cause trouble for you?' Mabel asked.

'And for you.'

'I can see why she set out to wreak her revenge on you, even though you didn't harm her deliberately, but what did she have against me?'

'Nothing,' said Persephone. 'She saw us together and realised we were friends. Then along came the opportunity to spread gossip about you and she took it. It was an extra way of hitting back at me.'

Mabel shook her head. 'I don't know whether to be furious or flabbergasted that somebody would want to hurt me like that.' Heat flushed through her and her muscles quivered as anger boiled up. 'It's because of her that Pops disinherited me. If I ever clap eyes on her again—'

'If you see her,' Persephone said calmly, 'you'll steer clear and if she makes a point of approaching you, you'll smile sweetly.'

'I most certainly shall not!' Mabel retorted.

'You have to,' said Persephone. 'You can't let her see how deeply she hurt you.'

'She got me *disinherited*,' Mabel fumed. 'But you're right, of course. I can see that.'

'I'm sorry to dump this on you, especially when we're here to admire all your hard work.'

'Not just mine,' said Mabel. 'I'll be writing a lot of thank-you letters.'

By concentrating on her pride in her achievement and her gratitude towards all who had helped her, Mabel was able to shove Davinia unceremoniously to the back of her mind – for now, at least. She provided Persephone with all the information she needed.

'There's nothing to say what the building is for,' Persephone remarked as they were walking around the exterior and Persephone stopped outside the front.

'The signwriter is at work as we speak,' said Mabel. 'A board is going to be fastened over the front door with the name.'

'The Mabel Bradshaw Nursery. Wonderful.'

Mabel didn't respond to that. 'Come and see the new lavatories. That doesn't sound very glamorous, but you should have seen the old earth closets.'

When Persephone had finished making notes, the conversation returned to Davinia.

'All the time I was Clarinda,' said Persephone, 'it never once occurred to me that appearing in the column might bring unwanted repercussions on someone's head.'

'I hope you aren't defending Davinia when you say that.'

'Crikey, no. Far from it. I only ever wanted to write an interesting column and give people the pleasure of seeing their names in print – and yes, I loved the secrecy that surrounded Clarinda's identity. But what Davinia did was deliberate and downright nasty. She intended to cause trouble for you and me.'

'She certainly managed that,' said Mabel. 'Bitch.'

'Mabel!' Persephone exclaimed.

'I'm sorry. It's not a word I'd normally use, but honestly, if anyone deserves it . . . Sorry,' Mabel said again.

'The best revenge you could have on Davinia would be to have the happiest of weddings followed by the happiest of married lives.'

'I was going to have those anyway,' said Mabel. 'Davinia or Clarinda or whatever she wants to call herself shan't make any difference to that.' She thought for a moment. 'The best revenge I could possibly have on her would be never to bother thinking about her again. She isn't going to spoil things for me. She might have *changed* them, but I won't let her *spoil* them. I'm better than that. Harry and I are better than that.'

Supported by her friends, Emily spent every spare minute preparing for the activity day at the orphanage. As the special day drew nearer, Mr Buckley and his young grandchildren were very much in her mind. What must it have been like for him to have to place them in the orphanage? He must have been desperate to hang on to them and take care of them himself, but as a man on his own, what choice did he have? Did his grandchildren understand that he hadn't wanted to give them up? Please don't let them harbour doubts on that score. She wished she could tell Philip and Norah how much Mr Buckley loved them.

It made her all the more determined to make the orphanage's activity day a big success. The handicrafts lady Mabel knew had agreed to take part and Persephone had nabbed a science teacher who had helped in the Wings for Victory Week. Emily wasn't entirely sure what he was going to do, but it involved dropping miniature pretend bombs onto a target and apparently his pupils had loved it.

Emily was surprised when Dot Green caught up with her at the end of a shift and took her into the buffet.

'Are you looking forward to Saturday?' Mrs Green asked. 'Don't take this the wrong way, but you're very young to be in charge and some of the adults won't believe you're up to it.'

'There's nothing I can do about that,' said Emily.

'I think there is. You have to behave in a certain way in order to be treated in a certain way. Take teachers. They all behave the same way, don't they? I mean, they have different personalities, but they all behave the way teachers do and so the pupils treat them like teachers. Well, you need to act like the person in charge. If you hang back politely because everyone else is older than you, you won't be in control. You wouldn't want somebody else to take over, would you?'

'No. I've put a lot of work into this. Thank you, Mrs Green. You've been a big help.'

'You're welcome, chick.' Mrs Green leaned across and said quietly and with a smile, 'You're allowed to call me Dot, you know, when we're not in company.'

'It wouldn't feel right.'

'Because of my great age, you mean?'

Emily felt colour fill her cheeks and didn't know what to say.

'It's a sign of your good manners that you want to call me Mrs Green. But I'll tell you summat. If it helps, Lizzie used to call me Dot.'

'Did she?' asked Emily.

'She'd have liked you.'

'Would she?'

'Now that you've climbed down off your high horse, she would.'

'I'm sorry I was such a snob when I first came home,' said Emily.

'It's how you are now that matters. And how are you, eh? Still hurting because of that lad of yours?'

'He's not my lad,' said Emily. 'He hasn't been for ages. I still miss him and there are times when I feel dreadfully lonely, but it doesn't hurt the way it used to. I've got a lot to keep me busy and I'm going to make the best of it.'

'Good for you, chick.'

It rained the day before the orphanage activity day, but Saturday dawned dry and bright, much to Emily's relief. The children helped to build the obstacle course and rooms

363

were set aside for crafts and indoor games. Some of the children had relatives who came along to help, including Mr Buckley.

Emily had felt nervous telling him what she'd organised.

'I'm doing it because you've been so good to me,' she said, 'and I want to do something for you in return.'

'Oh aye? Are you sure that's the only reason?'

'I'm not going to apologise for splitting on the porters, but I am sorry that you were hurt by it. Things used to be friendly and easy between us and they don't feel like that any longer. I – I miss it.' She waited but Mr Buckley didn't say anything, so she carried on. 'I've organised the day for the orphans because they deserve it – and so do you. You love your grandchildren so much. I hope you'll come. That's all.'

And Mr Buckley had come. He might not be a young man, but years of portering had made him strong and he used a wheelbarrow to ferry rubble from a nearby bomb site to add to the obstacle course.

Emily assigned jobs to her friends and they cheerfully mucked in, but it proved harder to get the other adults to take her seriously.

When a stout woman called Mrs Trent overheard Emily and her mother talking about the arrangements for refreshments, she automatically assumed it was Mummy who was in charge.

'I'm here to lend a hand,' she informed Mummy. 'What do you want me to do?'

Mummy was about to answer, but then glanced at Emily. 'My daughter is the organiser. She has a list of jobs. You should ask her.'

Mrs Trent's chin jerked in surprise. 'A slip of a lass like that – in charge? Don't make me laugh.'

Before her mother could reply, Emily stepped in. 'That's right, Mrs Trent, a slip of a lass like me. I think you'll find

I've got everything worked out. Please could you help set up the trestle tables?'

Mrs Trent gave her a look. 'Well I never.'

But she toddled off in the right direction.

'Well done, Emily,' Mummy murmured.

Emily was obliged to assert herself several more times, using a mixture of politeness and firmness, but at last the adults seemed to realise.

'Once everything has been set up and all the games and so forth are under way,' her mother told her quietly, 'you'll probably find everyone is perfectly happy for you to be in charge. That's always been my experience. Once the fun begins, others are less interested in being bossy and more interested in enjoying themselves.'

Emily didn't stop all day long. She went from the handicrafts room to the treasure hunt to the aeroplane bingo, checking all was well. She produced Daddy's starting pistol for the races and American chocolate bars as prizes, courtesy of the American fiancé of one of Miss Brown's land girls.

All in all, the day was an undoubted success. For Emily, the crowning moment came when Mr Buckley thanked her.

'My Philip and my Norah are having a splendid time because of you.'

'I'm pleased,' said Emily.

Mr Buckley looked as if he wanted to say something else, but then he didn't.

'I didn't report the pilfering out of pettiness, you know,' Emily said quickly, sensing that this was her last opportunity to clear the air. 'I did it out of honesty. I'm sorry if that makes me sound holier-than-thou, but . . .' She couldn't think of a way to finish the sentence.

Mr Buckley finished it for her. 'But you were definitely holier than the rest of us – and I don't mean that to sound nasty. I know you wanted to do the right thing – but maybe it was easier to do the right thing because your dad earns a tidy amount and you've never known what it is to be hard up. It's easy to be better than other people when you have all kinds of advantages.'

'I never thought I was better than you and the other porters. Believe me, if there's one thing I've learned since I left school, it's that I'm not superior to anyone.'

'I don't mean you have airs and graces. I just mean you've had a comfortable life compared to most. You've never had the need to . . .'

'To do any pilfering? You're right. I haven't. But that doesn't mean I can't understand. I know how you helped the old lady up your road and how you gave titbits to the orphanage cook to make life better in some small way for Philip and Norah. I know you're a good person. I know how much you love the children, and I know how guilty you feel for not being able to take care of them yourself.'

'And I know you only wanted to do what was right and honest,' said Mr Buckley. 'The rest of us, well, we were used to taking a bit here and a bit there. It's easy to see it as a perk of the job when you've always done it.'

Emily hardly dared to ask, 'Does that mean you can see why I wanted it to stop?'

'Put it this way,' said Mr Buckley. 'I think it was good of you not to name any names. You could have caused a lot more trouble than you did.'

Emily felt a flash of annoyance. 'Some would say it was the porters who caused the trouble by pilfering in the first place.'

'I don't mind telling you it frightened my socks off when that Mr Gordon stood up there and talked about theft. I think that's why there was so much anger about it – because everyone was scared. Listen, Emily. We're never going to agree about you spilling the beans about the porters. You did what you did and you had your reasons. But the main thing is that you've done this wonderful thing today for the orphanage and you've made a lot of children happy, including my own two. I shan't forget it. I know you did it to make it up to me so we can be friends again.'

'Did it work?' Emily asked. Her insides felt quivery. This meant so much to her.

Mr Buckley's features creased into a crinkly-eyed smile. 'It did.'

A flood of relief brought Emily's hand up to cover her mouth for a moment. Then she laughed.

'And you know what friends do on a day like this?' said Mr Buckley. 'They introduce each other to their families. I'd like to meet your mum and dad so I can tell them what a pleasure you are to work with and how proud they should be of you. Before that, though, I want you to meet my Norah and Philip.'

'I'd love to,' breathed Emily.

'Philip's doing the obstacle course at the moment.'

'I wouldn't want to pull him away.'

'This is at least his tenth go, so I think it's all right to get him to take a break from it for a minute,' said Mr Buckley.

They walked over to the obstacle course, where the boys – it was mostly boys – were climbing, jumping and running from one challenge to the next. Daddy had brought a length of rope and slung it over a sturdy branch so the children could swing from the top of one wooden crate to another. Some of the boys were clearly treating the course as a race while others were pretending to be soldiers, ducking as they ran and using their fingers as guns.

When Mr Buckley called, a sandy-haired boy broke away and came jogging towards him and Emily.

'Go and fetch our Norah,' called Mr Buckley before Philip could reach them. 'She's in the handicrafts room. Go on. Chop-chop.'

A minute later, the two children came running back. No one would have guessed they were brother and sister. Norah was dark and dainty next to her brother's lighter colouring and height. Philip had freckles too, masses of them. They showed clearly even though he was pink and puffed from exercise.

The little girl spared Emily a shy glance before she threw her skinny arms around her grandfather. 'I've nearly finished making a kitten out of felt, Grandpa. Maggie is looking after it for me until I get back.'

'Will you get it finished before the end of the afternoon?' asked Mr Buckley, looking down fondly at her. 'I'll look forward to seeing it. Your grandma loved cats. Now then, my little love,' and he gently disentangled himself from her embrace, adding to Philip, 'and you too. I want you both to meet someone special. This lady is Miss Emily Masters.'

'Is she the lady you've told us about?' asked Philip. 'The one you're training to be a porter.'

'That's the one,' said Mr Buckley, smiling at Emily.

'I'm going to be a porter when I grow up,' said Philip.

'I hope you get your grandfather to train you,' said Emily, 'because he's a very good teacher. I'd have made all sorts of mistakes if it hadn't been for him.' She smiled encouragingly at Norah. 'What do you want to be when you grow up?'

'I want to look after Grandpa.'

Emily's heart swelled. This little girl had lost so much – her parents, her grandmother, her home. Her grandfather was doing everything he could to make sure she didn't lose him as well.

'I think that would be a wonderful thing for you to do,' Emily told Norah. She glanced at Philip, including him in the moment. 'I know he's told you about me. He talks to me about you as well.'

'Does he?' asked Philip.

'He hardly ever stops,' said Emily. 'He loves you both so much.'

Norah slipped a hand into Mr Buckley's. 'We love him too, even though we can't live together.'

'Can I go back to the obstacle course now, Grandpa?' asked Philip.

'Aye, lad, you run along.'

'Will you come and watch me?'

Emily looked at Mr Buckley. 'You go and watch Philip and if Norah will let me, I'll go with her to see the felt kitten. Is that all right with you, Norah?'

The little girl clung to her beloved grandpa for a moment, then let go and took Emily's hand in hers. Together, Emily and Norah walked across the grass.

CHAPTER THIRTY-NINE

On the morning of the nursery's official opening, the Monday following Emily's activity day at the orphanage, Mabel sat up in bed, swinging her feet onto the mat between her bed and Margaret's.

'Now I know it's a special day,' Margaret teased. 'It must be if you're throwing back the covers.'

'Ha very ha,' Mabel retorted good-naturedly.

She had plenty to do before the ceremony got under way.

'Are you sure you won't want me and Mrs Grayson to make the tea for everyone?' asked Mrs Cooper.

'Positive, thanks,' said Mabel. 'The WVS have it in hand. They're providing volunteers to help staff the nursery, so it's important to have them involved in today's ceremony too. They'll be delighted with the ginger biscuits and honey-and-nut tartlets Mrs Grayson has made.'

'You can't have a proper opening ceremony without some goodies, war or no war,' said Mrs Grayson. 'Mrs Hannon from the WVS gave me the ingredients and the other ladies are making things too.'

'I wish I could be there with you,' said Alison, 'but I have to be at work.'

'You're not the only one,' said Mabel. 'Margaret, Dot and Emily are the only ones from work who can come – plus, of course, Joan, Mrs Cooper and Mrs Grayson.'

'Just try keeping us away,' said Mrs Cooper.

'It's a shame Persephone won't be there,' said Margaret. 'She could have added it to her article.'

'What's the order of events?' asked Mrs Grayson.

'The staff have to be there early,' said Mabel. 'Some of the mothers and children are coming early too, so that the little ones can get used to the place and start playing – supervised, of course. That way, once the ceremony is concluded outside and the nursery is declared open, people can go in and see it already up and running.'

'Much better than walking into an empty building,' Mrs Cooper said approvingly.

'If you'll all excuse me,' said Mabel, 'I'd better cut along.'

'Are you sure you don't want us to come with you and help set things up?' asked Mrs Cooper.

'No, thanks,' said Mabel. 'If you come in time for the opening at ten o'clock, that'll be fine. You're guests today. You're not there to muck in.'

She gathered her things together, putting Mrs Grayson's goodies into a string bag and her papers into an old leather satchel she'd got off the market. She'd copied the idea of having a satchel from Fay Brewer. When she reached the Extension, she pinned up the first four weeks of staffing rotas on the noticeboard, along with the nursery's rules and its general timetable, including story times and sleep times. Lastly, she pinned up a list of important names and telephone numbers.

Turning, she found that Fay Brewer had walked in.

'I can't be here for the opening ceremony,' said Fay, 'but I wanted to wish you well. I hope everything goes splendidly for your nursery.' She glanced at the lists on the noticeboard. 'I see you're prepared for all eventualities.'

'I hope there won't be many teething problems,' said Mabel. 'Now it comes to it, I feel bad about moving away so soon after it opens.'

'I'll be keeping an eye on it,' said Fay, 'and the WVS are very experienced. You've done a good thing here and a lot of mothers will be grateful. Anyway, I'd better scoot. I've got to get to a meeting. Good luck with the ceremony.'

'Thanks – and thanks for all you've done.'

They shook hands and Fay went on her way. Soon the WVS ladies arrived. They got the urn going and arranged the biscuits and fairy cakes on plates, covering them with fly nets. One lady prepared trays of cups and saucers, another trays of beakers for the children.

Presently the mothers started to arrive with their little ones. A WVS lady who was a retired teacher sat the children in a circle for a sing-song and a story before they started playing.

It was time for Mabel to go outside to greet her visitors. A couple of reporters from the local press had come and they were interested in seeing the changes and improvements to the building. Several WVS committee members were there, as well as representatives from the Corporation – though not, Mabel noted, Miss Brewster. Actually, she ought to be thankful for Miss Brewster. If she hadn't been so awful, Mabel might not have appreciated Fay Brewer so much.

Dot arrived.

'Thanks for coming,' said Mabel.

'I wouldn't miss it, chick. Look, here comes Joan with Max.' Dot went across to them. 'Let's have a look at him. He's a bonny lad.'

Margaret, Mrs Cooper and Mrs Grayson came along High Lane, accompanied by Emily. Mabel was pleased that Emily was here. She had settled into their group so well and Mabel was fond of her.

'Come and stand over here,' Mabel invited her friends. 'You'll see better.'

Above the building's double doors was the board on which the signwriter had done his work. This was now covered by a length of old sheeting with a tasselled cord tied at one end and hanging down.

Mabel glanced round to make sure everyone was present and correct, then she checked her wristwatch before stepping forward.

'Ladies and gentlemen, thank you all for coming. I don't propose to make a long speech, but there are some people I would like to thank publicly. First of all, my dear friend Mrs Joan Hubble, who, though she didn't realise it at the time, was the person who gave me the idea of setting up this nursery.'

Dot led the applause as everyone looked round at a blushing Joan.

Mabel went on to name and thank others who'd had a hand in setting up the nursery, then she moved over to the cord hanging from the sheet covering the name.

'There's a very special lady here today,' she told her listeners. 'She's my landlady, Mrs Cooper.' She was aware of a gasp of surprise over where her friends were standing. 'She has been a wonderful friend and wartime mum to me and to others. I'd like to ask her to step forward and pull the cord.'

Her friends gently pushed Mrs Cooper forward and she stood next to Mabel, looking flustered. Mabel put the end of the cord into her hands.

'Say "I declare this nursery open" or something like that,' Mabel whispered.

Mrs Cooper took a moment to gather herself.

'It's an honour to be asked to do this.'

She pulled. Nothing happened. There were a few sympathetic chuckles.

'Pull harder,' said Mabel.

Mrs Cooper tugged and the sheet dropped away, revealing the nursery's name written in fancy script.

The Lizzie Cooper Nursery

In amongst the polite clapping, Mabel heard the soft exclamations that came from her friends, but Mrs Cooper didn't move. She just stood and stared at her daughter's name. Mabel felt a twitch of unease. Had she made a mistake in keeping this secret?

Then Dot said clearly, 'Oh, that's perfect, that is,' and Mrs Cooper covered her mouth with her hand as tears spilled from her eyes.

'I hope you like it,' said Mabel quietly.

Mrs Cooper sniffed and nodded, reaching to clutch Mabel's fingers.

Holding Mrs Cooper's hand firmly in her own, Mabel addressed the small crowd.

'Lizzie Cooper was a lovely young girl who, like so many, gave her life in the course of her duty.'

'Hear, hear,' said Dot and clapped, which sent a wave of applause rippling through the group.

'Very appropriate,' said someone.

'If you'd all like to go inside,' said Mabel, 'you'll find some of the mothers and children who will be using our nursery. Refreshments will be served shortly.'

She ought to lead the way in, but she had something much more important to do. She enveloped Mrs Cooper in her arms and held her close as they stood together underneath the sign bearing Lizzie's name.

CHAPTER FORTY

Emily surprised herself by weeping when she got home. She had never known Lizzie, but seeing Mrs Cooper and Mabel together had affected her deeply. Poor Mrs Cooper – and poor Lizzie. Imagine being gone for ever.

Later, she got her mother to talk about Lizzie.

'She was a sweet girl,' said Mummy. 'You can imagine that, can't you?'

'You mean because of Mrs Cooper being so good-natured and kind?'

Her mother nodded. 'Lizzie joined the railways because she wasn't tall enough for the switchboard. Did I ever tell you that? She loved being a lad porter and I believe she was very good at it. She was helpful and cheery, a real ray of sunshine. You'd have liked her.' Mummy's eyes had been soft at the start of this speech, but now they turned serious. 'She'd have been coming up for her twenty-first birthday in October if she was still with us.' She shook her head. 'Twenty-one! Little Lizzie. She might have been married by now. She might have been a mother, like Joan.'

In that moment, Emily glimpsed how precious she was to her parents. She had always felt loved, of course, and knew herself to be the centre of their world, but had she ever truly appreciated what this meant? Right now, the knowledge reached deep inside her and she seemed to feel her heart stretching in all directions in an effort to accommodate the revelation.

On impulse, she asked, 'Do you think I'll ever get married?'

Mummy gave her a startled look, then smoothed her expression. 'If I say "Yes", will you immediately say "No, I won't. I'll never love anyone but Raymond"?'

Emily pressed her lips together. Her mind was full of thoughts. So was her heart.

'That's what I'd have said a few months ago – a few weeks ago.'

'I know,' Mummy said softly.

'And it would have been true,' Emily added stoutly.

'I know that too, darling. He'll always be your first love. That's a very special thing.'

'It wasn't all that special to him,' said Emily.

'I'm sure it was, to start with,' said Mummy. 'He loved you, Emily. It was perfectly obvious that he did, but . . .'

'But then he stopped.'

'I don't think he stopped just like that. I think it probably happened gradually.'

'It doesn't matter how it happened,' Emily retorted with a flash of obstinacy.

'No. It doesn't. I know it came as a bolt out of the blue to you.'

Emily felt a crumpling sensation inside and tears welled up. 'I couldn't believe it. It was the worst thing that ever happened. I've never known what I did wrong.'

'Darling,' Mummy said, reaching for her and taking her into her arms, 'you did nothing wrong. I'm sure of that and I'm sure Raymond would say the same. The change was all to do with him, not you. He was deeply in love with you, but – but not lastingly.'

Emily pushed free of her mother's embrace, though not harshly. She reached into her cardigan pocket for her hanky and performed a swift mopping-up operation. She was determined not to shed any more tears.

'Not lastingly?' she muttered. 'That makes me feel a lot better.' The tart words weren't intended to snub her mother, more to shore up her own strength.

Mummy, bless her, took the ungraciousness on the chin. 'That's the way it is sometimes and I wish with all my heart it hadn't happened to you, my darling. When it happened, I could cheerfully have crowned Raymond.'

'Did Daddy want to crown him too?'

'Oh, Daddy would have torn him limb from limb – and then glued him back together so he could rip him apart again.'

Emily laughed. She didn't mean to. It just came out.

Mummy took her hand and squeezed it. 'You asked if I think you'll ever marry and the answer is that I very much hope you shall. I dearly hope that you'll meet someone else when the time is right and that you'll love one another.'

'Lastingly,' said Emily.

'I hope so.'

'There's a part of me that hates him,' she whispered.

'Hates Raymond? For leaving you?'

'No, for making me love him in the first place. I always thought I'd fall in love once and it would be for ever. We'd get married and have a family and we'd be together until we died. That's the way it's meant to happen. I feel as if – as if Raymond has cheated me out of what I always wanted. If I'd known he was going to ditch me, I'd never have loved him in the first place.'

'I don't think that kind of choice enters into it,' Mummy said softly. 'And I'm sorry you were hurt. I'm sorry you've had to live through this pain. But let me tell you something important. It's very private and the only other person who knows it is Daddy, so it's something you have to keep secret. I'm going to tell you because . . .' there was a sad edge to her smile ' . . . because my little girl has grown up. Please don't hate Raymond for falling out of love with you. He never intended to hurt you. I know what it's like to fall in love for the first time. I also know what it's like to fall in love for the second time.'

'The second time?' Bewilderment flickered through Emily.

'I had a first love and I adored him, but . . . it didn't last. Then along came your father.'

'And you fell in love with him.'

'It wasn't quite that simple. It took a long time. But what matters more than anything is that the love Daddy and I have for one another is lasting. That's what I hope you'll eventually find with someone else. Second love doesn't mean second best. It means you know what it is to be hurt when you lose someone. It means you know how precious love is and it means you recognise lasting love when you see it.'

'Do you think that might happen to me?' Emily asked.

'My darling Emily, I hope so.'

CHAPTER FORTY-ONE

The day after the opening of the Lizzie Cooper Nursery, there was to be an evening tea party in Wilton Close. Mabel's heart filled with warmth. A tea party specially for her. She looked back fondly at the various tea parties her friends had enjoyed together. The first had been on what would have been Lizzie's eighteenth birthday and although it had been a sad occasion, the support it had given dear Mrs Cooper to have Lizzie's chums rallying round had meant the world to all of them.

Mabel helped Mrs Grayson make the sardine rolls, the steamed jam pudding and the mushrooms in potato pastry.

'With what the others are bringing,' said Mrs Grayson, 'we'll have a fine spread.'

'You're a marvel, Mrs G,' said Mabel, 'you and your magic mixing bowl. I just hope I can live up to what you've taught me or you can expect panic-stricken letters begging for advice.'

It was time to get ready. Mabel put on her peacock-blue linen dress with patch pockets while Margaret donned her collarless lilac dress with elbow-length sleeves. Then Alison joined them, wearing a light yellow dress, and she and Margaret did Mabel's hair.

'Have you decided on a wedding style yet?' asked Alison. 'I haven't forgotten the dot-dot-dot-dash fringe you tried out. Are you going to have that?'

'No,' said Mabel. 'Much as I want to be patriotic, I don't look my best with my fringe over my forehead. I look better with it fluffed to the sides. I'll probably wear a victory roll.'

'Everything will be perfect,' said Margaret. 'Your mum will see to that.'

As they went downstairs together, the bell rang and Alison ran ahead to open the door to Joel. Mabel and Margaret left the two of them to have a private kiss on the step. Soon the other guests started to arrive, everyone smartly dressed as befitted a celebration for the forthcoming wedding.

Persephone arrived with Miss Brown and Mrs Mitchell. She looked lovely in a bronzy-coloured dress that made her honey-blonde hair look an even richer shade. There was no Matt because he was working.

'Just as well, really,' said Dot, who was here with her husband. 'This would be a lot of folk to meet all at once.'

'Especially when everyone would be watching him closely, being the newcomer,' Alison added.

'We couldn't have that,' Mabel exclaimed. 'Today I'm the one you're not supposed to be able to stop looking at.'

As the others laughed at her quip, Mabel gazed round at them, all dressed up to do honour to her special occasion.

'I wish Harry could have been here,' she said. 'He'd have loved this.'

'After Saturday,' said Cordelia, 'you'll be together for the rest of your lives.'

'There's nothing better than a happy marriage,' her husband added.

Emily, wearing a pretty, short-sleeved dress in a soft peachy-pink colour with a floral pattern, was standing at the window. 'Here come Joan and Bob.'

She went to open the door. A moment later, Joan walked in, carrying Max, who decided to be shy and plugged his thumb in his mouth.

'God love him,' said Mrs Grayson. 'Don't you just love them at that age? Look at those chubby little knees.'

'Who's commenting on my knees?' asked Bob, putting a carpet bag behind a chair as he followed Joan into the room, giving Mrs Grayson a cheeky wink.

'Are we all here now?' asked Mrs Cooper. 'Let's get the kettle on.'

'I'll help,' said Colette.

'You'll have to put an apron over that lovely dress,' said Mrs Cooper.

Colette glanced down at her bluebell-coloured dress.

Soon they were all drinking tea, though it was rather a crush to fit everybody in the front room. The dining chairs had been brought in, but there still weren't enough seats. Not that it mattered. The younger ones sat on the floor, though Mrs Grayson protested when Mabel did.

'You're the bride. You have to have a seat.'

'I'm fine down here, Mrs Grayson, honestly.'

Several conversations struck up. Mabel didn't join in at first but spent time looking around at all these special people who knew one another so well. She wished for Persephone's sake that Matt could have been here today so he could start becoming part of their group.

After a while, Cordelia called for quiet and everyone looked her way. Mabel sensed a frisson of anticipation rippling through the room.

'It's time for us to give you your wedding present, Mabel,' said Cordelia. 'Mrs Mitchell, as you're related to Mabel, please will you do the honours?'

As Alison and Margaret quietly left the room, Mabel looked at Pops's cousin Harriet as she started to speak.

'Mabel dear, all of us wanted to join together to get you a special wedding gift. Since you and your friends seem to make a habit of having tea parties, Emily suggested that a pretty tea service might be a good idea. But could we find one? Certainly not a complete one.' Mrs Mitchell looked at Dot. 'It was your idea, so you ought to tell the next part.'

Margaret and Alison slipped back into the room, carrying a box between them. Mabel's heart beat faster. If they hadn't been able to get her a tea service, what was it?

'It was a bit of a cheek, really,' said Dot, 'but I remembered Persephone saying that Darley Court has several different tea sets and all but a couple have been packed away for the duration. So I wondered whether . . . well, as I say, it was cheeky of me, but it seemed so *right.*'

'It was entirely right,' broke in Miss Brown. 'Mrs Green's idea was for us to present you with one of the Darley Court services.'

'To ensure it comes from us all,' said Colette, 'we've each made a donation to the Red Cross as a means of paying for it.'

Alison and Margaret picked up the box again and put it on the table next to Mabel.

'Go on,' said Alison. 'Open it.'

'It comes with love from all of us,' said Cordelia.

'Lots of love,' added Mrs Cooper, 'and all good wishes for the future.'

With trembling fingers, Mabel opened the box and took out some pieces. The set was dainty, its cups, saucers and tea plates decorated with tiny flowers and a gold rim. She picked up a cup, turning it to examine the pattern.

'How pretty,' she said. 'Thank you all so much. I love it, though I don't know if I'll dare use it. I couldn't bear it if anything got chipped.'

'You must use it,' said Mrs Grayson. 'How else are you to enjoy it?'

'Better that than putting it away in a cupboard,' said Alison.

'Use it,' said Dot, 'and think of your friends in Manchester.'

Mabel nodded. 'You're right. It'll give me so much pleasure.'

She started to get up to go round the room and kiss everyone, but Cordelia forestalled her.

'We've got something else for you.'

'We couldn't give you a tea service without some tea, could we?' said Margaret, producing a shopping bag. 'We've all been saving up tea for you.'

'Two pounds of it,' said Mrs Grayson.

'Two pounds!' Mabel exclaimed.

'And there's scented soap as well,' said Emily.

Mr Masters joined in. 'I'm sure Harry would have preferred a gallon of petrol, which I gather is a popular wedding present these days, but I was outvoted.'

'Besides,' said Cordelia, 'imagine having to carry a full petrol can to Annerby and then all the way down south.'

Mabel sniffed the soap. 'Gardenia. The presents are wonderful. Thank you.'

Now she did get up and do the rounds, giving hugs and kisses, including a smackeroo for little Max, who chuckled in delight.

Just before Mabel could resume her place, Joan stood up, handing her son to Mrs Cooper.

'Don't sit down yet, Mabel,' she said. 'We need to borrow you for a few minutes.'

Joan stooped to pick up the carpet bag that Bob had popped behind a chair when they arrived. Then she led the way upstairs. Intrigued, Mabel followed, with Margaret and Alison behind her. What was going on?

Joan went into Mabel and Margaret's bedroom, placing the bag on Margaret's bed. As Margaret and Alison closed the door behind them, they were trying not to laugh. Joan opened the bag and carefully took out . . . her own wedding dress.

Mabel caught her breath. 'Why—'

'Because you're going to wear it,' said Alison. 'This is your wedding party and your friends who can't come to the wedding want to see you in a proper dress.'

'I can't. It's such a mad thing to do.'

'If your friends don't think it's mad,' said Margaret, 'then it isn't. We all want to see you in it.'

'It'll be fun,' said Alison.

'Think what it'll mean to Mrs Grayson and the others who can't come,' Joan added. 'They'll adore seeing you all dressed up.'

Margaret laughed. 'Why did you think we're all wearing our bridesmaids' dresses?'

Yes, Margaret in her lilac, Alison in yellow, Colette's dress the colour of bluebells, Persephone in that unusual but very attractive bronzy dress. It sounded obvious now that Margaret said it. And that dove-grey dress Cordelia was wearing – was that what she had worn when she was one of Joan's mothers-of-the-bride? And surely Mrs Cooper, Mrs Grayson and Dot were also in their mothers-of-the-bride costumes. That wasn't her imagination, was it?

Realising the trouble her friends had gone to on her behalf, Mabel was happy to be persuaded to wear the wedding dress, any lingering doubts slipping away as the others gathered round to help her get changed. There was a lot of giggling, but when she had got the dress on and the other three stood back to look at her, the atmosphere changed from giddy to serious.

'You look gorgeous,' said Alison, 'just like Lydia did when she borrowed it.'

'It's wonderful to see you in the dress I wore.' Joan had to wipe away a tear.

'Come downstairs so everyone can see you,' said Margaret. 'Think of it as practice for Saturday when you're wearing the real thing.'

Mabel held the long skirt carefully as she descended the stairs, followed by her friends. At the foot of the staircase, Alison dodged past to open the door for her to enter the front room, where the voices fell silent for a moment before the comments started.

'Oh my goodness,' said Mrs Cooper. 'How beautiful you look.'

'You make a lovely bride,' added Cordelia.

'And you'll make an even lovelier one in your own dress,' said Dot.

'What have you done with the furniture?' asked Mabel.

Everything had been pushed aside, leaving five dining chairs in a tight line, with some cushions on the floor in front.

'We can't have a bride without photographs,' said Joel.

'I know how disappointed you are that not everyone can come to your wedding,' said Joan, 'so we're going to have wedding pictures here.'

'You sit in the middle,' said Mr Masters, 'and we'll have Mrs Cooper and Mrs Grayson sitting on one side of you, and Miss Brown and Mrs Mitchell on the other. Emily, Persephone and Alison, you sit on the floor in front. Mrs Green, Margaret and Colette, stand behind. Have I missed anyone out?'

'Only your wife!' said Cordelia.

There were several photographs, mostly of the girls and ladies but some including the men.

Joan dumped Max on Mabel's lap for one picture. 'That'll give future generations something to talk about in the years to come.'

They all trooped outside into the evening sunshine for more photographs, laughing as they posed in front of the vegetable plot.

'Could we have a picture that shows the house behind us?' asked Mabel. 'I've been so happy living here.'

Mr Green had to stand in the road to take that one.

'I'm not sure how big you'll all look,' he said, but Mabel didn't care. She just wanted a decent picture of the house.

Number 1 Wilton Close, where she had been so very happy and which she would never forget.

CHAPTER FORTY-TWO

On Wednesday evening, Persephone met Matt at the bus stop in Chorlton. She had arranged for the two of them to have a bite to eat with the land girls 'and whichever Americans the girls have roped in,' she explained cheerfully to Matt. 'Hank will be there and he'll bring a chum or two with him. It'll be fun.'

God forgive her, supper in the old gatekeeper's lodge with the land girls, fun though it would be, was a compromise. How she would have loved to take Matt up to Darley Court to spend a little time with Miss Brown, but her parents would take a dim view of that. Larking about with the land girls was one thing, but leading Matt over the threshold of Darley Court would be to fly in the face of all that the Trehearn-Hobbs family held dear. It would flout all their wishes and expectations. Were Matt to hobnob with Miss Brown, Ma and Pa would interpret that as defiance of the first water – and maybe they would be right.

It was such a hard position to be in. She loved and respected her parents and had always sought their approval, but she couldn't turn her back on Matt to please them. After the long years of yearning hopelessly after Forbes, meeting Matt and getting to know him had brought joy into her life. Her relationship with Matt felt infinitely precious. She wanted to nurture it and see where it took them.

'Are we going straight to the lodge?' Matt asked.

'No,' she told him. 'They're not expecting us for a while. I thought we'd spend some time together first. Let me take you to Jackson's Boat.'

'We're going on a boat?'

Persephone laughed. 'No, it's a bridge. I imagine that many years ago a man named Jackson performed the service of rowing people across the Mersey to and from that point until in the end a bridge was built.'

'Is that true?'

'I don't know, but it makes a good story.'

Through the evening's golden warmth, they walked hand in hand across the meadows, which at this time of year were dotted with the purple flower heads of wild thyme and the dainty lilac blooms of the cuckoo flower. Bees crawled busily over the white clover.

The riverbanks sloped down steeply to the Mersey, with the bridge stretching from one side to the other.

'Lancashire this side,' said Persephone. 'Cheshire over there.'

Matt grinned. 'Cheshire over yon. You have to say it properly if you live in these parts. Shall we go across? Then I can say I've walked to Cheshire today.'

They went up the steps and crossed the bridge, their footsteps ringing on the wooden planks.

'What's that building on the other side?' Matt asked.

'A pub.'

Matt ran down the steps at the end of the bridge and, turning, placed his hands at Persephone's waist to lift her down. She burst out laughing, but when she found herself standing before him, the laughter stopped and she felt breathless. Then, becoming aware of people emerging from the public house, she stepped away from Matt, tearing her gaze from his.

The pub had a bowling green with benches on three sides. Persephone sat down while Matt went inside and bought drinks. They sat in the sunshine, talking, until it was time to head back across the bridge.

'I'm looking forward to seeing Darley Court,' said Matt.

'We're not actually going up to the house itself, just to the old gatekeeper's lodge.'

'I know. I only meant it'll be interesting to see the house from a distance.' Matt paused before adding, 'I realise you're not taking me there. I understand.'

Persephone stopped walking and turned to face him. 'What do you understand?'

'I understand that you can't take me there.'

'It isn't like that,' she exclaimed, then felt something inside herself crumple under his scrutiny because they both knew that was exactly what it was like.

Matt shook his head and moved his shoulders, not shrugging precisely, more in a gesture of helplessness. 'What are we doing, Persephone? You and me. How is this supposed to work? You come from the aristocracy and I'm a mere fireman on the railways.'

'You're not a "mere" fireman. What you do is essential work.'

'That isn't really the point, is it?'

For a moment, Persephone was so afraid, her eyes couldn't see. 'What are you saying? Do you mean that we shouldn't be together?'

'I'm sure that's what everyone else thinks,' said Matt. 'Your parents think it. They don't just think it – they *know* it.'

'Do your parents think it?'

'Probably. Actually, yes, they do. Don't get me wrong. It isn't that they don't like you, but both of them worry that this isn't, that it can never be, a real relationship. My mum said as much the other day. Real relationships follow a certain path, and – and how can ours follow that path?'

Persephone didn't pretend not to understand. 'Meaning marriage.'

'Not every relationship ends with marriage, of course, but at least it's a possibility when you start going out with one another. That isn't a possibility for us. It can't be. Couples are meant to come from the same background, from the same class.'

Persephone sat down and, tugging his hand, pulled him down beside her.

'So what are we to do? It's all very well saying we shouldn't be together, but it feels right – doesn't it? It does to me. I thought it did to you.'

'It does. I promise it does.'

Matt cupped the side of her face with a gentle hand and she leaned in to receive his touch. It wasn't just that they were intellectually compatible. It was a physical thing too.

Persephone looked into Matt's eyes. 'There are so many reasons why we shouldn't be together. Our families don't want it. The world doesn't want it. We're poles apart socially, but I've never met anyone I got on with so well.'

'I know,' Matt whispered. 'I feel as if I've finally found the person I've been waiting for.'

'So what are we to do? My parents are outraged. My father believes I've let the side down – not just the family, but every right-minded woman who has rubbed shoulders with new people during this damnable war without losing her sense of decorum. My sister would accept us as a couple, but only if you were my wartime fling – a secret one, of course.'

That coaxed a small smile out of Matt. 'No chance of that now.'

'I wouldn't want it anyway,' Persephone declared. 'I don't want us to sneak about. When two people are as perfect together as we are, they should hold their heads up. *We* should hold our heads up.'

'My family worry about me because nothing can ever come of this, of us. My mum says it's high time I settled down and, well, that can't be with you, can it? And – and there are jokes at work, only some of them aren't jokes. I get told I've done well for myself. One bloke said in my hearing that if I got you in the family way, I'd be set up for life.'

Persephone drew back a little, not withdrawing from Matt but from those hateful words. 'What a beast.' She gave a bitter laugh. 'He wouldn't be so free with his assessment if he knew my father's opinion.'

'I'm sorry. I shouldn't have told you that.'

She leaned forward again, gazing straight into his eyes. 'Yes, you should. We should tell one another everything. There shouldn't be secrets or hidden worries. We have to face this together.'

'Is that what you want?' Matt asked softly. 'To face it together?'

'Well, I certainly don't want it to end. However difficult it is, it's what I want. I know we're surrounded by people who think we're foolish or wrong, or just plain mad, but when it's just the two of us . . .'

'I know. When it's just the two of us.'

'I know we don't have "for ever" in front of us,' said Persephone, 'but we have now, which is as much as anyone can possibly have in wartime. Do you think we can concentrate on that and not worry about the rest? Do you think we can make the best of *now*?'

'We can. The two of us – for now,' said Matt and kissed her.

CHAPTER FORTY-THREE

On her last day at work, Mabel bade a tearful farewell to Bernice and Bette, whom she had known ever since her first day on the permanent way.

'I won't forget you,' she promised.

'We shan't forget you in a hurry neither,' said Bette, laughing to cover her emotion. 'That first time we saw you, you had your stockings on, not to mention a hat with a fancy rosette. To work on the permanent way!'

Mabel laughed too. 'I didn't know I'd be hefting a pick-axe for a living.'

'Anyroad, I reckon it's a good thing you're piking off to get married,' said Bernice, adding, when the others looked at her in surprise, 'You're taking our Joan with you, and that means I get to have my grandson until Sunday evening.'

It was an emotional day. Mabel and her friends met in the buffet after work.

'Your final time here,' said Cordelia.

'Don't or you'll make me cry,' Mabel protested, so they all kept the mood light and happy and Mabel drank in every moment.

When it was time to go, she hugged Cordelia, Dot, Emily and Persephone.

'I can't believe I'm not going to see you again,' she said.

'You're only going down south, chick,' said Dot, 'not to the ends of the earth. And you know what good letter writers we are.'

As they were about to leave the buffet, Mrs Jessop came out from behind the counter and gave Mabel a hug too.

'You and your friends are my best customers.'

'All we ever have is a cup of tea each,' said Mabel.

'Well, you're my most regular customers,' said Mrs Jessop. 'And that's the best kind.'

Mabel, Alison and Margaret went home to Wilton Close, Mabel keeping her lips firmly sealed against a remark about doing this for the last time. She had been increasingly aware the entire week of all the last times she was going through at the moment and this was an extra special one.

'Thank goodness you're coming to the wedding, Mrs C,' Mabel whispered to Mrs Cooper, 'or I'd have to bop you over the head and stuff you into my suitcase.'

Helped by Margaret and Alison, Mabel packed her trunk.

'Like boarding school,' she said.

'Except that we're all coming home with you,' said Alison.

All except Mrs Grayson. Mabel hugged her fiercely the next morning.

'Thank you for everything. And don't forget to send me recipes.'

'Easy ones,' Margaret joked.

Mrs Mitchell arrived from Darley Court to travel with them to Victoria. The taxi went via Torbay Road to pick up Joan and then Seymour Grove to collect Colette. It was a dreadful squash, but no one minded.

They spilled out and headed into the station, Mabel pausing one final time beside the memorial to the Great War, which commemorated the many men of the old Lancashire and Yorkshire Railway who had given their lives in the cause of peace. Railwaymen – like Grandad had been. How many lives were going to be lost in total in this new war?

Please keep Harry safe.

They had arrived early to be sure of being among the first to board the train so they could have seats together. The guard slammed the open doors, checked the closed ones before blowing his whistle and the journey began. They chatted and laughed all the way.

'This is the first time I've been away since before the war,' said Mrs Cooper.

'There are still plenty of people having holidays,' said Colette. 'Everyone benefits from a break.'

'I heard that the government is setting up holiday hostels for exhausted war workers,' said Margaret.

'The Lake District apparently has a reputation for feeling peaceful,' said Alison. 'So does the Derbyshire Dales.'

'Last week I chaperoned a lady and her little girl who were going on holiday,' said Colette. 'The child was clutching her most treasured possession – a nightdress case shaped like a rabbit. According to her mother, it had the week's rations in it.'

Mabel had a surprise when Persephone appeared, calling for everyone to have their tickets ready.

'I didn't say anything before because I didn't know if I'd be allowed to swap,' she explained. 'It's not quite the same as coming to the wedding, but it's the closest I could get.'

When the train drew into Annerby and everybody stood up to gather their belongings, Alison glanced out of the window and gave an exclamation.

'Look! A brass band.'

'They must be catching the train to go to a concert,' said Margaret.

'No,' said Alison. 'Their instruments would be inside proper cases for that. They look like they're about to start playing.'

The music began and after the first few notes, Mabel and her companions stared at one another in amazement before starting to laugh.

'They're playing "Here Comes the Bride". I can't believe it,' said Alison.

They piled off the train and stood to listen, along with lots of other passengers.

'It can only be for you, Mabel,' said Mrs Mitchell.

'Did your mother arrange it?' asked Colette.

'Definitely not,' said Mabel.

'I bet I know who did.' Joan looked around. 'There she is. Persephone! Come over here. Do we have you to thank for this?'

'Who, me? Whatever makes you think that?' But Persephone's smile gave her away.

'I think it's wonderful,' said Mabel.

'Is this for you?' asked a stranger.

'Are you getting wed?' asked another.

When Mabel said she was, congratulations filled the air as other passengers passed on their good wishes.

Mabel hugged Persephone. 'It's the best surprise I've ever had.'

'Call it an extra wedding present. I'm sorry I can't make it to your big day. I'd love to be there.'

'I wish you could too. Whenever I think of my wedding in years to come, I'll remember you and the Annerby Brass Band.'

'I think we can safely say you've made your mark on Mabel's wedding,' Joan assured Persephone.

Persephone gave Mabel another hug, holding her close for several seconds.

'Goodbye, Mabel. Good luck.'

*

The morning of Mabel's wedding was bright and warm. Mabel wandered around Kirkland House in her dressing gown, examining all the arrangements.

'I showed you everything yesterday,' said Mumsy.

'I want to see it all again. I can hardly believe it's happening.' Catching Mumsy's hands in her own, Mabel looked into her eyes. 'Harry is the right man for me. I want to be sure you know that. Even though Pops is going to disinherit me—'

'We said we wouldn't talk about that. I don't want today spoiled.'

'I was only going to say that in spite of that, I don't want you to feel iffy about Harry. He made a bad decision and he paid for it by very nearly losing me, but we've put all that behind us and we're going to be blissfully happy together, I promise.'

'I wish you both all the very best,' said Mumsy. 'You know that. I just want you to be as well suited as Pops and I are. Thank you for holding your wedding here.'

'Where else would I have it?' Mabel asked.

'Manchester. I know how you've grown to love the place and you have all those friends there. They mean a lot to you.'

'You mean more,' said Mabel. 'I wouldn't dream of getting married somewhere else and doing you out of the fun of organising everything.'

And Mumsy had come up trumps.

Without telling Mabel, she had prevailed upon the gardener to give up one of his greenhouses to gypsophila and now there were clouds of tiny white flowers everywhere, in vases of all sizes and styles borrowed from miles around. A string quartet was tuning up in a corner of the hall and Doris the maid had wound Union flag bunting up the banister rails.

The doorbell rang and Mabel went to answer it, barely hearing Mumsy's anguished cry that she was still in her dressing gown. Fortunately, the visitors were women from Pops's factory, bringing all the bread rolls and small cakes they'd been able to lay their hands on in the various bakeries in town that morning. Among them were Louise and her mother, Mrs Wadden, whom, at Mabel's behest, Pops had rescued from a desperately difficult situation in Manchester by providing jobs for them in his factory, as well as an apprenticeship for Clifford, Louise's brother. Mumsy had ensured the family had a good billet near the school the two youngest boys now attended.

'Thanks for doing all this,' Mabel said to Louise and her mother, indicating the bread and cakes. 'I know it was your idea.'

'This is nothing compared to what you did for us,' said Mrs Wadden. 'Things have worked out reet well for us.'

'It was a pleasure,' said Mabel, 'and only what you deserved.'

'It's a different life,' Louise said quietly. 'Folk used to despise us when we were in Manchester and they were scared of Dad and Rob. Being a Wadden was a bad thing then.'

'But not now,' said Mabel.

'No, not now,' Lou agreed. 'When we came here, we told the boys this was our chance to make summat of the Wadden name, summat good, so that we didn't have to be ashamed of it no more.'

'Good for you,' said Mabel.

Cook and Doris came bustling into the hall to lead the factory women through to the kitchen to deposit their bounty and Mumsy tried to shoo Mabel upstairs, though Mabel lingered to gaze at all the frothy gypsophila everywhere. Her friends had admired it yesterday when they

397

arrived, as had Harry and his parents, who had also come yesterday. Dr and Mrs Knatchbull were staying with the Wilmores while Harry and his best man had been sent down to town to stay at the Station Hotel so that the happy couple wouldn't run the risk of seeing one another today before the wedding.

The two of them had said a private farewell at the front door last night, whispering wonderingly that this time tomorrow . . .

And now it was time to get ready. Mabel's friends helped her into her dress, exclaiming over the beauty of the silver-striped white taffeta. And when it was on her . . .

'Oh, Mabel,' breathed Joan. 'You look like a princess.'

Mumsy carefully put Mrs Wilmore's veil on Mabel's head, batting Mabel's hands aside when she tried to help. Mumsy fluffed out the veil at the back.

'It's perfect,' she whispered into Mabel's ear.

Emotion swelled inside Mabel as memories assaulted her and she missed Althea as much as when Althea had just died. They had fallen out over a man and now Mabel was about to marry someone else. There was no accounting for the way life worked itself out.

Mumsy touched her hand and Mabel met her eyes, loving her mother for the understanding she saw.

'You make a beautiful bride, Mabel,' said Colette and the other attendants echoed her words.

Mabel gently let go of her thoughts of Althea and the past. From now on, for the rest of the day, she must live in the moment and make the most of her wonderful day. Her heart beat faster. Marrying Harry was what she wanted more than anything.

Mumsy sent the bridesmaids, Mrs Cooper and Mrs Mitchell downstairs before she would let Mabel go down.

'Go and show Pops,' Mumsy said softly, staying behind at the top of the stairs.

In the hall below, Pops looked up and Mabel saw the moment when his breath caught and his eyes widened. She felt like the loveliest girl in the world. The little girl in her wanted to race down the stairs and fling herself into his arms, but she made herself walk down sedately, relishing every moment.

When she reached the bottom, Pops took her hands and kissed her cheek, then had to fumble for his handkerchief to dash away a tear.

'My goodness, Mabs. You're the most gorgeous girl there is. I couldn't be prouder.'

'You're not meant to cry, Pops. It's supposed to be Mumsy who cries.'

Soon everyone else, including Mumsy, was on the way to the church, leaving Mabel alone with Pops. Well, not quite alone. Cook and Doris came to see her in her dress and give her their best wishes.

Then it was time to climb into the Daimler, driven today by one of the men from the factory. He held Mabel's bouquet for her while she settled in the back seat. The red roses, tied together with ribbons of white and blue, had a heavenly scent that filled the motor's interior. The bridesmaids and matrons-of-honour had bouquets in the same style, though smaller. Mumsy and all the other ladies were to wear corsages of a red rose with a little bit of gypsophila, while the gentlemen had red roses for their buttonholes.

In the motor on the way down the hill to the church, they overtook a soldier with his kitbag, thumbing a lift.

'We ought to stop for him,' said Mabel.

The young soldier was at the end of his seventy-two-hour leave and needed to get back down south.

'Need to get to the station, do you?' asked Pops. 'Hop in.'

The young man looked uncertain. 'Are you sure, sir?'

Mabel leaned forwards. 'Positive.'

'I hope this won't make you late for your wedding, miss.'

'I don't think it'll do Harry any harm if the bride is fashionably late,' Pops said in a dry voice, but he smiled at the same time.

When they got to the church, Mabel's attendants hurried to meet them at the gates, which made Mabel realise she was indeed late, but the main thing was that they had done a soldier a good turn. It would make an interesting story in years to come.

Inside the church porch, her friends gathered around her, arranging her veil and short train before taking up their own positions behind, Joan and Colette in front of Alison and Margaret. Pops offered her his arm and Mabel took it for the final time as a single girl. Inside the church, the organ music paused and when it started again, there came the rustling sound of the congregation standing up.

'Ready, Mabs?' asked Pops.

Mabel took a breath. 'Ready,' she whispered.

Mabel beamed as she and Harry posed beside the four-tiered wedding cake with its V for victory on the top. She hadn't stopped smiling since the wedding. She and Harry jointly held the knife as if about to cut the first slice. The photographer took the picture and everyone clapped.

Then it was time to remove the cardboard 'cake' to reveal the real one underneath the bottom layer. Quite how this was to be achieved had been a source of much angst to Mumsy, not least because there didn't seem to be a standard rule of etiquette.

'Mumsy's instinct was to have the cardboard cake removed discreetly,' Mabel told Joan.

'Discreetly? That whopping great thing?'

'I know.' Mabel grinned. 'Then Pops said that since everyone knows it's artificial, why not make a ceremony out of dismantling it?'

And indeed this was done to cheers and applause, the clapping taking on an extra warmth and depth when the V for victory was placed on the real cake.

'I'm going to keep the V for ever,' Mabel told Mrs Cooper. She looked around as someone touched her on the arm. 'Pops.'

Pops nodded to Mrs Cooper. 'Excuse us, will you? I'd like a private word with the bride.'

Mabel went with him to his den, which was furnished with leather wing chairs and paintings of railways that Pops had purchased as a tribute to Grandad. This was the one room that wasn't decorated with vases of gypsophila.

'I'm sorry to drag you away from the reception, Mabs, but I think you'll consider it's worth it. Darling girl, I want you to know that you aren't going to be disinherited after all. That is, I've yet to make up my mind about the factory, because I like the idea of a cooperative, but you'll come into a tidy sum in the fullness of time.'

'Don't say that. I'd much rather have you, Pops.'

'And I intend to stay around for a good few years yet. But you did hear me say you're not going to be disinherited?'

'Yes, and I'm delighted, of course. Thank you. What made you change your mind?'

'I reckon Harry has proved himself. We had a long talk yesterday about his plans for after the war and it's clear he is serious about providing well for you and your children. He wants to train as a pilot and fly commercial aircraft. We both reckon people will start flying abroad for holidays after the war – ordinary people, not just the rich. That's all

I wanted for you all along, my darling girl – a decent, trust-worthy man who'll work his socks off to give you the best possible life.'

'Thank you, Pops.' Mabel went to him. 'What matters most is that you've gone back to accepting Harry like you did to start with. You have accepted him again, haven't you?'

'I have,' Pops confirmed. 'But I'll tell you this, Mabs. This is the only chance he'll get from me.'

'It's the only one he'll ever need, I promise.' Mabel reached up to kiss him. 'Thank you, thank you.'

'Now be off with you. Get back to your party. You'll have to leave soon.'

Mabel groaned. 'Don't say that.'

She returned to the festivities, wanting to remember every detail. All too soon, it was time to get changed out of her wedding dress into her going-away suit – a three-piece with a belted, hip-length jacket and a simple collarless top and skirt, worn with a pretty straw hat. It was a real wrench to have to remove the wedding dress.

'Mumsy, have you heard of a lady called Barbara Cartland?' Mabel asked. 'She provides wedding dresses for loan to brides in the forces.'

'Are you proposing to send your dress to her?' asked Mumsy.

'No, I'm afraid I'm not that generous,' said Mabel, 'but I'd like you to make sure that any of the factory girls who needs a wedding dress has the option of borrowing mine. And you must send me a photograph of each girl who wears it. I'll add the pictures to the end of my wedding album.'

'I think that's a lovely thing to do,' said Joan.

'And now you must go down and say your goodbyes,' said Mumsy.

'I don't want this to end,' said Mabel.

'I know – and I don't want you to miss your train.'

Downstairs, Mabel and her new husband did the rounds of all the guests, accepting kisses, hugs and best wishes. Mabel lingered to share extra hugs with her friends from Manchester.

'I'll miss you all so much,' she said.

'We'll miss you too,' said Alison, 'but don't forget what Dot said. We're all good at writing letters. You'll be bombarded.'

'I hope so,' said Mabel.

'Depend on it,' said Margaret.

Mabel hugged Mrs Cooper. 'Thank you for looking after me.'

'It was a pleasure. You take care.'

'Goodbye, Mabel,' said Joan, holding her warmly and speaking close to her ear. 'Good luck.'

Such simple words. Goodbye. Good luck. What could sound more ordinary? But this was wartime, which imbued the words with the special meaning that came from absolute sincerity and the knowledge of death and uncertainty that everyone carried with them these days. Good luck. Best of British. Go carefully. Keep safe. Please don't die. We'll meet again.

Mabel hugged Joan hard, then they stepped away from one another, smiling and blinking back tears.

'Aren't you going to throw the bouquet?' Joan asked.

But Mabel had another plan. Sharing a warm glance with Mumsy, who knew what she was about to do, Mabel went over to Mrs Mitchell and held out the bouquet to her.

'I want you to have my flowers. I've got so much to thank you for. We all have.'

'Me?'

'Yes, you. You're the one who sent me to live with Mrs Grayson. If you hadn't done that, then she'd never have ended up moving into Mrs Cooper's house, and very likely Mrs Green would never have thought of asking Mrs Cooper to take in Joan when she needed it – and Mrs Masters wouldn't have recommended Mrs Cooper to the Morgans when they wanted a housekeeper. In a roundabout way, you're responsible for all of us having Wilton Close as our special place.'

Mrs Mitchell laughed. There was delight as well as surprise in her expression. 'A very roundabout way.'

Mabel held up the bouquet, closing her eyes as she inhaled the glorious scent of Mumsy's best roses, then she passed the flowers to Mrs Mitchell, leaning forward to kiss her cheek.

'Thank you, Cousin Harriet,' she whispered.

Everyone clapped and murmured approvingly. A swell of emotion rose from the bottom of Mabel's heart as she looked around at all these dear people, those she had always known and those whom the war had brought into her life.

'Goodbye, all of you,' she said. 'Good luck. I'll miss you.'

Then Harry caught her hand and hastened her towards the waiting Daimler. At its open door, Mabel turned for one final wave, one last blown kiss, then she bent her head and stepped into the motor, sadness turning to joy as Harry, her very own cheeky blighter of a husband, took his place beside her.

Dear Readers,

I want to start this letter by saying a massive thank you to all of you. You see, I get asked to write my Railway Girls books three at a time. After I wrote the first three (*The Railway Girls, Secrets of the Railway Girls* and *The Railway Girls in Love*), it was because you loved them and made them a success that I was asked to write three more: *Christmas with the Railway Girls, Hope for the Railway Girls* and *A Christmas Miracle for the Railway Girls*. Your continued love and support for the characters and the series has resulted in my being asked to write another three, of which *Courage of the Railway Girls* is the first. It's amazing to think this is book 7 – and it's all thanks to you. Consider yourselves well and truly hugged!

I also want to thank all the readers who join me regularly on my Facebook page at facebook.com/MaisieThomasAuthor. Between us, we have created a warm and friendly community. If you haven't found us yet, please come along and join in. You'll find all kinds of things from photos of my seaside home and my favourite garden plants to the regular 'What are you reading this weekend?' feature. You'll also have the chance to see my new book covers before anyone else and share insider information about forthcoming books (though without spoilers, I promise!)

There are opportunities, such as on publication days and book-birthdays, to celebrate by entering an exclusive competition to win a signed copy. This applies not just to my Railway Girls books but also to the books I write under the names Susanna Bavin and Polly Heron. And sometimes we do something extra special, such as creating the Readers' Roll of Honour, which you'll find in the back of this book.

I loved writing *Courage of the Railway Girls*. It was wonderful to have Persephone as a viewpoint character at last and I hope you'll enjoy living her story alongside her. As it unfolds, you might find you don't know as much about her as you thought you did.

And after what happened to Emily in *A Christmas Miracle for the Railway Girls*, it felt completely right and natural to make her a viewpoint character here too. She wasn't an official Railway Girl before, but she is now and I hope you'll all take her to your hearts.

As for Mabel, this is her fifth time in the viewpoint driving seat! I hope you'll find her storyline as satisfying and warming to read as I found it to write.

Much love, *Maisie xx*

If you loved

Courage of the Railway Girls,

Maisie Thomas's next book

Christmas Wishes for the Railway Girls

IS AVAILABLE TO PRE-ORDER NOW

Read on for bonus content from the author and an exclusive first look at the new book

Q&A WITH MAISIE THOMAS

CHARACTERS

Which of your characters is your favourite and why?

That's a difficult question to start off with! I know Dot is hugely popular with my readers and they are also very concerned about Colette. Personally, I have a soft spot for Mrs Cooper. She was only intended to have a brief walk-on part in book 1, but I liked her so much that I just had to keep her in the story. Losing her beloved Lizzie was the most terrible thing that could possibly have happened to her, but she carries on with quiet courage.

How do you get into the mind of your characters? What do you think makes a character compelling?

Usually, when a character first pops into my head, she is fully formed. And of course, because I've been writing about my lovely girls for some time now, I know them all very closely. What makes a character compelling? The way she copes with difficult problems. I love presenting my characters with moral dilemmas.

What role does friendship and/or community play in your stories and for your characters?

Friendship is the cornerstone of my Railway Girls stories. When I was asked to write the series, the instruction was: 'The heart of this series will focus on the core female characters and their friendships – and how they support each other through the hardships of war.'

What role does romance play in your stories and for your characters? What are the most memorable romances from books you've read?

Romance is important because it gives the girls and women the chance of experiencing a special kind of happiness. Because the stories are set in wartime, the romances have an extra edge of uncertainty and determination. I like to explore romantic relationships that wouldn't have happened in peacetime.

Memorable romances from other books? Captain Wentworth and Anne Elliott in *Persuasion*. And Ben in Catherine Cookson's *The Rag Nymph* is a wonderful hero.

THE WRITING PROCESS

Did you have to research anything while you were writing? How did you research it? What did you find out that made it into the book, and what was the most interesting thing you found?

Do I research? Heavens, yes! Creating the correct historical setting is essential; so, for example, every air raid in the books really did happen. I have several shelves full of WW2 books, including a whole shelf of railway books. I also have a railway-loving husband who gives me all kinds of help and information.

What advice would you give to any aspiring writers?

Don't stop writing today unless you know exactly how you are going to start writing tomorrow.

BACKGROUND

When did you start writing and what inspired you to do so?

I was a child writer and I have written all my life. I wrote for my own pleasure for years before I started making serious efforts to find an agent and a publisher. What inspired me in the first place? I honestly don't know. I just love telling stories. I also firmly believe that coming from a family of lifelong readers has something to do with it.

Of the books you've written, which is your favourite?

The honest answer is that my favourite is the one I'm writing at the moment – whichever it happens to be. This is because, when I'm writing, I'm deeply involved in the story as I live through all the experiences with my characters.

But if you want to know why some of the books are special to me … I love *The Railway Girls* because it was the first in the series and I remember writing Dot's first chapter and feeling myself sliding into the story and knowing how much I was going to love it. And writing *Christmas with the Railway Girls* was a huge pleasure because it was my first opportunity to introduce new viewpoint characters. And I love *Hope for the Railway Girls* because Margaret is a big favourite of mine.

What are you currently reading?

At the moment, I'm enjoying thrillers by Felix Francis, romances with a ghostly twist by Jane Cable and the wonderful Wartime Midwives series by Daisy Styles.

READERS' ROLL OF HONOUR

Joyce Ward (née Hicks), who worked in the Land Army in Ross-on-Wye. Remembered by her daughter, Chris Bartholomew, Swanley.

Kathleen Wilson, who worked in a munitions factory in Coventry. Remembered by her niece, Dawn Wilson, Hartshill, near Nuneaton.

John Prest Jobling, who was evacuated to Gunnerside in the Yorkshire Dales for five years. Remembered by his daughter, Beverley Ann Hopper, Sunderland.

Charles Leonard Green, Royal Army Service Corps, who died when his ship, the SS Yoma, was torpedoed. Remembered by his granddaughter, Tanya Cook, Tenbury Wells.

Cecil Oughton, who was in the Royal Artillery and died aged twenty-one on 2 July 1944 in Caen, France. Remembered by his first cousin twice removed, Amanda Oughton, Darlington, County Durham.

Anita Evans (née Green), who worked in munitions in Marchwiel, Wrexham. Remembered by her daughter, Lynn Dobbins, Rhosllanerchrugog.

Flight Lieutenant Gordon Stewart Richards, 406 Squadron, Royal Canadian Air Force, killed October 1943, aged twenty-two. Remembered by his cousin (several times removed), Jennifer Squire, Kemptville, Ontario, Canada.

Chrissie Weir, who was in the WAAF. Remembered by her great-great-niece, Paula Davitt, Edinburgh.

Edith Olivia Wolfe (née Nash), who was a lathe operator / machinist making parts for Howitzers in a factory near London. Remembered by her daughter-in-law, Judy Wolfe, Edmonton, Alberta, Canada.

Arthur Dean, Royal Engineers, who served as a dispatch rider at Dunkirk. Remembered by his niece, Vera Forrest, Merseyside.

Alan Heaword, who served in the Green Howards Regiment as a dispatch rider. Remembered by his daughter, Susan Webb, Stockport.

CHAPTER ONE

July 1943

Alison kept looking at herself in the dressing-table's triple mirror as she got ready to go out for the evening with Joel. The midnight-blue dress suited her, not just in colour but in style, with its fitted bodice and the gently flared skirt that would swing beautifully when she danced – not a wide swing, but a muted, discreet swing in keeping with the current fashion. Not just the fashion either, but the strict regulations concerning clothes and, above all, the rule that decreed no fabric should be wasted on unnecessary details such as pleats, turn-ups or fullness.

The midnight blue was a formal evening gown and had originally belonged to her sister Lydia, but Alison had suggested a swap.

'My apricot for your blue,' she'd said. 'I haven't worn the apricot for ages.'

'But it's a lovely dress,' said Lydia, fingering the material. She was obviously tempted.

'I know, but it has … unpleasant associations, you might say. I last wore it on the night that Paul met Katie. I've never worn it since.'

'Oh, Alison.' Lydia lifted her hand from the apricot dress and laid it tenderly on Alison's arm. 'But it's not as though you haven't found happiness elsewhere. Joel adores you.'

'I know, but I still have no desire to wear the dress I was wearing when my old boyfriend met the girl he later told me was the love of his life.' A little shudder rippled through Alison's shoulders. Oh, the hopes she had entertained on that fateful occasion! 'So, will you swap dresses?' she asked Lydia in a bright and breezy voice. 'You wouldn't be superstitious about the apricot dress bringing bad luck?'

'No.' Lydia smiled. 'I've always admired it, actually.'

'Hm.' Alison pressed her lips together, trying to look stern when really she was smothering a smile. 'I seem to remember you "admiring" a lot of my clothes when we both lived at home – yes, and helping yourself to them.'

That made Lydia laugh and her blue eyes twinkled. 'It's what sisters are for.'

Now Alison admired her reflection. Lydia's old midnight blue went well with her colouring. She had chosen the apricot because it was an unusual colour, but she could see now that it was more flattering to Lydia's fair hair than it ever had been to her own brown hair and eyes. Her gaze swept across the triple mirror. There was a long mirror inset into one of the wardrobe doors too.

She took a moment to look with pleasure around the bedroom she had recently moved into. To start with, when she had come to live in the house in Wilton Close, she had been given what used to be the boxroom, a small room with a ceiling that sloped down to about four feet from the floor. There had been space for a narrow bed pushed into the corner plus a cupboard and a chest of drawers. That might have sounded poky, but dear Mrs Cooper, who looked after them all so well, had made the room as comfortable as she could, keeping it spotless and popping sachets of dried lavender into the drawers, as well as making sure there was a hot water bottle between the sheets all through the colder months.

After Mabel's wedding in June, Alison had moved into the big bedroom with Margaret, taking over what had been Mabel's share of the space. Mr and Mrs Morgan, whose house this was and who had decamped to North Wales for the duration, had slept in single beds, each with its own little bedside cupboard. The girls shared the dressing-table and the wardrobe. There was even a fireplace, though fuel shortages meant that they only had the coal for the downstairs fires these days, and precious little coal at that. Thank goodness for the summertime. Last winter had been hard and the coming winter wouldn't be any easier. In fact, it was certain to be worse.

Alison had never met the Morgans but she was grateful to them for going to North Wales. Because of that, Cordelia had been able to recommend Mrs Cooper to them as a housekeeper who would take good care of the house in their absence and not kick up a fuss about being required to hand it back to them after the war. As well as looking after her lodgers, Mrs Cooper ran a little cleaning business called Magic Mop. It was possible for her to be out of the house earning a bit of money partly because Mrs Grayson, another lodger, had taken over the kitchen. Mrs Grayson, though never formally trained, was an expert cook and she found great satisfaction in providing tasty, nutritious meals for the household. Sometimes Alison got her to write down a recipe for her to take to Mum; and she knew that Mrs Grayson also sent recipes to Margaret's sister Anna in Shropshire; and now also to Mabel, who was taking care of her handsome RAF husband who worked at Bomber Command.

Satisfied that the blue dress suited her, and feeling far lovelier than she had ever felt in the apricot, Alison turned her attention to her dark hair. She wasn't a beauty like Persephone – *nobody* was a beauty like Persephone – but she knew herself to be good-looking in a fresh-faced kind of way. 'Natural and unaffected' was how Mabel had once described her looks and Alison liked to remind herself of that sometimes. She had good hair, she knew that. When it was properly curled and styled, it hung to a short way past her shoulders. Like many girls, she wore it in a simple pageboy cut that was easy to style away from her face. She curled her fringe too and wore it flicked back.

Alison had always enjoyed dressing up to go out and she loved looking her best. When she had been Paul's girlfriend, she'd wanted to look her best for him. It was different with Joel. *Every*thing was different with Joel. Yes, she wanted to look pretty for him, but she wanted to look her best for herself too. She had submerged herself in being Paul's other half. Much as she loved Joel, she would never submerge herself like that again.

Her pulse quickened at the thought of being with him very soon. People liked him because of his cheerful nature, but he had a serious side too and Alison was sure his patients must find him both kind and reassuring. As for herself, well … the way his blue eyes softened when he looked at her practically made her bones melt.

Venetia, Joel's attractive, clever, graceful sister, had done her level best to get rid of Alison in the early days of their relationship in favour of an old girlfriend she had wanted Joel to get back together with; but Joel hadn't wavered in his devotion to Alison, even though they hadn't known one another all that long at that point. Joel's steadfastness had been exactly what Alison had needed after the way

Paul had treated her. She had devoted herself to Paul heart and soul for a number of years – and then had come the occasion when she had worn the apricot dress.

It had been at a dance organised by Cordelia to raise funds for the War Weapons Week, held in the glamorous ballroom at the Claremont Hotel. Alison had worked herself up to expecting a proposal – just as she had many times before. She felt ashamed of herself now when she recalled how desperate she had been for Paul to go down on one knee. She had planned it a thousand times in her head, but Paul had never proposed. She had told herself he was biding his time, and maybe he had been, but then Katie had come along and … well, he hadn't felt the need to bide his time before popping the question to her. On top of being devastated by heartbreak, Alison had tasted bitter humiliation.

But that was all very much in the past. Alison had met Dr Joel Maitland and loved every moment of being with him. The heart that Paul had shattered had grown back together again, though it wasn't the same heart it used to be. Gone was the girl who had thought of nothing but marriage. She was happier now with Joel than she had ever been with Paul. With him, all she had ever thought about was getting a ring on her finger and buying fish-knives and a cut-glass fruit bowl ready for when they got married. She'd been all set to live with Paul's mother, the two Mrs Dunaways doting on the man they both loved. Alison had built up to every anticipated proposal with anxious elation and then felt crushed every time it had failed to materialise.

That had been the old Alison. The new Alison could only shake her head in wonder. She had grown up a lot since then, not just through her experience of heartbreak but also because she had an interesting job that she loved. The old Alison had seen work as something to be got through until her 'real' life started, when she became a housewife and mother. Even when war had broken out and women were needed in the workplace as never before, that had still been the way she had perceived the clerical post she'd been allocated on the railways.

But after Paul dumped her, she had been given a new post.

Miss Emery, the assistant welfare supervisor with responsibility for women and girls on the railway, had sent for her.

'As the war continues,' Miss Emery had told her, 'we'll need more and more women, the most experienced and capable of whom will find themselves being promoted through the ranks.' Then she had astounded Alison by adding seriously, 'You are just such a capable girl, Miss Lambert.'

As well as being astounded, Alison had felt resentful, because what she had wanted more than anything was to get back together with Paul, not be offered a new job; but she couldn't help feeling intrigued when Miss Emery went on to explain what lay ahead.

'I'd like to prepare you for a responsible role – not in the offices, but on the railway itself. To do this, I'd arrange for you to gain a variety of knowledge and experience, which will not only help to prepare you personally for what follows, but will also make it appear to other people that you are suitable for a post higher up. What do you think?'

That had been back in the second half of 1941, coming up for two whole years ago and Alison was no closer to finding out what the special job was that she was building up to. Her discreet hints seeking information had been ignored and the one or two outright questions she had dared to pose had been met by a coolly raised eyebrow and a murmur of, 'Really, Miss Lambert, you know better than to ask.'

Nevertheless, Alison loved going to work and was proud to feel she was playing her part in the war effort. She had gained experience in a variety of roles over the past couple of years. Every so often Miss Emery would place her into a new environment for a time – the marshalling yard, a signal-box, the various workshops – so she could see how everything worked. Her arrival was greeted with varying degrees of enthusiasm. Upon being informed that she was there to gain experience, her new colleagues either welcomed her and did all they could to teach her the ropes or else they resented the suggestion that their jobs could be learned so quickly. Moreover, even all this time into the war, there were still men who didn't like the idea of a girl in any position other than the lowliest. Most chaps were courteous and helpful, but there would always be those who chose not to be.

Although Alison had hated this new role to start with because she had been so ground down by heartbreak, she had gradually come to realise that work was more than a way of filling in the time before marriage. It was interesting and worthwhile in itself, something that had been a revelation to her. This knowledge had changed the way she viewed herself, increasing her self-respect. She could even be grateful that she hadn't had the chance to marry Paul, because that would have robbed her of the opportunity to become this new person, who was so much more than a housewife-in-waiting.

The old Alison had been well and truly left behind ... or had she? Mabel's wedding had stirred up all kinds of feelings. Being happy for Mabel had set Alison thinking about herself and Joel. Joel was deeply in love with her. Right from the start, he had made it clear that, after having a string of girlfriends, this was a serious relationship and he was in no doubt that Alison was the right girl for him. Thus far, Alison had been more than content to have a handsome, devoted boyfriend to spend her spare time with. Was it now time for more? Or was she just in love with the idea of it because of Mabel's wedding?

Acknowledgements

As always, I have to thank so many people.

Katie Loughnane, whose insightful editing made this a much better book.

The whole team at Penguin, including Rose Waddilove, Jess Muscio, Emma Grey-Gelder, Hope Butler, Marie-Louise Patton, Annie Peacock and everyone in Sales. Also Sally Sargeant and Caroline Johnson.

Jen Gilroy and Jane Cable for always being there.

All the reviewers and book bloggers who support this series, including Beverley Ann Hopper, Kath Evans, Julie Barham, Karen Mace, Zoe Morton, Yvonne Gill, Vikki Wakeham and Jo Barton.

And a big thank you to my Facebook followers.

SIGN UP TO OUR NEW SAGA NEWSLETTER

Penny Street

The home of heart-warming reads

Welcome to **Penny Street**, your **number one stop for emotional and heartfelt historical reads**. Meet casts of characters you'll never forget, memories you'll treasure as your own, and places that will stay with you long after the last page.

Join our online **community** bringing you the latest book deals, competitions and new saga series releases.

You can also find extra content, talk to your favourite authors and share your discoveries with other saga fans on Facebook.

Join today by visiting
www.penguin.co.uk/pennystreet

Follow us on Facebook
www.facebook.com/welcometopennystreet/